STAR WARS®
BATTLEFRONT™

TWILIGHT COMPANY

ALEXANDER FREED

DEL REY

NEW YORK

Copyright © 2015 by Lucasfilm Ltd. ® & TM where indicated. All rights reserved.

Published in the United States by Del Rey, an imprint of Random House, a division of Penguin Random House LLC, New York.

DEL REY and the HOUSE colophon are registered trademarks of Penguin Random House LLC.

ISBN 978-0-345-51121-8
eBook ISBN 978-1-101-88477-5

Printed in the United States of America on acid-free paper

randomhousebooks.com

2 4 6 8 9 7 5 3 1

First Edition

Book design by Christopher M. Zucker

To Susan, who earned it

THE DEL REY

TIMELINE

I THE PHANTOM MENACE

II ATTACK OF THE CLONES
THE CLONE WARS (TV SERIES)
DARK DISCIPLE

III REVENGE OF THE SITH
LORDS OF THE SITH
TARKIN
A NEW DAWN
REBELS (TV SERIES)

 IV A NEW HOPE
HEIR TO THE JEDI
BATTLEFRONT: TWILIGHT COMPANY

 V THE EMPIRE STRIKES BACK

 VI RETURN OF THE JEDI
AFTERMATH

 VII THE FORCE AWAKENS

ACKNOWLEDGMENTS

Books are written alone, but they rarely make it to publication that way.

Thanks first of all to Shelly Shapiro and Frank Parisi, who took a chance on me with this project (though Frank was wise enough to run for cover after tossing the grenade)—working with such thoughtful and adept editors is both humbling and a privilege.

Thanks also to Charles Boyd, Dana Kurtin, and Jeffrey Visgaitis, who provided valuable feedback during the writing process and helped forestall the worst of my nonsense. Due credit as well to all the writers from BioWare Austin who dragged me into the *Star Wars* galaxy in the first place; in particular, Daniel Erickson has been a tremendous backer and mentor over the years, and Drew Karpyshyn's support has been much appreciated.

Finally, while I could list a dozen and more authors whose work influenced *Twilight Company*, a special tip of the hat must go to the grandfather of space opera E. E. "Doc" Smith, without whom none of this would be possible. Clear ether, spacehound!

A long time ago in a galaxy far, far away. . . .

STAR WARS®
BATTLEFRONT™

TWILIGHT COMPANY

The Galactic Empire endures. Despite the destruction of its terrifying Death Star by the Rebel Alliance, its oppression spreads undiminished across the stars.

Under the direction of the Emperor and Darth Vader, an army of highly trained, single-minded stormtroopers quashes dissent and destroys resistance.

But on worlds like Sullust, Coyerti, Haidoral Prime, and untold others, rebel forces fight in the trenches, determined to maintain hope against the unrelenting Imperial war machine . . .

PART I

WITHDRAWAL

CHAPTER 1

PLANET CRUCIVAL
Day Forty-Seven of the Malkhani Insurrections
Thirteen Years After the Clone Wars

His name was Donin, and though that wasn't the name he'd been born with, he had the ink-rubbed brands to prove it. The black whorls and waves, freshly applied by the clan masters in honor of his induction, ran across his dusky shoulder blades under his coarse cloth jacket. They were one of four gifts he'd received upon joining the army of the Warlord Malkhan: a new name, the brands, a serrated knife, and an offworlder's particle blaster.

The masters had assured him that of the four gifts, the blaster was the most precious. Its grip was wrapped in fraying leather and its barrel was scored and crusted with ash. It had enough power left to fire a dozen searing bolts, and Donin had been warned not to waste a single shot or drop it if it began to burn his palms. Those were the acts of a child—not a full member of the clan.

He knelt among his new brothers and sisters—he'd yet to learn their names—behind a low stone wall that stretched across the hilltop. His slight frame, thin from youth and hunger, allowed him to conceal himself fully behind the barricade; for this reason he had been assigned to the front. Like his brands and weapons, that assignment was a privilege. He reminded himself as much when he began to sweat and tremble.

He glanced sidelong at his companions and looked for signs that they, too, were afraid of the coming battle. They were nearly all larger and older, carrying offworld weapons that appeared as scored and rusted as his own. They cleaned their knives and murmured to one another. Donin told himself he would die for them as they would die for him, in the name of the clan and its warlord. And if they won the day—

If I *survive the battle,* Donin corrected himself. Victory was inevitable for the Warlord Malkhan. Only Donin's own fate was in question.

—then they would celebrate. He'd heard stories of feasts, of troughs of clear water and skewers of bantha meat, of salts and sauces from other continents, other *planets.* He would gorge himself, he thought, and sleep in safety in the warlord's camp. He'd heard the clan's celebrations before, while hiding shivering in his father's home, and those joyful cries were what had finally lured him to the masters.

His father had said the Malkhanis were no different than any other faction on Crucival, but his father was wrong. No one else had such food or took so much joy in victory. No one else was as strong as Malkhan, or had the wisdom to procure such a trove of offworld technology. Donin's new clan would build a better planet.

Something far away howled in the dusty air, starting soft and rising rapidly. Donin squared his shoulders, half stood from his crouch, and thrust his blaster over the wall in one movement, as he'd been taught. He saw no target. A man's voice laughed behind him, and a broad palm cupped his dark hair and tilted his head back.

"Battle ain't started yet, boy. Just a ship headed to the tower. Get us all killed if you shoot."

His gaze redirected, Donin saw the sphere and crossbars of an off-world flier silhouetted against the clouds. It roared in the direction of the steel spire and faded from view.

Donin lowered himself to his knees again, and the hand on his head disappeared. He'd made a fool of himself. He silently pledged not to do it again. "We didn't see them much in the Gulches," he murmured—an explanation, not an excuse.

The man behind him grunted. "You'll see them a lot here. I'm serious about not shooting. Don't go within a stone's throw of the tower, either, no matter what happens. The offworlders in white may not come out much, but you bother them even a little . . ."

"I know," Donin snapped. He swiveled and looked up at the man, who could have been four times Donin's age, with milky eyes and pitted skin. Older than the warlord himself. But that didn't mean he'd been part of the clan any longer than Donin. "I know all about them. Their soldiers are clones. They make them in *batches.*"

The man grunted again, showing cracked yellow teeth in something that might have been a smile. "You don't say? Who told you that?"

"My father," Donin said. "He used to fight them." He gestured with his head toward the sky, toward the stars hidden behind yellow-gray clouds. "There was a war."

"Well, *you're* not fighting clones," the man said. "You're fighting the lowlifes who took the quarry last week and want our territory. That exciting enough for you?"

Donin scowled and stared. "I'm here to serve the clan," he said, and pivoted back to face the wall. One hand still clasping his blaster, he reached with the other to jerk down the collar of his jacket, displaying his brands to the man behind him.

Donin heard the man laugh, felt a slap on his spine that rocked him forward.

"I guess you are," the man said. "Just don't get your hopes up. Take it one fight at a time."

Donin nodded, shrugged his jacket higher on his back, and gripped his blaster tighter. He wasn't sure what the man meant. The clan was hope for them all.

It wasn't long before someone yelled that the enemy was approaching. The front line pressed against the wall and peered over. Donin saw specks against the brittle yellow grass in the valley below the hill, and soon those specks resolved into the shapes of dozens of men and women. Most held spears above their heads like pennants. Only a few carried offworld weapons—but those weapons were the size of tree branches, cradled by their owners in both arms.

The first of those weapons ignited with reverberating screams. Streaks of green fire spewed over the wall. The warlord's army became a mass of shouts Donin didn't understand. He steadied his blaster, reminded himself not to waste shots.

"All praise to the warlord!" someone called, and the shouting became a cheer. A rush of warmth filled the boy as he grinned and added his voice to the hurrah.

His name was Donin now. He was defending his new home. These were his brothers and sisters, their path was righteous, and he'd be part of their clan forever.

CHAPTER 2

PLANET HAIDORAL PRIME
Day Eighty-Four of the Mid Rim Retreat
Nine Years Later

The rain on Haidoral Prime dropped in warm sheets from a shining sky. It smelled like vinegar, clung to the molded curves of modular industrial buildings and to litter-strewn streets, and coated skin like a sheen of acrid sweat.

After thirty standard hours, it was losing its novelty for the soldiers of Twilight Company.

Three figures crept along a deserted avenue under a torn and dripping canopy. The lean, compact man in the lead was dressed in faded gray fatigues and a hodgepodge of armor pads crudely stenciled with the starbird symbol of the Rebel Alliance. Matted dark hair dripped beneath his visored helmet, sending crawling trails of rainwater down his bronze face.

His name was Hazram Namir, though he'd gone by others. He silently cursed urban warfare and Haidoral Prime and whichever laws of atmospheric science made it rain. The thought of sleep flashed into his mind and broke against a wall of stubbornness. He gestured with a rifle thicker than his arm toward the nearest intersection, then quickened his pace.

Somewhere in the distance a swift series of blaster shots resounded, followed by shouts and silence.

The figure closest behind Namir—a tall man with graying hair and a face puckered with scar tissue—bounded across the street to take up a position opposite. The third figure, a massive form huddled in a tarp like a hooded cloak, remained behind.

The scarred man flashed a hand signal. Namir turned the corner onto the intersecting street. A dozen meters away, the sodden lumps of human bodies lay in the road. They wore tattered rain gear—sleek, lightweight wraps and sandals—and carried no weapons. Noncombatants.

It's a shame, Namir thought, *but not a bad sign.* The Empire didn't shoot civilians when everything was under control.

"Charmer—take a look?" Namir indicated the bodies. The scarred man strode over as Namir tapped his comlink. "Sector secure," he said. "What's on tap next?"

The response came in a hiss of static through Namir's earpiece—something about mop-up operations. Namir missed having a communications specialist on staff. Twilight Company's last comm tech had been a drunk and a misanthrope, but she'd been magic with a transmitter and she'd written obscene poetry with Namir on late, dull nights. She and her idiot droid had died in the bombardment on Asyrphus.

"Say again," Namir tried. "Are we ready to load?"

This time the answer came through clearly. "Support teams are crating up food and equipment," the voice said. "If you've got a lead on medical supplies, we'd love more for the *Thunderstrike.* Otherwise, get to the rendezvous—we only have a few hours before reinforcements show."

"Tell support to grab hygiene items this time," Namir said. "Anyone who says they're luxuries needs to smell the barracks."

There was another burst of static, and maybe a laugh. "I'll let them know. Stay safe."

Charmer was finishing his study of the bodies, checking each for a heartbeat and identification. He shook his head, silent, as he straightened.

"Atrocity." The hulking figure wrapped in the tarp had finally approached. His voice was deep and resonant. Two meaty, four-fingered hands kept the tarp clasped at his shoulders, while a second pair of hands loosely carried a massive blaster cannon at waist level. "How can anyone born of flesh do this?"

Charmer bit his lip. Namir shrugged. "Could've been combat droids, for all we know."

"Unlikely," the hulking figure said. "But if so, responsibility belongs to the governor." He knelt beside one of the corpses and reached out to lid its eyes. Each of his hands was as large as the dead man's head.

"Come on, Gadren," Namir said. "Someone will find them."

Gadren stayed kneeling. Charmer opened his mouth to speak, then shut it. Namir wondered whether to push the point and, if so, how hard.

Then the wall next to him exploded and he stopped worrying about Gadren.

Fire and metal shards and grease and insulation pelted his spine. He couldn't hear and couldn't guess how he ended up in the middle of the road among the bodies, one leg bent beneath him. Something tacky was stuck to his chin and his helmet's visor was cracked; he had enough presence of mind to feel lucky he hadn't lost an eye.

Suddenly he was moving again. He was upright, and hands— Charmer's hands—were dragging him backward, clasping him below the shoulders. He snarled the native curses of his homeworld as a red storm of particle bolts flashed among the fire and debris. By the time he'd pushed Charmer away and wobbled onto his feet, he'd traced the bolts to their source.

Four Imperial stormtroopers stood at the mouth of an alley up the street. Their deathly pale armor gleamed in the rain, and the black eyepieces of their helmets gaped like pits. Their weapons shone with oil and machined care, as if the squad had stepped fully formed out of a mold.

Namir tore his gaze from the enemy long enough to see that his back was to a storefront window filled with video screens. He raised his blaster rifle, fired at the display, then climbed in among the shards. Charmer followed. The storefront wouldn't give them cover for long—certainly not if the stormtroopers fired another rocket—but it would have to be enough.

"Check for a way up top," Namir yelled, and his voice sounded faint and tinny. He couldn't hear the storm of blaster bolts at all. "We need covering fire!" Not looking to see if Charmer obeyed, he dropped to the floor as the stormtroopers adjusted their aim to the store.

He couldn't spot Gadren, either. He ordered the alien into position anyway, hoping he was alive and that the comlinks still worked. He lined his rifle under his chin, fired twice in the direction of the storm-troopers, and was rewarded with a moment of peace.

"I need you on target, Brand," he growled into his link. "I need you here *now*."

If anyone answered, he couldn't hear it.

Now he glimpsed the stormtrooper carrying the missile launcher. The trooper was still reloading, which meant Namir had half a minute at most before the storefront came tumbling down on top of him. He took a few quick shots and saw one of the other troopers fall, though he doubted he'd hit his target. He guessed Charmer had found a vantage point after all.

Three stormtroopers remaining. One was moving away from the alley while the other stayed to protect the artilleryman. Namir shot wildly at the one moving into the street, watched him skid and fall to a knee, and smiled grimly. There was something satisfying about see-ing a trained stormtrooper humiliate himself. Namir's own side did it often enough.

Jerky movements drew Namir's attention back to the artilleryman. Behind the stormtrooper stood Gadren, both sets of arms gripping and lifting his foe. Human limbs flailed, and the missile launcher fell to the ground. White armor seemed to crumple in the alien's hands. Gadren's makeshift hood blew back, exposing his head: a brown, bulbous, widemouthed mass topped with a darker crest of bone, like some amphibian's nightmare idol. The second trooper in the alley turned to face Gadren and was promptly slammed to the ground with his comrade's body before Gadren crushed them both, howling in rage or grief.

Namir trusted Gadren as much as he trusted anyone, but there were times when the alien terrified him.

The last stormtrooper was still down in the street. Namir fired until flames licked a burnt and melted hole in the man's armor. Namir, Charmer, and Gadren gathered back around the bodies and assessed their own injuries.

Namir's hearing was coming back. The damage to his helmet extended far beyond the visor—a crack ran along its length—and he found a shallow cut across his forehead when he tossed the helmet to the street. Charmer was picking shards of shrapnel from his vest but made no complaints. Gadren was shivering in the warm rain.

"No Brand?" Gadren asked.

Namir only grunted.

Charmer laughed his weird, hiccuping laugh and spoke. He swallowed the words twice, three, four times as he went, half stuttering as he had ever since the fight on Blacktar Cyst. "Keep piling bodies like this," he said, "we'll have the best vantage point in the city."

He gestured at Namir's last target, who had fallen directly onto one of the civilian corpses.

"You're a sick man, Charmer," Namir said, and swung an arm roughly around his comrade's shoulders. "I'll miss you when they boot you out."

Gadren grunted and sniffed behind them. It might have been dismay, but Namir chose to take it as mirth.

Officially, the city was Haidoral Administrative Center One, but locals called it Glitter after the crystalline mountains that limned the horizon. In Namir's experience, what the Galactic Empire didn't name to inspire terror—its stormtrooper legions, its Star Destroyer battleships—it tried to render as drab as possible. This didn't bother Namir, but he wasn't among the residents of the planets and cities being labeled.

Half a dozen rebel squads had already arrived at the central plaza when Namir's team marched in. The rain had condensed into mist, and the plaza's tents and canopies offered little shelter; nonetheless, men and women in ragged armor squeezed into the driest corners they could find, grumbling to one another or tending to minor wounds and damaged equipment. As victory celebrations went, it was subdued. It had been a long fight for little more than the promise of a few fresh meals.

"Stop admiring yourselves and do something *useful*," Namir barked, barely breaking stride. "Support teams can use a hand if you're too good to play *greeter*."

He barely noticed the squads stir in response. Instead, his attention shifted to a woman emerging from the shadows of a speeder stand. She was tall and thickly built, dressed in rugged pants and a bulky maroon jacket. A scoped rifle was slung over her shoulder, and the armor mesh of a retracted face mask covered her neck and chin. Her skin was gently creased with age and as dark as a human's could be, her hair cropped close to her scalp, and she didn't so much as glance at Namir as she arrived at his side and matched his pace through the plaza.

"You want to tell me where you were?" Namir asked.

"You missed the second fire team. I took care of it," Brand said.

Namir kept his voice cool. "Drop me a hint next time?"

"You didn't need the distraction."

Namir laughed. "Love you, too."

Brand cocked her head. If she got the joke—and Namir expected she did—she wasn't amused. "So what now?" she asked.

"We've got eight hours before we leave the system," Namir said, and stopped with his back to an overturned kiosk. He leaned against the metal frame and stared into the mist. "Less if Imperial ships come before then, or if the governor's forces regroup. After that, we'll divvy up the supplies with the rest of the battle group. Probably keep an escort ship or two for the *Thunderstrike* before the others split off."

"And we abandon this sector to the Empire," Brand said.

By this time, Charmer had wandered off and Gadren had joined Namir and Brand. "We will return," he said gravely.

"Right," Namir said, smirking. "Something to look forward to."

He knew they were the wrong words at the wrong time.

Eighteen months earlier, the Rebel Alliance's Sixty-First Mobile Infantry—commonly known as Twilight Company—had joined the push into the galactic Mid Rim. The operation was among the largest the Rebellion had ever fielded against the Empire, involving thousands of starships, hundreds of battle groups, and dozens of worlds. In the wake of the Rebellion's victory against the Empire's planet-burning Death Star battle station, High Command had believed the time was right to move from the fringes of Imperial territory toward its population centers.

Twilight Company had fought in the factory-deserts of Phorsa Gedd and taken the Ducal Palace of Bamayar. It had established beachheads for rebel hovertanks and erected bases from tarps and sheet metal. Namir had seen soldiers lose limbs and go weeks without proper treatment. He'd trained teams to construct makeshift bayonets when blaster power packs ran low. He'd set fire to cities and watched the Empire do the same. He'd left friends behind on broken worlds, knowing he'd never see them again.

On planet after planet, Twilight had fought. Battles were won and battles were lost, and Namir stopped keeping score. Twilight remained at the Rebellion's vanguard, forging ahead of the bulk of the armada, until word came down from High Command nine months in: The fleet was overextended. There was to be no further advance—only defense of the newly claimed territories.

Not long after that, the retreat began.

Twilight Company had become the rear guard of a massive withdrawal. It deployed to worlds it had helped capture mere months earlier and evacuated the bases it had built. It extracted the Rebellion's heroes and generals and pointed the way home. It marched over the graves of its own dead soldiers. Some of the company lost hope. Some became angry.

No one wanted to go back.

When the civilians came out of hiding and into the plaza, the open recruit began.

Sergeant Zab's squad—the squad Namir had once called, in a moment of pique, "morons who could make a hydrospanner backfire"— had somehow smuggled an astromech droid into the city surveillance center. From there, they'd accessed the public address system and broadcast the captain's message: Twilight Company would soon depart Haidoral Prime. Those on Haidoral who shared the Rebellion's ideals of freedom and democracy could remain to defend their homes, or they could sign on with Twilight to take the fight to the enemy. To go where the Rebellion was needed most. And so forth.

The captain recorded a new broadcast every time Twilight went looking to bolster its ranks, tailored to the needs and the circumstances of the local population. To Namir, all the messages sounded alike.

Open recruitments were technically against Rebel Alliance security policy, but they were a Twilight Company tradition and the captain was insistent the practice continue. So long as the Rebellion sent Twilight into hell time and again—and so long as Twilight *survived*— the company would replenish its losses from the ranks of the willing. On Haidoral Prime, seven Twilight soldiers had died. Namir hadn't yet seen their names. Twilight would need seven newcomers to balance those losses, and still more to make up for those who'd died elsewhere in recent weeks.

Dozens of men and women trickled into the plaza over the space of an hour, hand-checked by Twilight "greeters" for weapons and concealed explosives. Not all of them were there to be recruited: Barefoot women with callused hands begged Twilight to stay; hunched, elderly men screamed for the company to leave. A disorganized band of locals voiced their desire to keep fighting the Empire on Haidoral—these were given what few weapons Twilight had to spare and sent away with meaningless well-wishing and invocations of "the cause."

The genuine recruits were a motley assortment of young and old, pampered and desperate. Namir paced among them, watched their eyes, and passed his assessments on to the recruiting officer. A bearded and bedraggled man had the look of a street person but the carriage of a bureaucrat; Namir pegged him as an Imperial spy. A pug-nosed woman shifted her eyes to an escape route when Namir casually moved his weapon from one hand to the other; a petty criminal looking for an easy way off the planet, he thought.

That day's recruiting officer—Hober, a withered and creak-kneed quartermaster with a knack for card games—took Namir's recommendations with a shrug. "You know Howl's orders," he said.

Namir did. Captain Evon—"Howl" when outside earshot—liked to err on the side of welcome. He and Namir had spoken at length about that particular policy.

"Just keep an eye out," Namir said. "You have to be a special kind of crazy to jump aboard a sinking ship."

Hober snorted and shook his head. "Say that louder, and we can close up early."

Namir didn't say it louder. A bit of crazy wasn't always a bad thing. Still, he needed recruits he could train, not deserters or unhinged killers.

The line moved slowly. Hober engaged the potential recruits with questions, chatted about their pastimes and families as much as their combat experience. Hober was good at his job, good at judging who would last and who would panic and get someone killed. Namir paced and tried to stay out of the way; intellectually, he knew what the recruits felt like, knew they'd be more likely to come clean when relaxed. He'd been in their position less than three years before. But at the moment, he couldn't muster either interest or sympathy.

Someone in the line shouted. Namir turned to see three locals grappling with one another. Two of them were cursing and striking the third—a pale, gangly girl with a bolt of red hair. The apparent victim went down four times in as many seconds, popped back up after each hit, and seemed ready to keep brawling. Not a good fighter, but Namir gave her credit for persistence.

He fired three shots above the trio. They went still. The red-haired girl couldn't have been more than a teenager, and the other two looked scarcely older.

"Do I need to care what's going on here?" Namir asked, then cut the air horizontally with his hand before anyone could answer. "We'll all be happier if you say no."

The three youths shook their heads.

"Fight on my ship, and you'll be sealed in a maintenance closet until you starve to death," Namir said. "I won't waste blaster bolts on you. I won't waste oxygen shooting you out an air lock. You'll die slowly because I *don't care*."

Namir lacked both the callousness and the authority to carry out that particular threat, but the would-be recruits didn't know it. One of the older pair hesitated, then turned and stalked away. The other two lowered their eyes.

"How old are you?" Namir asked the red-haired kid.

"Twenty," she said, jerking her head back up.

That didn't seem likely, but there was no time for background checks. Nor would she be the first sixteen-year-old to enlist in the Alliance.

Namir turned and nodded his approval to Hober. The old quarter-master looked skeptical. Namir wondered if Hober would admit the girl into the ranks of Twilight's fresh meat, but he suspected the man would do so against his own better judgment.

It wasn't about being *welcoming*. These days, Twilight Company couldn't afford to be choosy.

Three hours into the open recruit, word came down that Namir's squad was needed outside the governor's mansion. It was a welcome distraction.

Twilight had locked down the mansion during the first day of fighting. The compound of multi-tiered domes was on the outskirts of the city, impractically far from the center of Imperial power but possessed of an impressive view of the crystalline mountains. After the initial skirmishing, Captain Howl had ordered half a dozen rebel squads stationed around its perimeter, within a stone's throw of its scorched but intact outer wall. No attempt to capture it had been made; with its occupants contained, the mansion itself had seemed strategically insignificant.

Since then, the situation had evolved.

"Mouse droid rolled out through a side entrance half an hour ago," Sergeant Fektrin said. "We figured it was rigged to blow. Turned out clean. It was carrying a written message from a 'rebel sympathizer' inside the mansion."

Namir, Gadren, Charmer, and Brand stood across from the mansion wall. The others rechecked their equipment as Namir and Fektrin spoke. Periodically, one of the mansion's windows slid open, spat a volley of hissing red particle bolts onto the street, then shut again. Fektrin's team barely seemed to notice.

"What'd the message say?" Namir asked.

"That Governor Chalis's men are holding captured rebel soldiers inside. Our anonymous tipster—and I quote—'fears for their safety.' "

Namir spat onto the road and watched his saliva sizzle where the bolts had impacted. "They know we've accounted for everyone, right? Do they think we're that stupid?"

"I told Howl the same thing," Fektrin said, "more or less." The ridges of his face crinkled in discomfort and the tendrils dangling from his cheeks and chin seemed to curl. Namir thought of those tendrils as a sort of beard, though he'd never asked if they were present on the women of Fektrin's species. "But the captain's worried the governor might have grabbed some locals. Wants it checked out.

"Besides," Fektrin went on, "if it's a trap, then what's the *point*? We lose a squad in there, we don't exactly lose the war."

Namir stared at Fektrin with as much skepticism as he could muster. "So the captain's theory," he said, "is that he can afford to gamble away our lives on the off chance we'll save a few civvies." Fektrin's tendrils twitched, but Namir kept talking. "Do I have this right?"

Gadren was frowning. Fektrin took it in stride. Namir had never seen Fektrin smile, but the alien had a deadpan sense of humor.

"*You* want to take it up with Howl?" Fektrin asked.

Namir swore and barked a bitter laugh. "Fine," he said. "But if we die, we're taking the whole mansion down with us."

Charmer came up with the squad's approach. Climbing the wall or besieging the main entrance would draw too much opposition; Fektrin would prep a frontal assault, but only for use as a last resort. Instead, Namir, Brand, and Charmer made their way to the rooftop garden of one of the neighboring residences. The occupants were more than cooperative after Namir burned three blaster holes in their custodial droid, and stayed out of sight while Charmer secured a magnetic grappling gun in one of the flower beds.

Brand watched the governor's mansion through the lenses of her armored mask. On her signal, Charmer fired the gun and sent the grapnel soaring through the resurgent rain. It struck the wall abutting one of the mansion's lower balconies, attached, and pulled the line taut. Namir traversed the gap first, sliding down the line and landing with a jolt on the damp stone.

Charmer came next, then Brand. Brand severed the line with a curved knife that she pulled from her jacket. The blade hummed softly with electricity.

"Where'd you get *that*?" Namir asked.

"Confiscated," Brand said.

Namir glanced at Charmer, who pulled a stun rod from his belt and extended the baton. It looked like it would snap in two with a bit of effort. He passed it to Namir, who shook his head until Charmer pressed the weapon into his palm. "I have my own knife," Charmer said, forcing the words past his stutter. "You need an edge."

Namir scowled but didn't argue. It was true he didn't have the taller man's reach.

"We're heading in," he said, tapping his comlink. "You hear screams, you know what to do."

Gadren's deep voice came through mixed with static. "I will weep at your funerals, and after grieving I will requisition a grapple that can support my mass. Many lives will be saved in the future."

"That's the spirit," Namir said.

Together, the three proceeded into the mansion. The rooms were dark and spacious in the Imperial style, appointed with lush carpets and glittering holographic mobiles that rotated and pulsed with the movements of the squad. Namir led the way through connected suites and into a tall, narrow hallway carved from mountain crystal. There, bronze busts and statuettes sat in niches along the wall.

Namir didn't recognize most of the subjects. The men and women in the statuettes nearly all wore Imperial military uniforms or robes of state. A bust of an elderly man with cheeks like melted wax and thinning hair bore a resemblance to the Galactic Emperor—Namir had seen him before in rebel propaganda videos. A horned figure might have been the Emperor's aged vizier. Namir dredged his memory for the name: *Mas Amedda.*

Charmer and Brand seemed more familiar with the lineup. Charmer scowled at a middle-aged man whose bulbous, alien eyes were set in a human face and whose neck was braced by a thick metal collar. The round collar gave the bust the appearance of a grotesque potted plant. Brand paused before the re-creation of a misshapen helmet of curves and angles and skull-like eyes.

"You know him?" Namir asked.

"Not personally," Brand said.

"Darth Vader," Charmer said. He didn't stammer.

The Galactic Emperor's personal enforcer: hound of the Rebel Alliance, born from the embers of the Clone Wars, perpetrator of every horror and atrocity known to civilization. So the stories went, anyway.

"Right," Namir whispered. "Can we get on with it?"

To Namir's surprise, Brand looked at him and spoke in a low, somber tone. "You should know these people," she said. "Darth Vader. General Tulia. Count Vidian. Look at their faces, and memorize every one."

Namir returned Brand's stare, cool and calm. Brand didn't back down.

"I get it," Namir said softly. "I do."

"You don't," Brand said, and began to walk again.

Charmer, three steps ahead, gestured before the stairway at the end of the hall. Two fingers raised, thumb moving across the palm. Two guards stationed at the top of the stairs, one patrolling.

Brand went first. In his darker moments, Namir resented the older woman's capacity for stealth—but not today, not when his own wet boots squeaked like rats on the polished floor. He followed her, tightening his grip on the stun baton, with Charmer so close behind he could feel the man's body heat.

Up the stairs. Two guards, neither in full armor. Local security. Brand stepped out of the mouth of the stairwell and Namir heard sizzling as the electrified knife found its first target. Namir charged forward, body low, looking for the patrol. Charmer would know to take the second guard behind him.

The sentry on patrol was less than five meters away, and Namir felt his guts clench when they spotted each other. An Imperial stormtrooper. The trooper was still turning to face him—Namir had time to close the distance—but the stun baton would be useless against that white armor.

He should have asked to borrow Brand's knife when he'd had the chance.

Namir raised his shoulder as he charged; he slammed into the stormtrooper and spun him to face the stairwell. Now at the trooper's back, Namir clung to the armor's cool surface and tried to pin the man's arms, prevent him from getting off even one shot with his blaster. *That* noise would alert the entire mansion, and their attempt at stealth would be compromised.

The stormtrooper reacted swiftly, competently. He threw his head back, grazed Namir's scalp where Namir's abandoned helmet should have protected him. If Namir had been standing straight instead of bending his knees, he would have taken the hit between the eyes. After a moment he smelled burning metal and plastoid, and the stormtrooper went limp as Brand twisted her knife under the rim of his helmet.

Namir tried to guide the body in a slide onto the floor, but it clattered more loudly than he'd intended. Charmer stood between the two security guards, both dead on the ground. Brand had already cleaned her knife by the time Namir said, "Keep moving."

The message warning Twilight about the governor's captives had included a rough map of the mansion. The hallway the team found itself in now was, at Namir's estimate, less than fifty meters from the captives' supposed location. If there was an ambush waiting, they'd be walking into it soon. Namir gave the rifle slung on his back a quick feel, confirmed he hadn't somehow lost its comforting bulk during the fight. Stealth would only take them so far, and he wanted to be ready.

Charmer took the lead next. Namir didn't correct him—somehow Charmer always wound his way to the front when an ambush seemed imminent, for reasons Namir couldn't understand and couldn't bring himself to ask about. Losing his face hadn't broken Charmer of the habit. Namir certainly wouldn't be able to.

Onward, down a cramped passage into a supply pantry that smelled of citrus. Namir assumed the scent was artificial until he saw that there was fruit—real fruit—casually stocked with the rest of the governor's boundless wealth; he drew one long breath of the aroma and then shook off the distraction. Past the pantry was a kitchen, sleek and metallic and packed with long-limbed droids nestled in their power stations. Charmer paused at the narrow door leading farther into the mansion and shrugged. The map indicated the captives were in the next room.

Namir glanced at Brand as she took a position across the door-frame from Charmer. "If anyone's been saving a flash-bomb," Namir said, "now's the time to speak up."

No one did.

Fine, Namir thought. *No smoke cover, no flash. We breach the old-fashioned way.*

It didn't bother him. The old ways were what he knew best.

He clipped the stun rod to his belt, took his rifle in both hands. Charmer and Brand mirrored him. Namir nodded; Charmer hit the door's keypad and they surged inside together.

What they found was a dining hall—or what *had* been a dining hall, now so strewn with printouts and holodisplays and maps and portable screens that it resembled the inside of a bureaucrat's skull. Standing amid the makeshift workstations were half a dozen Imperial Army officers—caps doffed, expressions haggard, sweat staining their black uniforms—who were so intent on their work that it took half a second before they looked up at Namir and his squad. Namir took aim at the first man to reach for his sidearm—a sharp-nosed colonel who'd been pacing alongside the dining table—and watched the rest of the group hesitate.

Brand and Charmer swept their rifles in steady arcs while Namir kept his eye on the colonel. "Prisoners," he said. "Where are they?"

"What prisoners?" the colonel asked.

Namir's muscles were taut. He kept his voice calm. "The ones you captured," he said. "Or the ones you *claimed* you captured."

"I have no idea what you're talking about," the colonel said. His right hand began to edge toward his belt. Namir cocked his head. The colonel froze again.

"He really doesn't," a voice replied, warm and resonant in the dining hall. Namir wanted to turn to look at the speaker, but taking his attention from the colonel would mean death. He kept his rifle aimed, kept his body turned toward his opponent, and trusted that Brand or Charmer would cover the remainder of the room.

The new speaker slowly resolved in his peripheral vision. She was emerging from one of the side entrances to the hall, a human woman whose olive-skinned visage was lined just enough to add gravitas to a once-youthful face. Her black hair was threaded with gray and white, and she wore a dark, formal suit trimmed with red and clasped with silver buttons. In contrast with the suit's obvious expense was a worn and stained duffel bag she'd slung over one shoulder—the kind a rebel soldier or a vagabond might carry.

"I'm the captive here," she said with bored disdain. "The fact the colonel doesn't realize it—"

As the woman spoke, she let the duffel bag slide from her right shoulder and land heavily on the floor. The words kept coming with that same, idle tone as, while the bag fell, she drew a blaster pistol from her left pocket. "—shows how little he pays attention." The blaster flashed red, and Namir's target fell to the dining table, a hole burned between his shoulder blades.

Namir wasn't sure who fired next. The sound of one bolt merged with another, and another after that. He dropped to his knees, swung to acquire a target, saw an officer with a something—maybe a weapon, maybe a comlink—in his hand and shot him. Flecks of stone spilled onto Namir's hair as someone blasted the wall above his head.

He scrambled forward, took shelter under the table, reached up and over, and fired wildly. The dead colonel's legs obscured his view of the other side of the room. The bolts slowed. He rolled out from under the table and loosed a volley at the first black-clad form he saw.

After that, only one officer was left. Namir didn't understand what the Imperial was aiming for, at first—the man had backed himself into a corner and his blaster was low, pointed toward the floor. Then Namir saw the pile at the officer's feet. Charmer was kneeling on the ground, moaning in pain, both hands clasped to one of his hips.

Namir began to turn his rifle on the officer, but the woman in the suit killed him first with a snarl and a flick of the blaster in her hand. Namir ignored her and hurried to Charmer's side.

Gently, he peeled back Charmer's hands and examined his right hip. The material of his pants was scorched through, the fibers melted into blackened skin. The injury wasn't fatal, but it had to hurt and Charmer wouldn't be walking out of there.

Namir bared his teeth in what he hoped was a smirk. "Quit moaning," he said. "It's already cauterized—you want it to bandage itself, too?"

Charmer laughed hoarsely and croaked an obscenity.

Brand methodically secured each door to the dining hall as Namir stood and looked to the woman who'd claimed to be the "captive." She was standing at the dining table, pouring a pitcher of water over her hands as if to clean them—not of blood, as Namir thought at first, but of caked-on dirt like clay. Her weapon sat beside the pitcher.

"Who are you?" he asked.

The woman barely glanced toward Namir as she wiped her hands dry on her hips. "My name is Everi Chalis," she said. "Governor of Haidoral Prime, emissary to the Imperial Ruling Council, and, of course—" Here her lip curled up, as if at a private joke. "—local artist-in-residence."

She began walking among the bodies, nudging each with the toe of her boot as if to confirm that it was dead. "Declaring myself a *captive* may have been an exaggeration," she went on, "but I needed your attention." When she came to the colonel, still sprawled across the table, she leaned in close, hoisted him by his hair, and spat between his unseeing eyes.

"Glad you're so loyal to your staff," Namir said, slow and cautious. When Chalis turned around, he had his rifle aimed at her chest.

She didn't seem bothered. "They weren't mine," she said sourly. "*My* staff—my advisers, my bodyguards, my *chef*—were taken away months ago. These men were here to *police* me at the behest of the Emperor."

Charmer was trying to stammer something; Namir only heard the word *chef.* Brand glanced from a side door to Namir, and then to the governor. "Shoot her," she said. "Haidoral deserves that much."

Namir scowled. The pieces weren't coming together, and he suddenly felt the weight of days without sleep, the thirty hours of fighting. "*Why* did you need our attention?" he asked.

"Thanks to the Rebellion, my days with the Empire are numbered." The governor smiled, but her tone was acid. "I understand you're recruiting. I want to join your company in return for asylum."

Namir took aim with his rifle. He wondered how many more guards were in the mansion and how long he had before they showed. He tried to guess how much Charmer's injury would slow down the squad's exit. He didn't have time to parse the lies at play.

Then came a low electric warbling and an oscillating flash of blue light. The governor's lips parted, but she said nothing. Her limbs stiffened, and she fell to the floor beside her bag.

Namir swung about. Standing in the last of the unsecured doorways was Gadren, two arms clasping his weapon and aiming the barrel toward where the governor had stood. He was breathing hard, enormous shoulders rising and falling. "We lost contact," he said. "I thought there was trouble. I am pleased to see I overreacted."

Brand eyed the fallen governor. "She's still breathing," she said. "Why a stun shot?"

Gadren crept to Charmer's side, pausing to assess the scarred man's injuries before gently lifting him from the floor and cradling him in two arms. Not until Charmer was secure did Gadren say, "I feared for the captives. A blaster bolt could have killed one."

"No captives," Brand said. Gadren nodded—not in comprehension, but in recognition that now was not the time for questions.

Namir stalked to the governor and checked the body. She was breathing steadily. No spasms, no choking, no irregular heartbeat. Stun bolts weren't reliable, but this one seemed to have done its job. Which meant the governor was still Namir's problem.

"We'll pack her up, take her to Howl"—he nodded toward Gadren— "if you've got room for one more. No need to be gentle."

Gadren roughly grabbed the governor by her collar and threw her over a shoulder, using one hand to keep the body in place. Namir wondered if Brand would argue, but she was lifting the governor's bag as she said, "They say kidnapping an Imperial is bad luck."

Namir couldn't tell if she was joking. "*Bad men crave bad luck,*" he replied. It was a saying he'd learned long ago on a more primitive world. "Now can we get off this planet?"

He was ready to be done with the rain. He was ready to sleep. He was ready to forget the piles of dead civilians and the opulent mansion filled with aromatic fruit and busts of murderers. The attack on Haidoral Prime hadn't been a failure, but it had been laden with troubles.

Now he was taking one of those troubles home.

CHAPTER 3

PLANET SULLUST
Day Eighty-Five of the Mid Rim Retreat

As evening approached in Pinyumb, the obsidian of the cavern roof slowly lost its refracted iridescence. The great towers of the city, rising from the cave floor like stalagmites, dimmed their upper lights until the dome was lost to blackness. The yellow sulfur that clung to the cavern walls seemed to turn sickly pale. The rustling of ash angel wings came and went as the creatures returned from foraging to nest.

With the ash angels came the people of Pinyumb, arriving in lifts and shuttles from the factories of the surface or departing their housing blocks for the night shifts. There were dark and pale humans, gray-skinned Sullustans, and rarer species, too. Pinyumb was cosmopolitan in its way—those willing to toil were welcome, and all others were outcasts.

Thara Nyende didn't linger in the streets or stroll along the turquoise streams that flowed by Pinyumb's walkways. She didn't stop to pick out familiar faces from the commuter crowds. Like everyone else, she had errands to run before curfew. She did, however, take the time to nod firmly in the direction of the stormtroopers posted at every shuttle and intersection. Only twice did the men or women inside the armor nod back.

Thara passed squat, steel-gray buildings that bore no signs but that she knew well—a public bathhouse, a hospice, a café—and then descended a short flight of steps hewn from the cavern rock to an unmarked door. She hoisted the leather bag slung over her shoulder and pushed inside, where her eyes slowly adjusted to the dim cantina lighting. No more than a dozen customers were present—nearly all men and nearly all old, no matter the species. They were broadshouldered and wrinkled, sturdy and scarred from years of work in the Inyusu Tor mineral processing facility. Most were gathered about a holotable displaying an offworld sporting event, but they spoke to one another loud enough to drown out the soft holocast.

"Uncle!" Thara called in the direction of the bar. "I'm here to spoil you."

The man who looked up from the array of nozzles behind the bar and started Thara's way looked old enough to be her grandfather rather than her uncle, and if his hair had ever matched her brightblond locks, the color had faded long ago. He clapped her on the shoulders as other heads turned and aged lips smiled at the young woman.

The voices around the holotable lowered.

"The only person getting *spoiled* is you," Thara's uncle said before accepting the leather bag from her hands. "Working half as long as the rest of us, and paid twice as much! But let's see what you've got anyway."

He placed the bag on an empty table and began to rummage through its contents. First out was a tube of ocher gel. Thara's uncle turned it in his hands, then shouted over his shoulder, "Myan! Got another tube of burn salve. Boys in dorm four still hurting?"

Thara remembered the accident with the dorm four workers.

They'd been scalded badly when the steam pipes in the magma extractors had broken. Some of the workers still hadn't returned to duty. Soon they'd be evicted from their residence.

Myan, a diminutive Sullustan, hobbled over to the table. He spoke in his native tongue—too quickly for Thara to fully understand, but the tone sounded grateful—and carried the salve away.

"Good start," Thara's uncle said. Thara smiled at him wryly and nearly caught him smiling back. One by one he pulled Thara's donations from the bag—extra food credits, flu tablets, mask filters for the men working in the deepest ore processors—and, calling his customers to the table, meted out gift after gift. Some of the recipients clasped Thara's hands, praised her and her family. Others refused to look at her.

As her uncle continued sorting through the bag, she drifted away and studied the nozzles on the wall behind the bar. He uncle had been repairing them, she saw now—replacing a fluid valve. He'd left his tools on the floor. She picked them up and started working, the way she remembered doing as a teenager.

"My son gave me a flyer the other day. Says he's thinking about joining."

Thara was close enough to the holotable now that she could hear the older workers' hushed voices. She didn't want to hear. She hadn't intended to eavesdrop. But she wasn't going to leave, either.

"After the accident with the magma release, he said maybe the Cobalt Front was right. Maybe we do need to stand up for ourselves."

"The Cobalt Laborers' Reformation Front," a second voice sneered, "is a band of terrorists. They probably caused the accident in the first place."

There was murmuring, reluctant agreement. "Protests are one thing. Riots are another."

Thara screwed the new valve into place. Cobalt Front members *were* terrorists according to Imperial decree. It was a pity; she thought they might have done some good if they'd stuck to talking about safety procedures and factory conditions.

"Is it our fault?" the first voice asked. "I know I protected mine. I didn't tell my son what we saw in the Clone Wars."

The third voice laughed. "Of course you didn't. Your kids would've never slept."

The first man continued. "But they would've *known*. They'd see why even a hard peace is better than—better than the alternative."

"Just pray the Rebel Alliance never notices Sullust. You think things are rough now . . ."

Thara tested the attached nozzle, caught a trickle of something green and sweet smelling in her palm.

"*No*," a new voice said in slow, ragged Sullustan, deliberately loud. Thara recognized the rasp of toxin-afflicted lungs; the condition was becoming increasingly common among the workers.

Someone tried to shush the new speaker as Thara rose from behind the bar. The toxin-afflicted man—a withered Sullustan with drooping ears and jowls—kept going. "This is not *peace*. We are *all* slaves, every one of us, and the Emperor forges stronger chains every year."

Thara's uncle was hurrying to the holotable. He squeezed the withered man's arm as the Sullustan propped himself against the tabletop and continued to speak. "I don't care who hears me," the withered man snapped. "What Nunb said was true: We traded our lives to buy a thousand years of darkness. The Empire runs on the blood of our grandchildren!"

Thara's uncle forced the man back into his seat. Thara looked around the table. The workers were all staring at her, silent.

"I'll be back next week," she said quietly. "If you need something, tell my uncle. I'll try to help."

No one spoke as she left the cantina.

She walked briskly down the street, as if she could pound her frustrations into the stone, sweat them out through the soles of her feet. She tried to put what she'd heard out of her mind, concentrate on the evening ahead. She was nearly late for her shift as it was; she couldn't afford to go on duty distracted.

She marched to the door of a sleek industrial building, looked into the mechanical eye of the scanner so that it could identify her. Past two more checkpoints and on to her locker, where she finally began to relax.

Donning her uniform always calmed her. She'd learned to dress and attach its components in less than a minute, but she preferred to go slowly, first stripping down and removing, one by one, the garments of Thara Nyende of Sullust and stowing them in the locker. Next, she pulled on her new skin—a tough black body glove that sealed itself as she climbed in, too hot to be comfortable until the smart material adjusted to her body heat and the temperature of the room.

She slid her feet into her white synth-leather boots and then—always left first, then right—snapped her plastoid greaves onto her legs. The soft click and hum of mechanisms assured her she'd attached the pieces correctly, and their perfect sculpt felt far more natural than anything she could buy as a civilian. Belt and crotch plate came next, then the torso piece—locked into the belt, finally making her feel clothed.

Shoulders, arms, and gloves came after the torso. Most days, she'd already forgotten her ordinary troubles by this point. Sometimes she noticed her breathing had steadied, her muscle tension drained into the support of the bodysuit and plastoid. She could have attached the arm sections faster with the help of a droid or a colleague, but this was *her* ritual. She liked doing it alone.

Finally, the helmet.

She took it from its place in the locker and lowered it onto her head. For an instant, she was in total darkness. Then it clicked into place, the lenses polarized, and the heads-up display blinked to life. Targeting diagnostics cycled over her view of the locker room, power levels and environmental readings blinking at the corners of her eyesight.

Like that, Thara Nyende faded into the background. A stronger woman, a better woman, stepped into place to do her duty.

She was SP-475 of the Imperial Ninety-Seventh Stormtrooper Legion.

CHAPTER 4

KONTAHR SECTOR
Day Eighty-Five of the Mid Rim Retreat

"You have no idea how the Empire really works."

The Rebel Alliance military transport *Thunderstrike* was not designed for comfort. Its corridors were lined with pipes and panels, and its doors were bulky and cumbersome, plated with heavy durasteel. Over the years, Twilight Company had stripped down and reconfigured the aging Corellian corvette, partitioning and repartitioning the ship's few open spaces until barely a square meter was left unused.

Thus, when Howl ordered the prisoner brought to his storage-unit-turned-office for questioning, the meeting was an intimate one. On one side of Howl's flimsy folding desk sat the captain himself, flanked by Lieutenant Sairgon and Chief Medic Von Geiz; while Sairgon stood stiff as ever, like an ancient and gnarled tree, Von Geiz had propped himself atop an offline holoprojector. Facing Howl and leaning back in her

chair with exaggerated ease was Governor Chalis, smiling like an em-
press. Behind Chalis stood Namir, who watched the governor's hands
as if she might be about to reach across the desk and strangle the captain.

"I'm not saying that to be insulting," Chalis went on. "But if you
think Haidoral Prime was anything more than a backwater, you're operating under dearly mistaken assumptions. My appointment there
was a *punishment,* not an elevation."

She spoke in a low voice, full of bored confidence. In the safety of
the ship, her Coruscanti accent—the accent of the Imperial elite, of
propaganda broadcasts and rebel satire—seemed overly enunciated
to Namir's ears.

"And why did you deserve punishment?" the captain asked.

Chalis cocked her head as if surprised by the question. "When your
Rebellion started encroaching on the Mid Rim, the Emperor set his
dog loose. You heard about the deaths of Moff Coovern and Minister
Khemt?"

"Tragic accidents, as I recall," Howl said.

"According to my sources, both died at the hand of Darth Vader.
Emperor Palpatine decided that incompetence at the highest ranks
was to blame for the destruction of his Death Star, and from there
began a culling.

"There were other deaths, less public," she added with a shrug. "I
was spared out of acknowledgment for my past contributions, and
because I had enough sense to limit my involvement with the battle
station. Exile to Haidoral Prime was the best I could hope for under
the circumstances."

Von Geiz peered at Chalis as if inspecting the skin of her forehead.
"And that's when you chose to defect?" he asked.

Namir suspected Von Geiz was present to put a kind face on the
company. He'd begun the meeting by checking Chalis over, asking
about aftereffects of the stun bolt, while Howl had waited patiently
and Lieutenant Sairgon had scowled. Von Geiz was a smart man, and
he knew the role he'd been asked to play—kind, fatherly, sympathetic.
But Chalis barely looked at anyone but the captain.

"Don't be absurd," Chalis said. "Even on Haidoral, I had time to read, time to sculpt . . . I had money for occasional luxuries." She turned in her chair and reached down to where Namir had placed her duffel bag. He'd already inspected it for weapons, though he'd only delivered it to the office under protest.

Unlike Von Geiz, Namir wasn't in the room to ask questions or manipulate the governor. Howl hadn't said as much, of course, but Namir knew he was present as muscle. Chalis's capture was being kept a secret; as first sergeant, Namir was a high-ranking grunt, authorized to witness senior staff discussions and duty-bound not to do a thing about them.

"And speaking of luxuries," Chalis said, "you've been more than hospitable and I've been ungracious." From the bag, she retrieved a glass bottle filled with a translucent violet liquid adrift with gossamer white threads. She turned it in her hands, set it on the desk with a heavy *thunk,* then withdrew a handful of yellow fruit, which she placed beside the bottle. "A gift from Haidoral to my hosts: local brandy and native figs. Something to celebrate our new relationship."

The lieutenant looked questioningly at Howl. Howl lifted one of the fruits and, with a smile, began peeling it as Chalis uncapped the bottle. "Normally when a recruit smuggles alcohol aboard, she knows better than to share it with the senior staff," Howl said, though his tone was light.

"Then you should vet them for better manners," Chalis replied. "Cups?" None were forthcoming, and with a shrug she took a sip directly from the bottle. When she removed the brandy from her lips and slid it across the table to Howl, she tilted her head to look up at Namir. "Perfectly safe," she said.

The thought of poison had crossed Namir's mind. He cursed himself for being transparent enough to show it, and Chalis for seeing through him.

The others passed the brandy bottle as Chalis started on the fruit, continuing to speak between bites. "So as I said, an exile to Haidoral was far from the worst fate. Then you came to my planet, and I realized I was doomed."

"Your mansion wasn't a target," the lieutenant said.

Chalis laughed bitterly. "Being shot by *rebels* wasn't my worry. Who do you think will be blamed for the failure of Haidoral's defenses? Who will be held responsible for the raid on her city, the theft of Imperial supplies? I could argue I worked *miracles,* holding your men off with a legion of stormtroopers spread across three continents; I could argue Haidoral was an obvious target *months* before I even arrived, and that I did all I could to shore up its defenses.

"But Darth Vader," Chalis continued, her patter slowing, her eyes intent on Howl again after dancing about the room, "doesn't take to rational, *reasoned* arguments. My reputation was already blemished. The moment your ship arrived in orbit, my life in the Empire ended."

"Too bad you didn't ask to defect *then,*" the lieutenant said. "Would've saved us some trouble."

Namir choked back a laugh. Howl bit into his fruit and said nothing.

"Some men delude themselves all their lives," Chalis said. "I feel no shame in taking twenty-four hours to reconcile with reality. What's past is past—it's time we discussed our future together."

No one else spoke. Chalis seemed to take that as a cue to continue. "I offer my full cooperation to the Rebellion. In return, I expect to be rewarded for my bravery in turning against our terrible Imperial oppressors."

Von Geiz finally cleared his throat, but Howl interrupted first. "We'll talk," he said. "But so far we haven't even heard what you have to offer."

Something tightened in Namir's chest. Not because the question was the wrong one to ask, but because he knew it was one Chalis had been waiting for.

"I'm not a fleet admiral," she said, and leaned forward, shoulders low as if she were ready to pounce. "I'm not here to share some weak point in a Star Destroyer's defenses. *My* knowledge is the Empire's lifeblood—everything that courses through its veins, everything that nourishes it. Food, raw materials, manpower . . . I know why a slave revolt on Kashyyyk spells doom for outposts along the Kathol Rift, and why General Veers can't afford another thorilide shortage along the Rimma.

"I know the monster the Empire has grown into. I understand its biology. Every hyperlane carries oxygen to its limbs. I know where to pinch to make it sputter and suffocate."

Howl nodded and tapped his knuckles on the desk. "You're a logistics expert."

The lieutenant said quietly, "Before you were governor, you did what? Ran labor camps? Starved planets if they didn't meet their quotas?"

Chalis was still staring at Howl and leaning in. She smiled at the question. "I was an *adviser*. I *advised*. My predecessor—Count Vidian—was the one who liked getting his hands dirty. I'm more interested in the big picture.

"Of course, none of that matters so long as you're on the run. The Rebellion needs to put some distance between its armadas and the Mid Rim—now that you've abandoned it—or you risk being overtaken. I've got suggestions for *that*, too."

Then she moved. Namir couldn't stop her. If the office had been larger, if the desk hadn't been the flimsiest of barriers, Chalis couldn't have pulled herself forward and leaned in to put her head beside the captain's. The brandy bottle tipped to one side and fell to the floor. Chalis's lips moved as she whispered something outside Namir's hearing.

Namir's hand was on her shoulder an instant later, dragging her back into the chair while she laughed. Howl appeared unfazed and certainly unharmed, eyes half lidding in thought. Von Geiz and the lieutenant looked on with bitterness and concern.

"I think," Howl said, as Namir's fingertips dug into the governor's suit, "we should end here. We all have a lot to think about. I'll speak to you later, Governor."

Chalis smiled and bowed her head.

If Namir's role in the meeting had been to protect the captain or the company, he felt profoundly certain he'd failed.

———————

After doling out the supplies stolen from Haidoral to the rest of the rebel battle group, the *Thunderstrike* peeled off with the Dornean gunship *Apailana's Promise*. The *Promise* was a mean, compact dagger of a ship that had run with Twilight previously; its crew of a few dozen Alliance navy veterans collectively owed the soldiers of Twilight Company nearly fifty thousand credits, according to a running tally on the door of the starboard barracks. The *Promise* also bore a pair of X-wing starfighters on its undercarriage; their pilots had earned a special infamy for never deigning to set foot aboard the *Thunderstrike*.

Howl hadn't announced Twilight Company's new assignment since leaving Haidoral, and the bridge crew and senior officers were staying tight-lipped about the ships' destination. Neither was unusual, but where there was no hard information, rumors took the place of facts. The engineering crew studied the *Thunderstrike*'s course and declared it en route to Wild Space, racing to escape Imperial territory by plunging headlong into the unknown. Veterans from the Chargona campaign murmured about a coming last stand against a blockade of Star Destroyers along the edge of the Mid Rim. It was telling, Namir thought, that no one spread rumors of imminent victory.

Still, wartime gossip was as good a distraction as any for bored soldiers crammed into a metal box with nothing to do but wait. The rumors wouldn't have bothered Namir if not for the presence of the new recruits: Trainees didn't focus well when they thought they were doomed.

Twilight Company had picked up twenty-eight volunteers on Haidoral Prime. It was a good haul, though a third of them weren't fighters—they'd serve as medics or engineers or crew for the *Thunderstrike*, and they weren't Namir's problem. The others needed to be put through their paces before being assigned to squads. As first sergeant, Namir had that special pleasure.

"You all know how to use a blaster?" he asked, after marching into the mess hall where he'd ordered the fresh meat to assemble. He had a fully charged rifle slung over his shoulder.

The nineteen remaining recruits sat around steel tables in the otherwise empty mess. The men and women looked at one another and nodded awkwardly in response to Namir's question.

"Good," Namir said. "I'm not here to mother you. Find a friend to take you to the weapons range, learn how to use the DLT-20A. A rifle isn't a pistol—it's got more kick and it'll burn your face off if you hold it too close. The twenties have a couple extra modes, but I don't want you spraying bolts everywhere until you can hit a target." As he spoke, he held up his rifle with one hand and swapped out the power pack with the other. It was a rote exercise, and he had to remind himself to slow down for his audience. "You get a Twilight soldier to vouch for you, tell me you can handle the basics? That's all I need."

Again, the awkward nods. Namir strode to one of the occupied tables, set the rifle on the tabletop, and sent it spinning toward the recruits at the far end. "That goes for more than just shooting, though. If you can't find one of my guys who'll trust you with his life, I really don't care how good a sharpshooter you are or what your grades were at Dirtrag Academy. You don't set foot on a planet until someone clears you. If you're too shy to partner up on your own, fine—come to me, I'll assign you a buddy."

He'd given variations on the same speech over a dozen times. At the start, he'd tried to train every recruit personally. It had been arrogant and stupid—the mark of a man who didn't yet trust the competency of Twilight's veterans—and he liked to think he knew better now. He paced across the mess floor, ensured he'd made eye contact with all the recruits, then flashed a half smile. "Also, you'll probably share a squad with whoever you con into saying you're ready. Try not to pick someone you want to strangle."

Nervous laughter. That was good—they were paying attention.

Or most of them were. At the corner of one table sat the red-haired girl Namir had seen fighting in the plaza on Haidoral. She was looking past him, staring at the wall, and her hands were vibrating against the tabletop. Namir stepped around her, slapped a hand on her shoulder, and felt her flinch like she was ready to jump and throw a punch. That she wasn't stupid enough to *do* it counted for something.

"What's your name?" he asked.

The girl scooted in her seat until she could look up at Namir. "Roach," she said.

Namir watched her. Her jaw was set. She no longer twitched. "That what you want to be called?" he asked.

"Yes."

Namir laughed louder than he'd intended. "More advice," he called as he glanced at the others. "If you've got friends back home you want to protect or you just feel like starting fresh? Now's a good time to pick a new identity. No one in Twilight cares who you were, but once you make us learn a name, you better keep it."

At least it wasn't another Leia. Half the fresh meat that joined up tried to call themselves after one rebel hero or another. They got relabeled by their comrades fast. Most of them died shortly after, victims of their own enthusiasm.

He turned back to the kid. "Roach," he said. "Tell me something: You read your field guide yet? The *White Book*?"

Roach stared up at him. "Yes, Sergeant," she said.

Namir cocked his head. It wasn't the answer he'd been expecting. "So you can tell me about the four-phase training process?"

Roach's teeth were chattering, but she didn't hesitate. "First two phases are same for everyone. Different phase three for ground and space forces. Phase four is special units."

"And what does the *White Book* say about recruits who can't pass training before deployment?"

This made Roach pause. "They start again at phase one," she said. "Unless an officer says they can't?" It was a guess, not a statement.

Namir let his amusement show. "I have no clue," he said. "Good for you, reading all that, but the bad news is you wasted your time.

"You all need to understand that the *White Book*—all those procedures and regulations High Command vomits at us—it's cooked up by generals who think they're running a government instead of a rebellion." He shrugged and retrieved his rifle, slinging it back over his shoulder. "Maybe Alliance Special Forces takes it seriously; I don't know. Out here, when someone above you gives an order, you *follow* it. When someone tries to teach you something, you *pay attention*. When someone shoots at you, you *shoot back*. Don't smuggle alcohol or spice aboard, don't be stupid, and if you have a problem with another soldier, come to Lieutenant Sairgon or me. We'll set things right.

"Short version: Twilight Company takes care of its own. So long as you remember that, you don't need regulations from on high."

Namir saw the older recruits nod in understanding. The younger ones, the ones who still weren't sure about what they were giving up, looked less certain. Many of them had grown up in an Empire that was nothing but rules and order. That was okay. They'd get there.

He wrapped up the orientation briskly, listing which sections of the *Thunderstrike* were off limits and answering the usual questions about pay ("stash what you've got under your bunk and pray the Banking Clan joins the Alliance") and comm network access ("put in a request, but don't get your hopes up"). By the end, he'd memorized the names of about half the recruits. If the others survived, he'd learn their names, too.

Namir was first out of the room. The others dispersed behind him, heading toward their assigned barracks or the weapons range. He noticed Roach tailing him, but he didn't turn to look back until she said, "Sergeant?"

"What do you need?" he asked.

Roach fell in at his side. Namir's boots hit the metal floor hard. The girl walked silently, and he saw she was still in footwraps appropriate for Haidoral's flooded streets and not much else; he made a note to ask Hober about finding her something, *anything* more combat-appropriate.

"I lied," Roach said.

Namir stopped, turned to Roach, and waited for her to elaborate.

"I don't know how to use a blaster."

Namir shook his head and tried not to smile. "Two hours," he said. "Meet me at the armory. We'll get you sorted."

He didn't wait for an answer before he resumed his pace. He didn't expect a thank-you. He'd voted Roach in on Haidoral. The least he could do was try to keep her alive.

The *Thunderstrike*'s makeshift brig was a secondary air lock along the ship's aft, plated with thick armor to repel boarders and fully controlled from the bridge. Its internal access panels had been welded shut. The exterior door remained functional; a prisoner could, in theory, be launched into space at the touch of a button, though Howl had made it clear that such a thing was never to be done. Namir had made it equally clear—many months earlier, in private, to select crew—that prisoners didn't need to *know* about Howl's squeamishness. Twilight Company's jail was naturally intimidating; why give up that advantage?

Namir doubted Governor Chalis was intimidated, but he could hope.

No one but the captain and his closest advisers ever saw Chalis, who remained in her air lock twenty-three hours each day. Periodically, the governor met with Howl in private. Chief Medic Von Geiz personally delivered Chalis's meals and brought her whatever she required for comfort—or at least whatever was available. In this way, Howl was able to keep the identity of Twilight's prisoner a secret from most of the company for a full two days.

Namir didn't know how word got out, but he wasn't surprised or bothered when it did. The presence of a captive was too tantalizing a mystery to last for long, and it seemed a healthy distraction from constant speculation about the rebel flight from the Mid Rim. Instead of wondering whether they'd survive to see planetfall again, soldiers debated what Chalis's presence meant. The recruits from Haidoral told stories of the governor's fickle tastes: how she would summon chefs and artists to her mansion only to return them to the streets hours, days, or months later. The turncoats—those Twilight Company soldiers, like Charmer, originally trained as Imperial cadets, who had switched sides after being armed and set loose—recalled older rumors of a woman who whispered to the Emperor's viziers, whose true talent was in manipulating her foes and converting them into allies.

The company's fascination with Chalis went too far only once, when one of the fresh meat—a squat, muscular young man named

Corbo who had a harsh red birthmark covering half his face—found his way to the air lock with a galley knife clenched in both hands. Corbo didn't resist when a passing technician urged him safely away, and Namir confronted him in private afterward.

"Any special reason you wanted to see her?" Namir asked.

"She killed my felinx," Corbo said.

"I don't know what that is."

Corbo shrugged. "Pet. Doesn't matter. Governor thought too many were turning feral, making the city look bad."

"That the worst thing she did?"

"No," Corbo said. "But it's what I can't forgive."

They were both silent awhile.

"I wasn't going to do anything, I don't think," Corbo added. "I just wanted to see her." He balled and unballed his fists. "I'll leave the company, if that's what you need."

Namir sighed. "Can I trust you not to do it again?" he asked, expecting he knew the answer.

Don't be stupid, he thought. *Just lie to me.*

"I don't know," Corbo said.

Namir swore inwardly.

"If I post a guard," he said, "tell him to shoot you if you show your face near the brig again—does that seem fair?"

"That seems fair."

"Good. Because I've got a lot of dead soldiers I need to replace. I need the lot of you in fighting shape, not abandoning ship."

So far as Namir was concerned, that resolved the incident. He made a point not to inform the captain.

Others weren't as discreet. "I have no love of the Imperial Ruling Council," Gadren announced in regard to Corbo's aborted attack on Chalis, "and I am not alone. But a woman stripped of all power deserves pity and contempt, not fury."

Namir, Gadren, and half a dozen others sat in the Clubhouse—a cramped, dimly lit crawl space above the ship's engineering section that jumped with each pulse of the hyperdrive. Set amid metal pipes running from floor to ceiling were storage crates cushioned with throw rugs and a dented table someone had stolen from a bombed-out cantina. Namir was skimming through post-combat supply inventories that boiled down to "not enough weapons," while Gadren, Ajax, Brand, and Twitch played cards. Roach sat near the card players—in Charmer's favorite spot, though Charmer was still in the medbay—observing. Namir didn't know how Roach had found her way to the Clubhouse; it usually took recruits months to get an invite, and he certainly hadn't invited her.

"She's got the captain's ear," Twitch muttered. "Don't seem powerless to me."

Ajax ignored Twitch, eyeing Gadren. "That mean you wouldn't take a swing at our prisoner if the chance came?"

"I shot her once already," Gadren said.

Brand glowered until each of them drew from the deck. Roach had stopped watching the cards, instead staring down at her hands as she wove her fingers together and pulled them apart with quick, awkward motions.

Ajax glanced at Roach and grinned wickedly. "Maybe fresh meat here thinks *she* should get a chance. The prisoner ran her planet, after all."

Ajax had joined Twilight after the obliteration of the Rebellion's Thirty-Second Infantry. He'd been one of five survivors among four hundred dead, and he still proudly wore the Thirty-Second's "Bleeding Roughnecks" badge. He was a jerk and a grenadier with better aim than most snipers. Namir found him tolerable in small doses.

Roach kept looking at her fingers. Gadren spoke to Ajax but watched the girl. "The fresh meat knows she is not alone. We *all* have scars, and we endure them together."

Roach squeezed her hands together until pink skin turned white. Finally she met Gadren's gaze. "You got scars?" she asked.

Twitch played a card that made the rest of the table wince. Gadren kept speaking as he reshuffled the deck. His voice was calm, easy, as if he'd answered the question a thousand times before. "The Empire took my kin," he said, "and sold them as slaves to a Hutt clan."

Roach cursed softly. Brand looked down at her cards, as if avoiding intruding on a private moment.

"If I had not found Twilight Company," Gadren said, and shrugged, "I would have died long ago. Sharing grief and grievances does us good when we face an enemy of such ebon depths. The Empire is a force unprecedented in any age, poised to end history itself. No one should confront it alone."

Ajax glanced at the pot, tossed in a credit chip, and smirked. "Shortest story I've ever heard a Besalisk tell. Good on you, Gadren."

Namir's instinct was to toss his datapad at Ajax, but he was only halfway through the inventory. Instead, he called, without looking up, "First: Don't be obnoxious. Second: He's Corellian, not Besalisk. Insult him right."

Ajax cackled. Namir didn't understand why until he saw Gadren smiling, too. Even Roach and Brand seemed to be holding back snickers. Twitch didn't look away from her cards.

"Corellia is a human world," Gadren said patiently, "and I lived there a long time. I consider it my home. But my species is Besalisk."

Ajax slapped his right hand on top of Roach's left. "The sergeant there?" he said to Roach in a mock-whisper. "He ain't *cultured* and *educated* like us."

Namir swore at Ajax in a cool, stilted tone. The others laughed, and Namir tried to let the moment of humiliation glide over him. Dwelling on it would only make it worse.

The card players picked up the game again. Twitch won the next round, to no one's surprise. Roach seemed to be struggling with something, looking between Gadren and the others, parting her lips now and then as if she wanted to speak. Of the players, only Brand seemed to notice, but she kept her usual silence.

"Six months," Roach finally said, "in an Imp detention center."

The others looked at her, perplexed. She hunched her shoulders and shrugged. "My grudge," she explained.

Gadren gruffly clapped Roach on the back. Twitch raised an eyebrow inquisitively, but didn't press Roach for the details.

Ajax grinned. "Guess it's story time." He took the deck of cards from Gadren and began to deal. "Winner of this round picks who goes next."

Namir watched Ajax closely, but he couldn't tell if the man was cheating or not. All he was sure of was that, two minutes later, Ajax *winked* when he claimed his victory and pointed at Brand.

Brand took it in stride. "I'm not here for a grudge," she said.

Ajax pressed her. "So why are you?"

"I took a bounty on the captain," Brand said.

Gadren shook his head. Namir knew he'd heard that much of the story before. The others were suddenly focused on Brand.

"What happened?" Roach asked.

"I changed my mind," Brand said. "Your story, Ajax."

Ajax was keen to share, and Namir decided to make his exit while the others were occupied. He didn't need to hear about Ajax and his lovers and their hunting trip again, and he didn't want to be around when *his* turn to speak came. He wasn't in the mood to argue and he wasn't in the mood to lie.

He ascended the ladder through the tight shaft leading to the aft end of the crew deck. He paused at the top, closed his eyes, and leaned against the gentle curve of the wall. He was glad Roach was finding a place in the company. He was glad Governor Chalis was a distraction from rumors of imminent doom. But he needed a break of his own.

Or he needed to get back to the fight.

Halfway to the barracks, Namir realized that Brand was walking beside him. He wasn't sure how long she'd been there or where she'd caught up. He couldn't even pinpoint the moment he'd noticed her company; she had eased into Namir's consciousness like stars emerging at night.

When Namir looked directly at his companion, Brand spoke in an easy tone as if they'd been talking for hours. "How do you think they'll hold up?"

Namir struggled to make sense of the words. "The new recruits?"

Brand nodded.

"Roach is trying. The others don't know jack about squad combat, but they can shoot and take orders. We've seen worse."

"You give them the meat grinder speech?"

"Figured it wasn't the time. They saw us on Haidoral. They're not under any illusions this life is glamorous."

The corner of Brand's mouth twitched. "Doesn't mean they know High Command sends us into hell every time."

"*Howl* sends us into hell."

"Howl keeps us alive."

"That, too."

Brand snorted. "You ever think you're too hard on him?"

Namir glanced down the corridor. There was a lot about Howl he didn't want to be heard saying, particularly by the recruits. "Howl's a genius," he said. "You won that argument on Blacktar Cyst. Just wish he wasn't mad as a glitterstim addict reading omens in his filth."

They walked together in silence until the door to Namir's barracks came into view. "You know it's going to get worse," Brand said. "With her on board?"

"Roach?" Namir asked.

"Don't be stupid."

Namir studied Brand's face, tried to read her expression. As ever, she was closed to him. "You know something? About what the captain's up to with Chalis?"

Brand turned and began to walk away before she even answered. "I don't know anything," she said. "But sometimes I guess lucky."

The attack came three days later in the middle of the night shift. The ship's klaxon brought Namir out his bunk with a groan of exhaustion and frustration, but he had his shirt and boots on in under thirty seconds. His bunk mates were scrambling to dress, as well; Roja asked Namir if he knew what was going on.

"You're kidding" was Namir's only answer. He was too tired for anything else.

The first rumble and the subsequent echo of rending metal made it obvious that the *Thunderstrike* had entered combat. The ship's corridors were full of Twilight soldiers rushing to shelter while the crew took to battle stations. Unless the enemy sent a boarding party, infantry had no place in a clash of starships, and the best Twilight's ground troops could do was stay out of the way and keep their distance from the hull. Meanwhile, the bridge crew, engineering, and the gunnery staff—along with the *Apailana's Promise,* if the gunship hadn't been destroyed in a surprise attack—would try to keep everyone alive.

Namir recognized the energy and purpose in the crew members and despised them with every step they took. They weren't to blame, but there was nothing worse than feeling useless and stupid during a fight.

Namir's assigned shelter was the mess hall. Twilight soldiers were pressed tight against one another when he arrived. The room stank of sweat. Someone called his name and waved from near the entrance— Sergeant Fektrin, one hand cupped over an ear and the other fiddling with his comlink.

Namir pushed his way through. Fektrin finished speaking into the comm as the ship rumbled again. "All shelters report in," he said. "Head count is a few short, but we assume it's just stragglers."

"Take their names when they show up, report any fresh meat to me," Namir replied. "Any idea who's attacking?"

"Something bigger than a pirate, smaller than a Star Destroyer."

The deck lurched, and several soldiers toppled into their peers. Namir kept his balance as Fektrin cupped his ear again before growling, "Section ten. Might be a hull breach."

Namir swore reflexively. So much damage so fast was never a good sign. But section ten was low-risk. Not much there except—

He swore again. "What about the brig? Is it intact?"

Fektrin looked confused, then winced as he was struck by comprehension. "Nothing from the guard, but that could mean comm trouble or—"

Namir was already heading out of the mess.

He knew that in all likelihood, the prisoner was secure in the air lock. Maybe she'd already been relocated. But he'd found an excuse to do something other than wait and he'd taken it.

As he approached section ten, Namir reached a blast door in the corridor. Someone had sealed off the hall. He checked the panel readings, saw there was still life support beyond the barricade, and decided to chance it. The air lock wasn't more than fifty meters out. How bad could it be?

Namir tapped in a code and felt an expulsion of heat break against his face as the door irised open. The corridor howled like a storm. Orange flame raged out of air vents and severed pipes, splashing into the wall and causing metal panels to warp and shriek. Namir stumbled back a step, then fell to his knees when the ship shook.

He swore again and wished he'd brought his helmet.

He pulled his shirt up to half shield his face and wrapped his hands in the ends of his sleeves. The fabric was, in theory, fire-resistant; in the field, he'd seen combat outfits fuse to men and women's skin before it caught flame—not strictly comforting, but proof of durability. He paused long enough to wonder about the fire's temperature—was it fueled by chemicals from the pipelines?—but shrugged away the question. He didn't have the expertise to apply the answer if he'd had one.

Namir resisted the urge to charge forward. He couldn't afford to stumble or fall if the ship took another hit. Instead, he set a deliberate pace, knees bent for balance and to keep his body small. The heat was searing, but soon the pain seemed to plateau—agony ravaged his skin, and it neither grew worse nor faded. He felt no different when he pushed through a curtain of flame than when he left it behind.

Then he was at the air lock.

The door was sealed. At the base, lying flat as if she'd been slammed unconscious against the door by one of the ship's upheavals, was the on-duty guard. Namir couldn't tell whether the woman was still breathing, but the flames hadn't reached her. A glance through the air lock's view panel revealed that the governor was still inside, sitting cross-legged at the far end of the room.

Suddenly Namir laughed. He had no idea whether he was authorized to open the air lock—whether his codes would open the door.

He might burn to death for nothing.

At least he wasn't waiting in the mess hall.

He pulled his shirt back into place and punched his access code into the lock. The door mechanisms groaned and stirred. *Guess the captain has some faith in me,* he thought.

The air lock interior was furnished with everything the stores of the *Thunderstrike* had to offer, though that amounted to little more than a trunk, a cot, a stained food tray, and a portable sanitation station. Several datapads were stacked on the cot, and in front of the cross-legged governor hovered a miniature holo-droid, projecting a shimmering blue web of spheres and lines. Chalis's hands played across the image, extending and rotating the lines, reshaping the web with expert precision.

Chalis was standing and the web was gone by the time the door was fully open. "I see you chose not to let me suffocate," she said.

Namir knelt and checked the guard's body as cooler air flooded in from the air lock. Still alive. He recognized her face but couldn't recall her name—one of the recruits Twilight had picked up on Thession.

He slid his hands under the woman's arms and half lifted her from the floor. He wanted to scream at the abrasions on his burnt hands. Instead, he gritted his teeth and managed to ask, "You really think suffocation was your worst problem?"

Chalis smiled and stalked forward, then stopped with a wince as she felt the heat of the corridor. Namir felt grim satisfaction at the sight of the governor taken aback.

"Air circulation isn't functioning," Chalis said, "so yes, that was my priority. Until you opened the door, I was *safe* from the fire."

Namir grunted and dragged the guard into the air lock while Chalis eyed the doorway. "Can we run for it?" she asked. Her voice had dropped an octave, all mockery gone.

"*I* could, maybe." Namir lowered the guard to the floor. He tried to catch his breath while ignoring the pain clinging to his skin like mud. "But I'm dressed for it. You'd roast alive."

Chalis closed her eyes and lowered her head. Then her neck snapped back up and she looked at Namir. "So we open the air lock's outer door. We create a vacuum. We cling to the walls for dear life. And when the oxygen has rushed out and the fires in this section have been extinguished, we close the door and get to safety."

It took Namir a moment to process the suggestion. Then he laughed hoarsely as he stepped back into the doorframe. "You've got it all figured." He edged far enough into the corridor to hit the control panel again, then ducked back into the air lock.

The interior door began to hum shut. Chalis stared and her tone became harsh. "What are you doing?"

Namir gestured at the guard with the toe of his boot as the door sealed with a metallic clang. "We open this section up to space, she's not in any shape to hold on."

Chalis's expression seemed to contort. Namir was sure she was going to shout, to rage. He wondered if he'd need to fight her off.

Instead, she simply said in a voice of dull resignation, "So you're locking us in."

"I'm locking us in," Namir agreed, "and hoping for the best."

Namir had trouble tracking time inside the air lock. The oxygen felt abrasive against his burnt skin. His head was throbbing, echoing every beat of his heart inside his skull. He tried counting the number of hits the *Thunderstrike* took in battle, but even that became difficult when he could no longer differentiate a new strike from the aftershocks of an old one.

Chalis sat across from him. "This is the second time you've come to rescue me, you know," she said.

"Be grateful," Namir said, "and shut up."

"You haven't earned any favors," Chalis countered evenly. "The first time, you thought I was someone else; then you shot me. This time,

I'm no better off than I was before you showed. I'm worse off, in fact, since all three of us are using what's left of the air." She didn't give the unconscious guard so much as a glance.

Namir exhaled in a hiss. The air *was* getting thinner, and it smelled of smoke. He was prepared to stare down Chalis if he had to, though—to ignore his cloudy vision and try to put her in her place by force of will.

As he squared his shoulders she smiled sourly, like a woman taken with her own dark humor. Not a woman worth saving. Yet not a woman who appeared to fear death, either.

Namir watched the guard's chest slowly rise and fall. "You may not be better off. She is," he said.

The governor shrugged, as if she didn't see the statement's relevance.

Namir closed his eyes and leaned against the bulkhead. "Any idea who attacked us? You're the expert . . ."

A distant rumble from below accompanied a jolt through the deck. Namir bounced an arm's width off the floor and couldn't quite stifle a gasp when he landed hard on his tailbone. Chalis didn't cry out, and Namir didn't bother opening his eyes to check on her.

She waited until the ship settled before answering. "At a guess," she said, a hint of strain in her voice, "I'd say my former colleagues are coming after me. Can't have Imperial secrets falling into rebel hands. Can't have another Tseebo, or a Death Star *incident* . . .

"By now, Darth Vader himself should be in pursuit. Whether that's his flagship out there, I can't be sure; if not, we may be spared so he can kill me personally."

Namir snorted. "What is it with you people and Vader?" he asked. "It can't be the helmet that scares people. Stormtroopers have helmets."

When Chalis replied, her voice held a note of curiosity. "Most rebels blanch when they hear the name," she said. "He may be mythologized, but he's earned his reputation. I could tell tales of how he slaughtered children, the Dhen-Moh genocides—"

"Spare me," Namir said. "That's my dying wish. Spare me the stories of the great *Lord Vader's* terrifying triumphs over the *Rebellion*."

After he spoke, he wished he hadn't added such a sneer to the word *Rebellion*. He cracked his eyes open enough to confirm that the guard was still unconscious. Chalis was watching him closely. "You don't think of yourself as one of them, do you?" she asked.

Namir closed his eyes again and made an obscene gesture in Chalis's direction. He'd learned it from Twilight's dead comm tech long ago, and he wasn't sure how commonplace it was. From Chalis's laughter, however, she seemed to get the point.

Neither spoke for a while, and eventually Namir realized that the shuddering of the deck had ceased. The battle, apparently, was over. Even better, the pain of Namir's burns had decreased to a steady but subtle throbbing. It probably meant he'd gone into shock, but he wasn't in any shape to worry.

Namir knew he was drifting in and out of consciousness, and he ceased to fight the pull of darkness when he heard the hiss of air vents coming back to life. His last thought was about the guard, the new recruit from Thession.

Her name was Maediyu. She never listened during training.

Namir hoped she would survive.

During his tour with Twilight Company, Namir had spent more than a few days in *Thunderstrike*'s infirmary. He'd broken bones, taken blaster shots, and seen shrapnel lodged in his flesh. In his experience, Twilight's medics offered two types of recuperation:

The first involved a blissful state of oblivion and submersion in a tank of liquid bacta. The tank was a sanctuary from pain and need, a welcoming home for as many hours or days as the medics deemed necessary—or, in less ideal circumstances, until bacta supplies ran low. The patient floated in pure, viscous *health,* emerging from unconsciousness gradually until full awareness was restored. The aches that came in the days following always felt worse for the loss of the bacta's pleasures, but they passed soon enough.

The second type of recuperation involved lying on a hard bunk stinking of cleaning fluid and shivering in too-cold air while slipping in and out of sleep. During moments of near-lucidity, the patient was afflicted with visions of blood-soaked medstaff making their rounds, alternating stinging shots with numbing balms. During sleep, the patient suffered confused fever dreams without narrative or logic: endless strings of images, of faces strange and familiar, along with inexplicable feelings of terror and alienation—as if the dreamer were alone in a world where every once-familiar object hid horrors.

Namir's recuperation from his burns took the second form. Hours after he'd been rushed to the medbay, during one miserable moment of clarity, he saw that Maediyu had been placed in a bacta tank. *Lucky girl,* he thought.

He was back on his feet within two days, his arms scarred and tender but his body largely restored. Von Geiz warned him not to return to full duty for another few shifts—a suggestion Namir was willing enough to take, given that Twilight's next combat assignment was nowhere in sight.

The attack on the *Thunderstrike* had apparently been a fluke—a chance run-in with an Imperial reconnaissance squadron—resulting in the deaths of three crew members aboard *Apailana's Promise,* half a dozen injuries aboard *Thunderstrike,* and minor systems damage to both ships. There was no evidence that the Imperials had been hunting Governor Chalis, who had been found unscathed in the air lock with Namir and Maediyu. The woman led a charmed life.

A day after Namir's release from the infirmary, after he'd read the latest reports and screwed up his courage, he arranged a meeting with Howl. He found the captain in the workroom off the operations center, pacing between upright displays and a holotable that projected topographic images of a world dense with waterways and jungles. Howl was speaking softly to himself, one hand tapping at the air as if beating out a rhythm to his words.

Captain Micha Evon was a tall man, with dark-brown skin and graying hair that seemed to tangle in his thick beard. Namir knew little of his past and had trouble imagining him existing prior to Twilight; he had founded the company (so Namir had been told) and it seemed impossible that he would ever leave. He rarely emerged from his lair, going unseen by the rank and file for days at a time while his senior staff passed down orders.

Namir believed with utter certainty that "Howling Mad" Evon was the greatest mind he'd ever fought with. He also believed Howl was responsible for the deaths of dozens of his friends—deaths that might have been avoided—and that the captain would sacrifice Namir in an eyeblink to win some esoteric victory for the Rebel Alliance.

Howl laughed at something while Namir stood inside the doorway, waiting to be recognized. When the captain finally waved him closer, he looked Namir up and down with an almost fierce intensity. "Sergeant," he said. "What have you heard about Mount Arakeirkos?"

"I'm not familiar with it," Namir said as Howl gestured distractedly at a chair. Namir walked to it but didn't seat himself.

"Neither am I," Howl said. "But at the top, there's a great clock set in stone, built by the Arakein Monks almost two thousand standard years ago. According to legend, whoever watches each swing of its pendulum for a day will have the life span of the universe revealed before his eyes." He resumed his pacing as he spoke, punctuating his words with small gestures and finally looking back to Namir.

Namir shook his head. "I'll take your word for it. Religious orders aren't my thing."

Private conversations with Howl were like exhuming a corpse. You had to dig and dig before you found what you were looking for, and even then it wouldn't be pretty. But Namir had learned that there was no rushing the captain when he had his own topic in mind.

"Time isn't just the provenance of philosophers," Howl said, as if correcting a child's mistake. "We live on a ship powered by energies that sunder cause and effect, beginning and end . . . hyperspace is a mystery more profound than gods and demons."

Howl dropped into a chair across from Namir, spread his hands, and bowed his head. "Yet we use it to make war," he said, "and here we are. Tell me what's on your mind."

"Governor Chalis," Namir said. "Were we attacked because of her?"

The last of Howl's effervescence vanished, as if incinerated in a flash fire. "We don't know. *Chalis* certainly thinks so, but she's not an unbiased source."

"The more she convinces us the Imperials value her, the more she can demand for her help. I get that," Namir said. "But you've talked to her. Do *you* think she's for real?"

"She could be."

"Because if she is—" Namir pressed on. He was sure he was overstepping; he was first sergeant, not the captain's strategist or second in command. He was in Twilight to execute orders, not question them. "—Twilight has a target on its back. A lot worse could come."

"Vader," Howl said. "Chalis said it to me, too."

Namir shrugged. "Vader or Captain Dirtfarm—doesn't matter *who* comes if they're backed by an armada. The best thing for us is to get rid of her."

Howl shook his head and tapped a long, slow rhythm onto the holotable. "I can't," he said. "We found her, and she's our responsibility."

"Turn her over to another company. Someone in the Rebellion must be equipped for this."

"Equipped for what?" Howl asked, without a trace of impatience. "We don't even know what we have, and we're still ten thousand light-years deep in Imperial territory and struggling to get to safety. No one nearby can watch her or protect her any better than we can, and I'm not prepared to take more dramatic action."

Namir watched his captain. He didn't doubt Howl was capable of lying to him; good commanders often lied to their troops. Yet his arguments had the ring of truth.

They simply weren't complete.

"You think it's a trap," Namir said. It was a guess. "She's a double agent, or she's being manipulated."

"It's a possibility," Howl said.

"You think you have a way to find out," Namir said.

Howl smiled, but he didn't answer. He stood and paced a few steps, stared at the door to the workroom, then held up a hand as if calling for silence.

"The Rebel Alliance," he said, "is falling apart. Things are as bad as they've been since—well, since long before you came aboard—and if the Empire wins, it wins completely. We need an edge, and we might have found one.

"I'm going to test that edge. If it cuts, I'm going to hone it. We're already taking the first steps.

"Chalis promised to assemble a schematic—a holographic map of the Empire's entire logistical network, showing its strengths and vulnerabilities. If she can do that, it *will* change the war. But we need to see if we can rely on her first."

Namir nodded slowly. "So what's our next mission?" he asked. *What did she tell you when you first met?*

Howl didn't reply. He merely opened the workroom door to the corridor and smiled again, sadly, at Namir.

Their meeting was over.

CHAPTER 5

CARIDA SYSTEM
Day Ninety-One of the Mid Rim Retreat

Captain Tabor Seitaron felt an internal buzz of distress as he stepped off his shuttle into the hangar of the Imperial Star Destroyer *Herald*. His boots seemed to cling to the polished floor and his intestines felt as though they'd been compressed under a stone. He couldn't recall the last time he'd experienced the tug of artificial gravity—perhaps four years ago, during the test flight of the *Rueful Confession*?—but he knew it hadn't always afflicted him so.

He felt *old*. He should have been on Carida, teaching military history to cadets who'd mastered the art of appearing attentive in class. Instead, he'd spent the morning being ferried from Academy to spaceport to hangar without the barest hint as to why.

"Captain Seitaron, sir! Welcome aboard."

Tabor looked to the ensign who stood stiffly at attention. His posture was adequate, his uniform neatly pressed, though his eyes were bloodshot and sunken. The boy—the man, Tabor supposed, though junior officers always seemed like boys nowadays—was backed by two stormtroopers whose arms were locked rigid at their sides. *At least,* Tabor thought, *they're following protocol.*

"At ease," he said. The trio relaxed their shoulders only a touch.

"We're grateful you could come," the ensign said, and began to lead the way out of the hangar—briskly at first, then abruptly slowing his steps to accommodate Tabor. "If you have anything stowed on the shuttle—"

"Nothing," Tabor said. "I was told the prelate wanted to see me?"

"He'll be ready for you shortly," the ensign assured him. "This way, please."

The stormtroopers fell in behind Tabor and the ensign as they braved the depths of the ship. Tabor had served aboard Star Destroyers even before they'd earned the name—during the darkest days of the Republic, when shipwrights used to building merchant vessels and gilded yachts had scrambled to learn the arts of war. He'd seen the ships evolve from overwrought behemoths barely able to power their frames to the greatest weapons in the Imperial fleet, each capable of transporting thousands of soldiers or laying waste to continents and orbital platforms. The *Herald* was one of the later designs, postdating Tabor's active service; though he knew its specifications, he didn't recognize the high-pitched hum of its engine or the droids that scurried among its data terminals.

Nor did he recognize the path the ensign followed through the cavernous hallways and operations rooms. As they walked, the ensign kept up a polite but incessant patter, pointing out the ship's features—its complement of walkers, its updated turbolaser targeting systems—and making a point to inform Tabor where to find the officers' mess, the crew quarters, and the bridge. He related the ship's upgrades to triumphs in Tabor's own career—"I'm sure that extra ten percent efficiency would have been useful at the Battle of Foerost!"—and Tabor

humored the boy, nodding approvingly and asking the obvious questions. But his mind wandered. *He's giving me the whole blasted tour.
How long does he think I'm staying?*

"When were you assigned here?" Tabor inquired, barely hearing
himself as they marched past duty stations.

"Four months ago, along with most of the crew."

Four months? That surprised Tabor. The ensign wasn't the only
man who looked exhausted. Officers flinched as Tabor walked past,
tapping at their consoles frenetically. He saw others slump their shoulders the moment they thought he'd looked away. He recognized a
mixture of diligence, fatigue, and suppressed terror typical of men
who'd spent *years* behind enemy lines.

He could have made delicate inquiries, asked about the ship's recent missions and the background of the officers aboard. Perhaps he
still would—it rankled Tabor to see morale in such a state—but that
could wait until he was home. The *Herald* was not his ship or his responsibility.

The tour was mercifully truncated when the ensign left Tabor alone
in the conference center with an assurance that the prelate would join
him shortly. Tabor took the opportunity to wipe his brow and ingest a
tablet the medics had prescribed to calm his innards. He checked the
time on a nearby console; at the Academy, it would soon be time for
lunch.

It was nearly an hour before Prelate Verge finally arrived.

If the ensign had been a boy, the prelate was practically a child—
barely twenty years old, at a generous guess, with gleaming sapphire
eyes and flowing black hair. He wore an outfit of deep-gray cloth,
augmented by a cloak in the style of the Serenno nobles and a single
bejeweled brooch. Tabor was left with the impression of someone
who would have been at home in the Republic Senate, gaudy and
elegant and alien all at once. Yet aboard the ordered refinement of a
Star Destroyer, the prelate was chaos personified—unconstrained by
regulations, a singular persona in the midst of diligently enforced
uniformity.

Tabor had heard of the prelate before his summons to the *Herald*, if only vaguely: the youngest member of the Imperial Ruling Council, a rising star among the ministers and advisers who gossiped and played politics on Coruscant. Emperor Palpatine himself had supposedly granted Verge his title, though what *prelate* actually signified, Tabor could not guess.

Prelate Verge strode into the conference room with a broad smile, reaching out to clasp Tabor's shoulder with harsh enthusiasm. "Captain," he said. "Welcome to my ship."

Your ship? Tabor thought. *You've never spent a day in the Imperial Navy.* But he nodded politely and said, "Thank you, Prelate. She's a fine vessel"—Verge released his grip; Tabor continued before the prelate could reply—"but I'm not sure why you brought me here."

The corners of the prelate's mouth twitched. Then his smile tightened and he backed away. "Of course," he said. "It's been a long journey for you, and you must be eager to begin."

Tabor wondered *what,* exactly, needed beginning, but this time he refrained from prompting Verge.

"I've been appointed a task," Verge said, "by our beneficent Emperor: the capture of Everi Chalis, former emissary to the Imperial Ruling Council and honorary Grand Architect of the New Order— now defector to the Rebel Alliance. I believe you knew the traitor, and I need someone at my side who understands how she thinks." He flashed a smile before adding, "So much as any true Imperial can comprehend the thinking of a traitor."

Tabor tried to keep the confusion from his face. Chalis had struck Tabor as capable in her way, an adequate successor to the genius of Count Vidian but better at promoting herself and outplaying her foes than anything truly remarkable. Had anyone asked Tabor whether Chalis might betray the Empire, he'd have denied the possibility altogether; such a woman had neither the courage nor the will to turn on her masters.

"With due respect," Tabor said, "you overestimate my understanding of the woman—we haven't spoken in years." He racked his brain, tried to remember the endless meetings and receptions on Coruscant; remember who had worked with Chalis and, of those, who hadn't yet retired or passed on. "Perhaps Tiaan Jerjerrod or Kenth Leesha could be of more use?" he tried.

Again, the prelate's mouth twitched. "I chose *you*," he said, "as the Emperor chose *me*. Chalis is dangerous, and this is not the time for humility."

Boyish fingers closed into a fist and reopened. Verge's voice fell to a whisper, and Tabor had to strain to understand. "You were once a great man; you served our Emperor and our age with distinction. Now you waste away at the Academy, and I am offering you the chance to serve truly once more."

With his final words, he raised his voice again. His tone was cold and lifeless. "To refuse this privilege would be as incomprehensible as Chalis's own acts."

Tabor stared at the prelate as he parsed the knot of verbiage.

He'd been in his own world so long he'd forgotten the language of the court: how polite men accused each other of treason.

Defiance rose in his throat. He banished it like he had the buzzing in his stomach. "I apologize," he said. "I meant no offense to the Emperor. I'd be proud to serve at your side."

Long-forgotten rumors surfaced unbidden in Tabor's mind. He recalled stories of a child of one of Emperor Palpatine's viziers, groomed for the Ruling Council, devoted to the Emperor's service above all else. That same child had embraced Palpatine's doctrine with a zealous fervor, sought to prove himself the embodiment of his Emperor's New Order.

People had *mocked* Verge to Tabor. They called him deluded and self-important. They said he'd built a manor on Naboo, the Emperor's homeworld, with a private shrine to Palpatine's glories. They said he'd once tried to *maim* himself, to scar his face as the Jedi had done to the Emperor. Perhaps they were correct.

If nothing else, Prelate Verge was a true believer.

Verge nodded stiffly, proudly. "Good," he said. "You and I will achieve great things—I'm certain of that."

Tabor offered a smile that felt more like a grimace and wondered when he would see his home on Carida again.

CHAPTER 6

PLANET COYERTI
Day Ninety-Seven of the Mid Rim Retreat

Swaths of green and brown and yellow raced past the open bay doors of Namir's drop ship. The roar of the wind and the fury of the engine combined into an inexorable howl that overwhelmed any other sound; so long as Namir fixed his gaze ahead, he seemed alone inside a hurricane.

A hand tapped his shoulder. He turned to see Brand hold up two fingers. Behind Brand stood Gadren, while Roach clung to one of the handrails, swaying with the rocking of the ship. In the recesses of the bay, two more squads of Twilight soldiers were crammed together on narrow benches, checking their blasters and their armor.

Two minutes until drop.

Namir nodded to Brand and turned back to the doors. The streaks of color were slowing with the drop ship, resolving into masses of broad-leafed trees spotted and drooping with disease. A heavy, vegetal aroma filled the humid air, along with something acrid Namir couldn't place. It wasn't the worst-smelling planet Namir had been to, but he guessed it would grow distasteful fast.

He cinched the strap of his rifle and adjusted his helmet. The masses of jungle now became individual trees as the drop ship descended toward the ground. One minute to go.

A faint, tinny voice sounded as Brand yelled in his ear. "TIE fighter incoming. Do it fast." Namir nodded again.

The ship descended farther until tree limbs and wet leaves slapped its underside. One branch leapt in through the bay doors before snapping off and falling away. Then the foliage cleared and Namir could see the tarry mire that served as Coyerti's surface.

With a fierce smile, he jumped.

The fall was less than five meters—short enough to survive or high enough to kill, depending on how one landed. Namir could feel the heat of the drop ship engines as he went down, but it was gone a second later when his feet struck the ground. He bent his knees as the dark soil compressed and his boots sank, then he fell forward and tried to roll. In another moment he was up again, filthy and sore but unharmed.

He surveyed the clearing. Brand was up already, as covered in mire as Namir. Gadren was rising with a groan a stone's throw away. Roach was on her back, and a jolt of concern ran through Namir before she sprang up, panting and grinning.

"Don't look so pleased with yourself," Namir called. "You ever try a rocket-assisted landing, you'll break your ankle."

"Assuming," Gadren added, "we keep you around after Charmer recovers."

Assuming you're alive, Namir thought, though he caught himself before saying it aloud. Better not to demoralize the fresh meat.

In the distance, in the direction the drop ship had flown, Namir thought he heard the sound of laserfire. He winced inwardly; if the drop ship went down, it would take the squads still aboard with it. There wasn't anything he could do now.

He pulled out a datapad and checked his coordinates before waving the squad together. "Come on," he said. "We're five klicks from our target. In this jungle, it'll be a long walk."

According to Howl's briefing, Coyerti was one of the Empire's military research outposts—a planet so rich in plant and animal life that it served as the perfect testing and development ground for biological weapons. On Coyerti, the Empire regularly deployed everything from neurotoxins to defoliants, manufacturing the most virulent poisons on-site for shipment across the galaxy and leaving Coyerti itself a rotting morass of half-dead trees and composting debris.

Yet the Empire hadn't gone unopposed. Native to Coyerti was an intelligent species that resisted occupation and had proved too hardy to wipe out. The same biodiversity that made the planet useful as a laboratory also shielded the Coyerti people from the Empire's custom plagues. What they weren't naturally immune or resistant to they were able to cure, and every attempt on their lives made the Coyerti angrier. If they'd been more populous or technologically adept, they might have reclaimed their world; as it was, they'd spent the past decade forcing the Empire to expend resources in an endless little war at the edge of the Mid Rim.

Without any formal negotiation, the Coyerti had become de facto allies of the Rebel Alliance.

Only now the Coyerti really were on the verge of annihilation. Three weeks earlier, High Command had received a garbled message stating that the onset of the Coyerti reproductive season had begun—a time during which, thanks to their peculiar biology, they would be effectively defenseless for a full phase of the planet's moon. By order of the Rebel Alliance, Twilight Company was there to engage enemy forces and protect the Coyerti people until the Coyerti could once again protect themselves.

It was a mission that had induced snickering among the Twilight regulars. Namir had offered his own share of crude comments. But in securing Coyerti, Twilight Company would harden the invisible border between the Empire's holdings in the Mid Rim and the galaxy's uncontrolled outer reaches. If Twilight could focus the battle on Coyerti, force the Empire to keep spending resources there, it could provide cover for the Rebellion's other retreating forces. It was, fates willing, the last rearguard action of the Mid Rim Retreat.

That was the official word. The truth was more complicated, and Namir suspected he knew only part of it. But his job wasn't to win the Rebellion's war or to understand the Coyerti. His job was to get Twilight through its latest operation intact.

That would be challenge enough.

Gadren nearly died in the first minute of the first battle. He *would* have died, *should* have, if not for a fluke—he'd charged into the Imperial camp, gripping his blaster cannon and shooting wildly while he tossed aside stormtroopers with his two free arms. He'd been entirely oblivious to the grenade that landed at his feet until it had been too late to take shelter.

Inexplicably, the grenade hadn't detonated. Whether by dint of a manufacturer's flaw, the corrosive effects of Coyerti's atmosphere, or incompetence on the part of the grenadier, Gadren's life was saved despite his own best efforts.

After that, the attack went more smoothly.

Namir's squad had coordinated its assault plan with Sergeant Zab's team before the drop. The target was an assortment of tents and perimeter sensors run by a skeleton crew—a newly erected scout post servicing the Empire's fresh assault on the Coyerti people, totally unprepared for an attack from fed, rested, and heavily armed rebel forces. The two squads approached from opposite directions and made no effort at subtlety. *Surprise,* not *stealth,* was the day's watchword.

Namir stayed close to Roach, taking shelter with her behind a fallen tree as they supplied covering fire. The girl was sweating, spending half her time diligently but fruitlessly lining up shots and the other half blasting randomly. Namir doubted she would hit anyone; that was fine with him so long as she followed his lead.

Brand had announced her intent to ambush any Imperials looking to flee or outflank their attackers on speeder bikes. Namir hadn't seen her since she'd slipped off into the jungle, and he counted that as a good sign.

Gadren and two of Zab's men pushed into the center of the camp, ensuring the Imperials couldn't pull together to mount a defense. Their job was the riskiest, and Namir might have joined them if Charmer had been present to work with Roach. Instead, he scanned the battlefield and tried to keep the stormtroopers' attention on him instead of on the soldiers coming for their heads.

The shooting was over within ten minutes. When each squad member signaled an all-clear, the teams converged carefully into the camp itself and began rigging what little equipment was present for detonation.

The acrid scent in the air was almost painful. Roach asked Namir about it, and he shrugged. "Blaster bolts rip up the atmosphere," he said. "Every time you fire, *something* gets vaporized. Every planet stinks a little different."

Roach nodded with a swift, jerky motion. She was sweating more than she had been while fighting.

After another five minutes, both squads were marching back into the jungle. Zab had wanted to steal the speeders, but Namir had talked him out of it—they'd be rigged with homing beacons, and no one on either team had the expertise to remove the trackers fast enough. Speed was imperative—there would be TIE bombers over the camp in moments, set to annihilate any straggling rebel forces.

That was how the war on Coyerti began.

On the second day of the Coyerti campaign, Namir and his squad mates spent the morning waist-deep in a stagnant bog. With improvised camouflage spackled on their heads and shoulders, they waited for an Imperial convoy to pass by. Namir had to warn Roach to secure her rifle when she started aiming at imaginary noises; she'd been twitchy ever since the first day's firefight, and boredom didn't seem to sit well with her.

Five hours in, a message from Lieutenant Sairgon came through announcing that the convoy had changed course at dawn. Namir cursed loudly enough to send marsh lizards scampering. He was cold and his thighs were cramped and he doubted he'd ever clean off all the muck—but in truth, he didn't mind the change of plans. The boredom was over and the squad could move on.

That afternoon, Brand and Namir refilled their canteens from a murky creek while Gadren and Roach kept watch. Sterilization pills would make the water safe to drink, but only after the canteens filtered out any solids. Namir stared at the container in his hand, waiting for it to click into readiness.

"Remind you of anything?" Brand asked.

"Kor-Lahvan," Namir said. "I remember."

"I thought you'd get us all killed."

"I remember that, too."

Brand held a fist level with her eyes and watched a four-winged insect crawl across her knuckles. "You were a brat back then," she said. "Kid from a galactic backwater who thought he'd been fighting longer than all of us put together."

Namir bit back a smile. "And I had been."

Brand shrugged. "Sure. But who would've believed it?"

The canteen clicked softly. Namir laughed, shook the mud from the filter, and clipped the container to his belt.

In the evening, green and orange glows lit the northern horizon. A dozen Twilight squads were attacking an Imperial fort, Namir knew—it had been part of the plan from the outset, the first large-scale engagement of the campaign. From thirty klicks away, all Namir could do was check for signals and watch the colors wash over the jungle canopy.

As evening became night, the colors grew more intense and black dots—ash or TIE fighters, Namir couldn't tell which—speckled the sky. Occasionally an echo like distant thunder passed among the trees.

Gadren kept Roach occupied, first walking her through the steps to check her gear and clean the moisture from her rifle. Later they laid out a dozen different ration packs, organizing them by flavor (as labeled) and actual flavor (as determined by experience). When they handed Namir a compact nutrient bar that tasted like chemically infused mucilage, he didn't argue and ate in silence.

Namir kept watching even after the more colorful blooms faded and were replaced by a guttering orange. When Roach and Gadren had zipped themselves into their bedrolls and the chittering of the night's insects had begun, Brand paused nearby before beginning her patrol.

"Tomorrow?" she asked.

"Could be," Namir said. "Might be another day."

Brand tilted her head as if listening to something far off. Her expression was untroubled, however.

"You think they did it?" Namir asked.

"Fort's trashed," Brand said. She sounded certain. "Don't know the cost, though. Carver is good, but you know how he gets."

Namir nodded. Brand started to turn away before Namir asked abruptly, "You really don't wish you were with them?"

Brand shook her head. "I'm here for a reason," she said. "That's good enough for me."

Namir turned back to the fire in the north.

"Get some sleep," Brand said.

On the third morning of the Coyerti campaign, Namir checked the portable satellite uplink for coded updates from the front. He received only a set of coordinates and a four-word message that, decrypted, read: AT-ST SEEK AND DESTROY.

Gadren took inventory of the squad's weaponry while Roach and Namir packed up camp and Brand kept watch. "Three grenades," Gadren told Namir afterward. "Together, they might take down a walker."

"Not a lot of room for error," Namir said.

Gadren nodded grimly. "I agree. So we use the detonators. One should suffice, and we would still have enough for—"

"No," Namir said. "Those are spoken for. We'll find a way."

Their target had left a trail of snapped logs and burnt trees, and shortly before noon they caught up with it: a two-legged, box-headed All Terrain Scout Transport that marched through the jungle, turning mounted blaster cannons to whatever obstacle stood in its path.

The squad's first engagement was a disaster. Gadren threw his grenade too hard against the vehicle's shell and sent it bouncing away. Roach was nearly crushed by a tree whose lower trunk was turned to cinders by the walker's cannons. Brand tried to climb to the walker's cockpit and sprained her ankle when she fell.

The afternoon became a series of hit-and-run engagements. The squad kept the machine's pilots from resuming their mission, forcing them to hunt. Gadren scorched the walker's metal sides with repeated shots. Roach managed to lob a grenade close enough to its spindly legs to visibly damage its mechanisms.

But the machine kept walking and incinerating trees. If the jungle hadn't been so humid, it all would have burned.

By evening, Namir had developed a new plan. The squad continued to strike and retreat to keep the machine in pursuit. Along the path of their withdrawal, the ground gradually turned from mud to water. It took hours of maneuvering, but by nightfall all four squad members were soaking wet and the walker was lying at the bottom of a marsh, its pilots sealed in the flooded, airless cockpit.

Namir ached from a day on the run, and at camp he stripped down to his underclothes to try to dry off. Brand was nursing her ankle, applying a nonregulation goo she swore by. Roach was trying to set up a heater to take the edge off the water's chill, pretending not to stare at the brands between Namir's shoulders or the tattoos on his legs. Gadren was standing at the edge of the camp, gazing out into the jungle.

Namir slapped Gadren hard between his shoulders. "Good day," he said. "I think we won."

Gadren raised a hand to hush him. "Listen," he said.

At first, Namir heard nothing but a faint breeze and the chirping of insects. Yet gradually, he discerned a low thrumming in the distance. It was neither a drumbeat nor a hum, but something in-between— unmistakably alive, with the resonance of a hundred deep voices. Once Namir understood the thrumming, he began to hear other noises, too—high-pitched peals like bells or notes of birdsong, clicks like wood tapping wood.

"It is the Coyerti," Gadren said.

Roach and Brand joined them, and both stared toward the distant sound—the singing, or chanting, or whatever it truly was. Namir looked between his companions and saw them transfixed, but he suddenly felt cold, and he smelled his sweat and the filth of the water in his hair.

"*Now*," Gadren said, "it is a good day. We have served this world. Cherish the memory, and let it warm you in the face of true evil."

Namir turned his back on the others and settled into his bedroll by the heater. "Don't amuse yourselves for too long," he called. "Tomorrow will be rough."

On the fourth day of the Coyerti campaign, the order Namir had been awaiting came at last. He marched the squad out from the bogs and into the highland jungle, where the rotting trees took on the sickly hue of pus. Gadren took charge of navigation, leading them through dark, narrow valleys that wound among the hills. Now and again, he stopped to examine a tree that was still whole and vital, running his enormous fingers over bark dusted in vermillion pollen—as if he'd found a gemstone in the planet's dross. Three times, Namir nearly scolded him for stopping, but Gadren never delayed for long.

They paused to eat at sunset, though Namir warned the others that the rest would be brief. Brand was limping slightly. Roach was soaked in sweat. Namir kept his attention on Gadren.

"How far?" he asked.

"Assuming we haven't been lied to?" Gadren asked.

"Assuming nothing," Namir said. "I want to know *when* we'll reach the coordinates; I'm not asking what's there."

Gadren smiled, showing teeth that could sever a human neck. "If we march through the night, we'll arrive by morning. According to the maps."

"We march until midnight," Namir said. "If we're half dead when we arrive, we won't have much of a chance."

"Assuming we've been lied to?" Gadren asked.

Namir smirked. "If we've been lied to, we're dead either way."

It wasn't until long after full dark that Namir realized Brand had been listening to the conversation. She matched Namir's pace despite her limp and said softly, "If it's a trap, I'll kill her."

Namir looked to Brand. He couldn't make out her expression in the dark. He wanted to ask, *What makes you so sure you'll survive?* But he'd fought with Brand long enough to know the answer. He'd spent enough hours with Brand to know what it meant for her to say such a thing.

Instead he said, "You don't want to promise that."

"I do," Brand said. "I swear: If Everi Chalis lied, I'll avenge you."

On the fifth day of the Coyerti campaign, Namir and his squad crested a stony rise covered in thick red ferns and came into view of what Everi Chalis had lovingly called the Distillery.

Three white bunkers connected by narrow passages sat in a triangle below the rise, smokestacks rising from each to deposit a fine mist into the humid air. Vegetation covered the bunkers' rooftops, occluding them from any satellite that penetrated the shroud of fog. Three patrols of stormtroopers moved about the structures, staying close to the walls—either they weren't concerned about maintaining a wide perimeter, or they'd already drawn back in preparation for a fight.

Howl had briefed Namir on the compound the day before planetfall. Governor Chalis, he'd said, had described the Distillery as the main processing facility for Coyerti's bioweapons. Inside, chemicals and toxins were refined and combined before being shipped on to spaceports for distribution offworld.

Chalis had promised that the destruction of the Distillery would set Coyerti's operations back years. And thus, while the rest of Twilight Company—including twelve recruits from Haidoral who'd been barely cleared for combat and who would hinder their comrades as much as their foes—fought to preserve a desperate species, Namir and his squad were to risk their lives on the word of a traitor.

The squad waited atop the rise throughout the morning, observing the patrol patterns and noting the handful of entrances to the bunkers. No one mentioned the possibility of a trap anymore. Namir guessed the possibility of a trap was the *only* thing on anyone's mind.

Around midday, a lightly armored transport skimmer brushed over the jungle canopy and landed outside the compound's cargo entrance. Brand rose to a crouch from where she'd been lying flat in the shale. She disappeared down the rise without a word. Namir could barely tell she was still limping.

"Should we get closer?" Roach asked. Her hands were trembling but her voice was steady. "In case someone sees her?"

Gadren saved Namir the trouble of responding. "If someone spots her," he said, "we all die. Give her room to work."

Namir pulled out a pair of macrobinoculars and tried to follow Brand's movements. Even the display's smart-tracking only caught an occasional flicker between trees. He saw no sign that the stormtroopers had been alerted; they were busy carting brightly painted yellow and red and blue barrels from the skimmer to the compound, with only two on active watch.

The next time Namir spotted Brand, the stormtroopers were nearly finished unloading the cargo and Brand was halfway back up the rise. She climbed the steep slope rapidly but without, so far as Namir could discern, any special urgency.

"Done," she announced, as she crested the top and crouched among the ferns again. "Set the timer for thirty minutes. Enough time to get down there. Not so much that they'll find the device."

"Will it be enough?" Gadren asked. "Which did you choose?"

Brand stared at Gadren as if he were speaking nonsense. "A blue one," she said. "It was closest."

Gadren grunted. "Then we must hope the *blue one* is deadly enough for our needs . . . but not so deadly it kills us, too."

"Next open recruit," Namir said, watching the stormtroopers lock and seal the compound's cargo entrance, "I'm bringing a medtech into the squad. And I'm not sharing with the rest of you."

———

Thirty minutes later, somewhere in the Distillery, a microdetonator attached to the underside of a blue barrel exploded.

Namir didn't see it happen, and the blast was far too small to be heard outside the bunker walls. But he knew the device had triggered when sirens began wailing from the compound and all its doors slid open simultaneously. He knew the plan was working when a stream of lab workers and security personnel hurried outside, looking more irritated than terrified and lining up with the rote certainty of people who'd drilled for disaster a hundred times before.

The squad descended the rise, circling away from the workers' gathering spot. Namir indicated one of the back entrances to the compound, now open and guarded by a single stormtrooper. The guard didn't make a sound when Brand slipped her knife inside the joint between his helmet and chest piece.

Inside, thick white fog sprayed from ventilators. "Neutralizer gas," Brand said. "Seen it before. Puts out chemical fires, liquefies toxic gases for cleanup. Mostly safe. Try not to get a lungful."

Gadren nodded. Namir glanced at Roach, but she didn't seem to be listening—she was staring into the corridor ahead, her mouth open and teeth chattering.

If there was a trap, Namir thought, this was the last chance for Chalis's allies to spring it. But it was far too late to turn back.

The four squad members worked their way through the compound as carefully as they could while knowing the workers might return at any time. They swiftly developed a system: In each room packed with laboratory equipment or thrumming vats, Gadren and Brand set explosives while Namir and Roach watched for reinforcements. When each room was rigged, they moved together to the next. Brand kept her mask in place, but no one bothered wearing the hazard gloves or rebreathers Quartermaster Hober had provided before planetfall; if the Distillery's toxins were loosed, half measures wouldn't do much good.

Midway through the second bunker, Namir and Roach entered a stockroom together. The neutralizer gas was too thick for visibility, but a cry of alarm made it obvious the room was occupied. Before

Namir could locate the source, Roach turned and fired; five shots, one sending a vague silhouette crumbling to the floor and the others sparking against a containment tank. Namir pressed himself against a wall, listened for footsteps, and hurried to confirm Roach's kill when he heard nothing more.

On the floor was a middle-aged human man dressed in a laborer's uniform. The gas had already extinguished the fire wrought by Roach's blaster, leaving two charred holes in his torso. He carried no weapon, no vial of toxins ready to be tossed at an intruder. He was an Imperial, however, and he was dead.

"We're clear," Namir called out. "Keep working."

Namir didn't stop Roach from approaching the body herself. She didn't kneel to inspect her work. She bounced slightly on her knees a meter away, twisting her hands around her rifle as if she were trying to strangle it, staring at the man's face. Namir gave her a few moments and then snapped, "Stay on watch. We're not done yet."

Roach didn't move. Brand was watching her. Namir started to march toward her, but Brand was at her side faster, touching her shoulder to guide her away.

The squad was half a kilometer out when the compound blew with the sound of a thunderclap. Brand had sworn they were being followed, but Namir gave his team a moment to turn and watch dark smoke rise into the sky. Anyone in pursuit would pause, too. Then, together, they pressed on into the uplands. Only Gadren seemed uplifted by their triumph; the others kept their heads low and said nothing, as if they'd proven themselves fools caught in Governor Chalis's trap.

There hadn't *been* any trap. They might have just saved countless soldiers from bleeding out their ears or watching their skin drop off their bones, or whatever Imperial bioweapons were primed for. So why, Namir wondered, did they all feel like they'd been beaten?

The climb took them above the jungle canopy onto an escalating series of rocky plateaus covered in thinner vegetation. Their orders were to rendezvous in the evening with a drop ship that would return them to either the front lines or the *Thunderstrike,* depending on the campaign's progress. Namir found himself hoping for the latter as he fought off a headache tumescing behind his eyes. Maybe the humidity was getting to him, he thought, or maybe the change in altitude had come too quickly.

Twice, Namir caught Roach lagging behind, bouncing on her knees to an inaudible beat, hands clenching her rifle. The first time, he lost his temper. "*You stay with your team,*" he yelled, after a lengthy series of obscenities. "I don't care if you're picking flowers or having a cry over some dead man—you keep up until your soles are bleeding, and then you crawl. Understood?"

Roach nodded jerkily and rejoined the line.

The second time she fell behind, Namir felt ire rise in his gut again, more powerful than before, but he didn't have the strength to scream. Instead, he waved the group to a rest.

Let them catch us, he thought, as he sipped from his canteen. *Can't get any worse.*

Then he looked at his companions.

Brand's forehead glistened with sweat and she was breathing heavily. Her nostrils flared with every breath. She sat on the ground, legs outstretched, adjusting her boot on her injured ankle. Roach hadn't bothered sitting; she'd just wrapped her arms around her chest, her head down as she shivered.

Gadren stood straight as ever, keeping watch.

Namir spit out a curse, tore off his helmet, rolled up his sleeves, and began inspecting his skin. He searched for a rash, a blister, any fresh blemish. He found nothing, and pounded his palms against the ground in frustration.

The others were watching him now. He slowed his breathing, tried to calm himself. "How bad do we look?" he asked Gadren, voice low and steady.

Gadren lowered his head and didn't answer.

"Does anyone know what *happened*?" he asked. "Did we breathe something? Were we sprayed with biotoxins and I just didn't notice?"

Roach didn't look up. Brand sounded bitter as she said, "Doesn't take much to have an effect. We might have cracked a container some-where."

Or maybe, Namir thought, *you shouldn't have picked the blue barrel.* But he loathed himself for the idea even as it sprang to his mind. Brand wasn't at fault.

"Whatever it was," Gadren said, "I seem to be immune."

"Maybe," Brand said. "Might just affect you slower."

"Also possible," Gadren conceded.

Namir squeezed his eyes shut and cinched the strap of his rifle, tried to evaluate his aches and the pain in his skull. "Okay," he said. "Okay. Anyone feel like they're about to die? Anyone not able to walk another hour or two?"

No one spoke up.

"Then we keep moving," he said. "Not much we can do here, so hold your guts in until we get to a medic."

When they finally reached the rendezvous point, there was no drop ship waiting.

Namir didn't have a backup plan. If the drop ship didn't arrive, they were all dead. Even Gadren, who still showed no signs of illness. Even Brand, who could live through anything.

Namir didn't tell his squad that. In the morning, as they picked at rations that none of them had the appetite for, he told them they'd wait for the drop ship as long as they could. There would be no at-tempts at communication; if they tried to send a message through the satellite uplink, odds were the Imperials would detect the signal. Be-sides, he didn't expect their transport had *forgotten* about the pickup. If the drop ship could come, it would come.

In a worst-case scenario, Namir explained, they would hike toward the front lines and hope to reunite with the rest of Twilight Company. He didn't tell the group that such an attempt would be suicide and he had no intention of trying it.

He didn't think anyone believed him anyway.

Roach had turned pale overnight, her clammy skin now glistening with moisture. Brand kept her dignity better, but Namir caught her slipping away from camp to vomit in the underbrush. Namir's headache came and went, which was a small mercy; during its worst periods, he saw colorful spots and was overwhelmed by vertigo.

After breakfast came the busywork. Patrols. Equipment checks. Scouting for food and water. Planning escape routes from the camp. Listening to static for unencrypted Imperial comm chatter. Listening to static for unencrypted rebel comm chatter. Listening to static for unencrypted Coyerti comm chatter. Equipment maintenance. Camouflage touch-ups. Wound inspections. Teaching Roach to use the uplink. Teaching Roach to disassemble and repair the uplink in case of emergency. Erasing patrol trails. Erasing trails left while erasing patrol trails.

Namir kept his people occupied until nightfall. Then they huddled around the heater while Gadren kept watch, none of them able to sleep.

Roach had pulled her knees to her chest inside her bedroll, then drawn the bedroll's length around herself. She was still shivering. Namir found himself watching her, and when his skull didn't feel too tight around his brain to think he realized how little she had said since the Distillery.

He wondered if she was thinking about her decision to leave Haidoral Prime, or about the man she'd killed. But he had nothing to say to comfort her. He wasn't entirely sure he wanted to. He'd been through worse at Roach's age, and if she lived, she'd be better for it. She'd be a better soldier, a better part of Twilight Company.

If she died, what did a few final hours of comfort matter?

"Roach."

Brand's voice was thick, but it cut through the night air. She'd lodged herself against a rock, sitting straight even through her pain.

Roach looked over at her, still silent.

"You want to know how I joined Twilight Company?"

Brand's words caught Namir by surprise; if he'd been less ill, he might have shown as much. Roach bit her lip and nodded. She looked like a frightened child—which, Namir supposed, she was.

"I won't repeat myself," Brand said, "and you'll respect my privacy." It was a statement, not a question.

Roach nodded again. Brand spat a wad of phlegm onto the ground and began.

"I used to be a bounty hunter," she said. "You know that. This is almost twenty years ago, not long after the Emperor took control. Not long after the Jedi died."

Roach shook her head, frowning in confusion. Namir had heard the word *Jedi* mentioned by rebels before—they seemed to be some kind of religious warriors from before the Empire—but that was all he knew. Roach seemed equally uninformed.

"Forget it," Brand said. "The point is, things were better then. Better than they are now. Better than they had been during the Clone Wars. People cared about the law. The Empire kept them safe.

"But the wars had done their damage. I worked Tangenine, mostly. Infrastructure there was hit bad by the Separatists and the syndicates stepped in, extorting folks in return for food, transport, basics. Imperial military tried their best, but the gangs and blackmailers still ran things below the surface.

"So they kept people like me on retainer. Empire didn't like bounty hunters even then, but on Tangenine there were killers and smugglers to catch.

"I felt good about what I did."

Brand's head dipped forward, and for a short while Namir was worried she'd passed out. Finally, though, she squared her shoulders, looked into the distance, and resumed speaking.

"I don't know when things went wrong. But as law came back to Tangenine, the Empire changed from what it was to . . . whatever it is we've got now. I brought a man in for stealing power converters and saw him jailed for life. I tracked down a gang leader, a spice dealer—the lowest of the low—and saw him pardoned because he bribed a magistrate."

The words were simple and her tone was flat, as if she were describing horrors she didn't want to relive. Namir saw Roach wanting to ask for more, for specifics, but she seemed to know better. Maybe she was afraid of what Brand would do if she pried.

But the pain and nausea in Roach's face were gone.

Brand didn't seem to notice the girl's unasked questions. "A few years back," she said, "I decided I needed a break. We'd finished rooting out one of the last big syndicates, and I was getting sick of the blood. Lot of people wouldn't surrender, knowing what would happen in prison . . ." She trailed off, started again.

"I needed a break. So for my next job, I picked a target that would get me off Tangenine, out of the Core Worlds. Away from cities and crime and bureaucrats."

"Captain Evon?" Roach asked.

"Captain Evon," Brand said. "I hadn't done much rebel hunting, but I figured it would keep me busy awhile." A hint of a smile played across her lips.

"Tracking down Twilight Company took time," Brand said, "but soldiers do stupid things when they're on leave. Talk to the wrong people—"

"That's a lesson for you," Namir muttered in Roach's direction, though he wasn't sure she heard.

"—and get cozy, mention their next assignments. Wasn't more than four months before I showed up at an open recruit on Veron and offered to join.

"I'll skip the blow-by-blow. Short version is, I lied, I smuggled in my kit, and I waited for a clear shot at Howl and an opportunity to escape. By the time my chance came, I'd gotten to know the troops. Saw that maybe they had a point."

"You changed your mind?" Roach asked.

Brand shook her head almost imperceptibly, as if anything more would send her spinning into oblivion. "Not until I had a gun to Howl's head. Man didn't seem scared, and we got to talking. He offered me a job, and I took it."

Roach nodded, not quite meeting Brand's gaze.

"No regrets," Brand said. "Not about joining. Not about my old life, either."

Namir buried himself in his bedroll and tried not to laugh.

Much later, in the dim light of predawn, Namir relieved himself in a gulch near the camp and made his way back toward his colleagues. Halfway there, he found Brand seated on a boulder, cleaning her knife. He sat down beside her.

For a while, Namir watched sunlight delineate the shadows. Finally he said, "How come you didn't tell her the whole thing?"

Brand shrugged. "She's too young," she said. "Besides, we'll all be dead in a few days. A few lies won't hurt her."

Namir nodded and dug into the dirt with the toe of his boot. Then he managed to smile. "If we're all dead, who's going to get revenge on Chalis?"

Brand shrugged again. "Far as I see, her information was good. We maybe saved a lot of people from—" She hesitated, then extended a hand and looked down at the palm. A rash was spreading up toward her wrist. "—this. Not her fault we weren't careful enough."

Namir's own rash had begun low on his neck. He'd discovered it while shaving.

"Howl doesn't know that," he said. "If we're lucky, Chalis will get blamed anyway. The troops could stone her to death."

Brand flipped her knife over and sheathed it. "You've got a mean streak, Sergeant." She wasn't smiling. It made Namir laugh.

"When we're dead," he said, "I'm going to miss these talks."

"Me, too," Brand said. She still didn't smile, but when Namir reached out his hand she took it and squeezed.

Two days later, the drop ship arrived.

Namir couldn't remember much of what happened afterward. He remembered Gadren shouting and Brand firing her blaster into the sky to indicate the squad's position. He remembered trying to crawl out of his bedroll toward the drop ship when the vessel landed and sent waves of dust and heat rippling his way. He remembered not quite making it; he was sure Gadren had been the one to scoop him up and carry him the distance.

He was reasonably certain he'd said unforgivable things to whoever tried to strap him into his seat. He'd found the strength to cinch himself into the harness and forced himself to stay conscious while being battered against the wall. Half dead or not, he refused to be the soldier who passed out during takeoff. That was Roach's duty as fresh meat.

Aboard the *Thunderstrike*, he tried to report the destruction of the Distillery to any medic who would listen, then realized that Gadren was still alive and could do the job just as well. He suffered days of tests, which he was later assured had taken only hours, and he remembered being told that he'd been exposed to only minuscule amounts of unrefined, unweaponized biotoxin. The effects were easily treatable.

Namir and his team were going to be fine.

The Coyerti campaign was over.

"The walker is staring us down, the X-wings can't get low enough to hit the cannon, and then we start hearing this drumbeat." Ajax smacked his palm against the dented metal tabletop, producing a hollow ring.

"Play your cards," Brand said.

Ajax ignored her. "But it's not a drumbeat—it's a whole blasted army of *Coyerti*. We hadn't even *seen* the things before, but I figure that whole 'reproductive season' thing must be over because they're *swarming*. Ten minutes later, the whole garrison is on fire and the lieutenant is begging us to stop lobbing grenades. 'We won, we won—save some for the next mission!'"

Half the Clubhouse laughed with Ajax while the other half scoffed. Gadren playfully slapped Ajax between the shoulder blades. "Maybe the Coyerti will invite you, their mighty savior, to the festivities next time." His voice became more somber as he continued, "May they continue their fight with skill and fortune."

"And without *us*," someone called. Namir didn't see who. He couldn't disagree with the sentiment, but he wouldn't have voiced it aloud in present company. Gadren frowned, as did—to Namir's surprise—Brand.

"So long as we're done with the jungle," Namir said instead. "I still smell it on all of you, and I swear there are gnats in the barracks now."

There was a round of agreement, and the card game resumed. Namir kept half an eye on the game while he read through post-conflict reports and counted up the dead and wounded. The relatively few who'd fallen on the front lines, fighting with the bulk of Twilight, had been mourned already. No one would mention them while sober; not for a while. The tally of the wounded was more severe. Namir dreaded the task of reassigning squad members to compensate.

All thirteen of the fresh meat assigned to the ground had survived. They'd acquitted themselves adequately, for the most part: Corbo, who'd brought the knife to Chalis's prison, had half a dozen confirmed kills. The bedraggled man Namir had pegged for a potential spy at the open recruit had taken a grazing blaster shot protecting a Coyerti native. Namir had seen only two reports of recruits freezing up entirely. Better than usual, really, and a hopeful sign that Twilight might rebuild its ranks in time for the next major offensive.

"So, Sergeant," Ajax called, after pushing a pile of credits over to Gadren. "Any news from Fisheye Company?"

Namir frowned. "What's Fisheye have to do with anything?" Fisheye was the Alliance's Sixty-Eighth Infantry, aquatic division. Twilight had crossed paths with the company once before, but Namir hadn't heard anything about it in months. Then again, he was still catching up on the day's rumors.

"Missed the big announcement in all the puking and hallucinating," Twitch said with a smirk, in an almost incomprehensible mumble.

Ajax laughed before explaining, "Turns out Coyerti wasn't the only target this week. Rearguard actions across the board . . . the Twenty-

First was on Bestine. Bitter Pill Company was on some trash heap of a planet; lost their troop transport but got a replacement."

"Then it was coordinated?" Gadren said. "One final effort to allow the fleet to complete its withdrawal from the Mid Rim . . ."

Twitch was still muttering. "Battleships aren't running fast enough? Toss your ground troops in the furnace. That'll fix 'em up."

The news of a coordinated action didn't surprise Namir. He hadn't expected it, but he *should* have—one company on one planet wouldn't ever be enough to distract the whole Imperial fleet. Still, something rankled him about the news, even if he couldn't say what.

"I'll check with the captain about Fisheye," he said, and stood with a groan. "I'm meeting with Howl in an hour, and I'm sure he'll be happy to share."

Namir's meeting was with Lieutenant Sairgon, not Howl, but he bullied his way into the captain's office anyway to deliver his report on the fresh meat's progress. He kept it short, and Howl appeared attentive throughout. But then, Howl treated everyone as if they were endless fountains of profundity, always worthy of patience and consideration regardless of what idiocy they were spewing. It irritated Namir to no end.

"And your team?" Howl asked when Namir finished. "You're feeling well again?"

"Good enough," Namir said. "Wish we'd known what we were dying for, though."

It wasn't what he had intended to say. It wasn't even what bothered him, though it was close enough.

"How do you mean?" Howl asked.

Now he was committed. " 'We're going to provide cover for our retreating fleet.' 'We're going to save the Coyerti.' 'We're going to test the governor's information at the Distillery.' Those are all nice, clear mission parameters, but they're not the same. Now we come home and learn the first explanation was the real one. Only it's *not*—not entirely—because it turns out we're only one part of a larger operation.

"You know I'm not one to question the grand strategy. I fight because Twilight fights. But I don't like to feel *used*, either."

Howl maintained that same, tolerant look. "We can't have more than one reason for what we do?"

"Not if we want to win," Namir said. "You pick a goal, and your troops get it done."

Howl started to reply, then raised a finger as if to silence himself. He squeezed his eyes shut, reopened them, and began again. "Our goal isn't conquest, but alchemy," he said. "The transmutation of the galaxy. We are a catalyst; where Rebellion comes into contact with Empire, change must occur. The substance of oppression becomes the substance of freedom—and as with any such change, terrible energies are released: war, victory, and defeat.

"But the alchemist's concern isn't those energies. They're a by-product, *not* the means of transmutation itself. The alchemist's concern is the purity of the catalyst. The rest will take care of itself." He shrugged then, and smiled. "Mostly, anyway. If we maintain the strength of our principles, the rest will follow.

"Your death on Coyerti wouldn't have halted the process. If all of Twilight Company had died, would the fleet have failed to escape? Would the Coyerti have been wiped out? Would we know any less about Governor Chalis's intent?"

The words meant nothing to Namir. He shook his head and grimaced. "I want to give my people a mission they can count on. Not a philosophy of war. Something that keeps them focused."

Howl smiled. "I think you underestimate your people. But we've had this discussion."

They had, beginning on Blacktar Cyst and recurring on and off since then. It never turned out satisfactory, but there were days that Howl's madness—his willingness to sacrifice Twilight to achieve his peculiar definition of victory—troubled Namir more profoundly than others.

Late that night, Namir went searching for Roach. She hadn't been at the Clubhouse. He hadn't seen her since they'd left Coyerti, though the medics assured him she was healthy.

One of Sergeant Fektrin's men pointed Namir in the right direction, and he eventually found her in a cramped cargo bay, back pressed tight against the bulkhead and arms wrapped around her knees. She was shivering and rocking gently, and she stared bitterly at Namir when he walked inside.

"You still sick?" he asked.

"No," Roach said.

Namir picked his way around the clutter of crates and spare engine parts and put his own back to the wall beside Roach. He didn't join her on the floor. Roach glanced up, then back to her knees.

"It's just the fighting," she said. "It was my first fight. First time I killed someone."

"And you're all broken up about the guy you shot?"

"Yes," Roach said.

Namir snorted. "That's garbage."

Roach looked up again. Namir shook his head. "Lot of people get messed up when they shoot people," he said. "Not you, though. Later, maybe; right now you've got bigger issues."

Roach kept staring.

Namir slid down the bulkhead next to Roach and stretched his legs. He tapped his heel against the metal floor, listened to the barely resonant thud.

"How long have you been clean?" he asked.

Roach was watching his foot. He saw her expression twist as indecision came and went on her face before she finally whispered, "Since Haidoral. Not much before."

"That why you were in a detention center?" Namir asked. "Spice addiction?"

Roach nodded. "Basically."

Namir kept his tone casual. "I probably should've seen it then.

You'd think I'd know the difference between 'sweaty and nervous' and 'going through withdrawal' by now."

Again, the long silence. When Roach spoke, the words were stilted as she forced each to emerge. "I'm clean now. I'm here to fight. I won't mess up."

"Yeah, you will," Namir said. "That's okay, though. We've all got problems."

Roach smiled weakly—an uncertain smile, an obligatory smile at her commander's sad little joke.

Namir reached over and took Roach's chin in his hand. Her skin was cool and damp. He turned her face toward his. "We protect our own. You understand?"

She nodded. Namir let go. She didn't understand.

Roach went on shivering. Her knuckles turned white where she gripped her knees, as if her hands were the only things holding the rest of her body together; as if she was afraid she might dissolve and spill onto the floor if she relaxed. Namir sat listening to the metallic groaning of the ship and the low, static roar of the engines before shifting closer to Roach and reaching an arm around her shoulders. He felt the damp of her shirt, smelled her sweat, heard her breath come rapidly like the respiration of a tiny, trapped animal. He gripped her loosely. Roach stiffened for a few moments before squeezing smaller and pressing into his side.

They sat together in silence through the night.

CHAPTER 7

PLANET CRUCIVAL
Day Four Hundred of the Tripartite Culture Effrontery
Fifteen Years After the Clone Wars

His name was Umu Seven now: Umu after the second son of the Hieroprince, and Seven because six other Umus also served the Opaline Creed. The boy had hoped for a name of his own, but the rules of the Creed were strict and there were worse fates than being Umu Seven forever.

He still wore the brands of old loyalties between his shoulders, buried under a bantha-fur cloak. When the Warlord Malkhan had died, the boy's oaths of submission had lost their meaning. He'd been lucky to find the Creed as swiftly as he had. Now as he walked briskly through narrow sandstone streets, he saw his brands mirrored on the faces of old men curled in spice-born stupors on the stoops of shops; on the wrists of women eating scraps in the alleys; on all the warriors of Malkhan who now lacked an army to serve, whose triumphs-etched-in-flesh now marked them as pariahs.

Umu kept his hood up, his eyes averted from the lost Malkhanis. He didn't fear for his safety, but he'd been given a task by the Creed. He could not hesitate or fail.

When he reached the bazaar, he elbowed his way through the crowd to the merchants he'd been told might aid him. Some he said nothing to—he reached out, pressed a handful of gold peggats into their palms to reward their service to the Creed, then drew away. Others he bartered with, and over the course of an hour he filled his sack with offworld batteries, wires, fuses. Devices and pieces of devices.

The Creed was rich in food and water and gold, but not so in technology. If it was to survive its battles against the heretic clans, it needed weapons that rivaled those of its foes. It needed soldiers who knew how to wield blasters and flamers.

Umu Seven had fought for Malkhan and knew how to wield the weapons of offworlders.

When he'd finished his business in the bazaar, Umu looped back into the alleys. He didn't retrace his path, knowing he might be followed—knowing that the objects he carried could feed and house a family for a year, or sate a spice addict for a month. On the first few occasions he'd run errands for the Creed, he'd been tempted to steal his way to freedom and a new life. He felt only so much loyalty to his masters, despite the communal recitation of oaths at morning and night, the constant readings from the Tome of the Hieroprince; at times he felt a raw, heavy guilt in his stomach over his own faithlessness. Yet as weeks had passed and he'd been entrusted with greater responsibilities, he'd found new reasons to stay true to the Creed.

"Hazram!"

He heard the voice as he felt the grip on his shoulder—a broad hand, a man's hand, with nails that dug into the fabric of his cloak. He heard the name, too, but it didn't register as one of his own until he'd thrown back an elbow, felt it connect with meat, felt the hand leave his body. Feet scraped at dust as his assailant stumbled backward, coughing in long, pained rasps.

Umu turned around. Standing in the alley was a tall, broad-shouldered, bald-headed man with a blasted and leathery face. He'd been strong once—that was obvious—but now his skin seemed as if it had been stretched to dry on a rack of bones. His vest and shirt were worn through in places, patched with leather scraps in others. He stared at Umu with wide, anxious eyes.

"You're alive," he said. "I knew you were alive."

"You need to leave," Umu said, curt and bitter. "The Creed is waiting for me."

Umu had not seen his father in nearly three years.

The man's chest heaved as if he'd been running. He squeezed his eyes shut, and when he opened them again they seemed clearer, focused but without the mad intensity. "I'll walk with you," Umu's father said with care and contrition, like a captive negotiating for release after a battle. "The Creed's in Templemarch, yes? I'll make sure you're not bothered on the way."

Umu turned his back on his father and began to walk again. His father followed behind him.

"Were you there?" his father asked, after they'd traveled in silence for some minutes. "When the Malkhanis fell apart?"

"Yes," Umu hissed.

The warlord's lieutenants had each staked a claim to Malkhan's cache of offworld weapons. The bloodletting that had followed had been worse than anything Umu had seen prior.

"I warned you that would happen," his father said. "It always does."

Umu said nothing.

"It happened in my war, too. Even after our enemies won, they still turned on one another."

"Maybe you should have fought harder," Umu said, his voice cool and level. "Maybe if *your* side had won, you would've known what to do."

Umu increased his walking speed. He heard his father's labored breath as he tried to keep pace.

Umu expected his father to argue. It had always been *easy* to make him argue about his war. One wrong word would get him started, defending his choices and his cause against—well, Umu had never understood whom his father thought he was arguing *with*. No one on Crucival cared about the Clone Wars.

"You can still come back," his father said instead, voice rising in pitch. "There's enough room, and enough food. I can hide you from the Creed—I know I can."

Umu flinched and planted his feet in the dust. He didn't turn as he spoke. "The Creed serves us meat and honey and wine every night," he said. "When I wake up, I smell fruit instead of someone's waste in the street. I made *oaths* to them. Why would I *ever* go back with you?"

His father didn't answer. Perhaps he'd walked away.

It was just as well. Everything Umu had said was true, but it wasn't why he stayed with the Creed. He didn't want to talk to his father about the Creed. Nor about the Malkhanis, nor about who he'd become since leaving home.

Not Hazram. Not Donin. Umu Seven.

There was a part of him, some vestigial instinct, that wanted to drop his sack and race after his father. To find him and—

But that was as far as the fantasy went. There was no "and." No joyous childhood to reclaim. There was only the fear of an opportunity lost.

It was dusk when he reached Templemarch and the ancient cloister where the Creed dwelled. He'd missed the evening loyalty pledge, and he'd need to be up at midnight to atone. Yet no one scolded him, and he was met warmly as he walked among his fellows, distributing his acquisitions to the engineers and the weaponsmiths and the trademasters.

As he rummaged through his sack, he was puzzled to find a small, bruised fruit—a sweet thorn pear, like the ones that stubbornly grew in the alleys. It almost fell from his hand when he realized that his father had somehow slipped it to him; his father had always been nimble, always able to play a trick when he set his mind to it.

Umu didn't want it. Trembling softly, he placed it in the cloister's storeroom before making his way to the sleeping court.

There, surrounded by the walls of the cloister, a hundred other followers of the Creed were stretched out on blankets or the yellow grass. Umu had to pick his way by starlight among the sprawled limbs of sleepers to reach his corner. In the shadows, plucking one blade of grass after the next, waited a girl perhaps a year or two older than Umu. She sat up with a tired groan and a smile.

"You're back," Pira Ten said.

"I'm back," Umu said. He squatted on the ground near the girl and grinned. "I saw an alien in the market."

"Shut up," Pira said, smiling broadly. "You're lying." She was pressing a hunk of bread and cured fish into Umu's hands. "Dinner. *Are* you lying? What was it?"

Umu laughed, and told Pira about the alien: yellow skin and horns, black eyes, like a demon out of myth. He *was* lying, but Pira liked aliens. Umu had concocted the story the moment he'd been assigned his task, embellished it when he'd left the cloister. He'd been looking forward to the lie most of the day.

He couldn't tell if Pira believed him. That was okay.

"So no trouble then?" she asked when Umu's story was done. She picked at the crumbs of Umu's dinner. Her voice turned more serious. "Keffan got robbed just outside the bazaar last time. Still can't move his fingers."

"No trouble," Umu said. "Mostly kind of boring."

Pira nodded. "Boring can be good," she said. "I know you're itching for a shooting war, but—boring is good. A break can be good."

"I'm not—" Umu started. Pira was holding back laughter, waiting for him to take the bait. Umu forced himself to bite back a protest, scowled, and began again. "When the shooting *does* start?" he said. "*Someone's* going to get stabbed in the back."

Pira cackled—too loud, though she managed to look half chagrined as others in the sleeping court glowered in her direction. Umu settled onto the grass, and the day's earlier encounters seemed to seep out of him, into the soil and deep into Crucival.

There were worse fates than being Umu Seven. There were worse things than being among the Creed.

He'd found his family, and he was content.

CHAPTER 8

METATESSU SECTOR
Day One Hundred Nine of the Mid Rim Retreat
Seven Years Later

The first attack came at midnight three days after Twilight's departure from Coyerti. The *Thunderstrike* was floating with its escort at the edge of a lifeless system dominated by a crimson sun, racing to complete a maintenance shift as it plotted a course out of enemy territory.

When an Imperial destroyer jumped out of hyperspace and moved into firing range, *Apailana's Promise* and its two X-wings responded swiftly enough to prevent any real damage to the *Thunderstrike*. The rebel forces were able to escape the frenetic battle at lightspeed, though one of the X-wings was crippled by a glancing turbolaser blow.

The second attack came thirty hours later. This time, the *Thunderstrike* was ambushed upon arrival in the Enrivi system, where Howl had hoped to put in for additional repairs. The attacking force consisted of a light cruiser and a squadron of TIE fighters. Even with one X-wing offline, Twilight managed to destroy the foe without difficulty.

The shock wave of the cruiser's death throes—the blossoming detonation of its engines and weaponry—obliterated the ship's own escape pods. As Howl later put it, the Imperial casualties were "deeply regrettable and unintended." This didn't prevent a raucous celebration from erupting afterward, in which Twilight soldiers broke out contraband drinks and toasted their pilots and gunners.

The pilots and gunners didn't participate. They feared they'd be needed again, and soon.

The third attack came after another nineteen hours, despite two course changes made by the *Thunderstrike* to shake pursuers. In a swift hammer blow delivered in the Chonsetta system, a group of TIE interceptors hidden in a comet trail ravaged the starboard side of the troop transport before Twilight managed to flee.

By this time, even the most skeptical company members were convinced the Empire was tracking them through the endless depths of space. This was a novelty—even ignoring the fact that tracking ships in hyperspace was virtually impossible, Twilight Company had never been considered so strategically significant as to earn the Empire's particular enmity. With the entire Rebellion on the run, why would anyone go to so much effort—sacrifice resources and lives—to wear down a single infantry unit?

There was only one plausible explanation.

As a precaution, Namir ordered extra security around Everi Chalis's cell. He doubted anyone would make an attempt on the governor's life—as satisfying as the thought was, not even Corbo seemed so reckless—but scared people did stupid things.

"I hear that three Imperial battle groups have abandoned rebel engagements to hunt us. Would you like to confirm or deny?"

The droid's voice sounded like rust: a harsh, grating, electrical noise that made Namir grind his teeth. Or maybe it was M2-M5's left claw that soured his mood—the jagged metal picks and assortment of mechanical tools that whirred, extended, and retracted from the thing's "wrist" seemed like the toy box of a torturer.

Namir didn't like droids. He'd never be comfortable with technology that could *think*. But M2-M5 was the best mechanic in Twilight Company, and Namir had been told—in so many words—to "get over your qualms and trust the walking scrap heap."

"Is that why we have engine problems?" Namir asked. "Because you're listening in on bridge communications when you're supposed to be working?"

"We have engine problems," the droid said, "because my ship keeps being attacked. And my ship keeps being attacked because we have engine problems."

Namir scowled. "Meaning?"

The droid trundled through the cramped engine compartment. Namir had to stay close to hear its voice over the noise of the hyperdrive. "You recall the strike made on us shortly after you brought your Imperial friend aboard?"

"I almost burned to death. I remember. And *I* didn't bring Chalis aboard. Howl decided—"

M2-M5 was waving its claw in front of a sealed hatch. A green light on one of the droid's instruments turned red. "You see?" it said. "*That* indicates a hypermatter particle leak. The damage is at the microscopic level, likely localized to one of several hundred radiation refractors in the *Thunderstrike*. It is not enough to impact efficiency—but it could leave a trail for Darth Vader to follow."

"We don't know *Vader* has anything to do with it. Don't listen in on Chalis, either."

The red light flickered rapidly. Namir suspected it was the droid equivalent of a shrug. Or an obscene gesture.

"You think the damage occurred in that first attack?" Namir asked.

"It is likely. I suspect even the Imperials did not identify our trail until Coyerti. Regardless, I do not have adequate equipment to render repairs."

"So cannibalize yourself for parts," Namir said, and stalked toward the nearest ladder out of the compartment. "Send a full report to the captain," he called. "This is going to be a problem."

Howl had the senior staff assembled an hour later. Namir stood in the back of the conference room, along with Chief Medic Von Geiz and Quartermaster Hober; the place reserved for Twilight members invited out of courtesy, who weren't expected to contribute to the discussion. Around the table sat Lieutenant Sairgon, bridge crew from the *Thunderstrike* and *Apailana's Promise,* and Everi Chalis—who had chosen to occupy the captain's seat, sipping tea from a tin cup while Howl paced around the perimeter.

The first proposal to abandon Chalis came from Lieutenant Sairgon, mere moments after Howl had summarized the situation.

"We've been lucky so far," Sairgon said. "The Empire hasn't had forces positioned to do more than harry us. But they're closing in, and we can't survive against a Star Destroyer—"

"A Super Star Destroyer," Chalis interrupted with a bitter smile. "Vader has a new flagship. But please proceed."

Sairgon didn't look at Chalis. "We send the governor out in a shuttle, odds are she won't survive—but the Imps won't keep chasing us with everything they have, either. I don't *like* the plan, but I don't see a way to hold on to her and live."

Chalis nodded sagely, as if she'd been expecting precisely this.

"No," Howl said, gaze dancing between his officers, making eye contact one moment, then breaking it the next. "I asked for your opinions and I appreciate your candor, Lieutenant. But we are not abandoning this woman.

"Talrezan Four. Hope Station. Unroola Dawn." He struck the tabletop with each name. "All lost while we were escorting the fleet out of the Mid Rim. General Amrashad is dead. Even Commander Skywalker can't blow up a Death Star every month.

"Our decapitation of Coyerti's bioweapons program is the only real victory the Alliance has seen lately. Chalis gave us that opportunity, and she's nearly finished her report delineating the Empire's entire logistical network. Once we have that, everything changes."

Then he smiled broadly, straightened his back, and spread his arms wide. "More suggestions? Keep them coming."

The discussions and arguments began in earnest then. Two crew members from *Apailana's Promise* wanted to head for Baskron Pirate territory and strike a deal for materials to repair the *Thunderstrike*. That would be a harrowing journey at best, even assuming the pirates were keen to negotiate. Commander Paonu, *Thunderstrike*'s naval captain, reluctantly spelled out his plan to transfer Chalis and select personnel to *Apailana's Promise* and split the *Thunderstrike* from its escort; the Empire would pursue Twilight Company, perhaps obliterating it, but Chalis and key figures could flee to safety. Even Von Geiz offered his input, asking if Twilight could lie low for days or weeks in a nebula or the atmosphere of a gas giant—somewhere that might scramble Imperial sensors while the company waited for enemy search parties to disperse.

Namir listened and tried to follow along. At first, he racked his brain to remember what little he knew of the sector map and hyperdrive mechanics. But his knowledge was too superficial, and even the terminology eluded his grasp. His skills were on the ground, limited to guns and people who carried guns. When his attention started to wander, he fixed his gaze on Howl, who nodded and asked his staff questions and never showed impatience. He looked utterly unworried, entirely in control.

You have no idea what to do, Namir thought.

"Your ship," Chalis said, "is compromised. Commander Paonu had the right idea."

Everyone at the table watched the governor, some with interest and many with suspicion. Sairgon started to interrupt but Chalis waved him off.

"I propose we locate an Imperial cargo transport. I can get us within range, and your soldiers—" She cocked her head as she uttered the word, looking directly at Namir. "—can board it. Once the vessel is under our control and all personnel transferred, you abandon this wreck and we resume our journey."

Sairgon shook his head. "And when we enter shooting range, how do we avoid damaging the transport? If it's supposed to be our new home, we can't afford to hit something critical. That's assuming the enemy captain doesn't wipe his ship's computers or rig it to self-destruct once he realizes—"

"Do you want me to plan the attack *for* you?" Chalis asked, suddenly leaning forward, eyes keen. "I thought you people liked a challenge."

The conference degenerated from there, voices rising until Howl pounded the table with a fist. He didn't allow the discussion to pause, however—he began gesturing to officers seemingly at random, prompting them to offer opinions and counterarguments. It was obvious there was merit to Chalis's idea, despite its crust of impracticality.

Howl's roving finger pointed to Namir. "Sergeant? Can it be done?"

Can what *be done?* Namir wanted to ask. He gnawed on his lower lip, running scenarios in his mind. "If you can get boarding parties over there," he said, "we could probably take a small transport. Wouldn't want to hold it, though, with Imps hiding in every closet and setting traps."

Howl nodded carefully and began to turn away. It wasn't a solution, but it was the truth.

So why, Namir wondered, was Governor Chalis staring at him expectantly, as if Namir had held back something essential?

"We could get in and out, though." Namir was talking again before he fully realized what he was proposing. "Take a section of the ship, hold open a corridor, and get an engineering team inside." He glanced at the quartermaster, then to Howl. "Could we strip an Imperial engine for parts, use them to patch up the *Thunderstrike*?"

Howl's lips quirked into a smile. "I don't know. But it's *certainly* an interesting idea."

Chalis mimed a slow clap, leaning back in her seat. No one else appeared to notice, and it slowly dawned on Namir that he'd said exactly what she wanted him to.

"You never visit anymore, Sergeant."

The strategy session was over. Half the officers lingered in the conference room to speak to Howl or one another, plotting details for the raid. Namir had expected Chalis to remain with them; instead she followed a step behind him down the corridor toward the mess.

"Maybe because every time you talk, my people end up in danger," Namir said, not looking back. "Charmer got shot. Maediyu was breathing smoke. On Coyerti—you're a curse on the company."

Chalis made a noncommittal sound, not denying the charge before answering, "A curse on the company . . . you really are from a primitive world, aren't you?"

Namir had never said a word about his background to Chalis. She kept speaking before he could interject. "If it helps," she said, "I really did want you to survive the Distillery. It would've been bad for my defection if your team had come back covered in pustules."

Now he stopped walking and turned to face her. He considered how hard he could slug her without leaving a mark. She wouldn't be the first prisoner of war he'd ever hurt; just the first that belonged to Twilight.

The things the Creed would have done to you . . .

Chalis let out an exasperated sound and shook her head. "Since you so clearly loathe me, I'll get to the point: If we're really raiding an Imperial transport, you're going to need me aboard. With my authorization codes, I can get your droids into the ship's computer in half the time. So this time, I *share* the risk."

The reasoning made sense. Namir wondered what he was missing. The governor didn't seem the type to volunteer.

"Why tell me?" he asked.

"I want you to keep me alive." Chalis's gaze was locked on Namir. The arrogance and disdain in her voice had curdled into bitterness. "I'm appointing you my security escort for when we're aboard."

That, too, took Namir by surprise, and he made an effort to keep his expression neutral. He wanted to tell her she didn't get to *appoint* anyone. He wanted to ask what she thought she'd achieve by using him. But she'd played him in the strategy session, prompted him to put forth the idea he was certain she'd had first. She'd known capturing a cargo transport was impossible, and she'd known a raid would sound better coming from someone other than her.

Namir was tired of fulfilling her expectations.

Instead, he kept his voice low and said, "You really shouldn't trust me."

"Everyone on your ship—Captain Evon excepted—wants me dead," Chalis said. "My choices are limited. My standards for *trust* aren't what they used to be."

The Redhurne system was a charnel house adrift with the corpses of planets. Its sun had gone supernova centuries earlier, burning worlds to cinders; now no sign remained on those planets' ravaged surfaces of life or civilization. The remnant of the Redhurne star, a collapsed post-nova fragment that glowed white with seething intensity, exuded radiation deadly to any unshielded creature.

But Redhurne was not empty. When the planets of the inner system had cracked open, their cores had been exposed to the star's toxic rays and been transmuted into exotic new materials—the building blocks of hypermatter fuel. Thus, in the waning days of the Republic, Redhurne had become host to parasites: scavenging drones that crawled across its planets and carried their bounty of volatile minerals and gases to orbital mining stations operated by skeleton crews.

Those stations still remained to feed the Empire. They were not Twilight Company's target.

Instead, the *Thunderstrike* and its escort lurked at the edge of the Redhurne system, nestled in the crescent of a shattered moon where neither scanners nor visual inspection could easily detect them. They awaited the transport that Governor Chalis promised would come— a freighter that would siphon off the mining stations' hoard and carry the day's take to more hospitable galactic climes.

The question that hung over Twilight Company was this: Which would arrive first—the *Thunderstrike*'s prey, or its pursuers?

It had been a full standard day since the last attack. Cornered as it was within the grip of the moon's gravity, the *Thunderstrike* was vulnerable—it would not be able to jump to hyperspace from its hiding spot, not without maneuvering into open space first. Howl had agreed to wait in ambush for four hours and no more; after that, the company would need to seek prey elsewhere.

Namir loathed the plan and he loathed his part in it.

He'd spent the last hours working with squad leaders to devise strategies and run drills. The boarding parties were all experienced in zero-gravity combat, EVA procedures, proper use of space suits and oxygen masks—everything required in case things went horribly wrong. This was a day not to test the fresh meat, but to put veterans and ex-stormtroopers and former pirates to work. Namir's own squad wouldn't be present—with the exception of Charmer, who'd participated in more boarding operations than Namir had ever seen. When Namir had warned him not to get shot again, Charmer had only grinned his horrible, scar-faced grin.

That left Namir alone on the *Thunderstrike*'s bridge, sweltering under layers of armor and gear while his fellow soldiers gathered several decks below. He would have no part in the initial insertion.

Howl had approved Governor Chalis's request. Namir was playing bodyguard for the day.

So Namir waited. He watched Chalis and the captain and Commander Paonu speak quietly to one another, observed the bridge crew tap at consoles and adjust levers. He'd never liked spending time on the bridge; when he was elsewhere on the ship, he didn't have to think about how it worked, about the mechanics at play and the naval officers who'd learned the difference between acceleration compensators and null quantum field generators—the officers whose expertise meant the difference between life and death in a sucking void.

Namir didn't mind space travel, but he bristled at reminders of his ignorance. The mere *existence* of the bridge needled him.

The *Thunderstrike* had been lurking for two hours when alarms went off and the bridge crew scrambled to see what had arrived from hyperspace. The officers' voices were nervous and giddy when they reported what appeared to be an Imperial heavy freighter, lightly armed and ponderously slow. The captain smiled tightly but showed no other sign of pleasure.

The Imperial vessel was a rugged durasteel cylinder that stretched half a kilometer long, bristling with ejectable storage pods and maneuvering thrusters. It might have been a warship once, before decades of use had left it obsolete and a hundred retrofits had stripped it of its might. "Ships," Chalis said softly, as if quoting someone else, "like men, must be used until they break."

The second scanning station reported that the freighter wouldn't pass near the *Thunderstrike*'s moon on its current course. That was unsurprising. Chalis took the bridge communications terminal and rapidly entered a series of authorization codes before opening a channel.

"Imperial freighter," she said. "We have been monitoring ion-storm activity in this system. For your own safety, please alter your approach vector as follows."

Chalis read out numbers. Namir watched the crew.

The freighter did not change course.

"If they knew who we were," the captain mused, "they'd raise shields. They'd run. Instead they're ignoring us."

"What if it's a trap?" Namir asked.

"Then I expect we're doomed anyway," Howl said.

Chalis repeated her message, more forcefully this time. Again, the freighter did not respond or change course.

We need to go, Namir thought. *Or we need to take a chance and attack. But we need to do something.*

He didn't speak. He wasn't on the bridge to advise the captain.

Chalis slapped a palm on the communications console, her voice suddenly louder: a snarl of perfect arrogance. "Imperial freighter," she said, "this is Governor Everi Chalis. If you do not adjust course within fifteen seconds, I will deal with you as I dealt with the crew of the

Mandible during the Belnar Insurrections. That will be my gift to your superior, Commodore Krovis, before I have him tried for gross incompetence."

She cut off the signal and, with it, the sneer on her face. Arrogance dropped away like a mask, and she stared at the scanners with all the tension of a soldier awaiting battle.

"It's changing course," an ensign said.

"Ready the boarding pods," Howl called, and the bridge went into action.

Apailana's Promise and *Thunderstrike* emerged together: the latter from its hiding space in the shadow of the broken moon, the former from behind an asteroid that had once been part of a planet. Flanked by two enemies, the freighter made the obvious choice, angling away from the weapons-laden gunship toward the *Thunderstrike*.

Its shields and weapons were fully charged by the time *Thunderstrike* came into range. This was not a problem; for all the damage the *Thunderstrike* had accrued over the previous days, it could still hold its own against a freighter. The squadron of TIE fighters that the freighter disgorged would prove more troublesome, but *Apailana's Promise* could pick the starfighters off one by one—if it could get a clear shot.

Sickly green bolts flickered across the gap of space, splashing against the *Thunderstrike*'s englobing shields like raindrops in iridescent oil. The rebel vessel returned fire in periodic crimson volleys, causing the freighter's own deflectors to shimmer and coruscate under stress. As the *Thunderstrike* maneuvered ever nearer, the freighter began to pull back—but by then it was too late, and velocity was on the side of the attackers.

As if a countdown had reached zero, the *Thunderstrike*'s boarding pods shot free toward the freighter. Each had been adapted from an escape pod—capsules originally designed to save lives—by trading their maneuverability and fuel storage for hardiness and launch power; by reinforcing them further; and by equipping them with magnetic grapples and laserdrills. Each pod carried a squad of Twilight Company troops, rattled and crammed together with only minutes' worth of air.

As the pods rocketed toward their target, the *Thunderstrike*'s gunners took on the task of protecting the pods from the TIE fighters. The destruction of a single pod would represent a loss of manpower and technology Twilight Company could ill afford. The loss of multiple pods would thwart any boarding attempt and force a withdrawal.

But the pods struck home. Their drills sparked to life and began the process of carving open the freighter's hull.

Namir reached out, grabbed Chalis's neck with a gloved hand, and tightened the rebreather mask over her face. "Just keep it on," he said. "If we get sucked into vacuum, I won't have time to help you."

"Of course," Chalis said, her voice muffled. "Anything else?"

The boarding pod was shuddering, jostling Namir against the sealed door as the laserdrill burned into the freighter. Chalis was barely a hand span away. Behind her, two more soldiers cradled their rifles.

Namir drew a blaster pistol from his belt, holding it out to Chalis in both hands. "It's a DH-17," he said. "Leave the settings the way they are and don't even think of switching it to automatic. Point and shoot if it comes to that."

Chalis turned the weapon over and smirked. "I have used a blaster before. You've *seen* me."

"You've wiped out whole ships before, too," Namir said. "Doesn't mean I want you commanding mine."

"I have no idea what you're talking about."

Namir placed a palm on the door, trying to judge the rocking of the pod. "'I will deal with you,'" he quoted, "'as I dealt with the crew of the *Mandible*.'"

Chalis laughed and shook her head. "The *Mandible* was an accident," she said. "A drunk captain ferrying volatile cargo. I got credit because—well, if you were the Empire, what rumor would you rather spread: That one of your captains was grossly negligent and got his men killed in a mishap? Or that a ruthless, high-ranking officer saw incompetence on her watch and executed those responsible?"

The pod stopped rocking. The sound of shearing metal echoed in the chamber.

"I've noticed how you handle the recruits," Chalis continued with a shrug. "Tell me you wouldn't scare them much the same? Assuming you could get away with it."

Namir barked a laugh and raised his rifle. "I'd do a lot of things if I could get away with them. Be grateful I can't, and step away from the door."

Chalis obeyed as well as she could in the cramped space. Namir tapped the door's keypad with his elbow and two half circles of solid metal slid out of view, opening the way to the freighter's interior.

Two sounds dominated the corridor: the distant reverberation of blaster bolts and the roar of air whipping down the passage. Namir's pod had been the last to leave the *Thunderstrike;* one of the earlier arrivals must have cracked the freighter's hull worse than intended, opening a leak into space. The corridor itself was tight, packed with heavy-duty piping along the walls and floored with black metal gratings. Not an ideal place for a fight.

But then, that's why Namir had come with Chalis late. The first soldiers to board an enemy vessel were always cannon fodder.

Namir signaled for the rest of his boarding party to emerge. The two soldiers took up stations in opposite directions down the corridor while Namir announced his arrival over his comm. A series of curt responses assured him that the other squads were active, along with the engineering specialists. One of the freighter's aft command stations had been secured, at least temporarily. That was where Governor Chalis was needed first.

Namir gestured for Chalis to follow. She nodded and tapped off her own earpiece. The other boarders stayed behind to protect the pod.

The rush of air was warm—almost *hot*, as if spewed forth by a furnace upwind. Namir was sweating as he crept down the corridor, his armpits moist and his gloves tight over his fingers. He kept his body in front of Chalis, trying to ensure he'd be the first target if they were spotted. He had to fight his training, keep himself from sprinting to cover; he'd played escort for civilians before and barely suppressed his instincts then, but for Chalis? Playing bodyguard seemed *unnatural*.

"It's the shield generators."

"What?" Namir shook his head, baffled.

"The shield generators," Chalis said. "They're right next to the oxygen units, and they overheat under stress. That's why it's summer in here."

"How do you know?" Namir rounded a bend, swept the corridor for enemies and saw none. The blasterfire was getting louder.

"I served on a ship like this a *very* long time ago. Part of my *apprenticeship*." Again, there was bitterness instead of arrogance in her tone. Then she added idly, "You know that stormtrooper armor has environmental controls? Internal cooling options?"

On the floor ahead, three dead stormtroopers were splayed across the grating.

Chalis kept talking. "You'd think it would be luxurious, but cooling drains power. Use in noncritical situations is a punishable offense. So many cadets try it anyway, thinking they won't be caught . . ."

Namir nudged a body with the toe of his boot, then stepped over it. He relaxed his shoulders and bit back a smile. "The Empire's famed discipline cracks in the heat?"

"That's the difference between our forces," Chalis said. "Imperial troops all make the same mistakes, and they never make them more than once. I can only assume Alliance troops are more creative and less agreeable."

Namir snorted. "Not *that* creative. It's the same garbage with every batch of fresh meat. I could tell you stories." Realizing what he'd just said, he winced: The woman *was* good at making others lower their guards.

"I'll take you up on that—" Chalis began. Then there was the sound of another shot, and a red particle bolt flashed across a branch in the corridor ahead.

"—another time," she finished, and raised her blaster.

Two quick bursts with the rifle. Namir aimed down the corridor, but he wasn't worried about hitting any particular target. He just meant to discourage stormtroopers from coming around the bend and peppering the hallway with plasma. There wasn't room to dodge. He didn't have the firepower to win. If the enemy pushed forward, the only option was to run.

He crept backward with Chalis a short distance behind him. They'd lost almost ten minutes maneuvering through the freighter and trying to circumvent the worst of the fighting. Repeated calls to the other boarding teams had been of little help—the freighter crew was intermittently jamming transmissions, and the squads Namir could reach had their hands full. That left it up to him and Chalis to take the long route to the command station alone, and Chalis's paranoia hadn't helped.

"Half the sections in this ship," she'd snapped, "can be opened to space or flooded with toxic gas. I'd rather avoid a preventable death."

Namir had agreed. But he still didn't like the delay.

A white form appeared at the end of the hallway. Namir's rifle jumped as he fired a pulse. His opponent sprawled on the floor. He crept backward another meter, felt his shoulder brush metal and lurched away. The wall was hot, scorched by stray bolts.

"You all right?" Chalis asked. She stood to one side, pressed to the opposite wall and working the keypad to a blast door.

"Fine," Namir snapped, gesturing in frustration to the portal. "We going?"

They went, racing down another set of passages before reaching the command station rendezvous. Sergeant Fektrin met them with a trio of engineers, an astromech droid, and two more soldiers. The numbers didn't add up right; Namir realized Fektrin had lost a squad member along the way.

Fektrin dragged the corpse of a young Imperial woman out of a chair and gestured Chalis and the astromech over with a sweeping gesture. Chalis scowled at the squat, boxy droid when it beeped incoherently, but she joined it at the dead woman's terminal.

Fektrin led Namir to the door and took up a sentry position across from him. Namir felt lighter the moment Chalis was out of reach, as if her mere presence had been oppressive.

No. That's not right.

Chalis wasn't oppressive. She was callous and manipulative, but Namir never felt personally threatened by her. His *responsibility* for Chalis—her life, her safety—was what weighed on him.

Why did Howl agree to this?

"Yours are at the pod?" Fektrin asked.

It took Namir a moment to understand. "Keeping an exit route. How about yours?"

"Cappandar took half a dozen shots before he hit the ground."

Namir knew Cappandar by name and reputation, but the alien hadn't spoken Basic—something about the way his lungs worked—and so they'd never been able to talk. He'd been one of the longest-serving members of Twilight; part of why Namir had approved him for the mission.

"One more to drink to when we get back," Namir said.

Fektrin's voice lowered. "Can she get us what we need?"

Namir spared Chalis a glance. She was arguing with the droid at the terminal and gesturing to the screen for the benefit of the engineers.

"She wants to get out alive," Namir said. "She'll do her best, for what that's worth."

Fektrin nodded. He didn't look amused. Namir supposed he couldn't blame him.

Namir listened to the other squads' comm transmissions as he waited. From what he could gather, the teams were trying to hold key positions while pushing forward into engineering, opening the way for Fektrin's technical crew. Ajax's men had set up a choke point at one of the main passageways. Charmer was making hit-and-run attacks on guard posts, trying to keep the enemy off balance and obscure Twilight's goal. Carver and Zab's heavy-fire teams were at the vanguard, smashing their way through blast doors.

"We're ready," Chalis said. "The engineers can salvage the parts they need from one of the upper drive compartments. We've rerouted the power so they won't be incinerated."

Fektrin relayed instructions through his comm. Namir felt his guts tighten, knowing what came next. He checked the power meter on his rifle to put off saying it aloud. Still at 70 percent.

"That's it for your job." He was looking at Chalis. "We'll work our way back to the pod and take off. Should be easier while the Imps are distracted."

Chalis looked around the room and gestured with her head to a private corner. When Namir joined her, she spoke quietly. "I'm in no hurry to die as gloriously as Cappandar, but I'll be no safer aboard the *Thunderstrike* if we fail here."

Namir studied the governor's expression, tried to read her and came up short. He spared a glance for Fektrin, who was organizing the others, and imagined a hundred ways the mission could end in disaster.

"Stick close to the engineers," he told Fektrin. "We'll tail you, keep anyone from coming up behind."

Fektrin nodded carefully, then stepped to the body of a fallen stormtrooper and kicked the man's rifle toward Chalis. It skidded across the floor with a hiss. Without a word, he led the engineers from the room.

Whenever Namir taught stormtrooper cadets—cadets who'd abandoned their units, reason, and steady pay to become Twilight Company fresh meat; cadets who, nine times out of ten, expected to become heroes of democracy and saviors of the weak instead of corpses abandoned on the battlefield—he had to teach them to fight alone. Or close enough, because even soldiers in a two-person fire team or a four-person squad certainly *felt* alone when outnumbered a hundred times over.

Fighting alone meant guerrilla tactics and dirty tricks instead of formations and shield domes and air support. It meant setting death traps and shooting people from behind and slitting their throats while they slept. It meant—as Namir recalled being told by one recruit days before she abandoned the company—performing acts that felt more like murder than war.

He wasn't surprised that Chalis had no qualms with guerrilla tactics. He was surprised she was *good* at them.

When Fektrin and the engineers had descended to the lower decks, Chalis had identified a gas cooling pipe running down the corridor to the turbolift. With a bored expression, she'd secured the rebreather tighter over her mouth and shot the pipe three times along its length. She missed only once in the attempt.

The coolant gas was invisible and odorless, carried along by the wind that twisted through the ship. By the time an Imperial security team came marching down the hall, the officers involved—not stormtroopers, but by the looks of them washouts, eighteen-year-old idiots who'd been assigned to a rusting freighter to keep them out of harm's way—were already unsteady on their feet. They couldn't aim straight, couldn't dodge. Namir huddled inside a doorframe and checked his scope, lined up his shots, and burned each of his targets through the chest. Chalis's initial shots came a moment too late, went too wide, but she soon corrected her aim and grip.

The kill zone did its work well. Namir and Chalis eliminated a second team and a third—whoever made it past Ajax and his team's blockade. Over his comlink, Namir listened to Fektrin and the engineers scramble to complete their salvage job; to the other squads desperately attempting to keep an exfiltration route clear. Twilight Company was hurting, but it was holding its own.

Twice, the *Thunderstrike* fired on the freighter, each time attempting to disable critical systems and stem the flow of Imperials into the combat zone. The busier the freighter crew was just trying to survive—the more Imperials who were repairing life support instead of fighting Twilight—the better. But there was only so much the *Thunderstrike* could do without killing its own people, and Namir and the others knew it.

When Fektrin and the engineers signaled that they'd finished their work, the squads changed tactics. The teams had stretched from their boarding pods into the interior of the freighter like elastic bands, dropping troops at key points and spacing themselves out. Now it was time for the elastic to contract, each team gradually withdrawing toward its initial position as the engineering team safely passed by. Namir found himself again staying close to Chalis, shielding her body with his own. They allowed the engineering team to overtake them and followed a short distance behind, out of sight but close enough to intercept pursuers.

As they approached the outer bulkhead, the engineers split up toward different pods. Fektrin sent the comm signal indicating it was time for a full withdrawal. The squad leaders acknowledged and began to pull back, contracting the lines further.

Chalis was smiling as Namir led the way back toward their own boarding pod. "Now we just hope your engineers were right about what they needed."

Namir grunted. "Sure. Once we're free and clear of the Mid Rim, we get to put this whole botched retreat in the past. Lick our wounds before the next massacre."

"That's the advantage you have with me aboard: The Rebellion won't have to count on winning victories through smug self-righteousness anymore."

Again, Namir couldn't hold back a smile. "You're one to talk about *smug*."

Yet it was good to hear someone say the things he couldn't around his colleagues.

Chalis laughed, and the sound wasn't affected or measured—it was a note of genuine delight that echoed as they crept together toward their escape.

They'd nearly reached the pod when an alert came in from the *Thunderstrike*: Enemy reinforcements had arrived.

An Imperial *Gozanti*-class cruiser had jumped out of hyperspace and set course for the battle. Howl had given the boarding teams five minutes to complete their evacuation; after that, the cruiser would enter firing range, and its turbolasers and proton torpedoes would begin reducing the *Thunderstrike* to a molten cloud adrift in space.

Five minutes was more than enough for Namir and Chalis, but Namir knew half the boarding squads wouldn't make it to their pods in time—not while they were still under fire from the freighter's security teams. If they turned their backs on their foes they'd be shot dead. The burst of comm chatter following *Thunderstrike*'s transmission confirmed Namir's suspicions, as Ajax, Charmer, Fektrin, Zab, and Carver—strained and cursing but never complaining—ordered their teams to do the impossible.

Namir stood motionless for only a moment. Then he turned away from the corridor leading to his boarding pod. Chalis moved between him and the rest of the freighter interior. "Five minutes," he said.

The joy had faded from Chalis's face. The creases of age seemed chiseled deeper into her cheeks, and Namir saw she'd been sweating. Her hair was plastered to her forehead. She looked at him gravely and shook her head. "We're going now."

Someone was shooting a blaster nearby. Namir aimed his rifle over Chalis's shoulder. "You offered your support," he said. "You had the chance to leave and you said you'd—"

"I said I wanted this mission to succeed. It *succeeded.* Your friends knew what they signed on for."

Four and a half minutes left. There wasn't time to argue.

"You know where the boarding pod is," Namir said, and pushed his way past Chalis and toward the remaining squads. The governor snapped something more, but he didn't hear what.

With four minutes to spare, Namir located Ajax's squad. In their haste to withdraw, Ajax and his soldiers had backed themselves into a corner. Namir shot wildly into a throng of stormtroopers until his rifle glimmered with warning lights, desperately drawing fire until Ajax's squad could break free. Ajax himself died shouting obscenities, with a grenade in one fist.

With three minutes to spare, Namir broke off from the remains of Ajax's squad as Fektrin announced over the comm that his team had been split. The engineers were safely away, but the rest of the group was scattered. Fektrin's men were being overwhelmed one by one.

With two minutes to spare, Namir found Fektrin's corpse. The alien's skin was somehow already cold. Namir realized he'd never touched Fektrin before.

With one minute to spare, Namir heard Charmer stutter into the comm and declare that his team had reached a boarding pod. Namir had never loved Charmer more than in that moment.

With no time to spare at all, Namir sealed the door inside Fektrin's pod and launched it toward the *Thunderstrike*. He did so alone.

"Eight dead. It's not a bad number until you look at who we lost." Lieutenant Sairgon spoke slowly, as if he were testing each word for flaws before pronouncing it. He turned a datapad over in his hands without looking, addressing the gap between Namir and Howl in the captain's cramped office.

Thunderstrike and *Apailana's Promise* had jumped to hyperspace under fire, and both ships wore scars from the battle. The *Promise* had lost its shield generator blocking volleys aimed at the *Thunderstrike*, while the *Thunderstrike* itself had been forced to seal off two decks due to hull breaches. Nonetheless, the engineering teams swore that the raid had been worthwhile; *Thunderstrike*'s course could not be traced again.

Chalis had arrived back aboard safely with the men who'd guarded her pod. If Howl knew Namir had arrived separately, he had not mentioned it.

"What about the recruits?" Howl was looking at Namir.

"Coyerti toughened them up—the ones who went, anyway. The others are mostly ready. They'll shore up manpower, but we can't just slot in a new Ajax . . ."

"If they're willing to fight and willing to learn, it's enough for now," Howl said. "They'll have time to train at the flotilla."

Namir glanced toward Sairgon. The man's expression hadn't changed, but then it rarely did. Sairgon was built from granite. "We putting in for repairs?" Namir asked.

"Yes and no," Howl said.

Sairgon was the one to explain. "The *Thunderstrike* and the *Promise* will rendezvous with three other battle groups in deep space. We've allocated a month to get both ships back in shape and let the men heal up. Alliance High Command should have new orders for the whole flotilla by then."

Namir winced. On the one hand, a month of rest and gentle training would be good for the company. Soldiers assigned new squads would need time to adjust. He had lists of troops with minor injuries—burns, lacerations, sprains—that had gone ignored since before Haidoral. But a month in deep space was bound to be mind numbing. By the end, he wouldn't be surprised if even the droids would be shooting holes in the walls to stave off boredom.

"All right," Namir said. "That sounds like a yes. What's the no?"

"Ah." Howl smiled—a warm, sad smile that made Namir want to slap him. "I told you that Governor Chalis has been working on a schematic—"

Namir cut him off. "—of the workings of the Empire. Every trade route, every factory, every neuron in its brain. I've heard her speech."

Howl bowed his head and turned to his holoprojector. He tapped a button. The overhead lights dimmed and a shimmering blue image filled the room—an intricate tangle that looked to Namir less like a machine or a monster and more like a plant floating within a fine mist. Gleaming droplets slid down a thousand stalks while spherical buds swelled and shrank. At a gesture from Howl's head, the whole image rotated and a hundred labels flashed into place. Here and there, Namir spotted the name of a star system he recognized—Coruscant, Corellia, Mandalore—but they brought him no understanding.

"She really is something of an artist," Howl said. "I can't quite parse it all myself, but I've already confirmed portions with High Command.

"Two weeks ago, our spies uncovered a Tibanna mining operation in the Pantrosian Eye. It's how the Empire was able to increase its blaster production rate over the past year. Chalis couldn't have known we knew about it . . . but it's there, in her masterpiece."

"So it's useful," Namir said. "What does it mean for us?"

"*We*," Howl said, "have received an invitation to High Command's secret base, per direct order of Princess Leia. While the *Thunderstrike* is being repaired, Chalis and I, along with an escort, will be leaving Twilight Company to discuss the next phase of the war."

Namir nodded carefully. His muscles felt suddenly fatigued, as if he'd been standing for hours. Howl's departure would cause some complaints among the rank and file, but losing Chalis? It was long past time, and it could only bode well.

Howl leaned forward across his desk, eyes wide and gleaming as he smiled. "Congratulations," he said. "You're part of the escort."

Of course I am, Namir thought, and he fought back a bitter laugh. Chalis was bad luck, after all, and he'd been carrying her like a charm.

PART II

REGROUPMENT

CHAPTER 9

PLANET SULLUST

Fifteen Days Before Plan Kay One Zero

SP-475 stood straight and stiff in her white armor, watching the lieu-tenant pace back and forth along the line. He stopped periodically to look a stormtrooper up and down: to examine a suit for scrapes or blemishes, catalog a soldier's equipment and peripherals, or—in the worst possible scenario—call out a trooper for inattention.

When SP-475 had started as a cadet—barely a year ago, when she'd been Thara Nyende and nothing but—she'd dreaded inspections. Every time she'd been called out for her errors, she'd taken it as a per-sonal insult. Anger and shame had burned in her guts for hours after-ward. As the weeks had passed, however, she'd gradually realized that faceless suits and alphanumeric designations ensured *no one* was sin-gled out. If the lieutenant called on you, it wasn't personal—you'd done something to endanger yourself and your comrades.

You corrected your error. The next day, it was truly forgotten. This was one of the reasons Thara loved the stormtrooper legion.

She'd joined with the intention of serving one tour of duty, making more money than she possibly could elsewhere and supporting her mother and cousins and uncle before returning to civilian life. Now she could see herself remaining forever.

"Command has issued a warning about the Cobalt Laborers' Reformation Front," the lieutenant was saying. He'd drawn back from the lineup and taken a position at the front of the small briefing room. "It's easy to laugh, I know—they were barely able to organize a protest, and we estimate eighty percent of their membership is in custody. A few disgruntled workers with pipe bombs shouldn't be a threat to the factories, to Pinyumb, or to Sullust."

SP-475 resisted the urge to pull Cobalt Front data onto her helmet's display. *Focus on the lieutenant,* she told herself. *He'll tell you anything you need.*

The lieutenant nodded to a droid, who obediently operated the controls to the holopit in the center of the room. Light flashed in the shallow recess, and images of human and Sullustan faces cycled through.

"But we've seen alarming indications that the Cobalt Front is attempting to cultivate ties with the Rebel Alliance," the lieutenant continued. "And if the Rebellion comes to Sullust, we have failed at our foremost duty: to keep and maintain order.

"Memorize the names on display. Nien Nunb, Sian Tevv, Corjentain Malaqua . . . these are rebels with known ties to Sullust. They are potential infiltrators. They may be smuggling in arms and equipment for a full-on revolution."

This was the part of the job SP-475 hated. She stared at the holograms, tried to lock the shapes of eyes and chins and ears into her brain. But on the street she'd be forced to make choices—take men and women into custody for hours or days because they looked *just enough* like her targets; waste their time and the time of interrogation officers . . .

She trusted the stormtrooper legion, trusted the lieutenant. She still didn't trust her own judgment.

The lieutenant began to say more, but something made him hesitate. He turned away from the troops and cupped a hand over his earpiece.

Then the garrison alarms began to sound.

The stormtroopers were too disciplined to break ranks, but SP-475 saw her comrades shuffle and glance about uneasily. Finally the lieutenant turned back toward them, and as one they straightened again.

"Stormtroopers!" he said, voice crisp and shoulders tense. "The situation has changed.

"The enemy has attacked."

The cavern-city of Pinyumb hid beneath the desolate surface of Sullust, on the southern side of Inyusu Tor—a volcanic peak shelled in black obsidian. Running from city to peak were sparking tram lines and hissing industrial lifts that led past the garrisons, past the aerial defenses, and up to the processing facility that crowned the mountain. Thousands of Pinyumb's people rode ground and air transports to the facility each day, worked its mechanisms as it drew magma up from the mountain's heart, filtered and sifted and purified molten rock to bring forth precious metals that would augment the Imperial fleet.

Despite a dozen levels of security—from stormtrooper-run checkpoints to worker psychological profiling to biometric scans—the facility's machinery was inherently vulnerable. It might only take one person to stuff the wrong pipe with rags soaked in a chemical cocktail and cause the extractors to grind to a halt, the magnetic separators to plunge into the magma flow.

It *might* only take one person. But until that one person was identified, SP-475 had to assume the worst.

There were other teams, more experienced teams, that cordoned off the facility itself. SP-475 spent the day locking down Pinyumb, blocking streets and conducting searches of random civilians. Half an hour in, a flash on her heads-up display told her she was authorized to indefinitely detain anyone she deemed suspicious. It was an authority she hoped not to need.

Early in the afternoon, she began receiving raid warrants from the Security Bureau. When a signal came in, she'd scramble to a residential complex or a bathhouse or a market, surround it with whatever other troops had been assigned, and search for incriminating items within. Residents who cooperated could observe. Any who resisted were subject to arrest. SP-475 never found a weapon or a bomb; just spice, black-market holovids, and Cobalt Front pamphlets. Enough for a few detentions. She wondered if the raids were random, or if the bureau had leads on the terrorists she wasn't cleared to know.

There were no further attacks.

Toward the end of her shift, she was assigned sentry duty at a tram station. She'd been partnered with SP-156. She'd worked with him before, trusted him as much as any colleague, though she didn't know his real name.

"You think anyone died?" he asked. "At the facility, I mean."

SP-475 winced inside her helmet. Nonessential chatter was against regulations while on duty, and the suits recorded everything.

She risked a brisk answer anyway and hoped the monitors would be lenient. "Not in the report," she said. "Probably not."

SP-156 nodded and shifted his grip on his rifle. "You think our side killed anyone? Down here?"

She wasn't sure why he was asking. This time, it seemed safer to remain silent.

When her shift was finally over, Thara was exhausted. She wanted to go home, to collapse on her cot and fall asleep without a meal or a shower. She felt like her armor had been holding her together; she expected to ooze out of her civilian clothes and onto the streets of Pinyumb.

But she'd promised her uncle another delivery of food and medicine and soap and simple luxuries. She'd been making purchases all week, stashing them in her locker. The old men were counting on her. So she dragged herself to the cantina and put the day's thoughts out of her head.

There was a crowd inside, packing the dimly lit tables and spilling onto the floor. She was surprised until she remembered the housing-block raids. The workers were drinking away the night because they had nowhere to go until the Security Bureau authorized their return. Thara winced at the thought and wished she'd planned better; she might have brought more food, a portable heater, fresh clothing.

She said as much to her uncle as he rushed over. He was smiling awkwardly. "It's fine, Thara. You don't need to spend your last credits on us."

She passed her bag to him, still apologizing. He grasped it in both hands, held it a short distance from his body as if expecting it to bite. She realized the old men were watching her again.

They were afraid. She understood. There was nothing she could do.

"I'll go," she said. Her uncle nodded, started to reach for her until he remembered he still held her bag.

She didn't mean to scan the room as she walked back toward the door. But she'd spent the past twelve hours studying faces for infiltrators, looking for concealed knives or blasters. Her eyes jumped about the crowd and she saw gray Sullustan hands slip discreetly under tables, clutching silvery ration packs. She saw a human boy step halfway behind a large woman, concealing the fresh white bandage around his upper arm. She saw a cloth duffel bag, deflated and empty, lying beneath a table in the corner.

She was trembling when she made it to the exit and climbed the stone steps back out into the cavern. None of it was evidence, she knew—not yet, not *really*, and she wasn't on duty anymore. She could even live with the fact that the workers hated her now—for no real reason, but she could take the blame and still help her family.

But if someone else was supplying the workers of Pinyumb—someone with money and resources the old men didn't have—then it wasn't something Thara could ignore forever.

CHAPTER 10

**THREE LIGHT-YEARS OFF THE
CORELLIAN TRADE SPINE HYPERLANE**
Fourteen Days Before Plan Kay One Zero

More often than not, there were no bodies involved in a Twilight
Company funeral. Sometimes it was because there were no bodies to
be found; air strikes and disintegrations had that effect. Usually it
was because Twilight was a mobile infantry unit and the dead were
decidedly immobile, too bulky to be carried while advancing or retreating.

So Twilight had developed its own traditions over the years to acknowledge the fall of a comrade. To recognize the eight killed in the
freighter raid, Quartermaster Hober stood in the *Thunderstrike*'s vehicle bay reading the name of each man or woman slain. Those closest
to the dead—friends and squad mates and, in rare cases, lovers—
looked on, squeezed together between speeders and drop ships,

smelling of grease and sweat. Others waited outside, listening to Hober's voice broadcast across the ship.

"Sergeant Maximian Ajax," Hober proclaimed.

Twitch shoved her way forward and stood before Hober. "Bleeding Roughneck till the end," she said, sharp and bitter.

She raised a blaster power pack in a shaking hand. It was rusted and dented, ready to be tossed away or recycled. Hober took it solemnly, inserted it into the vehicle charging station, and drained its dying sparks. That done, he placed it in a small metal case and Twitch retreated into the crowd.

It wasn't a long ceremony, and Twilight tradition ensured no one's eulogy was more than a few words. It didn't matter if you were a beloved veteran or fresh meat—you got one friend, one statement, and then the deed was done.

In death, all soldiers were equal.

The Clubhouse was always packed after a funeral. The card games had higher stakes and the contraband drinks were more plentiful. It wasn't a place for private or somber grief—it was a place for distraction, and the impromptu wakes ended in brawls as often as not.

Namir had his own need for distraction, but the Clubhouse wasn't providing it. He sat with his squad and forced a bitter smile when Roach asked when he was leaving.

"Tomorrow morning," he said. "Howl, Chalis, me, Roja, and Beak. Wish me luck on the shuttle ride."

"Beak is a fine soldier," Gadren said, "and Roja is . . . Roja. There are worse comrades to have."

Namir snorted. "They're not who I'm worried about."

"You going to meet the princess?" Roach asked. Her voice was even quieter than usual.

Charmer laughed. Brand shook her head. Gadren, however, gestured briskly for silence. "You mock," he said, "but who here was not inspired by one of the great heroes of the Rebellion? Or if not of the Rebellion, heroes of times past?"

Charmer bowed his head, smirking. "Wish I'd been—" He stammered out the words, but maintained the smile. "—good enough to blow a Death Star when I was young. But I'm—too old for idols."

"It was just a *question*," Roach muttered. "I saw her on a pirated holovid once."

Namir's forced smile was becoming a grimace. Brand glanced his way and offered what might have been a look of sympathy.

"For my part," Gadren said, his voice conciliatory, mediating, "I am merely glad the Alliance sees a future, even if I cannot. If Governor Chalis can provide a means to change the course of this war . . ."

That was the pattern of conversation for the evening. One by one, Twilight soldiers said their good-byes to Namir, wished him safe travels, and asked what he expected to find at the rebel headquarters. Men he barely knew speculated about the base's location, told him rumors of an asteroid fortress or an underwater city before offering up their hopes for the future.

Namir felt the desperation under the questions. These were soldiers who'd just seen their friends die, who'd spent the last months losing every piece of territory they'd gained. Of course they wanted hope. Of course they saw Alliance Command as inspiration.

Namir couldn't share that hope, and he couldn't bring himself to darken the mood of his comrades further—not when every other conversation in the room revolved around Fektrin or Ajax or Cappandar, people who'd sacrificed themselves to get Twilight to safety. Yet he was being separated from Twilight when the company needed him. At the rebel base, there would be a place for Howl, a place for Chalis— maybe even one for Roja and Beak—but not for Namir.

Maediyu passed Namir a bottle of something strong—she'd been unusually solicitous toward him ever since he'd saved her from burning to death outside Chalis's air lock—and that helped him endure the evening. Well past midnight, the tone of the gathering began to shift as the old grudges among the dead were recounted. When Twitch stumbled in and someone blamed Ajax for Fektrin's death, she threw the first punch of the day.

Seeing Twitch start a fight didn't surprise Namir. Seeing Roach, of all people, hold Twitch back and calm her *did* surprise him, but perhaps it shouldn't have. Roach was a scrapper.

After the fight, after the Clubhouse had nearly emptied, Namir found himself seated in a corner with Brand. He didn't remember when she'd joined him there, but she looked at him sternly and said, "Behave yourself when you're out there. Don't be stupid."

"You don't think much of me, do you?" Namir asked, his voice husky with exhaustion.

"Never did," Brand said.

"Is that why we get along?"

"That's me being tolerant, you not asking stupid questions. Usually."

For once, he caught her smiling. Or something close enough to it.

"I need you to look out for these people," Namir said. "When I'm gone. You have *sense* they don't."

"Can't promise that."

"You can," Namir said, quiet and intense.

"Not the way you want," Brand said. She didn't look at him as she spoke, measured and calm. "I turned my back on *sense* when I met Howl. There are things more important than surviving."

She hesitated. Namir searched for an argument before she interrupted with, "I will try. You know that."

He nodded. "Look out for them," he murmured again.

Brand reached into her pocket and held out a slender metal rectangle in the dim Clubhouse light. A datachip. She passed it to Namir, who looked at it curiously.

"In case of emergency," she said.

Without another word, she was gone from Namir's side.

Namir slept an hour that night before waking and packing his gear in the dark of the barracks. Even as a child, he'd learned how to sleep no matter his location or state of mind—though sleep never guaranteed *rest*.

The morning shift hadn't yet come on duty and the corridors of the

Thunderstrike were nearly empty as Namir groggily marched to the mess hall. Eating was something else he'd learned to do no matter the circumstances, and supplies would be limited on the shuttle to the rebel base. When he stepped inside the mess, he wasn't shocked to see another human face, but he hadn't expected to see Governor Chalis so early in the day. She sat at a table sipping from a steaming metal bowl, not looking at Namir as he entered.

That was fine with Namir. He wasn't looking for conversation.

When he'd filled a tray with what scraps the galley droid could provide—the fresh meat and vegetables they'd stolen from Haidoral Prime were long gone, leaving Namir with a breakfast of mashed grains swimming in artificial spices and a formulated nutrient drink with the texture and taste of gravel—he sat at the table adjacent to Chalis's and began to eat. He hadn't managed a spoonful before he heard her say, "You shouldn't have listened."

He exhaled between his teeth and stiffened on the table bench. "Listened to what?" he asked.

Chalis took another long sip from her bowl, then gestured around its rim. "The droid," she said. "That paste you're eating is a disaster. Better to take the kernels, soak them in hot water until they swell. The soup's an acquired taste, but it's better than what you've got." She glanced in the direction of the galley. "It also stretches out the supply longer, since that seems to be an issue for you."

"Aren't you supposed to be under guard?" Namir asked.

Chalis shrugged. "We leave for the base in three hours," she said. "In the words of Captain Evon: *How much harm can she do?*"

Namir grunted and swallowed a spoonful of the mash. It was, as promised, awful. "Where would you be without his support?" he asked.

"Where indeed?" Chalis replied.

They ate in silence awhile before Chalis spoke again. "It wasn't my idea, you know—bringing you on this trip. It doesn't benefit me. But I didn't tell your captain you abandoned me on the freighter, either."

"Should I be grateful?"

"No. But you also shouldn't hold a grudge."

Namir half laughed, half coughed around his mash. "Once you're safely away from Twilight? I don't plan to think about you one way or another. You've done your damage."

Chalis looked down into her dish and smiled. The silence stretched longer this time.

"*I* think," she said, "your captain believes you could *learn* something from this trip. He wants you to see the Rebellion at its best. Maybe come away inspired."

That thought hadn't occurred to Namir. The mash felt heavy in his stomach. He kept eating.

Chalis stood from her table and carried her bowl to the washstand. Namir kept his eyes on his food but couldn't help tracking her in his peripheral vision. She walked back toward him, seated herself at the opposite corner of his table. "I'm going to give you some advice, Sergeant, because you've been useful to me and I think you need it. You can listen or not."

This time, it wasn't the words that caught Namir's attention. Her voice shifted as she spoke, rising in pitch and losing that odd, artificial enunciation. It took on a new accent—not entirely foreign and not entirely familiar—that brought back memories of a world Namir hadn't seen in years.

Chalis shrugged, and when she spoke again, the accent was gone. "You're from Khuteb? Promencius Four? One of those Old Tionese colonial backwaters, I imagine, though I can't place the dialect."

"One of those," Namir said, almost too soft to hear.

"Fine," Chalis said. "So you've barely seen a working sanitation station by the time you're ten years old. The Rebellion comes and uplifts you, gives you food"—there was some scorn to the word, accentuated by a flap of her hand toward Namir's tray—"and shelter. Not much, but it's an improvement. Naturally, you pledge your allegiance to your saviors. Am I close so far?"

"By what definition is this *advice*?"

Chalis laughed. "Give me some credit, Sergeant. We're getting there."

Namir waited.

Chalis continued, "My point is, you survived and climbed out of a scum pit most people never escape. That's all well and good, but you're so grateful for the scraps you've got now that you've quit striving for anything better."

"*Better* like being governor? Or *better* like living in an air lock?"

Chalis shrugged again, unperturbed. "I'm not going to say this has been a banner year for me. Even Haidoral was a punishment, but it wasn't so bad—I had respect, I had comfort, I had time to sculpt. That's all I ever really wanted. If Vader hadn't been waiting for an excuse to execute me . . ."

As Namir listened, he noticed her accent shifting again—not to mimic anything he recognized, but in a subtle drawl, in stretched vowels. Her posture shifted as well, her square shoulders easing into an arc, her head and hands moving more casually.

For the first time, he felt the governor wasn't attempting to manipulate him.

"You know the rest," she said. "I'm here now, and if I need to overthrow the Empire to get my life back, so be it."

"Is that what you plan to tell Alliance High Command?"

Chalis wrinkled her nose. "Please—there are things they need me to say about 'Imperial oppression,' and I'll say them. That's called *diplomacy*." She paused. "The irony is, I don't think they're altogether wrong." She leaned forward, one elbow casually placed on the tabletop. "They believe the Empire is squeezing more of its citizens every year for the benefit of a shrinking elite—taking away *liberty* and *comfort* from the masses to feed the insatiable appetite of the Emperor and the Ruling Council.

"That much is true, and I have the numbers to prove it. Where the Rebellion deludes itself is in thinking the trend won't ever slow or stop. That the inevitable end is—" Here, her voice took a tone of mock-solemnity. "—utter desolation and hopelessness for every living being . . . save the Emperor himself."

She was enjoying herself now, energized. "They're so convinced of their *righteousness* that they don't see how infeasible their nightmare scenario really is," she said. "The Ruling Council doesn't need stormtroopers overseeing every moisture farm, or every habitable planet converted to a factory world. At a certain point, even Palpatine has to look at the Empire and say, *Good enough.*"

Chalis shook her head and sighed, an exasperated smile on her face. Watching her, Namir realized she wasn't simply *not manipulating* him—it was the first conversation he'd had in as long as he could remember with someone who didn't see the galaxy as an ideological battleground. That didn't make the governor any less appalling, but next to Howl's meandering philosophy and Gadren's zealous dedication, it seemed comfortably honest.

Or perhaps not. Pieces of a puzzle locked together in his mind and he laughed again. "You're lying," he said.

Chalis didn't look offended. "What about?"

"Overthrowing the Empire," Namir said. "You *needed* Twilight to escape Haidoral. You've been stuck with the Rebellion ever since, but you'll abandon it the first opportunity that comes along."

"Possibly," Chalis said. "But in the meantime, I belong to the Alliance." She stood from the bench and rapped her knuckles on the table before pivoting toward the mess hall door. "And at least I have a *goal.* Something to consider."

Then she was gone, and Namir was alone in the mess. The sense of comfort dissipated. He pushed the conversation from his mind, tried to forget the good-byes he'd said to his colleagues in the Clubhouse. He'd make his rounds and check over his troops once more before he left the *Thunderstrike.*

Don't think about the rebel base, he told himself. *You'll be back in no time at all.*

CHAPTER 11

METATESSU SECTOR
Thirteen Days Before Plan Kay One Zero

Captain Tabor Seitaron had spent the better part of a month aboard the *Herald*, observing the Star Destroyer's crew members as they hunted Governor Chalis under the leadership of Prelate Verge. His first impressions, he now realized, had been unkind.

In a young crew less than half a year out of spacedock, the diseases of fatigue and shell shock were ordinarily best treated through structure and discipline. For troops struggling to embrace their responsibilities, shorter, more frequent duty shifts encouraged greater concentration, and strict adherence to regulations gave incentive to those who chose *not* to concentrate.

But Tabor had hesitated to implement changes aboard the *Herald*. He'd seen too many commanders disrupt the functioning of their crews for little gain. Instead, he walked the kilometer-long span of the vessel from bow to stern over the course of days, making the acquaintance of ranking bridge officers and engineering specialists alike. He made a point to query them about their duties while making his rounds. Once a week, he even joined them in the mess and discussed trivialities—their families, their homeworlds. He read their personnel files in the evenings and annotated those for later review. He neither ignored nor blindly trusted the prelate's own assessments of his troops—assessments that tended toward the glowing or the despairing, with little middle ground.

What he found, in the end, was a dutiful crew that had lost its way. They were good men and women, loyal and able, but they no longer knew what to believe. *That* would destroy any soldier, but there was little Tabor could do.

For the blame, he determined, fell squarely on Prelate Verge.

Verge, too, Tabor had misjudged. The boy was a slavish idolater of the Emperor, to be sure, and he lacked military experience—but he was brilliant and fiercely charismatic in his way. When he asked after the child of Lieutenant Kourterel, promised the man that a detail of stormtroopers would see to his family's protection from rebels on Vanzeist, his sincerity was clear. When he stood before the display in the tactical center, plotting a dozen courses that Chalis's rebels might take from Haidoral Prime, he analyzed and dismissed scenarios so quickly that Tabor could only nod and pretend to follow the logic.

Yet Verge's idiosyncrasies counterbalanced the boy's finer nature. Tabor had learned as much during his sixth night aboard the *Herald*, at the prelate's impromptu gala.

The event had discomfited Tabor from the start. The prelate had ordered a docking bay converted into a concert hall, where holographic musicians played neoclassical paeans to the New Order and astromech droids served hors d'oeuvres from the officers' galley. The invitees—a mix of crew members determined, so far as Tabor could decipher, by random lot—seemed enthused enough, willing to feast and dance at the prelate's urging.

An hour into the evening, Verge stepped forth to proclaim the purpose of the gala. Earlier that day, he explained, he'd learned of an officer's failure to report vital information in a timely fashion. "He feared to wake me during the night," Verge said, "doubting that the information—a sighting of Governor Chalis's rebels over the planet Coyerti—was accurate."

Verge continued speaking as a pair of stormtroopers ushered the officer in question into the center of the docking bay. Tabor was surprised to see a look not of panic but of despair on the officer's face.

"His mistrust of the information was understandable," Verge said, "but by failing to bring it to me, he placed faith in *his* judgment over that of his superiors. That cannot be accepted, and it cannot be forgiven."

One of the stormtroopers produced a thin metal cylinder. Verge nodded, and the cylinder mechanically extended into a baton, one end dancing and crackling with electricity.

"I have decided to grant you all the privilege of administering punishment," Verge said. "If he lives, he will return to duty a chastened man. A better man."

Then Verge had left the gala. The attendees had done what was expected of them. And Tabor had slept poorly that night.

Tabor's constitution had suffered with age. Even as he adjusted to the Star Destroyer's gravity, he still woke each morning sore and cramped. He missed the selection of tea provided by the Carida Academy and he found himself increasing the size of text on the datapads handed to him by younger officers.

But his mental fortitude was as it had always been. He'd seen far worse things than the prelate's torments; inflicted worse himself, more than once. But how could a crew function when its commander acted unpredictably? One moment, Verge was quoting the Emperor to an enchanted audience aboard the bridge; the next, he was ordering an engineer stripped of his rank for the failures of a malfunctioning droid.

Each night following the gala, Tabor's desire to return home grew stronger. And so each day, he attempted to build his rapport with the troops and better equip them for their hunt for Governor Chalis. The sooner the mission was complete, the sooner he could resume his familiar routine.

Verge lent Tabor the support he required: When Tabor asked for permission to assign half a dozen officers to liaise with Imperial vessels in the Metatessu sector, Verge authorized it. When they learned that Chalis's ship was leaving behind a subtle particle trail, Verge encouraged Tabor to oversee the science team dedicated to the trail's analysis.

In the days that followed, Tabor became convinced that success was near. Few Imperial ships were poised to intercept Chalis in short order, but so long as she left a path there was no chance of her escaping. With a few days, the *Herald* itself could be in place.

And then came the news of the raid.

"One of our freighters! It was an obvious target—we should have been prepared!"

Tabor winced at the sound of his own voice. He clenched the report in one hand, glowered at the liaison officers on the bridge. But there were dozens of allied ships in the sector, and predicting which Chalis would strike at—had they even known with certainty that she'd attempt to hide her trail so—would have been nearly impossible.

One of the liaison officers was stammering an apology. Tabor waved it off, tried to show by his expression that he was venting frustration, not placing blame. This crew had seen too much blame.

The prelate stood at the bridge viewport, staring into the stars. Tabor strode past the duty stations, wondering how the boy would react. Yet Verge was smiling when he turned around. He looked almost amused, as if enjoying a twist of fate that affected him not at all.

"We were lucky," the boy said. "That trail was a stroke of fortune, but surely wars are not won through luck?"

Tabor found his ire melting away. "True enough," he said. He was too eager to get the job done and return home, as if merely *wanting* it was enough. It was a mistake children made. Once again, he'd misjudged Verge.

"What now, then?" Verge asked. "Chalis will take advantage of this, surely."

Focus, Tabor.

"The rebel ship," Tabor said. "It's taken considerable damage in the last week. They'll be looking to put in for repairs."

"Agreed," Verge said. "That will mean a base of some sort, or at the very least a flotilla equipped for the job."

The conversation soon moved from the bridge to the tactical center. An assortment of Tabor's favored officers joined him, calling up data and reports from other ships in the sector while Tabor stared at charts with Verge and racked his brain for anything useful on Chalis. Over the course of an hour, they narrowed down the area the governor could reach but not the particulars of any port; it was progress in only the most technical sense.

"We're approaching this wrong," Tabor finally declared. "If there's a base to be found through pure military theory, someone in Intelligence would've already found it."

Verge's eyes were closed as he leaned back against a console. "We already discounted finding the ship. Where does that leave us?"

"We can't find *her* ship, and we can't locate the base directly," Tabor said. "But our forces just chased half the Alliance out of the Mid Rim. How many other rebel ships managed to escape an engagement in this sector after sustaining damage—in the past week, say? How many others need repairs, as well?"

The officers began murmuring into their links and tapping at their consoles. A list flashed onto the main display. It scrolled rapidly through official designations of rebel ships—easily several dozen.

Tabor smiled with grim satisfaction and gestured toward Verge. "It's your hunt."

Verge pushed forward off the console and clapped Tabor on the shoulder. "It's *our* hunt." He turned and spread his arms, encompassing the rest of the officers. "All of ours!" he called, and laughed. Evidently, he understood Tabor's intent.

The men laughed with Verge. Some were transparently nervous; others apparently sincere, proud to share the moment with their commander. Tabor watched them and wondered:

What happens to them when the hunt is over?

CHAPTER 12

PLANET HOTH
Eleven Days Before Plan Kay One Zero

Namir hadn't dressed for the cold, and he regretted his choice of apparel the moment the ramp dropped down and a frigid tide surged into the shuttle. Specks of frost danced around the ramp's far end, melting slowly upon contact with the metal, and snow—true, white snow, the kind Namir had only seen twice in his life—paved the runway into the hangar.

"I take back my defection. Darth Vader can have me," Chalis murmured. Namir cast a glance at her, saw her dark hair dappled with pale flakes. Her hands were behind her back, where Namir had bound them in stun cuffs—a condition of Alliance High Command.

Together with the captain, Roja, and Beak, they descended the ramp into Echo Base.

The journey had been painfully long but uneventful. Howl himself hadn't known the rebel base's secret location—instead, he'd programmed the shuttle to follow routes provided, one after the next, via coded messages from the Alliance. Those routes had taken the shuttle far into the wastes of the Outer Rim and spiraling into the Anoat sector; when Howl had plotted a course to the Hoth system, the travelers hadn't known whether they'd find their goal or just another message there.

Chalis had passed the time reading classical fiction from Howl's data library or further refining her holographic schematic. Howl had found a holo-chess partner in Beak, and Namir had, by the second day, demanded they mute their battling game pieces. Roja had been the eager conversationalist of the group, ready to share anecdotes from his time as a dockworker with the unwary. Namir had tried to occupy himself by turning the engineering pit into an exercise room and working himself into exhaustion.

By the end, he'd been more than ready to leave the shuttle. He hadn't expected the vessel to be more comfortable than the Rebellion's hidden base, but now he was beginning to wonder.

Beyond the ramp, half a dozen meters down the hangar runway, a small group of rebels stood awaiting the shuttle passengers. They were all dressed for the weather, their matching jackets hooded and heavily padded. Three of them carried blaster rifles at the ready. *Good,* Namir thought. *At least they're not complacent.*

One of the group stepped forward—a pale man with a thick mustache and graying hair who wore the insignia of a rebel general. Proper insignia, like snow, were something Namir had rarely seen before.

The man introduced himself as Philap Bygar, and shook the hand of each of the Twilight emissaries as Howl introduced them by name and position. When Chalis—shivering in the chill—stepped up, Howl smiled tightly. "Governor Everi Chalis," he said. "An extraordinary artist and gracious guest of the Sixty-First Mobile Infantry. Former emissary to the Imperial Ruling Council."

"I'd shake your hand," Chalis said, "but I wouldn't want to make things awkward." She shrugged, lifting her cuffed wrists behind her back.

General Bygar nodded slowly and raised his hand in a salute. "The Rebel Alliance believes in redemption, Governor," he said. "Don't let our caution convince you otherwise."

"There's no shame in being wary," Chalis said.

Bygar stepped back and looked over the group. Namir felt his fingers numbing as the man spoke. "If I could thank everyone from the Sixty-First, I would," Bygar said. "You've had some hellish assignments these past few years, and you've survived things few other companies could.

"That's a reputation to be proud of, but not a pleasant one to earn— particularly when the reward is even worse assignments down the line. You're not wrong to think High Command sees what you've been through and sends you back for more. No one *deserved* to be sent to Praktin or Blacktar Cyst."

Bygar's praise surprised Namir. Under the circumstances, it was hardly necessary—the general didn't need to win over Howl, so Namir was forced to conclude that it was, in part, sincere. He felt a discomfiting mix of appreciation and resentment churn in his stomach.

The general continued. "What I can tell you is that we *know* what we're asking of you and the price you pay every day. *I* know it. And I'm grateful you're out there fighting for our cause."

Roja and Beak stood with their arms pressed to their sides, holding in their body heat. But their chins were up, their eyes focused on the general. Howl's expression was somber, and he nodded stiffly as Bygar concluded his speech. Chalis caught Namir's glance as he surveyed his colleagues and smirked. It might as well have been a wink.

"Now let's get you warmer and then to work," the general said, and the formality dropped from his tone. "It never gets comfortable here, and you don't quite get used to it, but there are ways to make it livable."

That, Namir thought, was the most he could hope for; along with as short a stay as possible. He already missed the shuttle, but he ached for the *Thunderstrike*.

Not comfortable, but livable was a phrase that stayed with Namir over the following days. Howl and Chalis were whisked away almost immediately to a grand strategy conference with Alliance High Command; Namir saw them in passing in the base's corridors and otherwise not at all. Roja and Beak were, with Namir's approval, split and assigned to teams appropriate to their skills under Echo Base commanders. Namir, too, accepted reassignment to keep himself busy.

The base was hewn out of the ice of a massive glacier, with natural caverns augmented by structural supports and linked by artificial corridors. Power cables and lighting rigs were strewn haphazardly about, and Namir was assured by a maintenance droid that one faulty element could deny heat to half the base. In its construction, then, Echo Base was almost comfortingly ramshackle. It reflected the abilities of the Rebellion that Namir knew.

The men and women posted at the base were less familiar. Their clothes and combat gear were a grade above anything Twilight had ever possessed, both in quality and uniformity: When the quartermaster handed Namir an A280 combat rifle before a patrol, Namir stroked the heavy barrel with something close to awe. Bundled in a thermal protective jacket and polarized goggles, Namir was nearly as faceless and unrecognizable as a stormtrooper. With that uniformity and orderliness came an emphasis on the importance of rank and hierarchy; it reminded him of stories Charmer had told about the Imperial Academy, and on his second day he learned why.

"Probably a third of the personnel here were Imperial cadets before defecting," a young man—Namir thought he'd introduced himself as Kryndal, though he hadn't been paying close attention—explained.

They sat together in the toolshed, warming power converters with welding torches. The converters had already failed due to internal icing, but if they could be revived they'd be returned to service in the base. It was grunt work, more suited to a droid than a human—but the job needed to be done, and Namir lacked the technical specializations Roja and Beak had.

Kryndal kept talking. "Maybe another third of us—some of the cadets, too—went through Alliance Special Forces training. Four months of misery, but they were the most important ones of my life. You want to learn how to use an antique slugthrower, disarm a proximity mine, or rappel off a ray shield, I recommend it."

Namir flipped a switch on his converter. No lights, no sound. Back to heating. "I've used a slugthrower," he said. "Other two never came up."

Kryndal shrugged. "Something to think about. High bar to qualify, but I'm guessing you wouldn't be here if your captain—"

"Not looking to retrain," Namir said, and Kryndal let the subject drop.

Two ships arrived at Echo Base on Namir's third day. The passengers' identities were classified—rumors among the rank and file claimed a highly placed Bothan spy was involved—but no one doubted the visitors were coming for the strategy conference.

That conference was, day by day, becoming the dominant topic throughout the base. When Namir hiked to the perimeter outposts through windstorms that tossed ice shards like shrapnel, he heard the comm chatter of sentries discussing attendees: General Rieekan, Commander Chiffonage, Princess Leia Organa. When Namir was in the mess, pilots asked him what he knew about Governor Chalis, told stories about her mentor Count Vidian. Roja, who'd bonded with the Echo snowspeeder technicians with shocking speed, came to Namir more than once to pass along the latest wild speculation: Chalis was the last piece of a puzzle the Alliance had been working on for months, and now there was a five-year strategy, or a four-year strategy, or a *one-year* strategy that would win the war at last.

It was wishful thinking. Even the troops speculating knew as much. But they hoped there was truth buried in the dream.

Namir understood. He'd thought similar things once, in other wars. He didn't have the patience for dreams anymore.

He didn't speak to Chalis again until the end of their first week on Hoth. He was leaving the command center after delivering a tactical assessment of Outpost Delta—busywork, perhaps, but he'd been told fresh eyes would be "valuable"—and spotted her in the frozen corridor.

Their direction and pace matched. Chalis was unescorted and uncuffed. Namir gestured at her wrists. "Winning new friends?"

"It took a day or two," she replied, without turning to look at Namir, "but we all came to an understanding. I receive a pardon from the Alliance for past deeds, and in return I agree not to seek official power in any postwar government."

"They don't want you around, either?" he said.

"You sound as surprised as I was."

Namir barked a laugh. They reached an intersection in the tunnels, and they both hesitated for a fraction of a second as they turned in separate directions. "If it keeps you out of Twilight," Namir said, "you've got my full support."

"Thank you, Sergeant." Chalis was walking away before she finished the words.

On the *Thunderstrike,* the mess served mainly storage-friendly staples in semi-edible combinations, broken up with occasional fresh vegetables, fruit, or meat procured during a raid. Ration packs were stockpiled for activity planetside: Their utility made them—militarily speaking—a luxury, and Twilight Company had no reliable means of acquiring more.

But nothing worth farming grew on Hoth's frozen and meteorite-cratered surface, and the Alliance's domesticated tauntauns—horned, stinking, ill-tempered "snow lizards"—were more valuable as mounts than as meat. That left military rations, delivered in massive crates and procured by means Namir couldn't guess, as the mainstay of every meal.

At a table with Kryndal and a handful of other Echo personnel, Namir enjoyed the dubious pleasures of an envelope of protein cubes suspended in thick orange goo: bland enough to be inoffensive, gelatinous enough to linger on the palate. He preferred to eat alone or with Roja and Beak despite their tiring praise of the base's virtues—Roja's bond with the technicians had grown almost familial, while Beak had declared his intention to join the Alliance Special Forces—but Namir's colleagues were nowhere to be found. There had been no empty tables.

Kryndal was tracing rings on the tabletop, naming planets and concocting a scenario in which, one by one, the Core Worlds miraculously began falling to the Rebellion. A blond woman and a snout-nosed alien were enthusiastically debating him, offering alternative plans—the assassination of the Emperor, or the liberation of slave worlds to bolster rebel troop numbers.

"Maybe I'm crazy," Kryndal was saying, "but it feels we're on the verge of something real. We can make it to Coruscant. The Empire wouldn't be fighting so hard if it weren't afraid."

Namir knew he'd be wise to stay out of the conversation. But it was the end of a long, tedious day of walking trenches and shutting out conversations too similar to the one he was hearing now. And Kryndal was just so *smug.*

"What happens at Coruscant?" Namir asked.

"What do you mean?" Kryndal responded. The others turned to Namir as well, waiting.

"For starters," Namir said, "you've got a capital planet full of what—ten billion people? More?"

The woman smiled, amused but not mocking. "Considerably more."

"Fine. Out of that *considerably more,* how many do you think want the Empire overthrown?"

Kryndal's tone was steady but insistent. "You don't live on Coruscant long without realizing—"

Namir interrupted. "I'm not finished. My guess is it's not as many as you think. In fact, I *know* it can't be that many, because if it were, you'd have a civil war on Coruscant *right now* instead of a bunch of rebel cells in hiding."

"It's not that simple," the woman said.

Namir was talking over her. "But suppose most of the population doesn't feel strongly enough to resist either way. They're not up for a fight. Fine. You've still got a hard-core element that's going to turn against the Rebellion the second you start bombing. One percent of

Coruscant's population is an awful lot of people, and I guarantee we're talking about more than that. Imperial loyalists, sure, but also anyone who doesn't trust the Alliance to run the place.

"You going to send fire teams into the streets to deal with them? Start cutting down civilians? One way or another, it's going to get bloody, and it's not going to stop for a *very* long time."

Kryndal's voice was still even, but his face was locked in a grimace. "The Alliance has a transition plan. Democratic elections—"

"—aren't going to convince anyone," Namir snapped. "And this is all your *best*-case scenario. Maybe the Alliance decides not to invade Coruscant at all. Too much trouble. It's way easier to contain the Empire's strongholds than to achieve total victory. But you know what I really think is going to happen?"

The alien said something, tugged at Kryndal's arm. Namir couldn't make out the exact words through the creature's accent, but the meaning was clear. Kryndal wasn't moving, however, and Namir rose out of his seat, leaning across the table to stare down at the man.

"I think," Namir said, "that as soon as any real victory is in sight, the *Alliance* will fall apart. You think there's anyone in that strategy conference who's not looking to come out on top? You think the instant their common enemy is weakened, you won't see half a dozen different rebel factions turn on one another?

"How do you think you ended up in this mess in the first place? After you won the Clone Wars, the Emperor snatched up power, other leaders missed their chance and started a rebellion. Victory always brings infighting."

"That's not how it happened." The woman was speaking again. "You've never met the princess or worked with General Rieekan. They're not just looking to seize power."

Kryndal was scowling in silence. Namir watched him, saw his hands flex against the tabletop. It wouldn't take much more. Namir knew he could still walk away, but he *needed* this.

"If you really think those people are heroes"—Namir was answering the woman, but his eyes were on Kryndal—"you're deluding yourself. Darth Vader's own stormtroopers are praising him the same way."

Kryndal threw the first punch. It wasn't meant to be a debilitating blow—Namir was exposed, and Kryndal could easily have aimed for his eyes or the point of his jaw. Instead, Kryndal struck Namir hard in the chest, shoving him backward and forcing the air from Namir's lungs.

Namir grasped Kryndal's hand before the man could pull away. He didn't bother to catch himself as he stumbled, instead dragging Kryndal forward onto the table and using him as a counterweight to stay upright. Kryndal sprawled for only a moment before getting his legs back under him and leaping at Namir.

As he grappled with Kryndal, Namir felt someone approach behind him. He threw back an elbow, felt it sink into the layers of a thermal jacket. He drove a knee forward into Kryndal's stomach, saw the world go dark for an instant when a gloved hand struck his face.

Voices were shouting. More bodies in jackets and goggles joined the fray. As he fought, knowing he had no chance of victory, Namir laughed.

The worst of the damage was a broken nose: Now donning the rebels' polarized goggles left Namir nauseated from the pressure on his nasal bridge. His right hip had turned deep purple overnight after being slammed hard against one of the mess hall benches. The knuckles of his left hand ached, too, though that, at least, was a mark of pride.

He didn't remember the details of the fight aside from how it had begun. It hadn't lasted more than a minute or two—just long enough for someone to separate him from the other combatants and drag him to the medical center under guard. He'd spent the night there and been greeted in the morning by General Bygar, who'd used the word *disappointing* more than once.

Howl, Bygar had explained, was needed at the strategy conference and so hadn't yet been informed of Namir's behavior. Namir was grateful for that much.

So with the approval of the medical staff, Namir had been given the most demeaning assignment Bygar could find as punishment. He'd

spent the morning lugging shipping crates—sometimes with the assistance of a grav-loader, often not—from the hangar bays to the Echo
Base interior, taking tiny, childlike steps all the way to avoid slipping
on patches of ice. The droids in the hangar directed him where he
needed to go, and he rarely had to speak to another living being.

It didn't bother Namir. He'd done far worse jobs.

One of the rebel ship captains eyed Namir as he hefted a canister of
bacta over his shoulder and marched beneath the undercarriage of a
light freighter. It was a territorial look: the suspicion of a man un-
happy admitting a stranger into his domain.

"What happened to you?" the man asked as he tugged burnt and
melted wiring free from one of the freighter's ramp conduits. There
was no concern in his tone. The bridge of Namir's nose seemed to
throb, as if a glance were enough to irritate it.

Namir looked at him. Brown hair, light skin, perhaps a decade
older than Namir. He wore no rank insignia, but that was more common among the ship crews than the permanent base personnel.

"You know those Special Forces goons?" Namir asked, deadpan.
"Turns out they take this Rebellion *seriously.*"

The captain cracked a smile, shook his head, and went back to his
repairs.

By late afternoon, Namir had taken to swearing at the droids in
response to their every demand. The droids complained but had no
recourse but to absorb the verbal assaults; Namir found the experience oddly satisfying. By evening, after he'd managed to unload most
of the day's cargo, the droids began sending Namir back inside the
base to tote shipbound supplies and maintenance equipment out to
the hangar. He wasn't sure if it was an act of revenge or a part of the
general's intended punishment.

The additional work didn't bother him. He didn't have anywhere
better to be, and he wasn't looking forward to returning to the mess or
sleeping among the base personnel in the barracks. He considered
bunking in Twilight's shuttle—but that seemed cowardly, the action of
someone ashamed of his deeds.

Namir encountered the freighter captain a second time while carrying a bin of mechanical parts earmarked for the freighter. He couldn't guess at the components' function, but when he boarded the ship, the captain—who was busy dismantling a ceiling panel—grunted and gestured at the floor.

Namir set the bin down. The captain crouched, sorted through the assortment of wires and rods and cylinders, and pulled out a small golden disk. "Hold this, will you?" he said, and pointed Namir to a secondary panel within the ceiling compartment.

Namir had to stand on his toes to do so. The captain began screwing the disk into a socket, ignoring the sizzling sound from the panel. The heat felt good on Namir's frost-numbed hands.

"Who'd you get into it with?" the man asked without looking away from his work.

"Kryndal," Namir said. "Didn't catch his last name. Or maybe his first."

"He deserve it?"

Namir shrugged in return. "I like to think we both did."

Namir didn't question the rebel captain when the repair job stretched out to ten, twenty, thirty minutes. When Namir asked about his crew, the man only shook his head. "They're out on other business," he said. "Don't ask."

When the task was finally done—or maybe when the captain had given up—the man produced a bottle of Corellian whiskey and dropped himself on the boarding ramp. Namir took that as a tacit invitation, and from there their conversation followed a meandering path lubricated by drink. The captain grumbled about his ship and told an unlikely, obscenity-laden story about how it had been damaged. Namir detailed exactly how he'd ended up on cargo duty for the day.

When Namir finished describing his encounter in the mess hall, the captain shook his head and offered a relaxed, mocking rebuke. "You can't just tell these people they're doomed. They ever wise up, I'm out of a job."

"You a mercenary?" Namir asked.

"Something like that."

"You must've wanted to take a swing at these guys once or twice . . ."

The captain laughed. "I don't bite the hand that feeds me. I don't need to start a fight I can't win, either."

"I could've won," Namir said.

"Then you sure didn't try too hard." The captain grinned and took another swig of the whiskey before passing the bottle. It wasn't particularly good—both men had agreed on that after the first sip—but it was potent and, Namir suspected, the only drink of its kind on Hoth.

"Anyway, you're too young to be this cynical," the captain said. "How'd you even join up with that attitude?"

"Long story," Namir said. "Kind of an accident. It wasn't for the *cause*, at any rate."

"I hear you," the man said.

They drank in silence awhile, and it was the captain who spoke next. His voice was quieter, his speech a touch slurred. The lights of the hangar had dimmed with nightfall, and even with the bay doors closed the cold was creeping inside.

"You remember when that battle station blew up?"

"Before my time," Namir said. "But I heard about it."

The captain nodded. "After that—I didn't notice at first, but for a while it felt like we could really end this war. You looked at those kids who shot down death . . . it didn't make any sense if you thought about it, but it *felt* like we were going somewhere."

"They all look like that," Namir said. "Fresh recruits."

"Not just fresh recruits," the man said. "Not all of them."

Again, there was silence. A red-and-white astromech droid rolled across the hangar floor, squawking at something unseen.

"Keeps us busy, though," the man said.

"Bad wars are good business?"

"To hell with that—even I'm not that cynical." The man shook his head vigorously. "But if it *did* end . . . you know the way we put up with them now? Even when they're downright insufferable? How long you think they'd put up with *us* after?"

Namir nodded very slowly. "Not so long," he said.

The captain didn't answer. Namir held up the whiskey bottle, watched the amber fluid slosh against the glass. He laughed softly before speaking again. "I'll say it if you won't: The war's damn well *better* for me. The minute we win, I've got nothing. So the idea that it'll keep going on forever? That feels *right.*"

It does feel right, he thought to himself. He felt warm as the notion of the ongoing war, never won and never lost, soaked into his bones, steady and comfortable. Even the fantasy, the briefest notion of a rebel victory made him queasy.

It had been that way for years, though he'd never said it aloud before. Never thought about it so consciously.

The captain looked troubled, however, as he wrested the bottle from Namir and drank with a grimace.

"If they knew you thought *that* . . ." the captain said, and trailed off.

Namir shrugged. "They don't."

"And that doesn't bother you?"

"I'm here to protect them. Doesn't matter what they believe."

The captain lifted the bottle to his lips again. This time he didn't drink. Instead, he breathed in the whiskey's aroma, lowered the bottle, and pressed it decisively into Namir's hands without turning his head.

"If it's a job," the captain said, "then it doesn't matter, and neither do they. You do what's right for you, you tell them what they want to hear, and you move on when the job's done. Otherwise—" He seemed to wrestle with the words as if fishing them out of the depths of his cloudy mind. "Otherwise, if it's more than a job, they deserve better. If you can't get behind what they believe in, maybe it's time to walk away."

Namir held the whiskey bottle close to his chest and felt its rim rub against his chin. Something in the back of his brain warned him that the wetness it left might crystallize in the cold. "I'm not a rebel," he said.

The captain said something as he stood and walked slowly, swaying, up the boarding ramp, but Namir didn't hear what.

Namir grasped the bottle in one hand as he descended to the hangar, angling toward the exit into Echo Base proper. He thought about Brand and Charmer and Gadren and Roach, and Ajax and Fektrin and the comm tech who'd died on Asyrphus—the woman whose name Namir had pledged to forget. He even thought about Roja and Beak and cursed them for traitors under his breath. They were *Twilight* soldiers, and they should've loathed Echo Base as much as him.

But they didn't, because they were also rebel soldiers. And so were Brand and Charmer and Gadren and Roach. So was the comm tech, underneath it all.

The freighter captain was right. They deserved better.

Namir woke up in a storage unit the next day with a whiskey bottle clutched to his chest, a pounding headache, cheeks numb from cold, and a mouth that tasted like Coyerti's biotoxins. When he managed to rouse himself and locate the duty roster, however, he found that his punishment was over and he'd been reassigned to patrol the perimeter outposts.

A day in the cold didn't seem like an improvement, but the other outpost personnel kept their distance and it gave Namir a chance to think. Two hours on scanner duty, two staring into the blinding whiteness of the horizon, and two on patrol, then back to the base to thaw. If he'd been able to wear the polarizing goggles on his broken nose, it would've almost been peaceful. Yet even with frost encrusting his eyelashes, he had the opportunity to dwell on thoughts that lingered from the night.

They deserve better.

In the evening, Roja and Beak found him—told stories about the incompetence of stuck-up base troops, mocked Alliance Special Forces. They didn't explain or justify their change of heart. Together, they reminisced about Twilight's battles on Mygeeto—before Namir's time with the company—and Phorsa Gedd, which Namir remembered vividly. Namir wanted to send Roja and Beak away, but he appreciated their intentions, if not their presence. He could smile and enjoy the lies for one night.

So the days went, and Namir settled into a routine until the morning when he was summoned to a meeting with Howl and Chalis. He'd

seen neither since before the incident in the mess hall, and he immediately knew what the summons meant: The strategy conference was
over.

They assembled in one of the secondary tactical control rooms off
the main command center. Howl and Chalis both looked at once exhausted and energized. Howl greeted Namir warmly, like an old friend
reuniting with a lost comrade. Chalis said nothing, smirking from her
seat and cupping a steaming metal thermos beneath her chin.

"Everything go as planned?" Namir asked as Howl waved him to a
seat.

"We have a goal, and the means to achieve it," Howl said. "Governor Chalis was the star of the show. Her information has proved in-
valuable."

Chalis snorted and gestured dismissively with her thermos. "I sat
in back and shot down all Rieekan's dreams."

"But you did it," Howl said lightly, "with such *authority.*"

Chalis laughed but said nothing more. Howl's voice dropped as he
turned somber again. "We've been retreating for so long, it's hard to
think about striking back. But the Alliance is almost ready. We can
win this war."

The words made Namir wince. They were far too familiar.

Howl kept going. "There's still much to do here, but my part is finished. Better minds than this one"—he tapped his left temple—"will
work out the details, and I need to prepare Twilight. I'd like to depart
on the shuttle tomorrow morning; Chalis will remain to advise High
Command."

"I'll check the ship over this afternoon," Namir said. "Make sure
nothing's frozen up."

The thought of leaving Hoth should have elated him. Instead, it
curdled in his gut.

They deserve better.

"There's one other thing," Howl said. "Chalis?"

"Captain Evon said I could make this a request, but not an order,"
Chalis said. "So it's your call." Where steam touched her face, her skin
gleamed as if she'd been sweating. "If I'm going to be stationed with

Alliance High Command—on Hoth or wherever else they end up—I'm going to want my own staff. That includes security, and as we've already established there aren't many people I trust not to stab me in the back.

"The job's yours if you want it, Sergeant. You have until tomorrow to decide."

Her expression was almost bored. Namir tried to read beneath the affect, see if there was something more to the offer, but he found nothing. Howl had set his face in stone.

The idea was tempting, in its way. Working with Chalis would be uncomplicated—free of unspoken debts and expectations.

He opened his mouth to respond, not sure what he was going to say, when a rebel soldier burst into the room half out of breath. She straightened and saluted as Howl and Chalis turned toward her.

"The Empire's found us," she said. "We're starting plan kay one zero. Total evacuation."

CHAPTER 13

ELOCHAR SECTOR
Two Days Before Plan Kay One Zero

Brand was restless.

Thunderstrike and *Apailana's Promise* had reached their rendezvous with the rebel flotilla ten days earlier, joining a dozen other ships in the void of deep space. Since then, the *Thunderstrike*'s crew had been working nonstop under Commander Paonu to repair or refit every square meter of the battered vessel. Parts and equipment were delivered by flotilla cargo haulers daily. Corridors had been sealed off, stripped of floor plating, and exposed to vacuum. Droids and engineers crawled like rats through ducts and tubes, welding panels and ripping out wires.

Meanwhile, with the crew busy, the soldiers of Twilight could only get in the way. In Howl's absence, Lieutenant Sairgon did what he could to occupy the troops—he devised training exercises and war games, granted squads "shore leave" to visit other ships in the flotilla—but without anywhere to land, there simply wasn't enough room for either work or recreation.

Still, most of Twilight's soldiers had developed a tolerance for boredom. Brand was an exception.

Not that boredom was a problem for her per se. She'd been a bounty hunter. She'd once spent eight days in the back of an abandoned landspeeder used by the Black Sun syndicate as a dead drop; she'd worn an environment suit built for intravenous feeding and waste elimination, exercised by tensing her muscles without changing position, and staved off hallucinations by mentally reciting half-remembered poetry. When her target had finally arrived to pick up a package of death sticks, she'd almost fallen over when she rose to stun and cuff him, but she'd *done the job.*

All she needed to overcome boredom was a goal. Something to focus on. Aboard the *Thunderstrike* she didn't have anything of the sort. She'd agreed, at Sairgon's urging, to act as the target of a training manhunt, but even that had ended when she'd elbowed one of the fresh meat in the ribs with too much force.

"You could talk to them," Gadren said one night. She'd gone to the Clubhouse with a vague notion of winning Twitch's stash of credits in a card game. Instead, she'd found the place crawling with fresh meat and encountered Gadren on her return to the corridor.

"I'd rather not," Brand said.

"You have training to offer, experience to impart—"

She cut him off. "There's a whole flotilla here. More than enough soldiers to coach them better than me."

"Perhaps," Gadren conceded. "Then join me and Roach awhile? Captain So-Hem of the *Sixmoon* has invited members of Twilight Company to visit his ship."

Brand stared at the Besalisk, who stood patiently awaiting her reply. She'd already decided to refuse, but she searched for a reason—a convenient lie, an existing commitment she could use as an excuse. She had no interest in an evening spent socializing with strangers.

Even Gadren must have known that by now.

"I don't need company," she said. "I need work."

Brand waited as long as she could for an answer—a second, or per-haps two. Then she marched down the corridor again, toward the port boarding pod array. The whole section was under reconstruction, which meant she could sit on the edge of the scaffolding as long as her suit's oxygen held out, alone except for the scurrying repair droids.

She had tremendous respect for Gadren, on both a personal and a professional level. She was in his squad—Namir's squad—for a rea-son. But he insisted on an *intimacy* with his comrades, wanted to tend to whatever personal troubles he imagined bothered them. Ordi-narily, Twilight was too busy surviving for that to perturb her; and ordinarily, Gadren could turn his prying onto Namir, who tolerated it better.

No easy escape today.

How much longer, Brand wondered, until the flotilla received new orders?

A strict routine kept Brand sane. Every morning, she woke up in the tool closet she'd converted into her private quarters. She exercised for two hours—first a jog through the ship, then training in the weight room. Then breakfast. Target practice. Equipment maintenance. One task after the next, productive or not, just to keep her hands and brain busy. It was a trick she'd learned during the four months she'd spent in a detention center.

She was negotiating with Quartermaster Hober, attempting to req-uisition a set of flash-bang grenades from another ship in the flotilla, when the *Thunderstrike*'s klaxons sounded. By the time she was half-way down the corridor to her assigned shelter, the alarm had stopped—but the *Thunderstrike* was in motion, the vibrations of the deck indicating that its thrusters had come online.

She marched toward one of the central turbolifts and watched for crew members, senior Twilight staff, anyone who might know what was happening. When she spotted Von Geiz boarding the lift, medkit in hand, she slipped in behind him.

Von Geiz eyed her curiously.

"Situation?" she asked.

He bit his lip, as if debating how much to say. Brand locked her gaze on him until he relented. "Another ship has arrived, just out of battle. They lost life support—we're taking the survivors aboard." He tapped at a panel and the turbolift hummed alive.

Brand nodded. More ships were showing up at the rendezvous every few days. It wasn't surprising one of them had barely made it.

Still, it paid to be cautious. When Von Geiz exited the lift and headed toward one of the upper air locks, Brand stayed at his side. She drew her sidearm from her belt—a modified DX-2 disruptor pistol banned by Alliance regulations and which she certainly wasn't supposed to carry openly aboard the *Thunderstrike*—and ran disaster scenarios through her mind.

The deck rumbled as something latched onto the *Thunderstrike*'s hull. When Brand and Von Geiz arrived at the air lock, full security and medical teams were already present, pulling floating medical gurneys burdened with bodies into the corridor. Brand observed the wounded as they passed by: a young man with blood crusted on his chin and nose shivered and stared at her; a woman with blackened palms hissed in pain, her eyes wide; a green-skinned Rodian whose twisted neck looked broken lay still.

It took fifteen minutes for the bodies to stop arriving. There were almost twenty wounded in total, with others dead aboard the damaged ship. At a signal from the bridge, the security team sealed the air lock. The remaining medics followed the last gurneys toward the *Thunderstrike*'s medbay.

Brand remained in the corridor, observing the air lock for some time. She kept her disruptor gripped in one hand.

Something was wrong. She wasn't sure what.

Now she had something to focus on.

CHAPTER 14

PLANET HOTH
Zero Days Before Plan Kay One Zero

The preparations for evacuation went swiftly. Echo Base was built to be abandoned—its designers had known the Empire would find it eventually, just as the Empire had located Alliance bases on Yavin 4 and Dantooine. All personnel had been assigned emergency transports long ago. When the alert came down, rebel troops began loading equipment and purging data with precision instilled by a hundred drills.

An Imperial probe droid had been the rebels' only warning. Scouts had found the machine floating through the icy wastes, broadcasting a signal to its distant masters. Whether the Empire would come in force or send additional probes first was anyone's guess, but the base was compromised and an attack would come.

Victory would be measured in the number of survivors.

Namir was running systems checks aboard the Twilight shuttle when he heard Chalis enter behind him. "I'm scheduled to leave on the first transport," she said as he watched diagnostics scroll on the bridge terminal. "The offer still stands—you're welcome to join me."

"I can't," Namir said. "I'm getting Howl off first."

Howl had volunteered to help coordinate Hoth's infantry in the event the base was besieged before evacuation was complete. That had made Namir's decision an easy one: Whatever else was troubling him, his priority was still Twilight's protection. Duty eclipsed all other thoughts.

"There might not be a fight," Chalis said. "Hoth's a long way from the nearest Imperial garrison. Besides which, Captain Evon can handle himself."

"You really think the Empire won't come?" Namir asked dubiously. He skimmed the diagnostics report, looked for anything labeled a warning. The rest was nonsense to him.

"I'd rather not find out. You know where to find me; if I don't see you again, Sergeant, good luck."

Perimeter Outpost Delta stood far to the northwest of Echo Base, a hundred meters outside the base's energy shield and barely within comm range when the weather was clear. It consisted of a three-person laser turret, a hand-dug trench in the ice, and a handful of light artillery emplacements. It was the sort of outpost Twilight might have taken in under a minute during a well-planned raid; against anything the Empire might field, it was doomed to obliteration.

But what couldn't be stopped could still be slowed.

Namir, Roja, and Beak stood above the trench line, bodies clustered together for heat. Two soldiers from Echo Base stood nearby, adjusting a tripod-mounted cannon, while three more enjoyed the shelter of the turret interior. Fresh snow was falling, but not enough to reduce visibility or interfere with transmissions. Namir wasn't sure whether that counted as good luck or bad.

His earpiece crackled with static. "Fleet of Star Destroyers coming out of hyperspace," a voice announced. "Keep your eyes peeled, Outpost Delta."

A fleet of Star Destroyers? Namir had seen the massive ships before—great, wedge-shaped dreadnoughts that dwarfed the *Thunderstrike*—but never more than one at a time. He'd witnessed a single Star Destroyer bombard a city into a crater of steaming sludge; seen skyscrapers melt and stone burn. One Star Destroyer had been reason enough for Twilight to abandon a planet.

Roja looked at Namir and started asking questions. How long before the Destroyers reached Hoth? How long before the transports could take off? Namir only half listened and shook his head. Howl might know the answers, but he didn't.

Beak saved him from responding, tapping Roja on the shoulder and pointing him south. A moment later, the sky shimmered like a mirage. Then the effect disappeared.

"Energy shield's at full power," Beak said. "That thing can hold against bombardment long enough. Now the Imps *have* to come down."

A ground war, then. It was preferable to bombardment from orbit, but it wasn't encouraging.

Namir, Roja, and Beak passed a pair of macrobinoculars among themselves, scanning the horizon beyond the white snowdrifts and watching the cloud-streaked sky. Roja saw the ships first—just black specks impossibly high above, drifting down like snowflakes. Through the macrobinoculars' magnification, Namir saw that each vessel bore an immense, solid metal form on the underside of its hull.

"Gozanti cruisers," Beak said, when he took the macrobinoculars back. "They're bringing walkers."

"You sure?" Namir asked.

"Clamped onto the undercarriage. Only thing it could be."

"Call it in," Namir said. Beak nodded and tapped his comlink.

Outpost Beta was the first to confirm the presence of troops on the ground. As Beak had predicted, the Empire had indeed landed walkers: All Terrain Armored Transports, four-legged giants that dwarfed the machine Namir and his squad had faced on Coyerti. That had been an AT-ST scout, devastating against infantry but vulnerable to light artillery and clever tactics. The AT-ATs had no such weaknesses.

"One of those things comes for us, it'll stomp us flat. Doesn't matter how much firepower we throw at it." Roja was shaking his head, but his tone wasn't panicked. He was stating a fact.

"Echo Base promised air support," Namir said. "If it's just walkers out there, we pull back. If there's another force coming, though—"

Something flashed in the sky, too quickly for Namir to trace to a source. Laserfire, maybe, but originating from where?

A dozen meters down the trench, one of the Echo soldiers cheered. She raised a hand toward Namir and spoke into her comlink.

"That was the ion cannon," Namir heard through the link. "Command center says the first transport is away."

Roja grinned. "Few more of those and maybe we'll head home ourselves, huh?"

Namir smiled slowly, stared into the sky as if he could watch the transport jump to lightspeed. "It's better than that," he said.

Beak started laughing. Roja appeared confused. Namir wrapped his arm around the latter man's shoulders and pulled him tight for an instant, grinning before letting him stumble away.

"Governor Chalis was on that transport," Namir said. "Forget Coyerti, forget the whole damn strategy conference. The woman was a curse; this is the best news we've had for *months*."

Outpost Beta was the first sentry post destroyed, annihilated in half a dozen laser blasts fired from the mandible-like cannons of an Imperial walker. Namir saw flames through the macrobinoculars, red and orange against white snow. As the walker trundled forward, the ground flashed blue under its footpads—proximity mines planted by Outpost Beta personnel, utterly impotent against the walker's mass.

It should have been horrifying—and it was, in its way. The enemy outnumbered the rebels and had a massive technological advantage. According to Roja, none of the rebel ground artillery could penetrate the walkers' armor—at best, precise, targeted bursts might disable the machines' weapons, but the piston-driven crush of their feet would be no less lethal to organic targets.

Yet along with the horror came a warmth inside Namir. He'd spent the last weeks without purpose, wandering a dusty mental labyrinth he hadn't yet escaped. Hoth might be a losing battle. It might be his death. But it was a battle he knew how to fight.

The walkers were angling toward Echo Base's main power generators. Destroying the generators would bring down the energy shield. Without the shield, the base and any unlaunched transports were vulnerable to the Star Destroyers. "Protect the generators" was the order from above and the priority of the rebel troops. Protect the generators. Hold out as long as possible. And when necessary, fall back.

Outpost Delta was on the western edge of the walkers' projected path. There were possibilities there: If the walkers ignored the outpost's threat, Namir's troops might be able to flank the machines as they passed. He ran through scenarios as he watched his breath steam. Could there be chinks in the walkers' armor, on the sides or rear or undercarriage? Could his squads act as spotters or give covering fire for the rebel air support?

"Sergeant!"

One of the Echo soldiers—the woman who'd cheered for the transports—was waving him over. He trudged through the snow to her side. "What's going on?"

"Command says snowspeeders have engaged the walkers. No damage yet, but they're slowing down."

Namir nodded, glanced into the northeast and tried to make out the battle. He saw nothing except splotches of darkness on the horizon.

The woman wasn't finished. "The bad news, sir, is that the Empire's sent recon forces fanning out. Troops are heading this way."

Of course. The Empire's commanders weren't stupid. They wouldn't let anyone flank the walkers if they could avoid it.

Namir wanted to call for the Delta troops to scatter—to let the turret and the trench and the artillery serve as bait while they hid and plotted an ambush. A straight-up fight against a superior force went against every instinct he had.

"Get ready, then," he said, and swung down into the trench.

Orders were to hold out as long as possible. He intended to do precisely that.

The enemy scout force consisted of a pair of floating gunnery platforms and an AT-ST escort. Each platform carried half a dozen stormtroopers wearing armor Namir hadn't seen before, stark white and almost invisible against the snow. They weren't skeletons; they were ghosts. And, he suspected, better equipped for the weather than he was.

"I want the turret and artillery focused on the platforms first," he said into his link. "They'll want us aiming for the walker so they can ride in, off-load the troops, and overrun us. Don't give them the chance."

The Echo Base personnel didn't argue. Roja and Beak crouched in the trench. Namir checked his rifle—the A280 he'd been assigned with his cold-weather uniform, the one he'd never used in combat before—and kept his eyes on the horizon.

The plan lasted less than ten seconds after the enemy came into firing range. As ordered, the turret gunners kept their weapon focused on one of the platforms even as the AT-ST charged forward, kicking up snow with its spindly metal legs. The first platform went up in a fireball, its passengers caught in the blast. But the rebel artillery missed the second platform, shots going wide by half a dozen meters. That vehicle's stormtroopers leapt into the snow and dashed toward the outpost.

Namir, Roja, and Beak fired at the AT-ST from their separate positions in the trench. Their goal was to distract the machine's pilot, to force the walker to retarget and give the turret a chance at a second shot. The walker was not distracted—it reared and fired on the turret, sending metal and ash and flames spattering across the ice. Namir was certain the three gunners inside died instantly, incinerated by plasma or crushed by the turret's walls.

After that, the battle took on two fronts. Namir called out for Roja and Beak to stay in the trench and take aim at the charging storm-troopers. The surviving Echo Base troops stayed on the artillery, try-ing to lock onto the walker as it picked them off one by one. Namir heard troops scream, saw flashes of red particle bolts, but he held his position, his chest pressed against the packed snow of the trench wall and his head and shoulders peeking above.

At any time, he knew, the walker might select him as a target. But if the stormtroopers reached the trench, Namir and the others were dead anyway; so he gripped his rapidly overheating rifle in his cold hands, took aim and fired at each stormtrooper in turn. He shot me-thodically, if not calmly, acquiring each new target as soon as he saw flames lick the armor of the last.

When there were no more stormtroopers in his immediate firing arc, he spared another glance for his surroundings. The artillery stations were in ruins. The walker had, unexpectedly, crossed the trench and now stood on the south side. Something was attached to its leg, hanging like a piece of debris—Namir thought it was scrap from the turret until he recognized the broken form of the woman who'd cheered for the transports, the woman who'd alerted Namir to the scouting party.

She had one arm wrapped around the machine's ankle joint, her hand trapped in the gears. Her legs weren't moving. But somehow she was still alive—her head was up, and Namir thought he saw her smile as she raised a grenade in her free hand. He wanted to call out to her as she disappeared in a fiery bloom and the walker plummeted for-ward, but he didn't know her name.

He turned back to the north side of the trench. He saw the handful of stormtroopers still alive cut down by Beak and Roja—the former still in the trench, the latter picking his way among the bodies on the ice. The second artillery platform had disappeared, presumably with-drawn back toward the AT-ATs' path.

The withdrawal didn't surprise Namir. Outpost Delta had lost its turret and most of its crew. It was no longer a threat to the invasion of Hoth.

The rebel snowspeeders were barely hindering the walkers. Not one AT-AT had been disabled by the time the fight at Outpost Delta finished, and the bulk of the Imperial forces had already progressed south past the outpost toward Echo Base. Delta's sole designated vehicle had been destroyed during the fighting and its tauntauns had scattered, which left Namir, Roja, and Beak with a long walk home.

As they marched atop a crust of frozen snow, the trio saw more rebel transports flash across the sky. If the base personnel could finish evacuating, Namir thought, the battle's losses might not be fatal to the Alliance.

The three didn't talk much during the trek. Roja cradled his arm strangely, as if injured. Beak's shoulders were hunched but his chin was up, the picture of grim determination. Namir scanned the horizon, trying to judge their distance from the walkers. The titanic machines were moving landmarks, and the farther south they plodded, the more unstoppable they appeared.

About a kilometer from the outpost, the three found a wheeled Imperial combat transport apparently abandoned in the snow. Broad scorch marks on its armored sides suggested it had been hit by cannon or snowspeeder fire, but when Roja climbed aboard he had it working again in minutes. Namir didn't know where its passengers had gone and he didn't especially care—it was a way to reach Echo Base before everything ended.

Roja and Beak drove. Namir sat atop the hulking machine, grimacing at the painful lash of the wind as he studied the detritus of the walkers' passing. He spotted crashed snowspeeders bleeding black smoke; burning turrets and charred bodies at other outlying sentry posts; cracked ice and depressions left by durasteel walker footpads. The wheeled transport—Roja called it a Juggernaut—raced over abandoned trenches with a sickening jolt, undeterred and unharmed.

Twice, Namir called for a stop when he saw other rebel soldiers stranded on the ice plains. There was no time to halt for the dying, to check for survivors at every scene of destruction, but aiding those still walking was a compromise Namir could make.

The Juggernaut's passengers numbered almost a dozen when an

AT-AT walker finally went down. Namir couldn't see the cause—the falling walker was the size of a fist on the far horizon—but it seemed to stumble as snowspeeders flitted about its legs. Its joints bent forward and then its whole body plunged headlong into the ice with a roar even Namir could hear—a low boom, less like a bomb than an avalanche. One of the rebels who'd joined Namir atop the transport grasped Namir's shoulders from behind and dug his fingers into the cloth of his jacket.

"One blasted walker," the man said—to himself or to Namir, Namir wasn't sure. "If we can take down one, we can take them all."

Namir didn't agree, but he didn't correct the man. If it had been Twilight soldiers dying and evacuating, he might have uttered the same lie.

The last five hundred meters to Echo Base were the worst of the journey. The hijacked Juggernaut had to travel between two walkers to reach the north entrance, and the mass of the machines seemed to blot out the sky. Then a final push through a line of Imperial stormtroopers nearly ended the lives of all aboard—Namir and the rescued soldiers pressed themselves to the icy metal roof of the transport, firing a sweeping barrage of bolts to force open a path. One of the soldiers fell from the Juggernaut, and Namir didn't see him again. Another rose into a crouch to toss a grenade and was shot through the chest for his efforts.

But the vehicle's armor plating held long enough for the Juggernaut to cross into friendly territory. There, its passengers disembarked to join Echo Base's last line of defense.

The soldiers remaining on the battlefield had already begun abandoning the turrets and artillery emplacements two and three at a time. Namir grabbed a man wearing a colonel's insignia after swinging down into a trench. "We just got in from Delta," Namir said. His lips were chapped and his throat was raw with cold. Under his jacket, he was sweating. "What's our status?"

The man rose on his toes over the trench wall and fired a volley of bolts before answering.

"Most of the transports made it out, but that shield's going down any second. Last word from the command center was to fall back and finish evac—all troops, all positions."

No point staying for a losing battle, Namir thought. But one part troubled him. "What do you mean, *last word*?"

"Walker took a few shots at the base. We think command got hit."

Namir swore, waved for Roja and Beak to follow, and left the colonel behind. The other passengers from the Juggernaut had already dispersed with the certainty and discipline of professional soldiers.

The interior of Echo Base was as chaotic, in its own way, as the battlefield. Lights flickered and klaxons rose and died haphazardly. Tunnels had partly collapsed, leaving chunks of stone and ice piled atop generators and tubing and, in some cases, bodies. The sound of settling and crackling snow all around promised more collapses to come. And though the base was emptier than Namir was used to, distant footsteps and blaster shots resonated throughout.

Namir led the way toward the command center, picking his way through the rubble where he could and doubling back to find alternative paths when he had to. As the group crossed an intersection leading toward the hangars, Roja hesitated and asked if they'd be better off sending someone to prep the shuttle. Namir thought about it and shook his head.

"If we split up in this mess, there's a good chance we'll never find each other. We locate Howl. We leave this planet together."

Roja nodded somberly. Beak offered an approving, profane oath. Namir hoped he wasn't dooming them all.

The main corridor to the command center had once been reinforced with metal beams. Now the beams and much of the ceiling filled the tunnel at an angle. No lighting fixtures remained intact. Namir peered into the darkness, waved for Roja and Beak to hold position, and clambered through. When he emerged on the other side of the wreckage he immediately barreled into another form— a woman, by the sound of her curses. She faced away from Namir, half crouched and dragging something as she shuffled backward.

The woman glanced behind her for only a moment. Namir recognized the angle of her jaw, her black hair threaded with gray and white.

"I could use a hand, Sergeant," Chalis snapped.

Namir felt irritated for reasons he couldn't entirely justify. "What are you doing?" He edged around Chalis, scraping his back against the wall, to look down at her burden: Captain Micha Evon, unconscious on the floor. His temple was bleeding. His face was encrusted with dirt and his chest was covered in snow.

"What does it look like?" Chalis returned. She scowled and tried to prop Howl up, hefting him under his shoulders. "I wasn't about to let Micha die."

The words didn't register until Namir had already grabbed Howl's waist, lifted him so that Chalis could work her way back through the half-collapsed corridor. Maybe the governor wasn't without heart after all.

Or maybe she just wanted someone in her debt.

Roja and Beak took Howl together when Namir and Chalis emerged from the tunnel. Roja asked the obvious questions and Beak shushed him as they started toward the hangar. Namir took the lead, rifle at the ready; Chalis followed barely a step behind him. Her forehead gleamed with sweat and her eyes were wide, overanxious. When a blaster shot echoed, he saw her flinch.

"We can circle around the east end," Chalis said. "We're in no shape for a fight."

Namir glanced back at Roja, Beak, and Howl, then down toward the nearest intersection. Another blaster shot. He couldn't tell how far they were from the source.

"Stay here. Give me two minutes to scout," he said. "We can take down a stormtrooper squad if we prep."

Chalis laughed—an ugly, barking sound. Namir had heard fresh meat make the same noise before a battle. It was the sound of imminent panic, of wild fear and self-doubt.

It was unlike Chalis. During the raid on the freighter she'd stayed calm and callous even during the firefights. On Haidoral Prime, she'd spat on the bodies of the dead.

"What's going on?" he asked.

Chalis just shook her head. Namir repeated the question, leaning in close, trying to demand her attention. Finally she looked up, lips twisted into a bleak and bitter smile.

"Those aren't just stormtroopers," she said. "They're from the Five-Oh-First Legion. Darth Vader's personal legion."

"Meaning what? Vader's here?"

Chalis squeezed her eyes shut and nodded. "His shuttle landed ten minutes ago. He's coming for me."

Roja said something Namir ignored. He bit his lip, glanced down the corridor again, then straightened. "If we run into Vader, we shoot him. But we have to keep moving."

Beak was protesting now, too. Namir slipped away down the corridor, body close to the wall and rifle cradled to his chest. He didn't have the time or patience for rebel—or Imperial—superstitions. The longer they remained on Hoth, the more difficult it would be to escape the base, let alone pass any blockade the Empire was hardening in space.

For all his arguments with Howl, he suspected the captain would have agreed.

The base seemed almost haunted. Its corridors were deserted, yet the sounds of movement and blasters and crumbling ice stalked Namir as he turned corners, sought any clue to the attackers' location. He didn't know the base well enough to anticipate an enemy's path, or where thin walls might allow demolition teams to enter. All he could do was engrave the tunnels—as they endured now, not as they'd been before the battle—in his memory and try to plot a path to the hangar.

He decided to turn back and rejoin his team when he reached a pitch-black passageway that should have led directly to his goal. A chill breeze wafted out of the darkness; enough evidence to persuade him that the hangar doors were open. As he pivoted, the toe of his boot nudged a soft pile on the ground and he nearly tripped. Catching himself in a crouch, he recognized the pile as Kryndal's snout-nosed alien companion from the mess hall.

The alien was dead, its body rapidly cooling. Namir rolled it over on the ice, saw a blaster hole burned through its chest. But that told him nothing beyond what he already knew: The Imperials were in Echo Base.

He didn't mention the dead alien when he returned to his team and waved them after him. As they moved together, he heard Roja telling Chalis, "If anything happens, your job is to protect Howl. We'll keep you two safe."

At the murky passageway, Namir flipped a switch on his rifle to activate the light mounted below the barrel. The dim arc swam with motes of dust and frost tumbling in the breeze. It guided them over rubble and three more corpses.

Namir didn't recognize two of the bodies, but the third, at a glance, resembled Kryndal. He didn't stop to be sure.

"They've been through here already," Roja said.

"One wave," Chalis said. "Don't assume there won't be a second."

Suddenly the corridor began to tremble. The ground shook without lurching, enough to force Namir to his knees. Shards of ice rained from the ceiling, striking painful blows along his spine. Behind the aching moans of stone was the rumble of an explosion from down the passage.

When the shaking ended, Namir saw a second light. Something had opened down the way.

The hangar wasn't more than a hundred meters ahead of them. Whatever happened next, they'd be able to run for safety. Namir glanced back at his comrades, saw that they were unharmed, and then looked to Howl. Chalis was bent forward over his body; she was breathing heavily, but she'd taken the blows of the falling debris for him.

She raised her head. Her eyes were wide with terror.

Namir turned back down the corridor. The light at the far end had been blotted out by six humanoid figures. Five of them were dressed in white, like ghosts, and they glided forward across the ice and rubble as if they'd been trained in Echo Base's own devastated hallways.

Flanked by the five stormtroopers was a figure in black.

"Vader is here," Chalis whispered, and it sounded like an accusation. "Vader is *here*."

CHAPTER 15

ELOCHAR SECTOR
Zero Days After Plan Kay One Zero

There was no light aboard the *Trumpet's Call* except the dim glow of the secondary bridge console. Brand preferred it that way. The enhanced optics of her pleximetal mask allowed her to pick out bloodstains and electrical circuits in the dark, and the shadows would give her cover in case she wasn't alone.

She'd boarded the vessel after the last of the injured had been evacuated to the *Thunderstrike*. She still wasn't certain what troubled her about the scenario, and she was well aware she might be looking for problems where none existed—occupying her mind through paranoia. In that case, she was wasting nothing but her own copious free time. But if the *Trumpet's Call* had been tracked to the flotilla somehow? Tagged with a homing beacon or sabotaged by a spy or blackmailed into reporting its position? She was prepared to deal with those possibilities, too. She was well acquainted with the extremes to which men and women—Imperial and otherwise, human or nonhuman—would go to accomplish their goals.

She'd swept for beacons already, found nothing but the bodies of more crew members. Most appeared to have suffocated. A few had burned to death. She couldn't determine when the ship's life support had lost primary power—onboard diagnostics were garbled, and while she might have been able to run the numbers based on the number of survivors and the oxygen supply remaining, she'd need a droid for the math. In the meantime, there were other avenues open to her through the main computer.

Its hyperspace jump logs were consistent with the crew's statements. The *Trumpet's Call* was a light freighter assigned to passenger transport and cargo duty. It had been operating among the purse worlds as a trading vessel, changing its identity records and name— *Eyesore, Careful Buyer*—whenever the Empire began to suspect something. Apparently *Trumpet's Call* was past due to be retired as an alias, as the ship had been attacked sometime in the last several days.

That was neither surprising nor suspicious. The crew had done a good job forging records, but the Empire was growing better at identifying fraud every year. Maybe, Brand thought, she'd retired at the right time; who needed bounty hunters when the Imperial security state ran so smoothly?

Regardless, the jump log neither confirmed nor alleviated her suspicions. She began attempting to access other computer files one by one. Many of the files were corrupt. Others were encrypted; another task for a droid aboard the *Thunderstrike*. Still, there was enough data to keep her occupied: cargo records, maintenance reports, a crew roster, personnel files . . .

She pulled up the roster and opened the captain's entry, only to immediately recognize him as the dead body she'd stepped over to reach the bridge. She skimmed the details—no personal history, just name and age and homeworld and visas and vaccination history, half of it likely faked—and opened the next record. She skimmed each dossier in turn and looked for something *off*—something that suggested tampering or a vulnerability the Empire had taken advantage of. She found nothing that indicated the men and women of the *Trumpet's Call* were anything other than victims.

Then she reached the last record. She stared at the screen.

Before she'd even finished her mental re-creation of the attack, she was running toward the air lock.

Earning a living as a bounty hunter meant learning to pick out and memorize faces. Surveillance was part of the game, and technological enhancement—cybernetic eyes, image-matching lenses—couldn't make an oblivious tracker observant. Brand's strengths weren't with people, but she'd compensated by training, running through black-market versions of the Coruscant underworld police recruitment test. She'd honed her mind, rewired her brain until it worked the way she needed.

She rarely doubted her memory. She didn't now.

None of the faces from the ship's personnel records matched the patients transported to the *Thunderstrike*'s medbay.

Whoever was aboard the *Thunderstrike*, it wasn't the crew of the *Trumpet's Call*.

She tried to open a link to the *Thunderstrike*'s bridge through her mask's comm as she tapped at the air lock control panel and watched the circular metal door roll open. No answer. She stepped into the air lock, waited for the pressure to equalize with the *Thunderstrike*'s interior, and tried her squad frequency. No response from Gadren, Roach, or Charmer, either.

Her mask's display told her the exact time of day. That was how she knew it took a full minute for the exterior door to open and admit the piercing sound of klaxons. As she raced aboard the *Thunderstrike*, she wondered if that minute could have made any difference.

Twilight Company had been infiltrated, and Brand was too late to stop it.

CHAPTER 16

PLANET HOTH
Zero Days After Plan Kay One Zero

Beak and Namir fired in unison, hefting their rifles and sending red streaks down the corridor toward the gleaming figures in white and black. Roja joined the assault barely a second later; he was behind Namir, but Namir could hear his swift, ragged breathing and his boots shuffling on snow.

One stormtrooper fell. The others were parting almost before Namir had fired, scattering to the sides of the corridor and taking cover behind mounds of stone and ice and metal support beams.

Darth Vader stood untouched in the center of the passageway.

The black-clad figure resembled the bust from the Haidoral governor's mansion in the arc of his helmet and the mad angles of the polished mask. But the bust hadn't conveyed his height or the amorphous billow of his cloak. Red and green lights winked from the chest piece of his armor, making him resemble something built rather than born.

Yet he moved like a man: There was flesh beneath the armor, and flesh could be made to burn.

The stormtroopers moved with the surety of professional soldiers, returning fire as soon as they'd exited the kill zone. Namir ordered his own team to cover and dived behind a curtain of dangling, broken piping and a massive block of ice. He was shooting again before he'd checked the status of Beak or Roja or Chalis. Or Howl. But the captain, dead or alive, couldn't be Namir's priority.

The stormtroopers began to advance, dashing across the space of the passageway two at a time while the rest of their squad kept Namir and the others pinned. One took a bolt in the stomach, though Namir couldn't guess who made the kill. He managed to spare a glance to one side and saw that Beak had ended up opposite him, while Roja, Chalis, and Howl were huddled together a short distance to his rear.

He looked back to the corridor. The figure in black raised a hand as a crimson bolt flashed toward him. The bolt hit his hand and bounced off like a tossed pebble, striking the corridor wall and sending flakes of ice crumbling to the floor.

"Force field!" Namir called.

He'd never seen one built into armor before. Yet force fields could be broken.

The stormtroopers halted their advance long enough for Darth Vader to claim the vanguard, taking long, unhurried strides like an Imperial walker disdainful of the stings of rebel snowspeeders. He made no effort to find shelter. He held no weapon Namir could see. In the back of his brain, a voice told Namir that Vader wasn't a threat—he was a bogeyman, built and dressed to intimidate instead of fight—yet the front of his mind screamed not to let the armored figure close in.

"Concentrate fire!" Beak yelled. His voice was forceful but shaking, as if he was trying to convince himself. "Burn the shield out!"

"Don't." Namir heard Chalis's voice through the sound of rifle fire. "We need to go *now*."

The stormtroopers were advancing again behind Vader. Turning and retreating would leave Namir and the others exposed; pushing forward would kill them even faster. Beak's plan was their best chance.

Namir swung his rifle toward Vader and pulled the trigger, holding it down and gripping the weapon's barrel with his free hand. The rifle tried to leap with every shot and the barrel grew hot against his gloved fingers. Between the dimness of the corridor and the red bursts before his eyes, Namir could barely make out his target.

Beak was shooting, too—Namir could hear the sound of energized particles scorching cold air across the hall, but he didn't dare look. Vader didn't hesitate or fall. Instead, something appeared in his hand between the pulses of crimson light and suddenly he *was* holding a weapon, a blade of coherent energy that danced with a twist of his wrist. If Vader had been protected by a force field, it appeared no longer necessary: His energy blade deflected bolts impossibly swiftly, humming and buzzing and crackling as it swept aside a storm of fire.

The temperature monitor on Namir's rifle blinked as the power pack began to overheat. He squeezed the trigger harder and the weapon flashed a dozen more times before shutting down with a mechanical click. The stream of bolts from Beak cut off an instant later.

Vader had advanced a dozen meters during the attack. Time seemed to stop as Namir saw a single snowflake, carried down the length of the corridor in the breeze, loop around the armored man's energy blade and vanish in the heat of the weapon.

Then Vader leapt forward and, in a single motion, landed before Beak and bisected the Twilight soldier with a swing of his blade. For a moment, the air smelled like burning fabric and plastic and muscle.

Namir was aiming his rifle again when he heard Roja shout an oath. A chrome cylinder just smaller than Namir's fist arced through the darkness toward Darth Vader: a fragmentation grenade.

Namir barely had time to hope before Vader lifted his blade and gestured to one side. Toward Namir. Like an obedient droid, the grenade adjusted its trajectory in mid-arc. The events seemed to follow the logic of a nightmare—Vader's capabilities seemed limited only by their horrific implications.

The grenade struck the wall behind the curtain of pipes, two meters down the passageway from Namir. He heard metal shriek and twist beneath the sound of the blast itself, felt something smash into his ribs. A rain of debris fell onto his shoulders and head. His chin was touching the ice of the floor, though he didn't remember falling. The back of his neck was pleasantly warm with what he realized had to be blood.

The rest of the world was darkness and noise.

Namir focused on his own body, listened to his heartbeat and began testing his limbs. He didn't try to stand or move—that was impossibly beyond him—but he could try to flex muscles, confirm whether he could feel his arms and legs and hands and feet at all. He was relatively sure he hadn't lost any limbs.

Nor had he lost his eyes, but his sight was slow to return. He saw shapes, but they refused to resolve into images he could recognize, as if he were a blind man suddenly cured and learning *depth* and *shape* and *color* for the first time. Some calm, cold part of him reminded Namir that this was normal. He'd been badly hurt before. His vision would return, unless someone killed him first.

Five more heartbeats. No one had killed him yet.

Someone had killed Roja, though. The first sight he recognized was his colleague's body on the ice a dozen strides away. Between Namir and Roja were six white-clad legs and two black ones. Stormtroopers, he thought. Stormtroopers and Vader.

He tried to scramble upright and felt something heavy shift on top of him. The world seemed to tilt. He wasn't going anywhere.

"You found me," a voice said. "Congratulations."

It was a woman's voice, in a strange, overly enunciated accent.

Chalis.

"Did you follow my shuttle to Hoth? Or did you pick up my trail later? Not that it matters, really . . ."

She was standing a short distance in front of Vader, neck tilted back slightly to meet the masked gaze of the Emperor's hound. Her hands were clasped together behind her head.

"I'm not going to grovel," she said. "I *like* my life, but you couldn't humiliate me by exiling me to Haidoral Prime and I won't be humiliated now. I made choices and I regret *none* of them. You were damn lucky to have me. You forced me into betrayal. If you want to execute me, *Lord Vader,* so be it."

Vader no longer held the energy blade. He raised a black-gloved hand, palm out toward Chalis. The governor's feet left the floor. Her legs were dangling in the air as the nightmare logic once again took effect.

Her eyes went wide. Vader's hand closed into a fist, and Chalis began gasping and clawing at her throat.

For the first time, Vader spoke. His voice was metallic and deep and resonant, his breath a rasping hiss underneath the impact of his words.

"Where is Skywalker?"

Chalis's head shook as she stared in bewilderment.

Namir repeated the words in his head, baffled.

There was a crackling sound like the branch of a green, healthy tree being twisted apart. Chalis kept clawing at her throat, her breathing increasingly ragged.

One of the stormtroopers approached Vader from behind, head tilted as if listening to his helmet comm. He hesitated, apparently uncertain whether to interrupt, then said, "Lord Vader. We've located the *Millennium Falcon.*"

Vader never looked toward the trooper, but he flicked his wrist again and Chalis struck the wall like a discarded toy before slumping to the floor. The stormtroopers responded by advancing down the corridor with their master in the center of a phalanx.

Namir closed his eyes and sought refuge from the nightmare.

CHAPTER 17

ELOCHAR SECTOR
Zero Days After Plan Kay One Zero

The blast doors aboard the *Thunderstrike* were sealed. Brand saw that as a positive sign—an indication that the bridge crew was attempting to isolate the Imperial infiltration team—until she found Charmer, Roach, and a trio of noncombat personnel and fresh meat trying to burn through one door with a welding torch.

"We're on our way to the command deck," Charmer stammered out, swallowing half the words in frustration. "We don't—don't know—"

"It was the wounded crew," Brand said. "They were Imperials. Must have slaughtered everyone on the *Trumpet's Call* before coming to the flotilla."

Roach was speaking rapidly into her comlink, but she seemed to be receiving no response.

Brand considered the situation. If the infiltrators had control of the blast doors, they'd probably taken the bridge. They would've taken internal comms offline already. They'd need time to take the better-secured systems—weapons, engine control, life support—but not a *lot* of time.

Brand eyed Charmer as he sheared through metal, sent sparks flying. There was no way he'd make it to the bridge quickly enough.

She'd already turned away and started down the passage when she remembered to say, "Keep going. I'll try another way." Even after all these years, teamwork still didn't come easily to her.

But Roach was following her. She recognized the footsteps, swift and ungainly. "Gadren's in the armory," Roach called. "I was going to meet him."

Brand glanced at the girl. "So?"

"That means he has guns. He can get out."

Brand mentally reviewed the armory inventory. "Maybe," she agreed. It wouldn't be a fast or subtle escape, but he had a better chance than Charmer. "If you make contact, tell him to meet me at the bridge. I'll wait as long as I can."

Roach started to reply. Brand stopped her with a look.

She left the girl behind before retracing her route to the *Trumpet's Call.* The damage to the light freighter was severe, but in some ways that was to her advantage: The main computer's safety systems, had they been online, would have prevented what she was planning. She slid into the pilot's chair in the dark of the bridge and transferred whatever power remained from life support to the engines. A warning light and a timer crystallized in one corner of her mask's display, alerting her of exactly how long her suit's emergency oxygen would last. The number wasn't encouraging.

Her stomach lurched as the artificial gravity cut out. She fastened the chair's safety harness over her chest and resumed work. Slowly, the *Trumpet's Call* unmoored its docking clamps from the *Thunderstrike.* As Brand had expected, the *Thunderstrike* did not unclamp itself from the *Trumpet's Call.*

As she activated the ship's thrusters, a dozen new lights appeared on the main console. Brand's teeth were vibrating before she felt the freighter shake. Metal howled, echoing through the ship's interior.

Brand wondered briefly which would tear apart first: the *Thunderstrike*'s clamps or the air lock of the *Trumpet's Call*.

Then she had her answer. Following a sound like the shrieking of a thousand tormented droids, the ship jumped forward and the detritus of the bridge—a datapad, a ration pack wrapper, a stuffed bantha toy that must have meant something to a now-dead crew member—began swimming back into the main passage. The thin air remaining on the *Trumpet's Call* was being sucked out of the damaged air lock, along with anything adrift in the zero-gravity environment.

It didn't matter to Brand. She kept the freighter aligned with the *Thunderstrike*'s hull and steered it—painfully slowly, thanks to the freighter's damaged thrusters and her own neglected piloting skills—in the direction of the corvette's bridge. Her suit clung to her, warming automatically as the ship's temperature dropped.

She barely noticed the freighter's communications light blinking among all the flashing warnings on the console. She flipped a switch and listened to a voice garbled by static, barely decipherable. She heard "Lieutenant Sairgon," "Empire," and "flotilla." She heard what sounded like a blaster shot.

Brand considered Sairgon a friend. Early in her tenure with the company she'd intruded on his privacy, dug around and learned who he had been before the war. He was an actor, a musician, a historian—a man of a hundred talents, none of which he ever admitted to in front of Twilight. She respected him for that.

She was glad to see the rest of the flotilla understood his message and his sacrifice. One by one, the dots on the scanner indicating other rebel ships disappeared until only the *Thunderstrike* and *Apailana's Promise*—loyal until the end—remained. The rendezvous had been compromised. Those able had fled to hyperspace.

That still left Twilight Company to save.

———

When the *Trumpet's Call* had crossed the bulk of the *Thunderstrike* from aft to fore, Brand returned to the freighter's ruined air lock and peered through the jagged hole left after the ship's violent unmooring. The hull of the *Thunderstrike* filled her view, smooth metal interrupted by sensor dishes and power distributors and ablative plating, like the circuit-etched surface of some strange machine moon.

Her mask filtered the shapes, magnified her vision. She knew the interior of the *Thunderstrike* as well as she'd known the streets of Tangenine. She had painstakingly memorized every deck, planned ambushes and escape routes in case of disaster. She felt a fool for not studying the exterior more closely.

She intended to correct her error if she lived through the day.

She spotted the object of her search: a maintenance hatch, built for droids but wide enough, she hoped, to admit a human. She didn't hesitate to push off the wall of the air lock and propel herself into space.

She plunged through the void between ships, into a sliver of blackness between two gray skies. In that void, she had time to wonder about the rashness of her actions. If she'd launched herself with too much velocity, she would rip her suit when she struck *Thunderstrike*'s hull. Even a microscopic tear in her gloves would mean her death. Yet she had jumped without fear or anxiety, without picturing her comrades or envisioning the infiltrators disintegrated by her hand. Even Namir, she thought, jaded as he was, would have admitted a thrill.

She felt nothing. All she had was a job and a purpose and a system.

She twisted her body to orient the soles of her boots toward the hull. When they struck metal, a sharp pain ran through the ankle she'd sprained on Coyerti—but though her whole body felt the jolt, neither bone nor combat suit broke. She leaned forward as she ricocheted back into space, stretched to grasp at the rim of the hatch and dig her fingers under a metal joint. Her arms ached as she held herself against the *Thunderstrike,* her velocity draining away.

Once she'd tentatively secured her position, she forced the hatch open with two disruptor shots. She had to wriggle to lower herself inside, but she was able to fit—the space was designed for an astromech unit, broad if not tall. Once again, her foremost worry was for the suit; a tight squeeze had the potential to shred the fabric.

As she descended, she spared one last glance at the void. The inertia of the *Trumpet's Call* had carried the freighter away, exposing the endless blackness and a thousand stars to her sight. She'd never been outside a starship so far from a planet before; a part of her wanted to linger, to achieve a sense of solitude that seemed just out of reach.

Then a new star winked into being, swiftly growing brighter: a ship arriving out of hyperspace. She magnified it through her mask, over and over, until she could make out its shape.

She wanted to be surprised. She wasn't.

The ship was an Imperial Star Destroyer.

CHAPTER 18

PLANET HOTH
Zero Days After Plan Kay One Zero

For some unknowable time, Namir could not tell the difference between reality and dreams.

Intellectually, he understood the distinction—knew it was imperative that he sift one from the other, knew his life and the lives of others were at stake. But what he clung to as fact seemed gossamer, prone to dissolve at a touch, while what he tried to discard as nightmare seemed fixed in his memory.

There were certain truths he was confident of: He was lying on the ice-slick floor of a half-collapsed passageway, drifting in and out of consciousness. He believed Echo Base had fallen—that he'd fought stormtroopers with his friends and lost.

He was less certain whether his friends had died. He had seen the bodies of Beak and Brand, could picture images of slaughter—of an

Imperial walker crushing Roach, of a blade of energy bisecting Roja—but were they real? He remembered climbing out of the rubble once, twice, only to be struck down again.

Namir recalled something Gadren had told him shortly after he had joined Twilight Company. The alien had taken it upon himself to educate Namir about the nature of the universe—about hyperspace and comets and stellar masses—and he'd spoken of a singularity in the galactic Deep Core. In the middle of everything, Gadren said, there was a black hole that devoured all light and energy, exerting a gravitational pull more powerful than a thousand suns. The entire galaxy rotated around this crux of darkness.

Namir remembered a man in black armor who could not be killed. Darth Vader.

In time, Namir defied a pressure upon his back, rose onto his hands and knees, and felt a ripple of nausea. He didn't believe he had ever felt nauseated in dreams, and took that as a reason to stand. He nearly fell, caught himself, and stepped forward. His chest heaved, but nothing emerged from his lips except his steaming breath. His ribs were sore where his rifle had lain beneath him.

He crossed the corridor to test his balance. He found Beak dead, cut in two.

Beak had been the one killed by Vader. Not Roja. Memories began to align.

Vader was real.

Namir leaned against the wall. *Stay awake,* he told himself. *Unconsciousness is death. Staying here is death.* Then he let the chill surface guide him several meters down the passageway. There he found Roja, a hole burned in his jacket over his heart. Roja lay atop Howl, who was cold when Namir knelt to touch him.

Howl had no obvious combat wounds. The untreated head trauma he'd suffered in the command center collapse had apparently proven fatal.

Namir laughed at that thought and raised a hand to gingerly touch his own head. The hood of his jacket was damp. His glove was spotted with red when he lowered it.

Howl always wanted you to be more like him. Maybe you'll get to die the same way.

He knew he should have felt other emotions—*any* emotions—at the captain's death. And Beak's, and Roja's. But numbness and shock were his allies. His priority was survival. Escape. Warmth.

Find Twilight Company.

But Twilight Company wasn't on Hoth. He remembered that now.

He'd been close to the hangar when the stormtroopers had attacked. He tried to recall which direction he needed to take down the passage and found the effort made him dizzy. The solution came to him when a snowflake touched his chin and melted there.

The hangar doors were open. Follow the breeze.

He trudged slowly down the corridor, his steps becoming more assured the longer he stayed upright. He hefted his rifle, examined it for damage. There were no warning lights. He thought of disassembling it, checking it over more thoroughly, but he couldn't risk the time when more stormtroopers might find him at any moment.

When he looked up again, Everi Chalis was standing in his way three meters down the passage.

She, too, was following the breeze upwind, swaying slightly as she walked. She moved even slower than Namir and kept one hand held to her chest. Namir tried to say her name, got it out the second time.

Chalis turned and swung a fist at him. He caught the blow easily and she seemed to lean into it, crumpling as she lost her balance. He started to reach out, but she pulled back and stumbled upright.

Her eyes were glassy and bloodshot. Her jacket was covered in snow and dirt and specks of blood. Beneath her chin, across her neck and down her throat, her skin had turned the intense red of a fresh bruise. She looked like she'd been hanged and freed from the noose too late.

"We need to go," Namir said.

Chalis's lips curled into something like a snarl. She said nothing.

Namir stared at her, waited. Chalis, too, seemed like something out of a nightmare, and he wondered whether he was unconscious after all. There was frustration and urgency in his voice as he asked, "Can you walk? We need to *go*."

He reached out to grip her shoulder. This time Chalis caught him by the wrist. When she spoke, it was in a hoarse, pained creak. "Yes," she said, the word drawn into two syllables.

That was enough for Namir. He strode past her and continued on his way. He didn't hear Chalis's footsteps at first, but soon they echoed a short distance behind him.

He followed the breeze. The farther they walked, the more attuned he became to the sounds of the base. The ice and stone were still settling, cracking, collapsing. He heard the popping of fires and electric wiring. Twice, he heard faint blaster shots. The battle was over, perhaps, but it hadn't been finished for long.

He heard Chalis, too. Mostly she was breathing through her nose with a soft whistle, but now and then she took a rasping, racking gasp of air. She said nothing as they passed through the darkness, climbed over rubble, and squeezed through doors frozen ajar.

The hangar, when they arrived, was dazzlingly bright. Beyond the great doors to the cavern, Namir could see a lush blue sky, and the rays of a low-hanging sun swept paths of intense illumination between patches of shade. Most of the ships were gone. Two X-wing starfighters were burning. Twilight's shuttle sat apparently untouched to one side.

"It's our lucky day," Namir said. He didn't smile, and Chalis didn't laugh.

The shuttle rattled and shook as it skimmed the runway toward the hangar doors. Namir had skipped the usual preflight checks—not because he feared to lose precious seconds, but because he'd never launched a starship on his own. He'd asked Chalis for instructions, but she had only sat in the copilot's seat and stared blankly out the viewport.

So warning lights blinked and sparks and fire trailed the vessel. But when it exited the hangar bay, it lifted into an endless expanse of blue above and white below, leaving the ruin of the battlefield and its war machines behind.

Namir wanted to stare into the sky, let himself be hypnotized by emptiness and return to the numbness of the dark passageway. He couldn't, he knew. Not yet.

"They'll be watching for ships," he said. "They'll have a blockade around the planet. We don't have the firepower to punch through."

His fingers were tingling as warmth crept into the ship. He watched Chalis, waiting for an answer. She didn't so much as turn.

"They'll shoot us down," he said, voice a little louder, a little harsher. "You need to talk us past, send a clearance code like you did when we boarded the freighter."

Chalis stiffened in her seat and seemed to suppress a wince, as if she'd just aggravated an injury. Still she did not speak.

Namir glanced at the control panels, tried to guess how long they had before exiting Hoth's upper atmosphere and finding themselves faced with a fleet of Star Destroyers. Outside, wisps of fog and cloud splashed against the viewport.

"*Chalis*," he snapped, and reached out to grasp her shoulder.

Now she did look at him, her expression full of loathing and bitterness. Still, the silence.

"I don't care if it hurts to talk," Namir said. "I don't care what happened back there. You're going to try this."

He kept one hand on her shoulder. The other fumbled with his rifle, still slung across his chest, and raised it toward Chalis. They were so close that the muzzle scraped the cloth of her jacket.

"You're going to *try*," he said.

Chalis kept staring her hateful stare. Then she turned to the console and with swift, jerky movements began tapping buttons and entering codes.

Next she opened a comm frequency. "This," she said in a voice so rough and full of breath that Namir worried no one would hear, "is Blizzard Force unit two-two-eight-seven. Requesting—" She stopped, and her mouth opened and closed like that of a gasping fish before she resumed. "—berth for captive shuttle."

She closed the frequency and leaned forward, her shoulders and chest heaving. She looked like she was trying to cough, but she made no sound.

The shuttle broke through gray clouds and the viewport turned black, stars glittering in the darkness like frost. The massive wedges of Star Destroyers stretched out to either side. Namir's instinct was to pour power into the engines, to speed away from Hoth and through the blockade.

Instead he waited. If he gave away the bluff too soon, the shuttle would be annihilated. *Get through the blockade first,* he told himself. *Get far enough from the planet to hit lightspeed. They'll be suspicious, but by then it will be too late.*

He tapped at the navicomputer, let it plot the first jump to hyperspace. He'd figure out where the flotilla's coordinates had been stored later—the ship must have logged them—but for now, anywhere away from Hoth was good enough.

A light on the console flashed. One of the Star Destroyers was attempting to contact them. Namir glanced at Chalis. She was staring straight ahead.

They were nearly through the blockade, nearly out of Hoth's gravity well, when sensors showed a handful of ships moving swiftly toward them.

TIE fighters, Namir imagined. But their opportunity to catch the shuttle had passed.

The navicomputer signaled that a course was plotted. Namir reached out and gingerly pulled on the hyperdrive accelerator. Stars became streaks of light and Namir felt himself crushed against his seat. Then the viewpoint became a whirl of azure energy and the ship settled again.

He checked the readouts as if expecting to see the TIE fighters still in pursuit, glanced around the cockpit as if a stormtrooper had stowed aboard. It took long moments for his body to accept that he was safe—

for the instincts of a hundred battles to subside and give way to true, deliberate thought for the first time since he'd woken.

He was alive.

Roja and Beak were dead.

The captain of Twilight Company was dead.

The rebel fleet was scattered.

He leaned back in his seat, shivering in the heat of the shuttle and clinging to the shreds of his numbness.

CHAPTER 19

ELOCHAR SECTOR
Zero Days After Plan Kay One Zero

"This is Prelate Verge of the Imperial Ruling Council. I come with an offer in the name of Emperor Palpatine, glorious ruler of our galaxy and our guide into this modern age."

The broadcast had started shortly after Brand boarded the *Thunderstrike*. It must have originated from the Star Destroyer, she thought, and been patched through *Thunderstrike*'s address system by the infiltrators on the bridge.

Prelate Verge. Brand had heard the name in passing, linked it with casual cruelty, but she couldn't recall the details and didn't have time to dredge her memory for more.

He had the voice of a child.

"All of you are traitors, in a sense—our Emperor welcomed each of you into the New Order, and each of you instead chose to rebel."

The maintenance hatch had led almost directly to the command deck, barring a short climb through a turbolift shaft offline and half dismantled for repairs. Now Brand squatted before the blast doors sealing off the bridge, pieces of the door panel scattered around her knees as she attempted to hot-wire the controls. Even if she'd been able to cut through, she would've rejected the option—if there were hostages on the other side, she needed the element of surprise.

She heard the sound of a blaster cannon muffled by steel barricades. The deck barely trembled. It might have been Gadren, carving his way from the armory. Based on the vibrations, he wasn't anywhere close.

"But one betrayal stings more than the others. I know you were joined by Governor Everi Chalis on Haidoral Prime. I know she is with you still.

"I cannot promise to spare you, but you have no chance against my vessel. If you do not turn Governor Chalis over to me, I will make a public example of all of you. Your executions will be slow, witnessed by your families and your homeworlds."

Brand couldn't laugh, given the circumstances. But she smiled bitterly. Governor Chalis had been gone for weeks, and she was *still* going to be the death of Twilight Company.

There was no time to wait for Gadren. Part of Brand was glad. She finished stripping a wire with her knife and touched it to the suit control unit on her wrist. Something inside the panel popped. The blast doors stuttered and slid open.

Brand fired at the first of the infiltrators before she'd even taken stock of the situation. It made her feel clumsy, reckless—if she'd been able to scope out the bridge before entering, she could have executed her foes in moments—but it was necessary. The disruptor burned bright, turned a woman standing at the comm station to rags and dust as Brand rolled through the doorway.

To one side, she heard the sound of flesh striking flesh. That was good. That would be the bridge crew, still alive and fighting back.

Her disruptor vibrated in her hand, nearly throwing off her aim as she fired a shot toward a man seated in the captain's chair on the central platform. She swept her gaze across the bridge, made a quick count. Eight infiltrators. Five *Thunderstrike* crew members still alive, already wrestling with their captors. Acceptable odds in tight quarters.

Prelate Verge was speaking again. Brand tuned him out to focus on the broad-shouldered Imperial coming at her from the left. She stepped back, drew her knife, and wrapped an arm around him, holding the edge of her blade to his throat. With her other hand she retargeted her disruptor at an infiltrator dashing for cover. Taking her own hostage wouldn't buy her more than a few moments, she knew, but that was all she really needed.

She heard five blaster shots. Only two were aimed at her. She didn't have time to check on the crew. Her captive tried to escape and paid the price.

The rest of the fight was swift and bloody. Brand sprinted from one target to the next, knowing she'd be shot down in an instant if she stayed at range and in the open. Her knife disabled two opponents—she didn't bother to check whether they lived—while the disruptor disintegrated another. When she caught her breath and wrinkled her nose to displace a drop of sweat, she saw the bridge crew had handled the remaining infiltrators.

What was left of the bridge crew. Two ensigns, neither of whom she knew. Commander Paonu was dead on the floor. She had no idea who was rightfully in charge of ship operations now.

"Get to your stations," she snapped. The ensigns moved.

She glanced at the tactical holodisplay, saw *Apailana's Promise* moving to interpose itself between the Star Destroyer and *Thunderstrike*. The gunship couldn't possibly know what was going on, but it was preparing to sacrifice itself anyway. *Stupid and faithful beyond reason,* Brand thought.

"They're firing," one of the ensigns called.

The holodisplay winked with a thousand tiny flashes as the Star Destroyer unleashed its weapons. The flares from the *Promise* seemed dull and lifeless in comparison.

The flotilla had scattered. The *Thunderstrike* hadn't completed its repairs but it was, Brand knew, spaceworthy. And Prelate Verge was right—neither the *Thunderstrike* nor the *Promise* stood a chance against a Star Destroyer.

The right call was obvious, even without Howl or Paonu. Brand hoped the captain would forgive her.

"Get ready to jump," she said.

"We need to get shields online," one of the ensigns—a yellow-skinned Mirialan with a face covered in black tattoos—called back. He was leaning over his control panel, not looking at Brand.

"We jump and we take the hit," Brand said.

She hated playing leader. She hoped the boy obeyed.

The *Thunderstrike* began to shake as the Star Destroyer's particle rain pelted its hull. Brand ignored the shuddering and entered a set of coordinates into the navicomputer, transmitted them to *Apailana's Promise*. She felt the deck shift as the vessel began moving.

She hoped that whatever was happening at the rebels' secret base— whatever Howl and Chalis were up to with Alliance High Command— was worth the dispersal of the flotilla and the hijacking of the *Thunderstrike*.

She wondered if she'd live to find out.

CHAPTER 20

PLANET SULLUST
Zero Days After Plan Kay One Zero

SP-475 was the third stormtrooper into the docking bay. She kept her head low and her blaster steady, as she'd been trained. She followed her partner to cover behind the charging station, swept for enemies while the rest of the team poured in. She trusted her helmet display to pick out motion, to alert her to any enemy she'd missed.

"Clear!" a static-distorted voice called. The speaker's designation blinked in her display, but it wasn't important. *Trust the call,* 475 told herself. *Trust your colleagues—not just your equipment.*

Twelve stormtroopers fanned out around a carbon-scored heap of a freighter registered as the *Keepsake*. If the Security Bureau's information was correct, it belonged to the most wanted terrorists on Sullust.

475 *hoped* the information was correct. She was ready for life in Pinyumb to return to normal.

Since the attack on the processing facility, the Empire had instituted aggressive new anti-terrorism policies. There were daily raids on the workers' dorms and the housing blocks, strict limitations on computer network access, new security checkpoints at the tram and shuttle stations leading from city to surface. And, of course, never-ending shifts for the Stormtrooper Corps; no matter what civilians said, there were never enough troops to meet the Empire's needs.

SP-475 had received a commendation for reporting a mysterious influx of supplies into the hands of workers. Her uncle had been taken into custody a week ago. He hadn't been charged. He'd be free once things settled down, she was sure, but she was tired of the bitter stares from his friends when she walked home to the troopers' dormitory.

She was doing her duty. Life was hard for the people of Pinyumb, true—but the best way to make things easier was to stop the rebels and resistance fighters who were blowing up factories and bribing innocents.

Her helmet's comlink crackled to life again: "Two teams: Check inside. Watch yourselves."

475's partner nodded and led the way.

Rumor was that the rebels liked to rig their equipment with improvised explosives. 475 had heard thirdhand accounts of stormtroopers who'd lost limbs to detonite blasts, whose armor had been pierced by shrapnel sharpened by diligent rebel hands. She'd never seen a bomb outside training.

What sort of monsters are these people? She'd read the file on Nien Nunb—rebel terror cell leader, native Sullustan, petty thief who'd embezzled from his employers before signing on with the Rebellion. But petty thieves didn't leave soldiers drowning in blood inside their helmets. Petty thieves might *murder* when backed into a corner, but self-defense wasn't the same as a coldly plotted massacre.

SP-475 was the second of eight stormtroopers onto the freighter. Her breath sounded too loud inside her helmet. The only light came from the docking bay.

"Night vision," came the command from 113. 475 had never seen his face, but she'd been told he was one of the original clone commandos who'd founded the Stormtrooper Corps. His voice sounded old. "Don't *touch* anything."

She let her visor switch over. The night-vision enhancements left a green haze over the corridor, but it was better than nothing.

The group stalked forward and came to a three-way branch. 475 pulled up a blueprint of the freighter model—a Corellian Engineering VCX-150—on her display. More than half a dozen rooms to search. Half a dozen chances to be ambushed or to trigger a trap. She tapped her partner on the arm and took the left passage, hoping for the best.

The search went slowly, at first. They scanned each room for comm signals and power sources—anything that might be used in a bomb— before entering. When they'd barely finished the first bunk room after ten minutes, however, the order came from the garrison to speed things up. If the rebels weren't aboard, headquarters wanted to know. Every second wasted in uncertainty was a second the foe could do more damage.

In the cargo hold, they found a chilled crate full of bacta packs sufficient to supply a hospital for a month or make a smuggler rich on the black market. Stuffed under a bunk, 475 discovered a trunk filled with enough specialized tools to dismantle a starfighter.

Similar reports came in from the others: datachips loaded with propaganda videos; fresh bandages; ration packs. No weapons. When the teams had finished sweeping their discrete sections of the ship, they gathered in the tight corridor outside the cockpit.

SP-113 was giving instructions on locking down the equipment, readying the ship for the forensic technicians, when 156 stepped away from the group, staring at a conduit access panel in the corridor. When 475 looked toward him, he shook his head briskly and indicated the wall with a gesture.

As one, the stormtroopers moved to block the corridor in both directions and leveled their rifles at the panel.

156 studied the panel—no wider than his arm span, set a meter high in the corridor wall—then finally gave it a solid strike with the

butt of his rifle. The panel shifted in its frame, already unbolted. 156 reached out and pulled the metal sheet away.

In a cramped compartment made even smaller by waterfalls of tubing and wires, a brown-furred alien crouched, scrawny legs pulled to its chest and its long snout sandwiched between its knees. Wide black eyes stared out at the troopers as half a dozen rifles took aim. 475's helmet identified the species before she could: Chadra-Fan.

The alien was trembling, but it didn't move. 475 tried to see its hands, but they were buried behind its legs. If it was holding a weapon, she couldn't tell.

"Where's Nien Nunb?" 113 barked. "Where are the others?"

"Not here," the alien said in a soft, high-pitched voice. "Somewhere in the city. Good luck finding them." It tittered weirdly. 475 took it as a nervous laugh.

She wanted to glance behind her, as if other rebels might begin crawling out of air ducts and maintenance shafts. She kept her focus on the Chadra-Fan.

"Who are their contacts on Sullust?" 113 asked. "Who are you working with here?"

Again, the weird laughter.

"What makes you think we're working with *anyone*?" the alien asked.

113 started to respond, but the Chadra-Fan kept talking between titters. "You've got them all so terrified they won't work with us at all. Oh, they'll take our food, but join the Rebellion?

"No, no, no. The attack on the processing facility? That was *us*. Our cell. Nobody else."

"Get him out of there," 113 said.

Three stormtroopers—those nearest to the panel—stepped forward. 475 stepped back, trying to establish a secondary cordon in case the alien tried to flee. She breathed slowly, forcing air in and out between her teeth. She'd been trained for this. Her comrades knew their duty. They could take a single rebel.

She nearly lost sight of the alien as the three stormtroopers closed in, but she heard its words: "Not okay. Not today."

And then the shout, screeched in static through her comlink: "Detonator!"

She froze a second too long. A body in white armor slammed into her, trying to push past, trying to run. The impact spun Thara halfway around and she scrambled away. She was no longer thinking about her team. She wasn't thinking about anything.

She felt a blow on her back, felt her legs kicked from under her, and her face smacked against the front of her helmet as she was propelled forward. There was a sound, a massive crack and roar barely dulled by her armor.

For long moments, she was too stunned to move. When she looked up again, she found herself lying prone halfway down the boarding ramp. She heard nothing but a distant ringing. She felt congested and realized her nose was bleeding.

Thara—475—had survived her first rebel attack. But the ship smelled of melting plastic and burning flesh and fur, and she wondered who else had been so lucky.

PART III

ASSAULT

CHAPTER 21

PLANET CRUCIVAL
Day Four of the Battle of the Tower
Nineteen Years After the Clone Wars

The dome over the tower gleamed with oily iridescence, as if one of the offworlders' great airships had bled out its gears onto Crucival. In the evening twilight, its glimmering outshone anything else on the horizon, and it shimmered brighter and coruscated more furiously with every energy blast that struck, every volley from the enemy. Green and yellow fire streamed in perfect lines from distant cannons, rippling the dome's unnatural surface. Burning, crackling shells descended upon the dome with a shriek, exploding in bursts that could have leveled a hillside.

Outside the dome, for over a kilometer around the bristling steel tower, the landscape consisted of ash, twisted metal, and the bodies of the dead. Here and there, blades of yellow grass nestled against the scorched frame of a downed flier. Trenches and stone walls had collapsed. A few brave, foolish men and women crouched low on the ground, firing occasional shots toward the invaders encamped just out of sight.

The battle was lost. The young man named Hazram knew as much. More important, it had never been winnable, and he hated himself for not seeing that sooner.

He dragged himself through the dust, fingers digging into soil and feet scraping through gravel. He felt something sharp press into his chest and carefully rose no more than a hand span to avoid cutting himself on shrapnel. When he was exposed, he scampered lizardlike toward shelter. When he found himself in the remnants of a trench, he rested.

To raise one's head meant death: incineration by one of the enemy's beam weapons as it swept across the battlefield; murder by a sniper's blaster shot; disintegration by one of the tower-masters' ambulatory machines, who seemed eager to target friend and foe alike; impalement on the shards of one of those same machines as it burst apart.

So *many* kinds of death.

In the trench, as Hazram patted himself down and felt for blood or injuries, he realized he no longer carried his particle blaster.

He laughed with a hoarse and queasy sound. The blaster had run out of power on the first day of fighting. It had been his payment—a clean and polished weapon to rival anything built on Crucival—for signing on to aid the tower-masters, the offworlders who called themselves the First Galactic Empire.

It hadn't seemed a poor bargain then. He'd fought for so many masters: the Warlord Malkhan and his clan; the Opaline Creed, with its hundred doctrines and righteous fervor; the Lady of Coins and her dust-shrouded acolytes; and more besides, all with their own labored reasoning as to why they, and only they, could justly claim Crucival as their own. But he couldn't remember the last time he'd cared about his masters' justifications for war, or believed Crucival under one ruler would be different from Crucival under another. When emissaries of the Empire had emerged from the tower for the first time in years, declaring that a foe was coming to the planet and that they would arm anyone who pledged to fight, it had seemed like one more opportunity. The best opportunity Hazram had seen in ages.

He was too old to keep joining the factions of Crucival one after the next. He was no longer a child, eager to pledge life and spirit to a cause. His past loyalties made him suspect or a pariah. He had few paths left, and if he could arm himself and his allies the way Malkhan had, found a faction of his own with power to spare—

—well, there were possibilities. And the Empire had only asked for one battle.

He'd brought Pira with him. Pira, who'd been at his side since the Creed; Pira, who was family. He recruited others like Tar and Mishru: men he had fought against before they'd lost their own masters. He'd found them in the city streets, hiding their brands and robbing passersby. Hazram's band had been nearly a dozen in total, soldiers ready to stop drifting from war to war.

When the Empire's troops in white had handed them their rifles, told them to defend the tower against rebels from the sky, Hazram had looked at his band and seen *survivors*. He'd seen the greatest warriors on Crucival.

They'd nearly all died in the first wave.

The tower-masters and their white-clad troops had withdrawn under the dome and let their mercenaries face the rebel vanguard. The Empire must have known the people of Crucival couldn't prevail. The mercenaries were fodder. At best, they were a delaying tactic. A thousand soldiers and a thousand particle blasters were nothing against the offworlders' arsenal.

Hazram hadn't seen it soon enough, and he cursed himself.

He climbed out of his trench, resumed his crawl across the battlefield and away from the tower.

He heard a low humming behind him. Over his shoulder he spied a metal sphere the size of a human head floating above the wreckage, its lone red eye flicking back and forth. It belonged to the Empire, not the rebels, but Hazram knew what it would do. When it saw something move, it stared. Where it stared, a flier would soon follow. With the fliers came a rain of destruction.

Against his better judgment, Hazram ran. A flier's bombs would leave nothing but a crater and dust. Not even ruins would be left.

He tripped once, again, catching himself both times. After the agonizingly slow crawl, he'd forgotten his own fatigue. Even before the battle, he'd barely been eating, stealing what he could from war camps or trading trinkets with the merchants of the city. He felt simultaneously light, *too* light, and as heavy as a mountain. When a long stride took him over the crest of a hill, he was in midair before he saw the sheer drop below him. He tumbled three meters down the face of an escarpment, landed hard, releasing a strained, breathy moan as his ankle turned beneath him.

He couldn't run again. He pulled his legs to his chest and edged backward against the escarpment, into a narrow ditch at its base. He heard the noise of thunder up the hillside and clouds of dust washed over him.

At least he'd survived the flier. They rarely bothered with a second pass.

"Hazram?"

The voice was small and confused, like a child's.

He let go of his legs, rested his ankle on the cool dirt. So long as he didn't move it, it didn't sting. He looked down the ditch and saw a figure stretched out a few meters away, shivering on her side.

Pira had changed since her days with the Creed. Hazram had watched her transform from a small, tough, long-haired girl to a tall, lanky, underfed woman who shaved her head to deny any handhold to an enemy. Her face was full of scars, and she'd taken a brand around her mouth during the year she and Hazram had spent separated. He couldn't see the brand now, thanks to the red crust covering her lips and chin.

"I thought the fliers got you," she said.

"Same here," he answered.

Pira didn't move closer. Hazram slowly dragged himself to her side, propping himself up. Pira didn't rise. She smelled like every wrong a human body could suffer.

"We lost pretty awful, didn't we?" she asked.

Hazram nodded. He saw that one of her legs was a mess of blood and cloth. "I made a bad call," he said.

Pira laughed. "You really, really did," she said. "But you weren't the only one."

He tried to shift closer, adjust himself so that he could get a better look at her leg. She pushed him away without force. "It's past infected," she said. "Unless you can amputate and cauterize, it's not going anywhere good."

Hazram swore quietly, without ire. "We can wait for a break in the fighting," he said. "Escape together."

"That was my plan," Pira said, and smirked. "Glad you figured it out."

They sat together, listening to the distant squawking of particle blasters and the rumble of bombs. Part of Hazram's brain—the part that had been fighting for the better part of a decade, starting barely after he'd hit puberty; the part that knew how to ambush an enemy camp at midnight and slit a sentry's throat, or find the weak point of a blockade—ran scenarios, tried to determine what it would take to carry Pira to safety and a surgeon.

The rest of his brain struggled with what to say while Pira was still alive.

"We should've gotten out a long time ago," Pira said quietly. "Whatever more there is, it can't be worse than this."

"Next time," Hazram said.

"Next time," Pira agreed.

The last thing they talked about before Pira fell asleep was bread pudding: the kind the Creed had made on holy days, with sweet fruits and a charred crust. That was when the sect had possessed gold and food to spare. Pira had adored the Creed's pudding, despite how it made her itch the morning after. Hazram had shared his bowl with her on the eve of the Hieroprince's Ascension, when Pira had been blindfolded and forced to abstain as punishment for misreciting the doctrines.

In the pre-morning light, Hazram left Pira in the ditch and resumed his crawl across the dewy battlefield. He told himself he would return if he could—if he could find medicine for the gangrene or a cart on which to carry her. By the time he left the hillsides behind, he still believed he had a chance.

That night, from the ruin of the Creed's cloister outside the city, he watched the hills burn. Then he knew he would not return after all.

The tower fell the next day. Victory, then, for the rebels. The Empire's soldiers in white had claimed the tower was a transmitter, that it communicated somehow with other planets; that was why they had wanted it preserved. Hazram wondered if the Empire would be back to build another, or if its rulers would give up on Crucival altogether. It was an idle, dispassionate sort of wonder.

Hazram's comrades were dead. He was weaponless and had no warband to protect him, no clan or faction to feed him. He spent the days following foraging for food—the birds nesting in the cloister had left a few eggs, enough to sustain him—or sitting in the weeds and grass in a weary haze. Now and again, his thoughts drifted to what he might do next: If he returned to the city, he would be recognized as a failure—as the man who had killed his allies chasing false hope, proving himself without value as a leader or a fighter. If he was fortunate, he might not be hunted and killed for his past associations. He would be able to eke out a living as a beggar or a thief.

Or he might become his father, an ex-soldier-turned-coward shunned or pitied by the city's other residents. He could die stabbed in the gut by a child, like his father finally had.

He could not return to the city.

Almost a week after the tower fell, his head throbbing from a lack of food and sleep and his unwashed clothes stinking of sweat, Hazram spotted a trickle of men and women leaving the city and walking the path toward the tower's ruins. Many were armed, but they didn't march as if to war—they were alone and in groups, as cautious as any prudent travelers but unafraid of being seen. Hazram watched them from a distance and trailed them without thinking. He had nothing else to occupy himself except survival.

They reached the battlefield by noon. The hills had already been picked clean by scavengers—humans stealing weapons from the fallen, scrap metal from machines; animals feasting on carrion—so Hazram was unsurprised when the line of travelers skirted around the destruction. Hazram thought of peeling off then, of searching for Pira and the others. But he'd seen enough of his dead to know it would give him no pleasure. He would find no satisfaction in revisiting the site of his failure.

So he wandered closer to the travelers, joining them on the path they beat through the yellow grass. As they crested a rise, he saw their destination: a circle of tents and generators and mechanical vehicles. It was an offworlder camp, and since Hazram saw no soldiers in white he presumed it belonged to the rebels. The group descended the rise, past the eyes of sentries who only scowled or smiled, looking the pilgrims over and waving them on. No one stopped until the camp proper; there, the travelers were approached, one by one, by rebels who took them among the tents to converse.

Hazram hadn't seen the rebels up close before. Their clothes were clearly of offworld design—they were perfectly sewn from brightly dyed, tough-looking fabrics—but they were stained and torn nonetheless. Some of the rebels wore helmets or heavy vests, while others barely seemed ready for battle, carrying only their sidearms. Those not engaging the travelers murmured to one another and laughed, or sat near their tents chewing on cakes in silver wrappers. They had the proud, weary look of soldiers after victory.

They looked too ordinary to have slaughtered Hazram's comrades so swiftly.

"Next?" The voice was powerful, resonant as a bomb blast.

Hazram realized he had found his way to the fore of the line. Approaching him was a monstrous, four-armed alien with a demon's head—a brown, bulbous, widemouthed mass topped with a crest of bone. One of its arms gestured Hazram forward, its nightmarish head smiling toothily, its eyes shining with impatience.

Hazram's comrades were dead. He could not return to the city. He stepped forward, and the alien led him between a pair of silver-green tents.

"We prefer to conduct these within a settlement," the creature said, "but we were warned our approach might be viewed as aggression. I promise you, we have no designs on Crucival."

"Not a lot here worth taking," Hazram said. He glanced about the camp, idly noting escape routes. He did not know what the alien expected or wanted. He did not especially care.

The creature shook its head with a wince, but left whatever troubled it unspoken. Instead it lowered itself to the dust, sitting cross-legged with a sigh. When Hazram had joined it, the alien asked, "So: Why do wish to join the Rebellion against the Empire?"

Was that why the camp was here? Hazram felt a fool for not realizing it earlier. They were recruiting.

He could have turned and walked away. Instead he stared at the alien for a while and finally said, "The Empire killed my friends."

It was true, in its way. Hazram held no grudge against them, but the tower-masters had arranged the execution even if they hadn't pulled the trigger.

The creature nodded slowly. Two meaty hands wove together. "You seek revenge, then?"

Hazram watched the alien and let the question tumble in his skull.

He could get revenge. He could wrest a blaster from one of the rebels, shoot everyone in the camp before he was overwhelmed. He pictured it, worked the scenario. There was no pleasure in it.

"Not really," Hazram said.

"Good," the creature said, and again offered that toothy smile. "Revenge is a fuel that burns too swiftly. But I will tell you this much: Should you join us, we, too, will mourn your friends."

Hazram barked a laugh. The creature clapped its lower hands together, as if pleased, before launching into an explanation of its warband's place in the galaxy.

It claimed to represent "the Rebel Alliance's Sixty-First Mobile Infantry," a company of troops that moved from star to star at the whims
of its superiors. Its unit had fought the Empire on a thousand battle-
grounds across a hundred worlds. It was bloody work, the creature
said, and the rewards were few. But when Hazram asked, it assured
him there was sufficient food and clothing and arms for all, "save in
the most dire circumstances."

"How often are circumstances dire?" Hazram asked.

The creature chuckled softly. It sounded like a drumbeat. "More
often than we'd like," it admitted.

It went on to question Hazram about his combat experience. Had
he fought in a unit before? Could he use a blaster? "So young," it said
with a shake of its head when Hazram told it a second time—it seemed
not to hear him the first—how long he'd been killing. When the questions were done, the alien spoke lovingly of exotic sights—endless
deserts, planets of islands adrift on clouds, countless species—that the
company had been privileged to encounter. It cautioned Hazram as
well that the company rarely retraced its path. If he signed on, he
would not find it easy to return to Crucival, though he would be permitted to depart the company if he wished.

Hazram pushed the alien's voice out of his consciousness as the
creature emphasized the just cause of the rebels and the terrors of the
Galactic Empire. That part of the speech Hazram could deliver himself; all calls to war were the same, and he'd been hearing them his
entire life. But the thought of leaving Crucival . . .

He would never have to go back to the city. Never have to face the
emptiness there, or forage in the bloodstained grass outside its walls.

His father had survived among the stars. He was certain he could,
too.

And if he could not, he could die a hundred planets away from
home.

The alien asked if he was truly willing to fight the Empire's evil for
little in return—if he understood what might be asked of him, and the
heartbreaking scale of the enemy's actions. "A war's a war," Hazram
said. "You can't show me anything I haven't seen."

That was the wrong answer. The alien's eyes closed and its head bowed and it let out a warm and pungent breath. Then it squared its shoulders and looked to Hazram again. "We have many hired guns already," it said. It was a rejection of the most oblique sort, but Hazram recognized it anyway.

Just like the factions of Crucival, the Rebellion wanted minds it might mold to its cause. Young minds. Idealistic minds. Hazram would not find a place there.

Yet the alien kept speaking, struggling for words. "But if we can show you nothing new, perhaps *you* can show *us* something? No man is only a weapon." The creature sounded almost hopeful. Hazram did not understand why, but it was giving him another chance.

He glanced around the camp, tried to guess at the rebels' needs. He didn't understand the workings of their technology—even the glossy sides of their tents seemed magical. Only their most basic weapons were familiar to him. He could sell them Crucival, tell them which factions to obliterate first if they wanted the planet, but the creature had already assured him of their intent.

He looked at the other travelers from the city. They shifted uncomfortably in line or spoke avidly or cockily or begrudgingly with rebel representatives. He saw one of the rebels glance at the alien, nod his head before sending the traveler at his side—a youth with a thick beard and tattered robe—to wait by a tent.

Hazram knew what he had to do.

"He's going to be a problem," Hazram said, and jutted a thumb toward the bearded youth.

"Oh?" the creature asked.

"Maybe he said the right things," Hazram said, "but he's trying too hard to impress. Show he's grown, show he's survived a tough life— maybe he has, for all I know, but I bet he can't even use a blaster."

"As I said, we have many hired guns already. Perhaps he has a spark. Dedication."

"Maybe," Hazram said, and shrugged. "But he's never going to *admit* what he doesn't know if he keeps looking for approval. You don't break him of the habit, he'll get someone killed on the battlefield."

The creature studied Hazram, its bulbous neck expanding and contracting. "How confident are you?"

Hazram shrugged. "Not hugely. Give me twenty minutes with him, I could be pretty sure."

"Why?" the creature asked.

Hazram smiled wryly. "You sign on to enough armies, you start to recognize the people to stick close to."

The creature nodded and strode away without a word. One hand beckoned Hazram to follow.

For nearly an hour they walked silently about the camp, drifting within earshot of the recruiters' conversations. Hazram said nothing unless prompted, but sooner or later the creature asked him his assessment of each of the travelers. Hazram noted a scarred, one-armed veteran who spoke passionately about his desire to serve a just cause, and told the alien that the man would be slow to learn offworld technology but otherwise a potentially excellent asset. He warned the creature about a woman wearing the brands of one of the most brutal successors to Malkhan: She'd be fierce, but she'd learned to fight in a spice-addled haze and she'd be a wreck if she were made to fight lucid.

At the end of the hour, the creature led Hazram back to where they had begun and asked, "What if I were to accept them *all*? If I told you my captain had ordered me to take on anyone who fought for the right reasons?"

"I'd say your captain needs to look out for his people better."

The creature seemed unruffled. "Could you teach them?" it asked. "Could you make them into soldiers you would fight beside?"

Hazram glanced about the camp again, at the travelers and the rebels.

"I wouldn't have much choice," he said. "If they were my comrades . . . I'd do what I had to in order to make them ready."

"Then," the creature said, "perhaps we have a place for you after all."

Hazram Namir did not fully believe he had left the planet Crucial until Gadren—the creature from the camp—walked him to the viewport of the starship *Thunderstrike*. He'd ridden a drop ship up from the planet's surface, nearly vomited down his shirt in the back of the windowless box as it rattled and clanged viciously, and he'd swayed unsteadily while descending a ramp into the *Thunderstrike*'s docking bay.

He'd never seen so much metal and plastic in one place before. The Rebel Alliance's Sixty-First Mobile Infantry didn't need to *conquer* Crucival. If it wanted the planet, it could *buy* it.

He stood alone at the viewport long after Gadren had moved on. Crucival seemed small and petty amid the stars, a mottled sphere of green and gray and yellow too insignificant to hold a single city, let alone nations.

He thought of what he was leaving behind to fly away in an alien cage. He had not expected to miss the yellow grass or the clouds. They had been fundamental to his existence; now they had been stripped away.

Yet when his mind turned to Pira, to his father, to everyone he had left far below, he felt as weightless and free as the ship.

He was out at last.

CHAPTER 22

PLANET ANKHURAL
Seven Days Before Operation Ringbreaker
Three Years Later

The last time Brand had been on Ankhural, its capital—if a planet with only one city and a handful of unmarked settlements could be said to have a capital—had been enclosed by a ray shield that filtered out the billowing dust of the surrounding silica plains. The streets had never been clean, but they'd had a seedy charm.

Brand no longer found Ankhural charming. She wore her mask as she walked through alleyways tagged by vivisector gangs, but her eyes had felt gritty since she'd woken. White-skinned, six-fingered men holding scalpels peered at her as she moved, fading into the shadows when they saw the rifle on her back and the knife displayed prominently on her hip.

She had already sold her disruptor. She missed it, but nothing on

Ankhural fetched a higher price than a lovingly maintained, excruciatingly deadly, and widely banned weapon.

The alleys took her beneath a broad awning and into near-darkness. Her mask enhanced the silhouettes of dozens of veiled men and women who whispered and haggled and grappled and kissed. Free traders from Wild Space met with representatives of the Crymorah syndicate, swapping favors for arms and spice. Umbaran spies bartered their services to survivors of the Death Watch. Any one of the market's denizens might have fetched a decent bounty; like a stray speck of sand, the thought of abandoning her cause and returning to a simpler life drifted through Brand's mind.

She shook the thought away and walked on. She reached the side of a shriveled, hobbling Weequay with a face like a desiccated corpse and matched his pace.

"No trouble?" she asked. Her Huttese was clumsy; she could have hired a protocol droid or bought a translation program for her mask, but she hoped the effort would win her some respect.

"No trouble," the alien said. "No inquiries. The gangs become curious soon, I think."

Brand reached into her jacket and withdrew a stack of high-value credit chips. She pressed them into the old Weequay's palm. "Tell the Grandfather of Vice I'm grateful for his help."

With that, she walked on. She felt a presence at her back until she exited the market, at which point her stalker, whatever it was, abandoned its hunt.

Could have gone worse, she thought.

By the time she arrived at the podracing track at the city's edge, the lenses on her mask were clouded with grime. She lowered the mask altogether as she neared the metal doors to the great arena—large enough to admit a hovertank but guarded only by a spidery droid. The droid inserted an appendage into a wall socket to acknowledge her arrival, and the doors slid open less than half a meter; she had to turn her body to squeeze through.

In the vast space beyond the doors, enclosed by the amphitheater but open to the swirling sky, the *Thunderstrike* rested in a bed of dust.

Dozens of Twilight soldiers moved about, dwarfed by the ship's hull: They carted tools and machine parts in from the city or hauled burnt and twisted scrap to junk piles, aided engineers stripping panels or welding scars. Others appeared to have nothing better to do than play dice or wait for trouble.

The *Thunderstrike* wasn't built to land, but it was capable of planet-fall in an emergency. The current situation certainly qualified. The ship had limped away from its battle with Prelate Verge, still only half repaired from its battles in the Mid Rim. To finish the repair job, the engineering crew needed to power whole systems down—and that meant finding a spacedock or a flotilla.

Or an unused racetrack in the middle of nowhere.

If the Empire found Ankhural—if the prelate tracked Twilight Company down, as he had before, or if the gangs became too curious and turned the rebels in—the *Thunderstrike* would be defenseless. *Apailana's Promise* was conducting its own repairs in orbit, operated by a skeleton crew; there was no one to protect the company anymore.

So they hid and they waited, and Brand tried not to think about what they'd do—what *she* would do—after the *Thunderstrike* was made whole. She tried not to think about how long they could afford to wait.

She had said she would try to look out for these people. She'd meant it, but she wasn't anyone's leader.

She nodded to the sentries as she approached the massive ship, watched M2-M5—now acting chief of engineering, wrapped in transparent duraplast to protect his joints from dust—blast snide remarks at the repair crews as he administered mechanical triage. She caught Quartermaster Hober's eye, shook her head, and hoped it was enough to communicate the gist of her morning's errands. No emergencies, no progress, and no real change.

Gadren and Roach were seated in the dirt. Two of the Besalisk's hands were bandaged, singed during his attempts to reach the hijackers on the *Thunderstrike*'s bridge. Roach rose and crossed toward Brand, but Brand didn't acknowledge her. She didn't dislike Roach—the girl had done her best on Coyerti, and no worse than anyone during the ship's infiltration—but Brand didn't have answers to her inevitable questions.

A shout from the gates saved her. Brand unslung her rifle, pivoted on her heel, and hurried back the way she'd come. The great metal doors were sliding open.

The sentries wouldn't have called an alarm if anyone from Twilight was still in the city. That meant a stranger was coming to visit.

The sentries formed a broad arc around the gate. Brand held her rifle steady, aimed at the crack through which two figures emerged. Both walked unsteadily, leaning lightly against each other for support. One was a bronze-skinned man, lean and compact. The other was a lighter woman with black hair. Each wore a stained and torn jacket too heavy for Ankhural.

Brand approached the pair and slung her rifle back over her back. The sentries cautiously lowered their weapons. She cracked a smile as Namir and Chalis stopped a few meters away.

"You made it," Brand said.

CHAPTER 23

PLANET ANKHURAL
Five Days Before Operation Ringbreaker

A few dozen soldiers had erected a tent city around the prow of the *Thunderstrike,* preferring to sleep in the dry and dusty open air over the bustling interior of the vessel. Namir didn't blame them; the ship echoed day and night with the sounds of sparks and welding torches, and the klaxon blared intermittently for reasons no one could determine. Outside there was at least a semblance of calm.

But while the troops spoke quietly, ate food scrounged from Ankhural cantinas, and cleaned their weapons in the evening glow, it wasn't a sense of *calm* they gave off. Namir watched them as he strolled down the orderly rows, saw them avert their gazes as he walked by. Shoulders tensed as a distant scream sounded from the city. They weren't calm. They were dejected, nursing a grief sure to curdle into bitterness.

Namir didn't blame them for that, either.

"How're you feeling?"

Roach was picking her way among strewn bedrolls and camp heaters at Namir's side. She wore a torn strip of cloth around her neck, ready to mask her face if the dust kicked up.

"Better," he said. "Hydrated. I needed the rest, but Von Geiz cleared me for duty."

Roach glanced over her shoulder, then back to Namir. "Good," she murmured. "Sorry we broke the ship."

Namir barked a laugh. His smile wilted almost immediately. *Sorry I lost the captain* was the only rejoinder that came to mind, and it seemed best left unsaid.

He looked Roach over, tried to guess why she'd come to him. A month earlier, he might have worried she'd be tempted by Ankhural's vices, or suspected she'd seen or done something traumatic during the attack on the *Thunderstrike*. But at some point, unremarked, Roach had become a Twilight soldier instead of fresh meat. She was part of the unit, as comfortable as anyone, and if she needed moral support she could turn to Gadren or Charmer or a dozen others in the company.

Which meant there was something she needed the first sergeant for.

Roach wiped her hands on her trousers, cast another glance over her shoulder, and said, "Some of the guys are talking about leaving."

Namir grunted, gave a curt nod. "Who?" he asked.

"Corbo," Roach said, "and the other Haidoral meat. Plus some of Fektrin's old squad." She hesitated again. "They still want to *fight*. Just—"

"They don't want to sit around waiting to get bombed," Namir said. "I'll handle it."

They continued walking together as Namir made his rounds and watched the tents. Even he wasn't sure what he was watching for. He knew exactly what the troops were feeling.

He didn't mind Roach's company. At least she didn't blame him for bearing news of Twilight's doom.

Howl was dead. The secret base of the Rebel Alliance was in ruins. High Command had fled to parts unknown. There were no new orders for Twilight Company, no grand plans to take back the Mid Rim and push onward to victory. All dreams had been crushed beneath the footpads of Imperial walkers.

It wasn't the news Namir had wanted to bring. Not when he'd left Hoth, and not when he'd found nothing but debris and a hollowed-out freighter drifting through space at the flotilla's rendezvous point. He hadn't let himself fear, then—he'd drawn on the numbness he'd felt on Hoth and reminded himself that Twilight Company *always* survived its battles. No matter how dear the losses, no matter how bloody the fight or how bad the defeat, it *survived.*

He'd focused on searching for anyone who was left. He owed them that.

He'd remembered the datachip Brand had handed him "in case of emergency" and followed its coordinates to Ankhural, a pirate backwater beyond the edge of Imperial space. He'd allowed a spark of hope to damage his numbness, imagined finding the *Thunderstrike* maimed but Twilight Company intact and determined to move on.

Instead he'd found a unit barely surviving on the dream of its captain's return.

At a glance, the men and women of Twilight seemed as numerous as ever. By its losses alone, the company had seen worse days; this wasn't the massacre at Asyrphus or the decimation on Magnus Horn. The casualties taken during the battle at the flotilla had been a blow, but not a crippling one, and the *Thunderstrike* could be repaired. But without Howl or Lieutenant Sairgon, with Commander Paonu and the rest of *Thunderstrike*'s bridge crew dead, the company had been decapitated—not a single ranking officer with command experience was left. The seniormost squad leaders and support staff had taken collective charge in the meantime, but stanching a bleeding neck was little use when the head was gone.

Now Namir had the dubious privilege of meeting with Hober and

Von Geiz and his fellow senior officers every morning in the conference room, reading the engineers' daily updates and Hober's supply requisitions and pretending they did it all for a reason.

He brought up what Roach had told him about desertions at the next meeting. Only Von Geiz and Carver seemed genuinely surprised, though Mzun—who'd stepped in to lead Fektrin's squad—let out a series of alien babblings that might have been outrage.

"We'll split them up, assign them to separate repair crews for a bit. See if that cools things down," Namir said. "And Corbo owes me a favor, so I can call that in. I just thought everyone should know this is where we stand."

"I will speak to them," Gadren said. He wasn't a squad leader, but he had experience and Von Geiz—who was technically the highest-ranking officer still alive—liked him. No one opposed his presence under the circumstances.

Namir forced a tight smile. "You're very good at speeches, but you'll just remind them who you're not. Unless you can solve that—"

"We can start with a funeral," Hober said. "It's past time."

Von Geiz nodded. Gadren bowed his head. Mzun said something Namir couldn't understand.

Namir looked impatiently at the others, waiting for someone to translate. No one did.

"We hold a funeral, every work crew we've got will want to be there. I'd say hold off until repairs are done," Namir said. Then he laughed bitterly and leaned back in his seat. "But I'm guessing I'm outvoted."

When Namir had returned from Hoth to find the flotilla missing, Chalis hadn't argued with his decision to search for survivors. She hadn't spoken at all after leaving the ice planet, despite the gradual fading of the bruise on her throat.

Her encounter with Darth Vader had left deeper wounds. Namir had seen troops cope with shell shock and trauma before, yet he had no warmth or patience to spare for the governor. His numbness was too valuable to lose. So he had let her sleep and sit alone. They had split a ration pack once a day from their swiftly dwindling stash. She had stayed out of the way, which was enough for Namir.

On Ankhural, he found her alone in the medbay an hour before Howl's funeral. Her neck was blotched with green and yellow and her hair looked caked with dust. She was extracting a long feeding tube from her mouth when Namir entered; it seemed rude to observe, as if he were interrupting something deeply private, but she didn't pause or acknowledge him.

When she'd hung the tube back at its station, Chalis looked at Namir from her seat on an exam table and waited.

"Howl's funeral is tonight," Namir said. "I thought you should know."

Chalis nodded but said nothing.

That rankled Namir, though it took him long moments to reason *why*. Chalis was only alive because Howl had taken her in. Chalis was still with Twilight because she'd tried to rescue Howl on Hoth instead of fleeing.

Namir didn't know what she really thought of the man. He didn't particularly care. But she had to be reacting, deep inside her head. She'd bound herself to Howl too tightly to shrug off his passing. And Namir deserved to see her response—he'd saved her life more than once, and he was tired of being ignored.

When it became clear she had no intention of answering, he chose a different tack. "He's not here to protect you anymore," he said.

At this, Chalis tilted her head slightly.

"Find a way to contribute," Namir said. "We need every hand we can get."

Chalis closed her eyes as if she hadn't heard and pressed a fingertip to her throat, tracing the bruise. Namir scowled at her and scraped his boot against the sterilized white floor. He was turning away when she finally spoke.

"Prelate Verge," Chalis said. Her voice was no longer the sickly rasp it had been on Hoth, but she sounded like a dying woman all the same.

Namir turned the name over in his head. Brand had mentioned it—the man who'd led the attack on *Thunderstrike* at the flotilla.

"What about him?"

"He's a child. A protocol droid fawns less on its master." Flecks of spittle flew from her lips as she forced the words out. She withdrew a handkerchief from her pocket, wiped the droplets off her knees.

Namir's irritation receded, replaced by bemusement. "So?" The battle at the flotilla was long since over. The enemy commander was the least of anyone's concerns.

"Why was a pathetic boy attacking Twilight," she said, "when Darth Vader was on Hoth?" Her eyes focused on Namir, a stern and deathly stare.

He didn't have an answer. He didn't even understand the question. Eventually, Chalis let out a long breath and lay back on the exam table. Namir stalked out of the medbay and decided to grapple with the problem of the governor another time.

"To 'Howling Mad' Micha Evon, first and only captain of Twilight Company and the best damn commander in the Alliance. The Empire is a safer place without him."

It was Charmer's toast, drawn-out and stilted but without a stutter. Namir raised his mug of steaming crimson fluid alongside Gadren, Brand, Twitch, and Nemenov—one of the X-wing pilots on leave from *Apailana's Promise,* making a rare appearance among Twilight's soldiers. Roach had volunteered to stay at the *Thunderstrike* on sentry duty. Another table of company troops sat just across the aisle in the roasting orange light of the Ankhural cantina, shouting their own toasts and stories of past battles.

"We'll make him proud," Brand said softly. The group drank together. Namir winced at the too-sweet, chemically fruity taste of the wine.

The funeral had been simple, in the Twilight Company tradition. In an effort to bolster morale, Namir and the other senior officers had agreed to allow squads out afterward on limited leave. It couldn't make things any worse, Namir supposed, and he had to admit it felt like some normalcy had returned. He was in the Clubhouse again, watching Ajax cheat at cards; he was on Vanzeist, celebrating a win against the Imperials with the locals.

"Came up to me on Bamayar," Twitch said into her drink. Gadren and Charmer leaned forward to listen. "After we took that stinking port—"

"Chenodra," Brand said.

Twitch shrugged. "Chenodra. Came up to me during the cleanup. Thought I'd messed up bad, with what Ajax and me had done. Howl started talking about the *buildings* instead—something about the arches and columns. Like I cared? Guy was a freak."

"There was no subject outside his interests," Gadren said. "Fektrin believed Howl had been a teacher before the war. It would explain much."

"Sairgon knew who he used to be," Brand said. "They were close."

Namir rotated his mug and smirked bitterly. "But Sairgon's gone, too, so the mystery remains. Howl dies a legend."

"We knew his heart," Gadren said, "and his passions. Was he really so mysterious?"

Namir shrugged. "Doesn't matter. Where I come from, *anyone* with the gall to lead an army dies a legend. It's the last thing you can give."

"I don't follow," Nemenov said.

The others shifted uncomfortably. It wasn't the right topic for the night, Namir knew. He blamed the drink for his rudeness and didn't stop talking. "It's a lot easier," he said, "to fight over a legend than it is over politics or religion. You don't even need to *pretend* to think things through. You die a legend, your followers are set with an excuse to keep warring for generations."

Gadren's tone was patient and conciliatory. "Then we must take pains to remember Howl as a man, not a myth, and avoid such a trap."

The others nodded tensely, all eyes on Namir. He forced himself to smile and conceded the point with a small, dismissive gesture. He hadn't come to the cantina to argue.

The conversation moved on. Between fresh rounds of drinks and filthy jokes from Twitch and Charmer's gentle goading of Nemenov, the group told stories of Howl and Twilight Company. Brand reminisced about the open recruit on Demiloch, when Howl had been shot by an Imperial spy pretending to be fresh meat; when he'd woken up two days later, he'd been incensed to learn that Sairgon had called an early end to the recruitment drive. Charmer spoke of the dark days after the company's losses on Magnus Horn, when the Alliance had tried to reassign the survivors to other infantry units; Howl had fought to keep his troops together and saved the company from obliteration.

Late in the evening, after Namir had bribed the bartender into ignoring the shattered mugs and broken chair at the second Twilight table, the mourners began to drift back to the *Thunderstrike* in twos and threes. Even tipsy, no one was stupid enough to make the trip alone. Eventually, Gadren and Namir were the only ones left.

"I never liked him, you know," Namir said.

"I know," Gadren replied. His skin looked like embers in the angry cantina light.

"I still can't picture a Twilight Company without him."

Gadren nodded slowly and folded two hands together. A low trilling sound came from his throat, as if he were holding back words that struggled valiantly to escape. "There is truth to what you said about legends," he finally admitted. "It is easier to fight when a symbol is close at hand.

"We are all dedicated to the struggle against the Empire. I doubt no one's bravery, nor anyone's understanding of the profound evil our age confronts. But Howl focused our hopes, and if Twilight is to endure . . . it needs that focus. A dream. A *goal*."

"Or something," Namir said.

"Or something," Gadren agreed.

"Right now," Namir said, "we've barely got a ship."

Gadren laughed, as if that concerned him not at all. "The captain," he said, "never worried about strength of numbers or equipment. He believed so long as he acted according to his tenets, Twilight could not be killed."

"He was a zealot," Namir said.

"*No*," Gadren replied, and the word came out with forceful resolve. "He was a man of reason. But I cannot explain him, either."

"Then I don't suppose it matters," Namir said, and finished the last of his drink. "Crazed zealot or inscrutable genius, we still don't have a future without him."

Namir had the cabin to himself that night. Roja was dead, and his other bunk mates had chosen to sleep outside. Without the sound of his colleagues' breathing, the total darkness felt desolate. Like a tomb.

Like a collapsed tunnel on Hoth.

Half dreaming, Namir saw the armored figure in black murdering his comrades with a beam of light. He saw Chalis rise into the air untouched, heard the cartilage in her neck crackling like leaves.

Was that why the others fought? Was that the "profound evil" Gadren insisted threatened everything that existed? Utter depravity backed by inexorable might; an endless shadow passing over all the stars, shaped like a Galactic Empire. Darth Vader was only its leading edge.

Nothing in Namir was eager to confront that darkness again. But he was starting to understand why the men and women of Twilight Company wouldn't turn aside when confronted with the hopelessness of their cause.

His thoughts drifted, bobbing on the sea of putrid wine he'd consumed. He remembered Chalis mocking the Rebellion's fears of total desolation, and his days with the Creed—the first time he'd come to see his fellow soldiers as family. He remembered the last time he'd drunk heavily, with the rebel freighter captain on Hoth.

He'd made a promise to himself that night: *If you can't get behind what they believe in, maybe it's time to walk away.*

They deserved better.

He loved them all. Gadren and Brand, Charmer and Roach, Twitch and Hober. Roja and Beak. The comm tech Twilight had never replaced. Pira.

He couldn't turn aside, either. He couldn't abandon them when they were bleeding in the dust of a planet like Ankhural.

By the morning, Namir's head felt no clearer, but he was certain he had to act. He had to find the goal Gadren had spoken of, find Twilight hope in the wake of Howl's death. Give the company a means to fight the Empire.

He had no idea how.

CHAPTER 24

ELOCHAR SECTOR
Nine Days Before Operation Ringbreaker

Prelate Verge had devised the punishment himself. The crew members who had failed him against the *Thunderstrike*—the gunner who'd targeted the vessel too slowly; the scan officer who'd failed to anticipate the enemy's jump to lightspeed; the Special Forces commander who'd assembled the infiltration team—would be used as calibration subjects for the interrogator droids until they confessed every act of disloyalty they'd ever committed.

In the week since the attack, only the gunner had been released. The scan officer was dead. The Special Forces commander still screamed.

Captain Tabor Seitaron did not dispute that punishment was necessary. Mistakes *had* occurred, and Governor Chalis, by all rights, should have been the one suffering under the droids' apparatus. Tabor should have been home again, rolling his eyes at some cadet's plagiarized essay on the Battle of Christophsis.

But Verge's proclivity for gruesome torment would only instill more fear in his crew. Fear was like heat applied to steel: Applied correctly it might forge a blade; overused, it turned metal to slag.

"We are men of different eras," the prelate said after breakfasting with Tabor outside the interrogation chambers. As they walked away, Tabor could still hear the commander's screams. "You helped build the machine that is the Empire. You oiled its mechanisms, turned its wheels—you created order, and I commend you for that."

"We did our duty," Tabor said, "and tried to rise to the Emperor's challenge."

Since his assignment to the *Herald,* Tabor had found himself—to his own surprise, and against his better judgment—beginning to enjoy the prelate's company. The boy's enthusiasm for expounding on his own ideas, his desire to uplift those around him into his strange world, was surprisingly infectious. His familiarity and sincerity, his curiosity about Tabor, were similarly alluring—even Tabor's most capable students had seemed more concerned with career advancement than with grappling with new ideas. Verge had already climbed higher than Tabor ever would, and yet he remained eager to unlock his own potential.

But there were limits to Tabor's tolerance, and after a morning spent watching unspeakable acts while trying to digest pickled eggs and dumplings, his interest in conversing with Verge was at its nadir.

"Nonetheless," the prelate said, "the machine was built. And—this is important, Captain—I believe that machine is why we don't always see eye-to-eye."

"Have we disagreed in some important matter?" Tabor asked, letting a hint of surprise into his tone.

"We have not," the prelate answered, "but I know you're not fond of my choice of disciplinary measures. You see more *efficient* ways to maintain the machine."

Tabor focused his attention on Prelate Verge and squared his shoulders. This was not a time to be inattentive or sloppy; whatever relationship he'd built with Verge, he never forgot to be wary of the boy's ire.

"I have my own habits, certainly," Tabor conceded. "But this is your ship, and every leader commands his troops in his own way."

The prelate's lips twitched: a sure sign of growing impatience. "You're not comprehending, Captain. I *acknowledge* your ways may be more effective in making the machine of the Empire run smoothly.

"But the machine is already built," he went on. "The Emperor has constructed a new society, a new way of living. My duty is not to lay its foundation, but to live as our Emperor commands—as a member of the civilization that you so deftly engineered." Verge frowned a moment and drew to a halt in the corridor. "What does the Emperor demand of each of us, Captain?"

Was the question a trap? Tabor wondered. But he chose not to second-guess himself. He would not, could not try to predict the prelate. "Our loyalty and obedience," Tabor answered.

"*Total* loyalty," Verge echoed, "and *total* obedience. That is correct." The prelate smiled as he continued, turning to face Tabor in full. "In exchange, our Emperor rewards us with the privilege of extravagant actions empowered by our most puissant emotions. You were taught restraint, while I have learned the virtue of excess.

"For so long as our loyalty and obedience are absolute, our excesses can do no harm to our master. My generation will be glorious slaves, Captain, and while Lord Vader believes himself the Emperor's first acolyte, I believe I am the first true child of the Empire."

The words were proud to the point of arrogance. But there was a tremor in the prelate's voice, and his smile looked stiff and forced.

"Then you believe," Tabor said, wondering if his neglect for caution would be his downfall, "that so long as we're fully loyal, failure is impossible?"

"I do," Verge said. "Thus, any whim may be fulfilled, so long as we are true to our Emperor."

And any mistake, Tabor thought, *is tantamount to treason.*

Tabor realized suddenly that the boy was terrified.

He forced himself to show no reaction. Instead he attempted to reassure the boy the only way he could conceive. "Then let us endeavor to remain true," Tabor said, "by ensuring the capture of Governor Chalis."

Verge pivoted and began to walk again, nodding briskly. "Of course," he said. "Her ship is now in hiding. We won't track it again, I think."

"Then we determine her next move," Tabor replied. "Darth Vader and his forces scattered Alliance High Command. That means she's isolated now. What would she do on her own?"

"What indeed?" Verge said. "We'll talk, Captain. We'll study her options, and we'll assemble a plan." He slowed his pace and reached out to touch Tabor's arm.

Tabor turned to look at the boy.

"This last failure," Verge said, the tremor in his voice returning for a fraction of a second, "was the fault of our crew, and they have been justly punished.

"But there must not be a *second* failure."

In that, Tabor thought, they were in agreement.

CHAPTER 25

PLANET ANKHURAL
Three Days Before Operation Ringbreaker

The *Thunderstrike*'s communications array had melted in the attack on the flotilla. *Apailana's Promise* wasn't equipped for interstellar encryption. So Namir and Brand spent most of the morning combing through cramped shops and junkyards, searching for a dealer who would sell them the parts they needed to make contact with whatever was left of Alliance High Command.

They didn't find anyone willing. Ignoring Twilight Company was one thing; the citizens of Ankhural seemed happy to turn a blind eye, particularly when a few credits were in the mix. But no one wanted to get *involved*, and Twilight's engineers had already reported difficulty obtaining wires and tubing and scrap metal. Illegal transmitters and code sequencers were a step too far.

By noon, Namir and Brand had silently agreed to make do with someone *unwilling.* In a curio shop where animal tusks and vials of silver fluid were piled alongside datapads and retinal spiders, Brand whispered something into the proprietor's ear while Namir held a scalpel-flourishing droid at gunpoint. The proprietor disappeared into the back before returning with a box of metal devices marked with the Imperial crest. He shouted something in an alien language as the two left the shop, the box safely nestled under Namir's left arm.

"What did you say?" Namir asked.

"Something that will only work once," Brand said, glancing over her shoulder as she led the way through the city's back alleys.

It was more of an answer than Namir had expected. He decided to press his luck. "What did *he* say?" he asked.

"He thought we were a couple," Brand said.

Namir laughed until Brand cast him an irritated look. His joy faded, however, as they approached the podracing track, and the fears and burdens that had claimed him the night before enveloped him like a shroud.

He still had no idea how to give Twilight Company what it needed.

Once the communications rig was in place, getting a response was a matter of patience and prayer. The *Thunderstrike* sent three messages to three separate Alliance relay stations, hoping one would be routed to a ship or a base that hadn't been destroyed. That in itself was a risk—if the Empire had located the relays, there was a chance the messages could be traced. Namir didn't understand the mechanics, but he trusted the word of the surviving bridge crew; ensigns or not, they were still Alliance navy, and that meant they'd read operating manuals for equipment with names Namir couldn't even pronounce.

The senior officers traded comm duty for the rest of the day and into the night—any channel opened to the Alliance wasn't likely to stay open long, and someone from Twilight had to be ready to seize any opportunity for communication, however brief. Namir had come to relieve Von Geiz early in the morning when he arrived in Howl's office and saw the old doctor staring at a shimmering blue hologram.

"—most of High Command survived, but the fleet is scattered and the Empire is hunting strays." The image pixilated, turned to static, reassembled into the upper body of a non-uniformed boy younger than Namir. His words were difficult to pick out; a droid would have sounded more human. "I can't guess when they'll reassemble."

Von Geiz nodded slowly. "And the princess?" he asked.

There was a long delay before the boy answered. Namir couldn't tell whether the cause was human or technical. "Gone missing. We know she's alive—the Empire's committed massive resources to finding her—but that's all."

Von Geiz nodded again and looked to Namir. Namir gestured to the medic, prompting him to proceed.

"Is there *anyone*," Von Geiz asked, "with command authority who we can reach? Or a general order for surviving ships?"

Again, the delay.

"Not that I'm aware of," the boy finally said. "I'm sorry, *Thunderstrike*. Good luck."

The hologram blinked out. Von Geiz spoke softly, watching the air above the projector as if he expected the call to resume. "As we surmised, we're on our own."

Namir leaned against the wall in the cramped room and folded his arms across his chest. "Howl trusted you," he said. "What would he do now?"

Von Geiz laughed. "Something only Howl could do, I'm sure," he said. "Better to ask ourselves this: What can we do *without* him?"

Namir steeled himself before the door to Howl's quarters. He knew what he would find inside and he knew he needed to stay calm. But when he tried to picture the exchanges and arguments that might ensue, tried to ready himself for unpleasantness, his mind found no purchase and slid into the gray void that had haunted him since Hoth. He was too exhausted to predict anything.

To hell with preparation and speeches. He tapped the keypad and stepped through the doorway.

The room wasn't luxurious, even by Twilight standards. It was barely larger than the captain's office, with a bunk spanning its length and a trunk and a small desk dominating two walls. The private, closet-sized bathroom was its only concession to the privileges of rank. Its decorations were spartan; Namir suspected Hober had cleared out Howl's belongings before the funeral.

Seated on the bunk was Everi Chalis. She looked small, huddled over a datapad with her head bowed low and her knees together. Her finger rapidly danced across the pad's screen. When Namir stepped forward, he caught a glimpse of a face taking shape under her hand.

"New art project?" he asked.

Chalis tapped the screen again and erased the sketch. As she looked up, Namir saw that the bruise on her neck had nearly vanished.

"Just an exercise," she said. Her voice was hoarse, but not unnatural.

Namir wondered if that was as close as she would come to healing. Then he banished the question from his mind. It didn't matter.

"I need your advice," he said.

Chalis looked back down at the blank screen and began sketching again.

"You told me," Namir said, "that all you really wanted was comfort, respect, and a place to sculpt. You said you'd overthrow the Empire to get your life back." He felt an urge to snatch the datapad from her hands, but he suppressed it. "I don't see how any of that has changed. You're still stuck with Twilight Company. Even if you were free, my guess is the people of Ankhural would sell you to the Empire in an eyeblink."

Chalis said nothing. Her body was too low over the datapad for Namir to observe her linework.

"You know the Empire better than anyone here," he said, forcing his voice not to shake with irritation. "High Command is out of the picture. Without a plan, we're all dead."

"Are you a true believer now, too?" Chalis asked. Namir had to strain to hear her.

"No," Namir said. "But I'm not abandoning Twilight, either."

Chalis made a soft, noncommittal sound.

Namir waited. He studied the woman before him, tried to remember if she had always been so gaunt: if her shoulder blades and cheekbones had always been so prominent; if the white streaks in her hair had stood out so brightly on Haidoral Prime. He watched the muscles in her arm twitch like those of a dying animal as she moved her fingers over the pad. He tried not to wonder what was happening in her mind.

He knew her too well to believe he could sway her.

As he turned to leave, however, she spoke again.

"I grew up like you did," Chalis said, though she didn't look up. "Not on your particular colonial disaster, but close enough."

"Crucival," Namir said. "It was called Crucival."

Chalis didn't seem to hear him. "We had *nothing*," she said. "My mother tried to sell me to a Trade Federation exploratory vessel when I was six. I was too small. Out of pity, the captain gave me a packet of nectrose crystals.

"Imagine this little girl who sleeps on her mother's stained mattress in the ruins of a bombed-out paper mill. Nectrose—you're supposed to sprinkle it in water—it makes things sweet and fruity, but I didn't know that.

"I didn't have fresh water. I'd stick my fingers in the crystals and lick them off. I rationed them, gave myself a treat once a week for *months*. I broke out in hives every time. It was the most wonderful thing I'd ever encountered.

"That was how I knew I had to leave my world. It was how I realized I was living in filth, eating garbage and drinking poison, when off-worlders were so rich they could throw nectrose packets to children."

Something had changed in Chalis's voice. It took Namir time to recognize it beneath the rasp, but her accent had changed. Once again, the strange overenunciation was gone, and the way she spoke was suddenly familiar.

She almost sounded like she was from Crucival.

"I got into the Colonial Academy. *How* isn't important. I trained as an artist. I made it offworld and found I was still the lowest of the low, a pretty savage rich sponsors put to work as a novelty. Under the Republic, I had nowhere to go. I could scrabble and claw against the sides of the pit until my hands bled and never climb out.

"When the Empire rose, it wasn't kind to me. But it rewarded success. Count Vidian saw some . . . quality in my sculpture. An ability to visualize concepts in a way he couldn't. He offered me an apprenticeship and my art fell to the wayside.

"I did horrible things, Sergeant. I proposed mining the atmosphere of an inhabited planet, leaving its people wheezing the rest of their lives. I found ways to make slavery efficient again. I told a moff I loved him and slit his throat as a favor to another.

"But I thought it was *worth* it. I climbed to the top of the hierarchy by being a damn good adviser. I earned the respect of men who thought generations of 'good breeding' was the key to success."

Her tone had become bitter, and specks of spittle dotted the front of her datapad. Her shoulders rose and fell even before she began coughing. What started as a dry rasp became wet and mucosal, like the heaves of a woman rotting on the inside.

Namir merely watched, waited. He felt neither sympathy nor pity.

Finally the coughing subsided. A few moments later, Chalis resumed. "Now I know the truth," she said. For the second time since he'd entered the room, she looked up at Namir.

"The truth?" he asked.

"I never had respect," Chalis said. "The moffs never considered me an equal. Darth Vader never considered me a threat. The Emperor sent *Prelate Verge*—a brainless sycophant—after me while Vader was . . ." She waved a hand dismissively. ". . . chasing rebels.

"The Ruling Council never saw me as anything but a runt of a sculptor from a backwater planet. I gave up everything to defect and they barely even cared."

Namir felt heat prickle beneath the skin of his forehead. The words drew forth something he'd thought he had left behind on the journey to Hoth: a frustrated, fitful anger at Chalis for the curse she'd brought onto Twilight Company. The curse *he* had brought onto Twilight Company by not killing her on Haidoral Prime.

"Lieutenant Sairgon and the others," he said, voice low and steady, "are dead because of how *little* the Empire cared about you. So are Fektrin and Ajax—but you don't know their names, do you?"

She was still looking at him. Namir stepped forward and knelt in front of the governor, placing himself level with her. Her eyes were bloodshot, her pupils dilated.

"You owe this company," he said, "and you owe me. Stop pitying yourself and help me save these people."

"I gave the Rebellion everything I had on Hoth," Chalis said. She looked back at her screen. Squatting so close to her, Namir could see the rough image of a wide-eyed, bearded man who might have been Howl. "My debts are paid."

When she said nothing else, Namir stood and exited the room. His mouth was suddenly dry and his heart was beating rapidly.

Now he had nothing left to hope for.

The fight was over by the time Namir got word. Twitch was covered in other people's blood, while Jinsol had a broken nose and Maediyu had come back to the podracing track holding the skin of her cheek in place with one hand.

"It could have been random," Brand said. "One of the lower-level gangs looking to score cheap blasters, maybe hold our people for ransom."

Namir had found her standing on the top tier of the amphitheater, looking out into the city. "But you don't believe it."

Brand shrugged. "I think it's a message," she said. "I think the real powers in Ankhural want us out."

"And who are those *real* powers?"

"Does it matter?" Brand asked.

"Probably not," Namir said. "Besides, the ship's about ready for takeoff. There's still work that has to happen, but we can handle it during flight."

"Assuming we have somewhere to go."

Namir flinched at the statement, though Brand's tone was unassuming.

"Tomorrow morning," Namir said. "Senior staff meeting. We'll figure something out."

Brand's head tilted slightly as she tracked some distant movement in the streets. Whatever she was watching, Namir couldn't see it. Maybe she just didn't want to show her skepticism.

"No one would object if you showed up," he went on. "You've earned a lot of leeway—"

"No," Brand said.

"No?"

"I'm not a captain," Brand said. She was absolutely still, like a gargoyle atop the amphitheater. Then she broke the spell and faced Namir. "I'm not even a soldier."

"Meaning?" He heard the irritation in his voice, tried too late to conceal it.

"Meaning if there's a better way to fight the Empire, I'll take it."

Namir swore and kicked at one of the steps. "You really need to say that out loud? I know what happens to this company if we don't come up with a plan—I don't need you threatening to walk, too."

Brand's fists flexed, her fingers curling in and out. Finally she nodded. "Sorry," she said, and began to descend.

Namir grunted and followed along. "We'll figure something out," he repeated softly.

When they reached the podracing track, Brand turned toward the gates first, then back to touch Namir's shoulder. "I'm glad you found us," she said. "We all are. Most of the fresh meat would be rotten by now without you."

"Don't worry about it." Namir shook his head and smiled tightly. "You heading into the city?"

"Hunting," Brand said. "Don't tell Twitch I finished a fight for her."

Namir spent the night cursing everything he didn't know.

On Crucival, he'd known the factions, known the landscape, known that defending a hill was easier than defending a cornfield. He'd been able to recognize when a battle became hopeless and known how to run or surrender to keep his unit alive.

What did he know about fighting a galactic war? The Rebellion's strategy had always been a mystery to him, and that hadn't mattered. His job was to win planets on the ground, to slog through mud and creep through the night and terrorize the enemy.

There was no rebel territory to hold. Those few planets that had fully committed to the Alliance were cordoned behind Imperial blockades, inaccessible to the *Thunderstrike*. Hitting soft targets—lightly guarded Imperial worlds that Twilight could descend upon, devastate, and flee—was almost viable; but without a strategic goal, the company would hemorrhage deserters. Not to mention the actual casualties.

Even a lie seemed impossible. Namir imagined choosing a planet—any planet—and committing to its conquest. But Twilight Company was mobile for a reason; if it ever lingered, ever became a permanent threat, the Empire could bring massive firepower to bear and annihilate the unit.

Every goal he concocted was a phantom, fading at a touch.

He ate breakfast—rehydrated powdered eggs imported to Ankhural and purchased in bulk by one of Hober's assistants—an hour before sunup after a sleepless night. As he walked the perimeter of the *Thunderstrike*, it occurred to him he had forgotten to shave—but he saw no use in hiding his exhaustion. He surveyed the strange tent city and waved to the sentries. He thought he saw Brand trekking in from the gates and wondered if she'd found her prey.

He sat in the amphitheater seats watching the dawn of a foreign sun. He wondered if he could convince Brand to take him along, if she left.

Not that he would go. He *couldn't* go. Not when the company needed him so badly. His promise—*if you can't get behind what they believe in, maybe it's time to walk away*—still held, and he'd chosen to back his friends.

However disastrously it turned out.

He was already late for the senior staff meeting by the time he reboarded the *Thunderstrike*. He resigned himself to a morning of bitter debate and pointless arguments, and hoped that another mind would prevail where his had so badly let him down.

When he arrived in the conference room, what he saw made him freeze in the doorway.

The senior officers of the company sat around the table or stood along the walls, as usual. But while they spoke to one another in low tones, all of them were oriented toward the far end of the table—toward Howl's place.

There, Everi Chalis stood with a datapad, keying instructions into a floating holo-droid that hovered over the table. She looked entirely unlike the woman Namir had seen the previous day. She was straight-backed and certain, the bruise on her throat totally invisible—cosmetically concealed, he presumed. Even her hair was different, cropped close around her head in a fashion the Imperial military might have approved of. Only her exhaustion remained unchanged—the gauntness of her cheeks and the redness in her eyes.

She looked away from the 'pad and the droid, across the room to Namir, and she smiled.

"We're all here," she said. "We may as well start."

Chalis's voice was rough, and she paused often as she spoke. Sometimes she turned away from the table entirely, and her shoulders shook and heaved. But except for those brief signs of infirmity, she seemed utterly in control of herself and the room. She never stumbled. She locked gazes with any officer who seemed ready to turn away, smiled with the self-effacing certainty of a rebel determined to overthrow a mighty empire.

"This is the Alliance's moment of weakness," she began. "The Emperor intends to deliver the killing blow at last, hunting down the scattered members of Alliance High Command as they flee deep into the galaxy's Outer Rim.

"But in the Emperor's would-be triumph, there is also an opportunity. High Command and the rebel flagships are dispersed, not destroyed. Princess Leia Organa is the target of an unprecedented manhunt."

For a moment, Chalis's lips froze into a smile. Namir recognized the bitterness he'd seen the previous day. Then it vanished and she continued. "Emperor Palpatine, the moffs, Darth Vader—they've done what they do best, deploying overwhelming force to scour the Outer Rim of their enemies. And to cover those vast territories, they've moved whole fleets out of position. For the first time in years, the Core Worlds' defenses are enervated."

There were murmurs about the room. Carver spoke up, openly skeptical. "How do you know?"

Chalis flicked her hand dismissively. "I was at Hoth," she said. "I recognized the ships they brought to bear. I've also been monitoring whatever unsecured broadcasts make it to this sandpit, and—most important—I know what resources the Empire has and what it doesn't. Pulling fleets from active war zones or the Mid Rim border is too risky. Drawing from the Core Worlds for Vader's operation just makes sense."

To Namir's surprise, she waited for a counterargument. Carver offered none, and she continued.

"This vulnerability," she said, "isn't a license for conquest. If we try to strike at the Imperial Palace on Coruscant, we'll be obliterated before the drop ships hit atmosphere. But I know how the Imperial war machine functions. I want to make its gears grind and shatter."

She snapped her fingers. The holo-droid bobbed over the table and its projectors flared, generating the image of a planet Namir failed to recognize. The planet appeared ordinary enough, covered in clouds and water and land; it might have been any of a hundred worlds Namir had visited already, except for the single ring that circled its equator.

Were terrestrial planets supposed to have rings? Namir tried to remember what Gadren had taught him.

"This is the planet Kuat," Chalis said. "Its shipyards are the primary source of the Empire's Star Destroyer fleet. I propose we destroy them."

The holographic image flickered and resolved on a magnified portion of the ring. Up close, it appeared to be an immense scaffold in space, bridged and augmented by enormous habitats bristling with machinery. Inside the scaffold, like prisoners caged and left for dead, were the skeletons of wedge-shaped ships, their metal skin only half covering their bodies. Tiny bright dots drifted to and from the skeletons, alighting on the ships or returning to the habitats.

"If we succeed," Chalis went on, "our attack will cripple the Empire's fleet-building capacity and deny repairs and upkeep to current vessels. Star Destroyers may be nearly indestructible, but they're the most resource-intensive ships this galaxy has ever seen. Kuat possesses the *only* shipyards capable of supporting and maintaining more than a handful at a time.

"Furthermore, stopping the production and repair of Star Destroyers will inhibit the Empire's capacity for fast infantry deployment. No longer would one ship be able to carry thousands of stormtroopers and a full squadron of armored transport walkers. The Empire's strategy for planetary containment would need to shift."

Namir watched the senior staff. Some were checking their datapads, taking notes or cross-referencing data. Others watched Chalis or the hologram. Von Geiz spoke up. "The Alliance tried to attack Kuat before," he said. "We're only two ships . . ."

"Kuat's defenses are oriented toward space combat," Chalis said smoothly, as if she'd been expecting the question. "We're an infantry company, and no one's ever tried a ground invasion of the shipyards." She snapped again, and the hologram magnified further, showing tram tracks and enclosures against the backdrop of space. "The orbital ring has a total inhabitable area of less than three hundred thousand square kilometers—smaller than a typical planetary subnation, and susceptible to unique forms of attack. Imagine urban warfare in a city where you could sever whole blocks from the mainland at the touch of a button; where any damage to the infrastructure was a blow to the enemy. Yes, it will be bloody—but I believe Twilight can succeed."

Namir sensed a wave of discomfort in the room, though no one argued openly. He tried to picture what Chalis was proposing and found it meant nothing to him. Even the numbers were beyond his comprehension.

"All that said," she went on, "the Kuat star system's space-based defenses are formidable, even with fleet elements diverted to the Outer Rim. We need to soften them further in order to safeguard the *Thunderstrike*'s passage to the shipyards."

The droid's projection changed to a star map. From a point near the bottom, a line zigzagged toward an upper dot Namir could only assume represented Kuat.

"To that end," Chalis said, "we must take an indirect path to Kuat and strike these designated targets. No sieges, no prolonged attacks— these are surgical strikes against logistical hubs. We destroy these, and the Empire *must* react by reassigning ships and officers—either to repair the damage or to compensate by bolstering efficiency elsewhere. Directly or indirectly, these reassignments will cannibalize Kuat's own defenses."

"You can't possibly know that, either." Carver again, voice steady despite his confrontational tone.

"I understand the flow of resources within the Empire better than anyone alive," Chalis said. "It's why Captain Evon accepted me. It's why Alliance High Command needed me. I *absolutely* know it."

She gestured at the droid and the hologram flickered out. The conference room seemed dark without the azure glow. "Sergeant Namir and I have been discussing this plan since we fled Hoth," she said. "It will be risky. We'll need to move fast, both on the ground and in space, just to give ourselves a fighting chance. We'll need to maintain operational secrecy so that the Empire doesn't anticipate our true goal. And once we reach Kuat, everything could go wrong—I can't predict the future. But if you want to turn this war around, I believe this is our best chance."

She didn't look at Namir when she said his name. It came out so casually he might have missed it if not for the others glancing toward him. He knew if he didn't deny his ownership of the plan immediately, any attempt later on would cost him all credibility.

And if he *did* deny he'd been involved, Chalis would be branded a liar and her whole presentation would be thrown into doubt.

He chose to say nothing.

He barely listened after that. The senior staff began to argue. Hober inundated Chalis with questions about her targets, about Kuat's shifting defenses, and—after a coughing fit that ended only when Von Geiz intervened—she answered them readily. Mzun and Gadren and Carver debated the tactics of a shipyard invasion. The second in command of *Apailana's Promise,* there to represent her ship, shook her head silently in the corner.

Namir thought about the promises he'd made. He thought about Gadren's words and about Hoth. He thought about Kryndal, the idiot Alliance Special Forces soldier he'd fought with at Echo Base, and wondered if his lunatic plan to take Coruscant was any less practical.

But then, this wasn't the plan of a mad ideologue. Even if it looked the part.

"Do we have any alternatives?" he asked. "Any better plans at all?"

The chatter around him quieted and stopped. The senior officers watched him. In those seconds of silence, he prayed someone would answer in the affirmative.

"Would you leave the room?" Gadren asked Chalis. His voice was stern, almost too deep for clarity.

Chalis nodded politely and exited, the droid floating behind her.

"Howl trusted her, at least in part," Gadren said, now facing Namir. "Howl trusted *you* more than you realize. And all of us respect your service to this company. So I ask you: Is this what we must do?"

I don't know, Namir thought. *How could I?*

"Yes," he said.

"Then you have my support," Gadren replied. "Though if we are voting, I will remove myself and thank you all for your forbearance."

"Do we need to be that formal?" Von Geiz asked. "Technically command falls to me, after Howl and Sairgon and Paonu and—well. Sharn, would you object to a voice vote?"

The *Promise*'s second in command shook her head. "Your company, your show. The *Promise* will back you either way."

"In that case," Von Geiz said, "all in favor of the assault on Kuat?"

There were sounds of assent—forceful and determined, reluctant and soft—throughout the room. Only Hober, Mzun, and Gadren remained silent, and all three maintained neutral expressions. Namir couldn't read them.

"The vote is in favor," Von Geiz said.

Namir felt no relief. Twilight Company would have died without a plan, but that was no guarantee it would survive with one. Still, he made himself smile. It was *his* plan, apparently, and now wasn't the time to show doubt.

"I suggest we break for a while and start preparing for takeoff," Hober said. "But there's one other thing we should decide first."

Namir looked at Hober quizzically, before the quartermaster's intent struck him. Beneath his stony expression, he fumed and wondered just how thoroughly Chalis had choreographed his fate.

Waves of silica crashed against the wall of the amphitheater, spilling dust toward the shrinking tent city. Namir's sleeves flapped in the wind as he tried to shield his eyes and mouth. If the *Thunderstrike* wasn't prepped for departure within the hour, it would be caught in the fast-approaching windstorm; the company would be stuck on Ankhural another night.

Much as he was coming to loathe the planet, he wasn't sure he minded that idea.

He turned away from the wall when he heard the sound of leather striking leather—the slow clapping of gloved hands from a few tiers down the aisle. Brand looked up at him, lips curled in amusement.

"Congratulations, Captain," she said.

Namir grunted and began to descend the steps toward the track. Brand fell in at his side.

"Still first sergeant," he said. "Temporary command only, since they sure as hell weren't putting the governor in charge."

"It's her plan, then?"

"Yes."

Brand shrugged. "It's yours now."

Namir glanced over and saw that she'd raised her mask. "You think it's the wrong call," he said.

"The plan?" Brand shrugged again. "I have no idea. People have a lot of doubts, but they always do. And the troops trust you. It's good for morale."

Namir laughed. "So I shouldn't worry about a mutiny?"

"Not even a little," Brand said.

They crossed the podracing track together toward a cluster of soldiers carrying tents and generators back to the *Thunderstrike*. A few saluted Namir and laughed, but they kept their distance. Over the wind, Namir could hear the low moan and whine of the corvette's engines coming to life.

"Thank you," he said softly. "For saving the company."

"My pleasure, Sergeant. You'll do right by it." Her tone was steady, serious—but then she reached out suddenly and gripped his shoulder, and he thought he heard a note of humor in her voice.

"Who knows?" Brand said. "With luck, maybe we'll even win."

CHAPTER 26

PLANET MARDONA III
Four Days into Operation Ringbreaker

The *Thunderstrike* and *Apailana's Promise* flew in such tight proximity that their shields bumped and clashed, coruscating through the visible spectrum and releasing enough energy to atomize any TIE fighter that passed through their field. Any squadron that attempted to weave between the rebel vessels was destroyed as surely as if it had been crushed between their hulls.

But for every starfighter that disappeared in a green-white cloud of burning oxygen and Tibanna gas, a hundred more swarmed into the rebels' path. The *Promise* had already pulled its X-wings out of the fray rather than sacrifice them in an unwinnable dogfight. Twilight's volleys could only thin the enemy masses, not disperse them; and if there was hope for the two vessels that plunged toward the blue-gray oceans of Mardona III's southern hemisphere, that hope lay in speed, not firepower.

The *Thunderstrike*'s bridge trembled and bucked as it skimmed atmosphere. Namir gripped the railing of the command platform until the knuckles of his dark skin began to pale.

Chalis smiled tightly at his side, her own arm looped more casually about the rail. "You look nervous," she said.

"I'm normally on a drop ship for these things," Namir said. "It's a lot more worrying when you can see what's causing the bumps."

"You should've been on the bridge during Coyerti," Chalis replied with a shrug. Namir thought he heard an edge to her tone, and wondered if she was feigning calm for him or for the crew. "We'll be fine—won't we, Commander?"

"More than fine!" came the call. "We'll be majestic! Laughing seahawks diving for prey."

Commander Tohna was a transfer from the *Promise*—a squat ball of muscle and a former helmsman who'd arrived to take charge of the bridge crew and run the *Thunderstrike*. He'd come with high praise from the *Promise*'s officers, but Namir didn't yet know what to expect from the man. It had been Tohna and the *Promise* crew who'd devised the insertion onto Mardona during the planning meetings, after Chalis had assured them that no warships would be present and that Twilight's largest worries would be ion cannons on the surface and satellite defenses in orbit. Thus, the plan to accelerate rapidly toward the planet and dive swiftly into Mardona's atmosphere over water—beneath the satellites and out of range of the continental cannons.

Something metallic rumbled in the hull, but Tohna didn't seem concerned. "We've outrun most of the fighters," he said. "Drop ships can go on your command."

"Go," Namir snapped. The men and women at the bridge stations tapped at their consoles or spoke into their links. The *Thunderstrike* rumbled again as its hangars opened onto Mardona's gray storm clouds.

Chalis unlooped her arm from the rail and stepped closer to Namir, lowering her voice. "Your squads know the mission," she said. "If we don't make it down, the operation won't be compromised." Between her rasp and the ship's roar, he struggled to comprehend her words.

"I know," he said. "We're going anyway."

Mardona III was—by Chalis's scorn-ridden description—a warehouse world. Not a bustling trade port or a production facility, but a place for the Empire to stockpile equipment and materials for delivery to nearby systems in times of need. The warehouse worlds were part of a larger Imperial initiative to allow for rapid reallocation of resources and to eliminate dependency on outdated trade routes. More important, they were a vulnerability the Alliance hadn't yet learned to exploit.

The mega-spaceport that served as Mardona's primary warehousing hub consisted of dozens of enormous black metal buildings that rose from the rocky surface. They were almost crystalline in design, cuboids with their sides perfectly sheared at odd angles. The buildings extended deep underground, where the main storage facilities were contained and where an elaborate system of tramways allowed automated transfer of goods according to shipping schedule and projected needs. The entire mega-port was large enough to house millions, but its systems were largely mechanized; a few hundred thousand dockworkers and administrators and droid controllers were enough to keep the warehouse world running.

If Twilight Company could disrupt the planet's operations—upend Mardona's ability to supply its neighbors—the Empire would have no choice but to make new accommodations, scramble for other ways to maintain the flow of resources. Personnel and security would need to be reallocated to conventional trade routes. Chalis had shown Namir schematics, star charts, explained how a pebble could become an avalanche. The moffs themselves wouldn't recognize the Kuat shipyards' degradation until it was too late; but Chalis knew the workings of the machine.

"Efficiency," she'd said, "is predictability. The Empire is nothing if not efficient."

War, however, was neither efficient nor predictable.

After the drop ships had landed and the *Thunderstrike* had fled the star system, the company's first twelve hours on Mardona were spent descending from the surface and stealing through the tram tunnels. Once the squads had entered the underground, they made no attempt to hold open routes to the surface; instead, dozens of strike teams sabotaged tramways, disabled surveillance equipment, and ambushed security forces independently, spontaneously splitting and merging and regrouping. They were rats infesting the machinery, too dispersed to exterminate easily. When the Empire shut down power to the underground in a five-block radius, forcing the soldiers to switch to night-vision goggles and personal respirators, it was a temporary measure only; Twilight's attacks continued elsewhere, and shutting down a whole section of the spaceport inhibited the Empire as much as it did the enemy.

Namir fired his weapon only once, when his two escort squads were ambushed by a swarm of spidery maintenance droids—each a fist-sized sphere with magnetized legs and a welding torch. The machines scuttled over rails and across ceilings, racing to sear their victims. Aside from a few minor burns and the promise of a sleepless night, the squads emerged from the ambush intact.

During the next twelve hours of the company's attack on Mardona, the real work began.

Even discounting the ongoing repairs to the *Thunderstrike*, Twilight's engineering crew had been busy since leaving Ankhural. Each squad had come to Mardona armed with two dozen ion mines: crudely improvised explosives mass-produced by the crew from batteries, motion sensors, and whatever casings were available. The mines came in duffel bags and sheared-off piping, in food containers and cracked helmets. They were, in Brand's words, "glue for Mardona's gears."

The squads planted the devices at junctions, along kilometer-long tram lines, and at the entrances to underground warehouses. It was one duty Namir could participate in without taking on more risk than his subordinates would suffer. He listened to the distorted sound of blaster shots echo in the tunnels as Maediyu—the woman who'd treated him with almost unbearable deference since he'd saved her from burning to death outside Chalis's cell—gripped the soles of his boots and boosted him to the level of the tunnel's lower pipework. With a graceless grunt, he clambered onto a broad metal conduit and reached down as Maediyu passed him a tattered backpack and a roll of adhesive tape.

"Here?" he called toward Chalis, who watched with arms folded a dozen paces and a short fall away.

"Farther down," Chalis said. "Let the tramcar build speed."

Namir shrugged and crawled along the length of the pipe. Maediyu followed directly below, holding her rifle at the ready.

When Namir and Chalis had linked up with her squad, she'd appointed herself their personal bodyguard. She was attentive and cautious, good at her job. Namir missed Gadren and Roach and Charmer and Brand, but Charmer had his own squad full of fresh meat now. The others were needed on the offensive—striking at security posts, keeping the Empire distracted while the mines were planted.

Namir looped the tape around the bag, tried to keep it out of view from the track. He jostled it, made sure it was secure, then slipped a hand into the bag and felt for a button. He pictured a tramcar turning the corner and the mine detonating as it passed below. Ion mines didn't deliver much concussive force, but the explosion would fry any circuits in the car and the surrounding tunnel. The vehicle might derail or not. Either way, it would block the route until a maintenance crew removed it.

By the time Twilight Company was off Mardona, there would be thousands of ion mines planted through the tram network. It would take months for the Empire to clear them all—and during that time, the whole system would need to be shut down.

It was a clever plan, devised by Chalis and the engineers and the squad leaders. But "clever" could go wrong very fast.

On the second full day of Twilight's attack on Mardona III, Namir ordered the squads to cluster in the tunnels below one of the mega-port's housing blocks. Reports had come in overnight of Imperial armored vehicles descending into the tramways, sweeping through whole sectors. Any squad caught in such a sweep was doomed; Twilight couldn't afford to stop mining, but teams in the field needed a fallback position.

A housing block was a safe choice, a *reasonable* choice, likely to contain food, water, and computer resources a warehouse would not. Namir listened to Gadren and Mzun's and Zab's concerns about risking civilian lives and chose to proceed anyway.

A dozen squads poured into the block at once, surrounding the perimeter and demanding the residents retreat to their apartment pods. There was no resistance; the civilians were unarmed and unprepared for an attack, and those too stunned to react were ushered back into their homes by Twilight soldiers. With the halls cleared, the squads sealed off all but a handful of entrances and posted sentries down the tunnels. Charmer's team was the first to venture back out.

Chalis volunteered to speak to the residents while Namir saw to the block's defenses, setting up barricades and kill zones. "I'm used to dealing with people like this," she said. "Just give the word."

"If I put you in charge of civilians," Namir said, "the recruits from Haidoral will beat me to death in my sleep. I'll handle it."

Chalis didn't argue, and he was grateful.

One resident from each floor was brought from his or her pod to the block's education center, where the meeting could be broadcast to every apartment. When Namir arrived, half the civilians began shouting as soon as he walked in; the others stared in horror or whispered to their neighbors to be silent. When he started to talk, however, they all listened. Having Maediyu at his back, rifle in hand, likely helped.

"We're not here to hurt you," he said. "Believe me when I say you're the least of our concerns. Tomorrow morning, anyone who wants to leave will be escorted into the tunnels. Trams are shut down, but hopefully your governor will accommodate you.

"If you don't want to brave the tunnels or your family isn't up for the trip, we won't force you out. If you want to stay, keep your pod doors sealed. Don't attempt to communicate with the outside. And we won't be responsible for your safety if the Empire attacks."

It wasn't an inspiring speech, and it wasn't intended to be. Namir needed the civilians out of the way and at least a little cowed—if they tried to sabotage Twilight's operation from inside the apartment block, the situation would turn messy fast.

There were questions—practical ones, mostly, about access to food and medicine. A withered, yellow-bearded old man wanted to know if residents could speak to their neighbors within the block. A squat young woman eloquently described how she'd come to Mardona on the promise of work and good pay, and begged the Rebel Alliance to leave for a world where it was *wanted*. A stern, balding dockworker wanted to know what would happen to residents who hadn't been home during the attack, who might try to return. "My son is out there," he said. "Do you plan to shoot him when he comes for me?"

Namir answered as well as he could for half an hour before a runner informed him he was needed elsewhere. He waved away the remaining questions and had the civilians escorted back to their pods. He didn't intend to ignore them, but he still had a company to run and a planet to ruin.

By the fourth day of the attack, Namir was stewing irritably in the claustrophobic embrace of the housing block. While the squads slipped out through maintenance shafts and air ducts to continue mining the tramways, or defended the barricades against periodic Imperial assaults, he was stuck in the administrative office Twilight had converted into a command center. He studied maps and datapads and listened to sentry reports, and kept his muscles busy by pacing a meter from Chalis's desk.

The governor seemed untroubled by her surroundings. More than untroubled, at times—when they were alone together, Namir sometimes saw her staring, apparently oblivious to the world, into a blank screen. Those were the only moments he remembered the husk she'd been after returning from Hoth, and she always returned to her more vibrant self as soon as she sensed his attention.

Those moments, and whenever he saw her suppress a cough.

The civilians who'd chosen to remain proved a persistent distraction. Barely an hour went by when Namir wasn't forced to deal with a resident sneaking between apartment pods, or requesting additional food supplies, or reporting a neighbor for possessing a blaster. One of Twitch's team members was caught stealing jewelry and loose credits from an abandoned pod; Namir didn't especially care, but he scolded the man publicly for the sake of keeping peace. A family that had come to blows—Namir had no idea why—needed to be forcibly separated and locked in separate pods. "We're not your blasted *police*," he muttered more than once.

Yet the overall operation was proceeding apace. Every day, the Imperials sealed off more entrances into the tunnels, and every day Chalis discovered alternatives in city blueprints or Brand scouted fresh routes. The housing block was buried deep enough to be defensible against heavy vehicular attacks, and if the Empire used large-scale weapons against the block, it would collapse half the mega-port's tunnels in the process. Squads continued their minelaying every hour, returning to the block exhausted and filthy and eager to resupply.

Namir took satisfaction in that. He tried not to show it.

At the end of the fourth day, Namir was picking at the contents of a meal tray (some sort of mashed tubers, flavorless but superior to the *Thunderstrike*'s fare) when he was summoned to one of the block's upper floors to deal with a "discipline problem" involving a squad member in an empty pod. *Another looter,* Namir thought, and dragged himself through the block's mazelike passages. The only decorations were whatever tiny portraits or icons or sprigs of plant life the residents dared post on their pod doors. Life under the Empire was bleak, Namir supposed, but it didn't look uncomfortable.

The source of the "discipline problem" became obvious as soon as he reached the twelfth floor. A rhythmic bass caused the walls to thrum, and he followed the noise down a hallway and around a corner. Gadren, smiling toothily, stood across from a pod door.

"You called your commanding officer here for *this*?" Namir asked. He had to nearly shout to be heard over the pounding.

"She is your protégée," Gadren said, and shrugged his massive shoulders. "Your squad may now belong to me, but I did not wish to overstep."

Namir glowered at Gadren, then stepped to the entryway. When the door slid open, the hall flooded with sound—not just the bass, but eerie notes spawned by instruments Namir couldn't imagine, human and alien voices mixed in incomprehensible song. Namir's bones ached at the vibrations, and as he walked into the apartment, over the stained yellow rug and past a table covered in glass animal statuettes, he saw the woman responsible.

Red hair matted with sweat, barefoot yet otherwise garbed in full combat gear, Roach danced with wild enthusiasm, swinging and twisting her gangly body about the living room. It was nearly a minute before she noticed Namir; when she did, she grinned shamelessly and slapped a hand against the audio controls in the wall.

The music stopped.

"This isn't your home," Namir said. "Try to have some dignity."

"There were complaints about the volume," Gadren added behind him.

"But I can stay, right?" Roach asked. She was still smiling. Namir couldn't remember ever seeing her smile.

He couldn't remember her ever looking like a *child* before.

"You can stay," Namir said. "Keep a channel open in case your squad needs you."

Gadren followed him back outside the pod. When the door closed, he laughed in his alien bellow. "I know you have other duties," he said, clasping a leathery hand on Namir's shoulder. "I know they are supremely important. But I thought you deserved to see that."

"You're a monster," Namir said. He felt lighter as he returned to the command center.

His good mood lasted a full hour until a message came in from the sentries: Charmer's team had been ambushed during a mining run. Only one of his squad had survived.

Corbo's arms were wrapped and bandaged by the time Namir reached him. The young man from Haidoral was lying on a bed in the company's makeshift hospital—an apartment scrubbed clean and staffed by a pair of Twilight medics. Corbo shivered on his back as he told his story.

Charmer's squad had been attacked by an armored Imperial vehicle—not a tank or a walker, but a segmented metal worm that glided on repulsors and sped along the tramways. It had been armed with flame weapons and stun beams—anything more powerful, Namir suspected, would risk collapsing the tunnels. Charmer had barely ordered the others to run before being incinerated.

Namir didn't press Corbo for details of the fight or how he'd escaped. As Corbo stumbled over half-recalled horrors, Namir asked him simply: "You're sure the others were killed? Not captured?"

"Yes," Corbo said.

Namir felt something heavier and sicklier than relief congeal in his stomach—something that replaced doubt with focus, but pressed on his guts nonetheless. "Then get some rest," he said. "We'll avenge them."

Three Twilight soldiers had died during the previous days of running and hiding and planting mines. Now three had died in one night. Namir wasn't sure if it was his own restlessness or the soldiers' he sensed as he walked through the apartment block—not until Brand found him in the kitchen they'd turned into an armory.

"We haven't hit back—*really* hit back—since Coyerti," she said. "If you want to hurt them, you won't be short on volunteers."

"We'll hurt them," Namir said. He clipped a pair of spare power packs to his belt, patted himself down to ensure his equipment was secure. "Tomorrow we get back to work, but tonight . . ."

"Does Chalis know you're going?" Brand asked.

"I owe it to Charmer."

"It was a question," Brand said. "Not an argument."

Two teams went hunting for the machine that had burned three soldiers alive. Brand took point, scouting for enemy patrols or trace energy signatures; a machine so large running on repulsors might leave a footprint. The others fanned out from the ambush location, sweeping an arc through the tunnels behind Brand.

Most of the hunters had known Charmer well: Carver, who'd been classmates with Charmer at the Imperial Academy. Namir and Brand, of course. Twitch came at Namir's request—he needed soldiers with heavy-weapons expertise to take down the machine. Maediyu was there for Namir. Gadren had elected to stay behind. Namir had rejected the idea of bringing more fresh meat; the Haidoral recruits had been friends with Corbo and the dead men, but they didn't have the experience for a death squad.

The teams intercepted the worm as its crew was disembarking outside an Imperial sentry post. The heavy weaponry wasn't necessary. The enemy officers were caught in a storm of blasterfire; if any survived, they didn't last under the savage kicks and stomps of the squad members. A single grenade lobbed through the machine's hatch brought the worm to the ground, spewing chemical fumes and crackling with electrical arcs.

By the time the sentries inside the Imperial outpost were ready to reinforce their allies, the squads' mission was done. But Namir didn't call for a withdrawal until the weight of the reinforcements became too great—until the Twilight teams had killed a dozen more officers and stormtroopers and exacted the price for a squad's decimation. Bodies were heaped at the gates of the sentry post when Namir and his colleagues finally fled into the tunnels.

Back at the housing block, the company members still awake—and there were many, even in the quiet hours before dawn—cheered the squads' return. Some of the soldiers who'd taken part in the mission went on to the cafeteria to share triumphant stories over breakfast. Brand promised to bring word to Corbo and Roach.

Another contingent of soldiers had been searching apartments, convinced one of the residents had been feeding information to the Empire resulting in the ambush of Charmer's squad. They'd found a transmitter with the yellow-bearded old man who'd spoken at the first civilian meeting, and beaten him half to death before Gadren had intervened.

"I'll take care of it," Chalis told Namir as he returned his equipment to the armory. She'd given him the whole story on his arrival. She hadn't said a word about his participation in the death squad.

He didn't want to care, but he made himself ask: "How?"

"We'll sweep his apartment, drain his accounts, and if he owns anything useful add it to Hober's inventory. Burn the rest. Leave him with nothing—not even food or clothing—and send him into the tunnels."

Enough to appease anyone who wanted blood, Namir thought, but not so harsh as to leave soldiers like Gadren with a lasting grudge.

"Good enough," he said. He went back to his quarters—an apartment pod that had apparently once belonged to a collector of vintage mechanical clocks—and slept.

He was in charge of Twilight Company. His friend had died under his command. And he'd made it right. That had to suffice for the night.

Leaving Mardona III was no simpler than arriving. Chalis had given the company six days for the mission, after which Imperial reinforcements would arrive to cut off its escape. Even staying that long, she'd insisted, would be a risk.

Namir signaled for the *Thunderstrike* and *Apailana's Promise* to return for pickup on the evening of the fifth day. The company had laid four-fifths of the ion mines; that would have to be enough. The squads dispersed again, abandoning the housing block and seeking lightly guarded egresses onto the surface.

Mardona's security forces were prepared and all the exits guarded, as Twilight had known they would be. The squads' timing would need to be precise—they had to surface during the brief window in which the *Thunderstrike* and its drop ships were in the planet's atmosphere. If the squads arrived on the surface too early, they'd be exposed and overrun by Imperials. Too late, and they'd be left behind when the *Thunderstrike* was forced to flee.

Namir expected the extraction to be bloody and desperate. He expected to lose as many as three or four squads. Maybe a drop ship, as well.

Instead, mere hours before the squads were scheduled to ascend, rain began falling on the mega-port. Thick, heavy drops whipped northward by the wind pelted buildings and sensors and sentries. Clouds blocked out sunlight. Even electronically enhanced vision became useless. The streets began to flood and water trickled into the tunnels.

The squads made their final ascent through mist and gales, slogging up slick steps and climbing cargo lift shafts. Namir's soaked boots clung to his toes, and he fired wildly into the darkness toward the enemy. Victory was impossible in a squall of such force, but Twilight Company didn't need victory—it only needed to push forward, to reach the drop ships that rocked wildly against the wind.

The storm saved Twilight Company. The squads escaped Mardona III with one fatality and a handful of injuries.

The *Thunderstrike* resumed its course for Kuat.

"Sergeant Pol Andrissus," Hober proclaimed. It was Charmer's real name, though Namir couldn't remember ever hearing it said aloud.

Carver and Gadren had argued over who would eulogize Charmer at the funeral. Gadren had ultimately conceded, and it was Carver who approached Hober and the charging station, handed over the blaster power pack ready to be drained. "Ladies' man," Carver declared, and there was nervous laughter throughout the crowded vehicle bay.

Was that how Charmer would want to be remembered? Namir wasn't sure. It seemed mean-spirited after what had happened on Blacktar Cyst—after the fight that had stolen Charmer's good looks, after the shrapnel in his brain had cost him his ability to form a sentence without stammering—but then, Charmer had never given up the nickname, either. Namir hadn't ever asked him about it.

He swore softly under his breath. Carver withdrew and Hober went on to the next name. Namir felt a grip on his arm, flinched and turned to see Roach beside him, watching him with obvious concern. He forced a smile and gently removed her hand.

Seven names, seven dead, seven batteries drained and eulogies delivered. He'd seen plenty of friends and comrades die before. Yet he felt cold and clammy, like he was still drying off from the storm on Mardona III.

When the ritual was over, Hober stepped away from the charging station. Instead of ending the broadcast to the ship, however, he paused as Governor Chalis edged her way among the soldiers and emerged into the clearing. Namir hadn't even known Chalis was present—he hadn't seen her at the start of the ceremony—but she'd dressed for the occasion, wearing a black suit she must have scavenged on Mardona and an ornamental kerchief. She murmured something to Hober, who hesitated a moment before moving aside.

"I'll be brief," she said to the crowd. Her voice was too rusty to hear easily, and the soldiers seemed to go rigid as they strained to listen. Namir saw more than a few of them scowling, though most seemed merely puzzled. "The men and women who died on Mardona—I didn't know them well. I barely knew them at all."

Twitch turned her back on Chalis and pushed her way out of the bay. Chalis seemed not to notice, and continued.

"What I *do* know," she said, "is what the Rebellion means to all of you. Captain Evon showed me by his own example when he welcomed me aboard. I saw the Rebellion's heart firsthand when I served with High Command.

"The soldiers who died on Mardona Three did so believing the Rebellion was worthy of their dedication. They weren't there because of *orders*; they believed that a great victory, even in these dark days, was still possible. I intend to do whatever is necessary to prove them right.

"I'm not claiming that's enough," she added swiftly. "We're different from the Empire because every life *means* something—our soldiers aren't faceless stormtroopers, but our friends and lovers. Our dead were rebels, yes, and they were lady-killers and jokers and they struggled with their own demons.

"I intend to fight for victory not because it's *enough*—" Here she paused, surveying the room, eyes skimming over her audience. "—but because it's the *least* we can do to honor the fallen."

She smiled, then—a small, sad, tight smile—and bowed her head, returning to the crowd. The company members' response was muted, but Namir heard soft affirmations, saw heads nod.

"Onward to victory," a man's voice muttered. Namir didn't see who spoke, but he thought it sounded like Hober.

"I didn't mean to upstage you. You *know* that. I just thought they needed to hear—"

Namir smiled bitterly and shook his head. "It's fine," he said. He sat on the trunk in Howl's quarters, watching the governor as she perched at the edge of the bunk. "You're probably right . . . a little inspiration is good for them."

"Next time," Chalis said. She took a swig from a bottle of brandy—not unlike the one she'd first brought aboard the *Thunderstrike*—and passed it to Namir. "You get the *next* speech, even if I have to write it myself."

Namir turned the bottle over in his hands and wondered where Chalis had found it. The influx of contraband after Ankhural could turn out to be a problem.

He'd gone to the Clubhouse after the funeral. He hadn't been unwelcome, and he'd stayed long enough to listen to a few stories, hear about Charmer's heroism on Tokuut and the shore-leave incident on Sigma Station. But conversations had a tendency to stop when he walked by. Bottles got hidden behind support beams . . .

No, he thought. The problem wasn't that the troops were uncomfortable around him. The problem was that anything he said seemed trivial, like an abdication of responsibility for his part in the deaths. And he didn't have any speeches to give, any words of wisdom or solace for grieving friends.

He could lead the squads of Twilight Company. He would *try* to lead them. But he had nothing to say to them when they mourned. He couldn't take part in the grieving when he was also the cause.

So he'd come to Chalis, and she'd welcomed him.

"Next time," he agreed.

"We did well, though," she said. "It'll be a while before we know what resources the Empire cannibalizes on Kuat to make up for Mardona, but that's my problem. You got them in and out alive. Mostly."

"I watched. The squads did the work."

"Welcome to command," Chalis said. She smirked and retrieved the bottle from Namir's hands, taking another quick swallow. "Speaking of which, you should rest—you don't get time off between missions anymore."

Namir grunted and rose from the trunk. Chalis mirrored him, rising from the bed. She crossed to the door before he could intercept and gestured to the bunk. "Yours," she said. He started to argue and got a glower in return. "I already moved my many possessions into Sairgon's old quarters. It's past time you started staying here."

"We could seal the door," Namir said. "Make sure *nobody* gets the room."

"Do you really want to bunk with your men?" Chalis asked. Her tone made it clear what answer she expected. "Do you really think they're better off with their commander in the next bed over?"

Namir watched Chalis awhile. She seemed to be holding back a smile.

"Get the hell out of my quarters," he said at last, and she laughed as she departed.

CHAPTER 27

PLANET SULLUST
Nine Days into Operation Ringbreaker

For the past two weeks, Thara hadn't felt much like SP-475 at all.

The explosion on the rebel terrorist vessel had left her with a jagged scar across her forehead and a right ear that went deaf at intervals. For the first few days after the incident, she'd suffered from headaches that left her pressing her forehead against cold metal floor panels at night and praying for unconsciousness. The medical droids assured her it was nothing unexpected and soon approved a return to light duty: surveillance reviews, munitions maintenance, and the like.

No one had visited her or wished her well. Her uncle might have done so under other circumstances, but he was still in holding awaiting trial or release.

On her first day back, as she cross-checked automated supply records with her own hand-counted inventory of blaster power packs, 113 joined her in the brightly lit armory. He'd led the team on the day of the explosion, interrogated the rebel agent himself. Somehow he'd survived, too, even as close as he'd been to the detonation.

Maybe, Thara thought, *he really* was *one of the original clones.* The commandos had been built to last. Other members of the team hadn't been so fortunate: She was glad she couldn't remember the sight of body parts blasted and strewn through the ship, but she could still imagine.

"You're one of the new ones," 113 said. More a statement than a question. "Accelerated training to bulk out the corps. Pinyumb your first assignment?"

"Yes, sir," Thara said. She was dressed in a variant of a cadet's uniform, in an open-faced helmet that left her every expression exposed. She felt blind without the glow of her old uniform's display.

"Huh." SP-113 stared at her through his own helmet. Thara wondered if he was reviewing her record. "You survived. Give you credit for that. But you need to do better."

Better than leaving my comrades to die? she wondered. It seemed a low threshold to clear.

"Yes, sir," Thara said.

"However long the med droids said to stay off patrol? Cut it in half. We're shorthanded, and the bosses want Nien Nunb and the rest of the cell found before they cause more trouble."

The alien aboard the rebel ship had claimed the cell lacked supporters in Pinyumb—that the local civilians were too scared to help. No one believed it. Not Thara and her comrades, and certainly not her commanders.

Still, Thara opened her mouth to protest. "Sir?" she asked. She shouldn't have been speaking, but she fumbled for the words anyway. "I thought—"

"You thought what?"

"Hoth, sir. I thought the rebels would be . . . less dangerous. Less active. Less something."

The garrison stormtroopers didn't gossip much—certainly not

while on duty, when chatter was forbidden; and official policy discouraged bonding during off hours. Troopers who grew attached to their comrades became inflexible, slow to adapt to new postings with new squads. Still, talk got around during meals or in the locker room, and Thara had heard about an attack on a prime rebel base in the Anoat sector. The enemy had been routed, the base obliterated. Darth Vader himself had led the troops to victory, the elite of the elite marching through fire and ice against a thousand rebel traps.

113 made a short, scornful sound like a laugh as he turned away. "We're a long way from Hoth," he said. "And there're always more rebels."

One week after her conversation with 113, Thara's full status was restored. She donned each piece of her uniform with care and diligence, reminding herself of her name and her mission and her duty to Sullust and the Empire. But the faint scratches on her armor and the dead silence in her right ear distracted her, and she fumbled as she locked her helmet into place.

Nearly thirty stormtroopers stood at attention as the transport touched down onto the hangar floor. Another thirty were stationed out of sight or in the adjoining tunnels, ready for any surprise attack by the rebel cell. Still more teams were searching housing blocks in Pinyumb and locking down the Inyusu Tor processing facility; someone in charge had decided that the transport's safe arrival was worth shutting down city business.

SP-475 stood behind a maintenance crew, staring toward the tunnel through which the transport had descended from the surface. She imagined rebels deployed between dim rays of sunlight, prepping explosives in the shadows.

The transport hissed, and her attention turned to the boarding ramp. Pinyumb officials rushed forward, meeting the first wave of arrivals and occluding her view. Half a dozen white-armored figures surrounded the group and escorted them down a tunnel. Chatter played in her helmet: team leaders reporting that nothing was amiss.

"Who are these guys?" one of the maintenance workers asked.

Now a second wave of arrivals marched down the boarding ramp: black-clad officers, helmeted security personnel, and more storm-troopers. First ten, then twenty, then more than SP-475 could count.

"Labor oversight," another worker replied. "Some rebels hit a sup-ply depot on Mardona the other day. Need to make up production somewhere."

SP-475 hadn't heard that. She bristled at the idea that Pinyumb needed more troops, more overseers to do its part—but she forced the instinct down. 113 had told her that they were shorthanded, and they still hadn't found Nien Nunb. Maybe reinforcements weren't such a bad thing.

Then she heard a high-pitched whine in her helmet. Her comrades began shouting.

The overlapping, static-distorted voices were impossible to deci-pher. In a second, a commanding officer would override the others and make her orders clear. She wanted to freeze. She wanted to run. The last time she'd seen her fellow troops fall into chaos, men and women had died.

Her chest ached. She wasn't breathing.

In the periphery of her vision, she saw another trooper gesture be-hind her and up the cavern wall. Her rifle was in her hands as she turned. She stumbled half a step back and bumped into one of the maintenance crew.

The helmet directed her attention to a mechanical sphere no larger than her fist, floating a dozen meters above the cavern floor and weav-ing toward the tunnel to the surface. She didn't question what it was. She brought up her rifle and squeezed the trigger three times. Her visor polarized against the red glare. Two shots chipped the stone. The last clipped the sphere, sending it spiraling onto the ground and leav-ing a trail of sparks.

Nothing exploded. No one died. It was a long time before she heard the comm chatter again or noticed the two troopers kneeling over the fallen sphere.

"Spy cam," came a crisper voice. "Knew the rebels couldn't stay away." It was 113. "Nice shot, Four-Seven-Five."

SP-475 wanted to tear her helmet off and vomit.

But she'd done her duty. She'd overcome her hesitation. Her shift was just beginning, and if the rebels were at work, she had to be ready. She had to push through.

CHAPTER 28

FIFTEEN LIGHT-YEARS OFF THE RIMMA TRADE ROUTE
Ten Days into Operation Ringbreaker

The dockyards of Najan-Rovi fell in less than a day. The gas giant's floating habitats lacked a dedicated stormtrooper battalion, relying on Imperial fleet troopers and a complement of TIE fighters for defense. By the time the *Thunderstrike* had delivered its payload of Twilight Company strike teams, the dockyards' doom was sealed; by the time Twilight jumped to lightspeed and departed Najan-Rovi, almost a hundred Imperial luxury transports and light freighters were in flames.

"'Executive shuttles' for senior officers and special envoys of the Ruling Council," Chalis had explained during a briefing to the squad leaders. "Stored and resupplied in Najan-Rovi but built by the Corellian Engineering Corporation. Once they're destroyed, Corellia will need to increase its production; the officers *must* have their toys."

Increased production on Corellia meant shipbuilding resources and security transferred from Kuat. After Najan-Rovi, Twilight Company was one step closer to its true objective, and the squads celebrated on their return from the dockyards. It was gratifying to see, though Namir was surprised that Chalis retreated to her quarters rather than accept congratulations in the drop ship hangar.

Thunderstrike's next destination was Obumubo, a frigid moon covered in a sea of icy liquid metal. There, Twilight was tasked with the obliteration of an Imperial garrison. "There are certain people I want promoted out of Kuat," Chalis said at the senior staff's morning meeting. "Once they're gone, they'll take their security with them. Kill the right man on Obumubo and we create a job vacancy."

Von Geiz—one of the gentlest people Namir had ever known—asked if the target could be assassinated. "Must we risk the whole company to destroy one man?"

Chalis said nothing at first, her lips twitching in an expression that never quite became a smile. Then she began coughing, spitting into her sleeve as her chest heaved. It was over a minute before she recovered enough to reply.

"The Empire can't suspect our intentions," she said, her voice hoarse and her tone cold. "The military employs very smart people who are doubtless wondering about our attacks. If the *possibility* of our striking Kuat crosses their minds, our entire operation ends. So yes—we risk the company."

Von Geiz did not argue further.

The attack on Obumubo was bloody. No Twilight soldier had died at Najan-Rovi, but injury and exhaustion had taken a toll. The garrison was smartly defended by experienced troops who'd held Obumubo's sea creatures at bay for months. The battlefield favored the defenders. Two Twilight infantry personnel and a medic drowned in silver waters while disembarking the drop ships. A dozen more died in the first assault.

It took two days of fighting before the company managed to erect its siege weapons on the fluid landscape. Cannon fire brought down the garrison at last, and the *Thunderstrike* sped out of the system, its drop ships safely recovered as a phalanx of destroyers arrived.

It was, Chalis promised, another victory. One step closer to Kuat.

The night of the *Thunderstrike*'s departure from Obumubo, after a late visit by Namir to M2-M5—Namir still loathed the engineering droid, but it was more amenable than most of the crew to delivering reports at odd hours—Namir heard a noise from the mess hall and made his way to investigate. He found a dozen soldiers gathered around a portable holoprojector on one of the dining tables.

The projector was running an Imperial newscast. The digitized image of an attractive young woman proudly announced a string of Imperial triumphs over rebels in the Outer Rim. "Since the destruction of the Alliance base," she declared, "over fifteen rebel outposts and seven members of the enemy leadership have surrendered. Emperor Palpatine is reportedly considering public trials for select combatants in the hope that others—witnessing their fair treatment—will follow their example and turn themselves in."

"Is any of it true?" Namir recognized the voice and saw Roach seated at the corner of the table.

He shook his head. "I don't know," he admitted. "It's propaganda, so it's not *all* true, but—" He sighed, uncertain how much to share. "We still haven't made contact with High Command. The fleet's out there, condition unknown."

Was he being too direct? Too oblique? He barely remembered what it was like, speaking to his colleagues without second-guessing himself. Roach nodded briskly. The others were either watching the newscast or avoiding his gaze. He wanted to leave, but he was their commander. He owed them something better.

"Let's just make sure that when the fleet comes back, we've given the Alliance an edge."

It was the best he could come up with, and he couldn't tell if the stern nods and raised fists he got in response were genuine signs of enthusiasm or concessions to a commander's authority. Maybe it was best not to know.

Maediyu was among the first casualties on Nakadia. Namir stayed by her side in the medical tent as she sweated and bled, thrashed and stank. Bright, blotchy rashes covered her face, and she insisted Namir was her mother, didn't remember his name when he told her he wasn't. Eventually he gave up on the truth and stroked her hair as her organs slowly liquefied. He left her alone only twice, both times to empty his stomach and wipe the bile from his lips.

Namir had known Nakadia would be difficult. He hadn't expected the deaths there to be so horrible.

The planet was an agricultural world of boundless hills and neck-high stalks of stiff, leafy flora. Twilight had come to devastate Nakadia's plastoid factories, where millions of tonnes of farm crops were processed into armor-grade polymers and synthetic resins. Namir hadn't realized such conversions were possible—he couldn't imagine how plants could be transmuted into industrial materials—but no one else seemed surprised and he'd kept his questions to himself. Looking stupid in front of his colleagues wouldn't inspire confidence.

He'd left Governor Chalis behind on the *Thunderstrike* and joined the squads in the initial wave of assaults. They struck covertly under cover of night, advancing and retreating invisibly through the forests of stalks. It was a good strategy, but it was grueling for troops who'd barely had time to rest since Obumubo. It required men and women with barely treated injuries to march sleepless through difficult terrain.

And then Maediyu and the others had returned from a sortie, staggering and bloody-eyed. The medics had recognized what was happening, but they didn't confirm Namir's suspicions until after Maediyu was dead.

"These aren't pesticides. They've got military bioweapons," Namir told the squad leaders that morning. He kept his voice calm, despite the boiling fury in his guts. "Be careful."

Sixteen other soldiers fell to airspeeders spraying toxins before a scout team located their point of origin. Gadren, Mzun, and a dozen other alien soldiers accompanied Namir—who'd wrapped himself in as much protective gear as he'd been able to scrounge—to a launch pad and warehouse high in the hills. They burned the warehouse to the ground, watched metal blacken and curl and listened to poison sizzle inside.

Twilight Company won Nakadia, too.

When Namir returned to the *Thunderstrike,* he marched directly to Chalis's quarters, not stopping to remove his armor or stow his rifle. He knocked on the door and didn't wait for a reply before keying it open. If it hadn't been unlocked, he might have blasted the control panel.

"It was the same toxin," he snarled.

Chalis sat on her bunk, sketching something on a datapad. She made a few strokes across the screen, considered her work, and set the device down before looking up at Namir. "Give me context," she said. Her voice was calm, but her eyes were hard. "You're talking about the bioweapons on Nakadia? I heard—"

"The bioweapons," Namir said, "that came from Coyerti. We destroyed the Distillery. We destroyed the stockpiles. That stuff should be *gone,* and instead my people are dead."

"Sit down," Chalis said. Namir made no motion to do so, and she shrugged. "I'm sorry for your losses—"

"You aren't."

She shrugged again. "I'm not in *favor* of them. Are you going to listen, Sergeant? Our next planetfall is in three days, so if you're just going to vent I'll get back to work."

"Talk."

She closed her eyes and pressed her forefinger to one of her temples, as if massaging a headache. She spoke slowly, cautiously, apparently constructing an argument as she went. "You're a fine commander. You're a good judge of what your people need and what they can accomplish. But you still think like a man from Crucival."

"Meaning?"

"Meaning you don't understand the *scale* of the enemy. It took me—it took me longer than it should have, too. I don't fault you for it."

Namir's ire had drained from him. The strap of his rifle felt too heavy around his neck. His bitterness remained, however, and every word Chalis spoke grated.

"We—you and your squad—destroyed enough biotoxin to save millions. Maybe more. But the Empire has been building its arsenal for decades. How much do you think is stored in dusty armories and warehouses across the galaxy?

"If I'd known there was *any* present on Nakadia, I might have chosen a different target. I didn't. We'll be better prepared next time."

"How many more *next times* should we prepare for?"

Chalis rose slowly from the bunk and met Namir's gaze. He saw her chest heave as she suppressed a cough. "You've seen the plan," she said. "It won't be long until Kuat."

"I really hope not," Namir said. "I think Hober's tired of conducting funerals."

Namir found a speech had been added to his datapad an hour before the ceremony in the vehicle bay. It talked about how Twilight Company would honor the squads' sacrifices; about how Nakadia was a reminder of the depths the Empire would sink to; about how on a world that could have fed trillions, the enemy had chosen to deploy poison.

He didn't read the speech at the funeral. Instead, after Hober wrapped up the usual proceedings and Namir did nothing, Chalis strode to the fore and recited it herself. The reaction seemed largely positive, which didn't especially surprise Namir. It was a good speech. The governor was winning the company over one day at a time, and the troops were getting used to her proclamations.

He visited neither the Clubhouse nor Chalis that night. Instead he laid in his bunk—Howl's bunk—wondering what the captain would have done differently. Whether the captain would have done *anything* differently, or whether Twilight was the same as it had always been— bleeding, fighting, desperate to win but losing just as often—and it was just Namir's perspective that had changed.

He regretted arguing with Chalis, and it troubled him to think that she was, in fact, the only person on the ship who understood his position. The thought of telling her as much flitted across his brain before he swatted it away. Chalis was not his friend, and whatever warmth there had been between them had frozen over on Hoth.

That thought, too, seemed *off* somehow, but it was close enough to the truth.

Over the following week, Twilight Company fought two more battles—in the mountains of Naator and the miasmic canyons of Xagobah. The company won. Soldiers died. The grueling pace continued, and even Chalis agreed that a day spent resting and resupplying was in order. Chalis and Von Geiz proposed that the *Thunderstrike* would put in overnight at Heap Nine—a junker world beneath the notice of the Empire, where scavengers picked at the garbage piles of a long-dead civilization.

As shore leave went, it wasn't much. Namir anticipated that much of the company would choose to remain aboard the ship. But he nonetheless found himself in an open-air cantina with a handful of his colleagues, drinking noxious local brew and trying to flirt with a green-skinned woman who seemed unimpressed by his lies about life as a meteor miner.

Gadren found him three drinks after the woman had left. "You made a fine effort," he said, "but now is the time to acknowledge defeat and regather your dignity."

Namir tried to straighten in his seat and discovered he was still slouching forward. "I'm betting you didn't tell that to Brand."

Gadren cast a glance toward the far end of the cantina. Namir hadn't seen Brand for a good hour. "That is because she is better at this than you," Gadren said. "And no one is troubled if she looks the fool."

Namir barked a laugh and pushed his drink away. "Subtle. Fine. Howl never sat around looking like an idiot—"

"—in public," Gadren said, his tone patient and conciliatory. He slipped an arm under Namir's shoulder, pulling him to his feet. "What Howl did in private is another secret he will take with him, but I have no doubt he was as flawed and foolish as the rest of us."

Namir grunted. Gadren left an arm around him, half supporting Namir as they walked together along the main street of the settlement—a dirt road flanked on both sides by junk shops and scrap traders—and ignored the shouts of hawkers and thieves. "You remember the fighting on Dreivus?" Namir asked. "The way we celebrated after?"

Gadren made a hollow sound of amusement. "I remember. You made an impression on the fire dancers." He paused, scratched at his wattle with one hand. "Twitch brought up Dreivus the other night. We miss you at the Clubhouse."

Namir didn't answer. Gadren kept talking. "There is another campaign that has been recurring in my memories. This one was before your time—before Brand's, before even Lieutenant Sairgon joined us. Have I spoken of Ferrok Pax?"

Namir thought about nodding, making his excuses, and slipping away. He enjoyed Gadren's company, but he wasn't sure how long he could bear it. Still, there was nowhere to go. The drop ships wouldn't return to the *Thunderstrike* for hours yet. "I don't think so," Namir said.

Gadren nodded sagely. "I was new to the company, barely able to hold a blaster without singeing my fingers." He wiggled meaty digits, as if inspecting them for scars. "We were barely two hundred strong, and we marched for days through the ruins of a proto-species kingdom in an effort to flank our foe.

"Had we taken to the skies, our attempts at stealth would have been futile. But we left behind a trail of soldiers who could no longer walk or whose hunger ravaged their bodies as our supplies dwindled. We lost brave men to dreadful beasts; others vanished, consumed by alien technology we lacked the knowledge to defend against.

"Then came the battle. We won that day, against a laughing menace and her fiendish warriors, and we extracted the rebels we had been sent to save. But only thirty-seven Twilight soldiers survived the clash."

Rough even by Twilight standards, Namir thought. "Which would be why I haven't heard the story before," he said. "There aren't many left to tell it. Not exactly uplifting."

"No," Gadren said. "It is not. But it is etched in the history of our company—Howl's company. He led those two hundred to their deaths, and he led those who lived in the aftermath. He rebuilt the company from the ashes of its sacrifice."

Namir straightened and looked into Gadren's alien eyes. He smiled, but he heard a challenge in his voice. "And you think, what—I'm leading the company into another massacre?"

"No," Gadren said again. "I think you fear the sacrifices we have made, and the sacrifices to come. Howl felt the death of his men as keenly as any of us, but he never grew hard or distant. I told you at his funeral that I cannot explain him; yet I know he believed sacrifice was the *strength* of Twilight, and he wielded that strength to good purpose."

"If I were afraid of sacrifice," Namir said, "I never would have agreed to Chalis's plan in the first place."

"As you like," Gadren said. "But we follow you, not Chalis. And we will gladly give you what you need to reach the shipyards of Kuat."

After the respite of Heap Nine came the asteroid mines of the Kuliquo belt. Namir planned the attack personally, selecting the twenty soldiers he trusted most to sabotage machinery in an airless, lightless death trap. At Gadren's urging, he agreed to send Roach. She returned from the mines with a hunk of gold the size of her fist and presented it to Namir as a gift.

He placed it on the desk in his quarters and later toyed with it in both hands as Chalis briefed him on the situation at Kuat. She'd been recording Imperial comm traffic, decrypting low-priority signals in the evenings, and she seemed pleased with the results of Twilight's actions. "The One-Oh-Seventh Stormtrooper Legion specializes in putting down slave revolts and worker uprisings. Three full battalions have now been pulled from stable, predictable Kuat and reassigned elsewhere, thanks to us. And"—she added swiftly, raising a finger—"thanks to the reliable idiocy of so many old friends on the Imperial Ruling Council."

"*Reliable idiocy,*" Namir echoed. "It wasn't long ago that you were desperately worried about our plan being discovered."

"By intelligence analysts, absolutely. But by the people I worked with for a decade, and who decided I wasn't a *threat* after I left? No, I'm really not concerned with what they think now." There was no lightness in her tone, no attempt at charm. There rarely was when she and Namir were alone.

"So what's next? If we hit many more targets, we'll be in no shape to take on the shipyards no matter how weak they are."

"Two more stops," Chalis said, "though resistance will be heavy. We're moving toward the heart of Imperial space—if half the enemy fleet weren't still chasing Alliance High Command, we couldn't even get close. As it is, we need to hit fast enough and hard enough that the Empire can't surround us."

"Two more," Namir repeated. He rolled it around in his head as if the number meant something real, as if opposition and battleground and days in combat versus days in motion didn't matter at all. "I can give you two more."

"Good," Chalis said. "Because this opportunity disappears as soon as the Empire regroups. We take Sullust next, then Malastare. When those are done, Kuat falls. Victory is in sight, Sergeant—we just need to reach for it."

Sullust was a mining and manufacturing center for the Empire, a once-proud and influential member of the Republic that had been reduced to the position of a scrabbling vassal—a source of fuel for the Imperial machine, and little more. Its cities were buried like gemstones below the scorched and blasted surface, housing billions of native Sullustans and generations of immigrants from offworld.

Seated alone in the *Thunderstrike*'s mess hall, Namir listened to talk about the coming battle. Zab, of all people, spoke the Sullustan native tongue. Hober had heard rumors of movements to resist the Empire emerging on the planet over the years, quashed by the Imperials every time they began to blossom.

Namir knew only what he was told and what he read in the *Thunderstrike*'s spotty computer records. He'd never seen a Sullustan before. Or maybe he had and just didn't realize it.

The day before the *Thunderstrike* was scheduled to arrive at Sullust, he made another effort to contact Alliance High Command. The farther Twilight Company encroached into Imperial territory, the more difficult it would be to open a secure channel; this was, so far as Namir was concerned, the last opportunity to find another path forward. After this, the company was truly committed.

No, he thought as he toyed with Roach's gold in his quarters and stared down at his terminal. That was what he could tell Chalis, but it wasn't the truth. This wasn't the last opportunity for Twilight. It was simply the last opportunity for him to sidestep his promise.

If you can't get behind what they believe in, maybe it's time to walk away.

He'd decided to give Twilight what it wanted: a fighting chance against the Empire's evil. Only the Rebellion could relieve him of that responsibility now.

After two hours of waiting, the *Thunderstrike* received a reply from a rebel relay station. When the hologram flickered into existence at Namir's desk, he frowned at the woman who appeared in the image, trying to remember where he'd seen her face before. "Careful what you say, *Thunderstrike,*" the woman said, "and make it fast. This channel may not be secure."

Hoth. Namir had met her on Hoth. He'd argued with her and Kryndal; she'd punched him in the jaw. He wanted to laugh, but he suppressed it and merely smiled instead. He wondered if she recognized him.

"Understood," he said. "We may be out of contact awhile and we haven't received new orders. Anything we should know?"

"Final orders still stand," the woman said. "High Command has *not* regrouped. Vader is still leading the hunt." She scowled a moment, seemed to consider how to phrase her next thought. "Do you still have your . . . cargo?"

Namir cocked his head before the meaning hit him. Apparently she recognized him after all.

"Safely aboard," he said. "Why do you ask?"

The woman paused again. The hologram flickered. Namir wondered if the communication had been cut off, but then she spoke, voice distorted by static. "No reason," she said. "General Bygar had high hopes, was all."

The general who'd welcomed Namir and Chalis to Echo Base. The man who'd kept Namir's "discipline problem" from Howl.

"But Bygar's dead now," the woman continued. "So is the old plan. You're on your own, *Thunderstrike*."

"Aren't we all?" Namir asked, and the hologram abruptly flickered out.

The *Thunderstrike* and *Apailana's Promise* jumped out of hyperspace less than half a million kilometers from Sullust—so close that, upon the vessels' entry into realspace, the sudden clench of the planet's gravity nearly tore both ships apart. Namir lurched forward in his seat restraints in one of the *Thunderstrike's* drop ships and heard metal pop in the hangar bay. Emergency klaxons blared. An instant later, the voice of Commander Tohna came over the comm roaring laughter and triumph.

Sullust's orbital defenses were too formidable to risk facing in a straight-up fight; that was the only thing Twilight's senior staff had managed to agree on. Tohna's "solution"—jump in barely a stone's throw from the planet, deliver the drop ships, and jump out before the defenders could coordinate a counterattack—had possessed the potential to obliterate the company in a nanosecond if the jump were miscalculated, but Namir hadn't heard any better alternatives and approved the plan anyway. There were many fates worse than a quick and foolish death.

The other downside to Tohna's approach was that it left no time for a first wave of ground teams to clear a beachhead. The drop ships would descend together, and Namir and Chalis and the medics and engineers would arrive alongside the company vanguard. Word was that Hober had sent armor and fatigues to Chalis's quarters with a note reading, "Not available in black."

Namir had no complaints. He'd assigned Chalis to a separate drop ship—better to spread the risk—and he felt almost comfortable sandwiched between his colleagues' armored bodies, their rifles clacking together as the ship's thrusters discharged and its occupants swayed. This was planetfall in all its dangerous, sweaty, nauseating glory, as he'd experienced a hundred times before. He had to fight to avoid blacking out as they struck Sullust's atmosphere.

He didn't know whether he succeeded in staying conscious throughout the flight. All he was sure of was that the drop ship eventually slowed and the thunder of its engines quieted. He was the last man onto the surface, dropping two meters from the bay doors onto a slab of cracked and yellow-stained obsidian. A cloud of ocher motes rose where his boots impacted and he tasted ash through the filter of his breath mask.

The drop ship soared back into the blue-gray sky, pursued by dark specks—other drop ships or enemy aircraft, Namir wasn't sure. He surveyed his surroundings and saw that he stood on a narrow shelf jutting from a massive black slope; the shelf faded into the distance on either side, apparently wrapping around the mountainside. Below him, shallow crevices led down the slope like riverbeds to distant metal structures embedded in the base of the mountain—bunkers and transport stations, he thought. *Secondary targets and potential threats.*

Above Namir, the slope rose and became increasingly sheer toward the mountain's apex. Gripping the peak of the mountain was another metal structure: a compound of spires and support frames like a parasite feasting on the mountain's skull.

Comm signals cut through static, announcing other squads' safe arrival. Namir waved the other soldiers from his drop ship to gather as they finished scanning the perimeter. "We've got twenty-four hours before pickup," he called. "Don't plan on eating, sleeping, or emptying your bladders—we're in hostile territory and I need you ready to work."

Someone shouted, "Yes, Captain!" and Namir winced. Were they all calling him that now?

He bent down, scooped up a shard of obsidian, and tossed it over-hand down the slope. "Down there," he called, "buried underneath the enemy camps, is a Sullustan city. If you end up there, turn around and start climbing. You won't need maps for this mission."

"Up top," he continued, and turned to look toward the peak, "is the Inyusu Tor mineral processing facility. That's where the Empire bur-rows into this mountain and extracts ore from the magma inside. This facility supplies almost ten percent of the raw manufacturing re-sources for the planet, so . . . it's big. It's important. It's our target."

He looked around and saw heads nodding. In the distance, around the shelf, other squads were approaching. He cinched his rifle strap and smiled like a soldier ready to die for an idiot commander.

"Let's go get it," he said.

Even unprepared for an attack and only lightly guarded, the process-ing facility should have been unassailable by infantry. Ground forces would need to trek up the unforgiving rock while enduring a barrage of blasterfire from above. Move too swiftly and the squads were sure to be slaughtered. Move too slowly and the Empire would have time to scramble air support.

Upon reaching the apex, the teams would need to force their way inside the facility itself. Breaching a wall would be too time consum-ing with the tools Twilight had available—the facility was built to withstand volcanic heat—which left only the main entrances. These would be protected by the entirety of the facility's security force; at best, Twilight Company could expect a standoff until additional Im-perial units arrived from below the mountain.

Nonetheless, Namir sent all but four squads, a team of engineers, a rearguard selection of scouts and sentries, and a handful of medics to attempt the assault.

He observed with Chalis from a mobile camp less than fifty meters downslope from the fighting. It was a place the injured could retreat to and a command hub for senior staff out of the fray. It was not a site for squads to withdraw to when hard-pressed; twice, Namir had the grim task of informing squads that there could *be no withdrawal.* He watched the crimson flash of blasterfire sizzle in volleys against mountain obsidian, saw his colleagues desperately taking cover behind stones smaller than speeder bikes. He lifted his macrobinoculars high and saw stormtroopers and fleet troopers lined neatly before the processing facility walls, ready to move to shelter the moment the rebels closed in.

As the squads climbed upward—ten, twenty meters over the course of an hour—the camp moved with them. The scouts reported Imperial airspeeders rising from the garrisons below, and Namir sent word down the chain of command: *Advance.* Get closer. If the squads were near enough to the apex, the airspeeder pilots would be reluctant to drop sweep bombs for fear of damaging the processing facility. That wouldn't save the squads from the speeders' blaster cannons, but with luck, cannon fire could be evaded.

The teams climbed the mountain. The enemy began to withdraw to the facility entrances. As the airspeeders flitted into view, Namir—crouched as low to the ground as he could manage—signaled to one of the medics. "Get me the Plex," he called.

Chalis watched him from her position flat on the ground. She said nothing. Maybe she didn't understand what he was doing, or she knew he needed a distraction to maintain his sanity. Maybe she didn't care.

The PLX-1 was a cumbersome weapon, bulky and weighty and half as tall as a man. The control labels had long since worn off the Plex that Namir accepted from the medic; Namir imagined it as the sole survivor of Twilight's earliest incarnation, when Howl and a handful of others had first been tasked by the Rebellion. He didn't need the labels to adjust the settings or confirm its payload.

With the Plex hoisted on one shoulder, Namir rose to his feet and marched down the slope, away from the camp. He heard the shouts of his soldiers over the comm and tuned them out, kept his head turned away from the flickers of crimson. As he lifted his weapon's barrel toward the gray sky, he smiled as he was briefly left alone in the world.

An airspeeder soared into view. As Namir had predicted, it veered toward him. He was an obvious target, the lone man standing in view on the mountain slope. He turned toward it, pulled the trigger on the Plex, and felt his shoulder snap back as a rocket roared into the air reeking of exhaust and accelerant.

The airspeeder tried to swerve, firing its cannons as it did so. Shards of stone stung Namir when blaster bolts impacted nearby. Then the airspeeder was gone, consumed in a ball of flame and black smoke. Namir drew a breath, turned back up the slope, and tapped his comm.

"Where do we stand?" he asked.

"Ready for phase two," Chalis said.

Namir couldn't feel the mountain shake beneath him when the tunneling crew entered the processing facility. Intellectually, he knew it wasn't *possible*. But he thought he felt a tremor in his soles anyway when the designated moment arrived, and he clenched a fist in triumph.

While the bulk of the company had been climbing toward the apex, four squads and a team of engineers had descended to the transport stations embedded in the mountain's base. There, they'd stolen a pair of mining vehicles and proceeded to burrow their own way beneath the slope, up the mountain, and into the facility.

Later, the burrowing squads would talk of tearing their way through an underground wall and terrifying the Sullustan workers. At the appointed time, Namir ordered the aboveground squads to press forward, and shocked Imperial security teams and stormtroopers found themselves trapped between enemies both inside and outside the facility.

Once again, Twilight Company won.

It had been Chalis's plan, and Namir had doubted it—doubted that the mining vehicles would be stored where she claimed, doubted the machines could burrow their way up the mountain fast enough to win the battle. But Chalis had had faith in the systems of the Empire and the reliability of its quartermasters. She'd been able to access Imperial stock records and provide Twilight's engineers with vehicle schematics.

"You were right," Namir said. They stood together in the security office, looking down through the window at the workers marching out of the facility toward the industrial lifts and tramways that led down the mountainside. Twilight soldiers kept the Sullustans moving at gunpoint.

Chalis nodded. Her chest heaved as she suppressed a cough. Namir wondered how she was handling the air supply; the facility filtered the atmosphere, making the breath masks unnecessary indoors, but the smell was still sulfurous and foul.

When the last of the workers were gone, the transports were disabled and the squads finished scouring for any remaining resistance. Then the engineers began their second task of the day: programming the magma extractors to flood the facility interior. The new program would be run after the drop ships arrived to exfiltrate Twilight, at the last possible minute. The facility would be utterly annihilated as the *Thunderstrike* fled back into deep space, and the Empire would be deprived of one of Sullust's most valuable resources.

Until then, Twilight's soldiers had roughly twelve hours to pass. Namir assigned patrols both in and out of the facility. He kept a comm channel open and listened to sentries report—with perfect regularity, every thirty minutes—Imperial airspeeders passing overhead. He wasn't overly concerned. The Empire had no interest in destroying its own investment, and it didn't know what Twilight was planning.

Late at night or very early in the morning, he paced across one of the walkways overlooking an exposed magma stream. The flow smelled noxious even through the shimmering heat shield and cast everything in a lurid red glow. When Namir noticed that Brand had arrived at his side, her skin looked like polished bronze.

"Final numbers?" she asked.

"Four dead, sixteen injured," he said. "We were lucky."

Brand nodded and wrinkled her nose. Namir wanted to laugh at her suppressed, too-dignified reaction to the odor.

"Anyone you knew well?" she asked.

"Not too well," Namir said. Names and faces he recognized. Men and women and aliens he'd sat with in the mess or trained as fresh meat. They were all Twilight, all family, but none like Maediyu or Charmer or Roja or Beak or even Ajax; or the comm tech he'd pledged to forget on Asyrphus. Today's losses were ones he could pretend didn't matter, people whose ghosts wouldn't haunt him aboard the *Thunderstrike*. He drifted to the railing of the walkway, tried to stare down into the magma, and failed to look long at the flow's bright surface.

Brand followed him. "Yeah," she said. He couldn't tell what she was agreeing with.

They stood together that way awhile. Namir thought of all the hours he'd spent silent and alone with Chalis—on Mardona III, on the shuttle from Hoth—and was quietly amazed that two people, both utterly motionless, could be *present* in such different ways. Brand became one with her surroundings, like a boulder on a mountainside. Chalis was like a nail in a pane of cracked glass; solid as steel, but in fundamental tension with the world around her.

"Why are we doing this?" Brand asked.

Namir frowned. "Chalis says—"

"Not Sullust. The whole campaign. Kuat."

Right. *This*.

"I made a promise," he said, "to support Twilight Company and the Rebellion. Everyone here—" *Everyone but me and Chalis.* "—joined to strike back at the Empire. I'm giving them the best way I know to do it."

"Huh," Brand said.

In an instant, Brand's reserve seemed to turn aggressive. The silence that had been comforting now irked Namir. "What?" he asked. "Say it."

She shrugged. "I'm just thinking. You ever ask Howl why he did something?"

"I really don't need you comparing me to Howl right now—"

She kept speaking as if he hadn't replied. "He never gave you one answer. That's because he never did *anything* for one reason. Never did anything that wouldn't count as a victory, even in a military defeat."

"Not to his mind, anyway. Maybe."

She shrugged again. "The point is, if all we're doing is spitting in the face of evil? Hitting back just to *hit back*? Maybe Gadren and Roach see some proud warrior sacrifice garbage in that, but you and me are too old for it."

He straightened up, stared at her. She met his gaze, face unreadable as ever, and all he could think was *How dare you?* How dare she question him now, weeks after Ankhural instead of earlier, when it would have *mattered*? He wanted to say something that would sting, something that would hurt her. It would be only just.

He knew her secrets. But when he found his ammunition he let it sink back into the ocean of his mind. Instead, he said, "Do you have anything useful for me? Or are you just questioning my ability to command?"

"Neither," Brand said, and walked away.

Namir swore silently into the fire.

The *Thunderstrike* was scheduled to arrive around midday. By early morning, Twilight soldiers had packed any gear worth salvaging from the facility. The engineers had programmed the extractors to flood the compound with magma at the flip of a switch. Namir had sent alternative drop ship assignments and locations to the squads in case the Empire's air support made pickup at the facility impossible.

Namir was squatting just outside the main entrance, watching the skies through macrobinoculars and wondering about Twilight's next mission—the strike on Malastare, the *last* strike before Kuat—when he received a signal from *Thunderstrike* indicating it had arrived in orbit. "We've got heavy TIE presence," Commander Tohna said. "We're going to come in low, use our own firepower to cover the drop ships while the *Promise* and her X-wings watch our flank. Should be a good show."

Namir waved at a sentry, and a slow stream of Twilight squads began hustling out of the facility. An engineer cast him a questioning glance, but he shook his head. "Not yet," he called. "Wait for the drop ships." No point in being hasty.

He waited for the shadow of the *Thunderstrike* to cross the clouds and listened to Tohna's updates. A dozen TIE fighters destroyed, a dozen more incoming. Three minutes until he released the drop ships. Two minutes. A dark shape took form high above, and the macrobinoculars enhanced its edges until it looked like a starship. "One minute," Tohna said. "Get ready to board—we're cutting it close!"

Then a dozen new specks flitted into Namir's view and Tohna began cursing. Far above came a sound like thunder.

Namir couldn't see what was happening at first. He demanded an update from Tohna, but the commander either wasn't listening or could no longer hear him. Yet the form of the *Thunderstrike* among the clouds continued to grow, continued to descend, now sporting a red-and-green halo as blaster cannons and turbolasers ignited the air.

The soldiers nearby watched uneasily, murmured questions that Namir couldn't answer.

He winced as a burst of static pierced his ear, started to adjust his link before a new voice cut in. "Twilight? This is the *Promise*," a woman's voice said. "We've been ambushed—whole blasted swarm came in from behind the moon. They were waiting for the *Thunderstrike* to hit atmo . . ."

Namir swore too loudly. A dozen heads turned to look at him. The *Thunderstrike* seemed to be descending faster. "Pull back," he said into his link. He sounded calmer than he felt. "We can hold out here. Pull back *now!*"

But the order came too late. The *Thunderstrike* was no longer lowering itself by thrusters and repulsors. Its prow had tipped forward and it trailed black fog. Fire swallowed its hull, brighter than the gleam of blasters.

Every soldier in Twilight Company stood at the entrance to the facility and turned to watch the troop transport spiral through the air. It leveled itself briefly then dipped again until its roar was constant, like the crash of ocean waves. Then it passed out of sight around the curve of the mountain and the ground rumbled.

The word *retreat* came in over the comm, the woman's voice repeating over and over until a burst of static ended the transmission.

The *Thunderstrike* was down. The *Promise* and her starfighters were gone, if not destroyed.

Twilight Company was trapped on Sullust.

CHAPTER 29

PLANET SULLUST

Thirty-One Days into Operation Ringbreaker

Stormtroopers must remain in uniform at all times while in view of the public.

It was a simple rule, a basic rule, drilled into every cadet's brain until it became instinct. Thara Nyende believed in it, knew it was integral to maintaining the public trust. A stormtrooper without a helmet was an individual with her own name and needs and goals. You couldn't trust individuals.

A stormtrooper in uniform represented the Empire. That *meant* something.

None of which explained why she'd removed her helmet in the security office of Pinyumb Transport Station Four. It was unlikely she'd been seen, but it was still possible. The black visor stared up at her from the console while she chewed on her ration bar. When her armor's memory was downloaded, she'd probably be caught, her indiscretion flagged and automatically appended to her record.

She was just so tired.

Was a five-minute break and an early lunch too much to ask?

For the past three weeks, she'd worked ten-hour shifts daily. She'd received no further treatment nor counseling after the horrors she'd experienced aboard the rebel terrorist vessel. Her hearing still came and went in her right ear. She knew other troopers on other worlds had been through far worse, and she didn't complain. Still, she flinched whenever she opened the door to an apartment pod to search for rebel supporters.

But if the hunt for the rebels had been the only burden, she could have suffered through it. Since the raid on the warehouse world, the Empire had been demanding longer shifts from the civilian workers as well. This, in turn, meant more overseers and security teams to enforce standards. New transports arrived almost daily from offworld, while other enforcers were hired locally and rapidly trained. The entire city was tired, and Thara had nowhere to turn for respite. The Rebellion was to blame for this, as well—the raids were continuing across nearby sectors, and Sullust had to make up the difference where it could.

She'd visited her uncle's cantina one night. She'd been discreet. She only wanted to see how it was functioning in his absence, while he was still awaiting trial or release from the holding pens.

"If Cobalt Front hadn't decided to bomb factories instead of write letters to the governor," one of the old men had said, "maybe we'd have someone to speak up."

"Cobalt Front *never* cared about workers' rights," another had argued. "The Rebellion was behind it from the start."

"It doesn't matter now," said a third—a man with bandages wrapped around his steam-burnt eyes. "Blame doesn't matter. Pray the storm passes, and that the harvest is richer after the rain."

But the storm hadn't passed.

Instead the Rebellion had sent an army to Sullust.

———

Thara hadn't fought during the invasion. She hadn't been at the processing facility or the surface garrisons, and when they'd sent her on patrol at night—assigned to a stormtrooper squad full of offworld veterans who could recognize a blaster's specifications by the sound of its trigger—she'd trembled every time she saw a distant figure on the mountain. She'd nearly shot at a speeder bike piloted by an allied scout; only her sergeant's angry, snapped order had stopped her.

She was *willing* to fight. She'd go to the facility if she was ordered, shoot at rebels and avenge the colleagues she'd already lost. And she was willing to follow the protocols delivered to her at the morning briefing: instructions for a crackdown in the city, should the citizens of Pinyumb or rebel infiltrators take the opportunity to strike. Door-to-door searches, roundups of subversives and suspected subversives, lockdowns of all housing blocks and workplaces ... she knew her duty. She hoped drastic measures wouldn't be necessary, and she was prepared to enact them if they were.

But after so many weeks of hunting and seeking and waiting for the next bomb to go off, so many ten-hour shifts that ended with her face-down in a coarse pillow and crying, she needed a moment—just a *moment*—for herself.

So she chewed her ration bar slowly and tried not to meet the gaze of the helmet balanced on the security console before her.

She hadn't quite finished eating when her comlink blared an emergency signal.

She threw the bar and wrapper to the floor, scooped her helmet up and donned it as data cascaded onto the display. There was an emergency on the surface. Stormtrooper teams were being deployed to the streets of Pinyumb and the upper garrisons. All units were expected to be combat-ready.

She felt a wave of guilt for neglecting her duty and pushed it aside. She was SP-475 of the Imperial Ninety-Seventh Stormtrooper Legion and she'd been ordered to report to the transport station's upper levels. *Were the rebels coming down from the mountain?* she wondered. *Was the city going to be attacked?*

Twenty other troopers crowded into the cargo lift as it rose to the surface. When she stepped off metal and onto rock, her display flickered as it updated to accommodate the outdoor lighting. She heard wind, and behind the wind a shrieking, rumbling sound. Behind the rumbling was the sound of blasters, distant and tinny.

Her fellow soldiers were looking up, pointing at something in the sky. As she scrambled to her post, she saw a ship plummeting toward the mountain, wrapped in black smoke and fire. It was enormous. It was a rebel vessel. It had to be.

When it struck the side of the mountain, the crash sounded like the explosion she'd survived in the spaceport.

This time, she was sure all of Pinyumb would suffer.

PART IV

SIEGE

CHAPTER 30

BREMA SECTOR OUTSKIRTS
Two Days Before the Siege of Inyusu Tor

Captain Tabor Seitaron was pleased.

He'd forgotten the difference having a plan made. Intellectually, of course, he'd always understood the value, had lectured to his students about the importance of *purpose* to a ship's morale. Yet in his weeks aboard the *Herald* he'd discounted the fact that he, too, was part of the Star Destroyer's crew. When his men looked at Prelate Verge askance and feared for their future, Tabor shared in the toll.

And when Tabor had seen the common thread between Governor Chalis's targets—not in a revelatory flash, but in the gradual, almost unnoticed dawning of an inevitable idea—when he'd shared that knowledge with the prelate and they'd strode confidently out of the tactical center . . . well, the mood aboard the *Herald* had changed, and Tabor's had changed with it.

He felt almost young as he paced the bridge and nodded approval to the men at the duty stations. The facts seemed straightforward now, and the solution similarly so.

Fact: Governor Chalis and her infantry company were striking soft targets along the Rimma Trade Route.

Fact: Governor Chalis's expertise was in the logistical machinery of the Empire.

Extrapolation: Her goal was not military. Rather, she sought to deliver a crippling blow to the Empire's infrastructure.

By what exact means, Tabor neither knew nor needed to know. His only concern was to discern the existing pattern and analyze Chalis's next step. Stop her midway down the path, and who cared about her final destination?

He had worked with Prelate Verge to whittle their list of Chalis's potential targets down from hundreds to dozens. Of the targets that remained—manufacturing facilities, spacedocks, shipping lanes— they'd separated out any that failed to match Chalis's secret pattern, any that lacked the thread that bound them inexorably to the governor. They had been too late to stop her at Nakadia and Kuliquo, but both proved that Tabor could predict her actions.

That left only a handful of possibilities. Sullust. Malastare. Tshindral. They set to preparing each for an attack. "She'll flee if she sees a foe prepared," he'd told Verge. "She's too much of a coward to do otherwise. We must keep our distance until she steps into the trap. When the time comes, the kill is yours."

That time was fast approaching. He was sure of it.

The communications officer rose from his duty station, stood stiff as he signaled for Tabor's attention. "Captain!" he said. His voice trembled slightly, but his lips crept into a smile. "We have a signal coming from Sullust!"

"And?" Tabor asked.

"The *Thunderstrike* and her escorts are in-system. You were right."

The duty officers began to applaud. It was a breach of protocol Tabor could forgive—this was their triumph as much as his, and they deserved to linger on it. They deserved a reminder that they had earned their positions aboard a Star Destroyer, earned the power to ruin planets and battle fleets.

Yet he did not smile. "Bring the prelate to the bridge and get me a tactical feed," he said gruffly. "I'll need a channel to Vixus Squadron, as well."

The bridge crew set to work. Tabor withdrew to the tactical center to consider his options. Sullust would not, in all likelihood, repel the *Thunderstrike*. That was for the best; Verge had insisted on leaving the regional governors uninformed of their systems' target status for that very reason. But Verge had also divvied up his forces well, secreting squadrons of TIE interceptors near Chalis's most likely victims.

"Well done!" the prelate's voice declared. Tabor felt the boy's hand squeeze his shoulder. "Are they following standard procedure?"

"Delivering drop ships to the planet surface? Yes, Prelate." Tabor swept his hand over the tactical hologram, switching from a view of the star cluster to the feed direct from Sullust. "Vixus is ready to move, but I expect the rebel troop transport will flee as soon as insertion is complete . . ."

Verge shook his head briskly, dismissively. "There's no hurry," he said. "Our quarry is Chalis, not a gaggle of rebel soldiers. Unless we're absolutely *certain* she's with the ground forces?"

"No evidence of it either way," Tabor said.

"Then her ship remains the priority. And her ship will be back once the ground mission is complete."

Tabor smiled grimly. "Agreed. I'll have Vixus move to Sullust and prepare for the *Thunderstrike*'s return. It might also be wise to contact Sullust ground forces and ensure the rebel company isn't entirely obliterated. Unlikely, but if they get lucky . . ." He shrugged. "We need to be sure the *Thunderstrike* has a reason to come back."

Verge laughed, throwing his head back unashamed. The sound was exuberant and joyous, full of life and passion. It buoyed Tabor's own spirits further—but only for an instant, before he recalled where the boy's delight came from: his mad obsession with extravagance, his half-concealed terror, and his messianic belief that he was the forerunner of a new Imperial way of life.

Suddenly Tabor felt old again. His muscles seemed too atrophied to hold his body straight. But he smiled again and went about his tasks. Perhaps victory and Tabor's example would mellow the boy. Refine his genius into something more mature.

Within the hour, Vixus Squadron was on its way to Sullust. The *Herald* had set course as well, though its arrival would come later. It was a pity, Tabor thought, that the crew wouldn't witness the fall of the *Thunderstrike* in person after all that they'd done . . . yet he was sure the aftermath would prove satisfying.

"When this is over," Verge said as they stood together at the bridge viewport, watching the azure vortex of hyperspace ripple about the ship, "you will be rewarded, you know. You and I will go before the Emperor together. Your role in this endeavor has been essential."

Tabor wished only to return to his home: to his classes and his tea set and the natural aroma and sky and gravity of Carida. He knew the prelate better than to say as much.

"Thank you, Prelate."

Verge chuckled and touched a fingertip to the viewport, sliding it down the pane as if he could feel the pulse of hyperspace. "Nor, I think, will the crew of this ship forget you. I do not know what our future will entail, but I look forward to seeing their next performance."

Tabor turned his head and brought the duty stations into his peripheral vision. He studied the men who'd applauded him, whose fears he'd tamped and whose purpose he'd delicately nourished since coming aboard. He tried to imagine what they might want as a reward.

"I'm sure you'll do right by them," Tabor said. "And they will do right by you."

CHAPTER 31

PLANET SULLUST
Day One of the Siege of Inyusu Tor

Namir had half a dozen search-and-rescue squads ready to go. It wasn't the mix he might have wanted—too few medics and engineers, too many demolitions specialists—but all were combat-ready and they could travel fast. The rest of the company would stay behind at the processing facility and fortify for an attack.

Because an attack had to be coming, and Twilight Company had nowhere to run.

He signaled the first wave to head out. Scouts riding speeder bikes pillaged from the facility hangar shot down the mountain slope, angling toward the plume of black smoke rising into the sky. The rest of the squads would need to reach the *Thunderstrike*—whatever was *left* of the *Thunderstrike*—on foot. He gave the nod to Carver, who began speaking into his link. Boots struck obsidian and stone and team leaders shouted marching orders.

Namir adjusted his helmet and breath mask, cinched his rifle strap, and started to follow when a voice cut in over the comm.

"They're dead, and we need you here. Stop this," Chalis said.

Namir didn't answer. Instead he joined the soldiers scrabbling down the rock toward their lost ship. He tried to remember how many people had been aboard the *Thunderstrike*—more than thirty permanent crew members, any company members not cleared for ground combat . . .

. . . and injured soldiers unfit for duty.

How many were they? Von Geiz would know, but he'd stayed aboard the *Thunderstrike,* too.

Damn it all.

The trek to the transport was brutal. An early fall scraped Namir's hands raw as he slid down a bank of gravel. Reports from the scouts urged him forward, kept him moving despite the rough terrain. The ship was still partly intact, the scouts said; the reactor hadn't detonated on impact. There might still be survivors.

When the vessel came into view, however, it was hard to maintain hope. The *Thunderstrike* was only intact in that it hadn't shattered altogether. Even from far up the mountain, even through the smoke, Namir could see a massive breach through the center of the vessel. If it had tried to rise into the air, it would have fallen in two.

Shortly thereafter, the scouts reported Imperial airspeeders en route. If there was any chance of rescuing the living, it had to be done before bombing runs reduced the wreckage to a crater full of scorched metal.

Onward. Namir listened to the first wave of search-and-rescue teams call out every victory and loss. They tore aside doors and found members of the bridge crew trapped under consoles, hurt but alive. They found the broken parts of M2-M5 scattered across the medbay; the sardonic droid's final act had been to try to protect the wounded. By the time Namir arrived on the scene, Von Geiz—his face stained with blood as red as a warning light—had begun triage: counting the dead, sending the worst casualties toward the processing facility on speeder bikes, ordering the rest to rejoin Twilight on foot.

Namir was glad to defer to the old medic's expertise. He kept the conversation brief as they sheltered beneath a hull fragment and listened to blaster cannons pelt the stone around them. "How many unaccounted for?" Namir asked.

"Another twenty, perhaps," Von Geiz said. "We can't reach the lower decks."

"Keep trying," Namir said. "But if we start losing our line of retreat, we all pull out together."

Von Geiz nodded. He'd been with Twilight a long time, and he knew when a patient was too far gone to save.

As the afternoon wore on, the squads formed a chain between the shipwreck and the processing facility. Namir would escort a handful of limping and bruised crew members a hundred meters up the mountain slope and hand them over to the next squad, assuring them that shelter wasn't far. Zab's team built a makeshift sniper's nest above the wreckage to provide cover while others salvaged canisters of liquid bacta and medical devices. As night fell, Namir bent his knees as Commander Tohna leaned heavily on his shoulders, clasped the tatters of his glove to the larger man's breath mask as the *Thunderstrike*'s skipper tried to howl in pain. "Too many enemies, too close," Namir told him. "We can't give away our position."

Heavier bombers finally arrived shortly after dark, smashing fresh holes in the *Thunderstrike* and sending shards of metal and bone flying. Fewer casualties emerged from hiding even as Imperial ground troops appeared on the horizon and their scouting parties delivered constant volleys of blaster bolts. Namir didn't remember sending the order to withdraw, though he knew he must have done so. His mouth tasted like ash and his lips were cracked as he began his final march back. He'd stopped sweating hours before, and his legs ached with every step up the slope. He wondered for only an instant about the situation back at the processing facility, then forced that question from his mind. *Survive first,* he told himself. *Then find a way to save Twilight.*

Of the soldiers who'd joined the rescue parties, five were unaccounted for when Namir stumbled back into the processing facility, winding his way through a maze of barricades improvised from industrial equipment. "If they're not back in an hour, assume they're dead," he told Twitch, who stood guard at the innermost sentry post. "If they come in later, we can believe in miracles."

He felt simultaneously hollow and heavy, a shell of a body wearing skin of lead. Men and women hurried to his side as he walked under dim yellow lighting through the main access corridor. None brought him water or food or a change of gloves. Instead, they burdened him with reports and updates about *Apailana's Promise,* which appeared to have fled Sullust intact; a team was attempting to make contact and determine the gunship's position. They told him about Imperial infantry forces circling the base of the mountain and slowly closing the noose. They guessed at the likelihood of repairing the *Thunderstrike*—not inconceivable with the proper resources, but impossible under fire—or what could be stripped and salvaged from it instead.

Namir tried to absorb it all, comprehend the reports and provide direction when required. When the last of the urgent demands on him had been addressed, he pulled aside one of the Haidoral recruits whose name he couldn't recall. "What do you need, Captain?" the man asked.

Namir didn't correct him. "I want to see the field hospital," he said. "I want water. And I want to meet with Governor Chalis."

After he'd drunk his fill, after he'd stilled his stomach after breathing in the vile odors of the aid station, he found Chalis in the administrator's office. The vast space had been hastily ransacked—likely by the administrator when Twilight had first arrived—and niches on the wall that might once have held plaques or awards were now empty. An upholstered couch was scorched on one end, and beside it a stack of boxes held facility records. Chalis sat at a desk apparently carved from a single piece of mountain stone, gripping the edge of the rock with her fingers as if she expected to crush it into dust.

"Someone planned this," she said, voice taut and bitter. She didn't bother to ask Namir about the rescue operation. "The moment we landed they were preparing to cut off our escape."

And whose fault is that? Namir wanted to ask. But he didn't want to know the answer. It hardly mattered now.

"So what comes next?" he asked instead.

"Our enemy—for the sake of convenience, we'll assume it's Prelate Verge—brings reinforcements to annihilate us. I'd expect a Star Destroyer in-system shortly. Just one should be enough."

"One would've been enough for Hoth, too." He dropped himself on the couch. "How fast do those things move?"

"Faster than a stripped-down rebel corvette past its prime. I wouldn't give us more than a day or two at most."

He wanted to drift off, stop *thinking* for a moment. He made himself speak. "Then we get off the planet first, somehow. Head farther into the Outer Rim, lick our wounds—"

"What?" Chalis's tone was suddenly sharp. Namir straightened in his seat.

"They *know*," he said, frustration giving him strength again. "The prelate figured out the plan. You said over and over that if that happened—"

"No one knows what we're doing," she said. She started to continue, then began to cough, chest heaving and head bent forward. Namir wanted to avert his eyes but Chalis never turned from him, as if trying to hold him in place until she could resume. When the fit subsided she spoke slowly and hoarsely. "Even if the prelate saw some pattern," she said, "that doesn't mean he knows our goals. We can adjust. We can survive one loss. The window of opportunity is still open."

Namir watched her. Her hands still clutched the stone of the table.

"Unless," she added, and smiled a forced, deathly smile, "you want to announce to the company that we're giving up?"

Namir began to laugh.

He couldn't have justified why. It wasn't a raucous or a joyous sound, and he tasted ash rising from his lungs, gritty on his lips. Chalis maintained her frozen rictus, and finally he shook his head. "You're the one who likes giving speeches," he said. "If it comes to that, maybe you should tell them yourself."

They watched each other. Eventually Chalis's smile faded. She stood from the desk and walked to a table in the corner of the office where a tin pitcher sat. She lifted it, glanced about, then shrugged and brought the pitcher to the couch. Namir took it and drank gratefully. The lukewarm water tasted bitter; it reminded him of the well water of Crucival.

"As I see it," Chalis said, "we have two challenges ahead. First, we need to survive the coming siege and—if we can't avoid it—whatever blow Verge's reinforcements deliver. Second, we need a way off Sullust.

"I *suggest*—and I'm open to alternatives—that you take care of the former. Devise a way for us not to die. I'll get to work on the latter."

She still stood over him, above the couch. Namir drew himself upright and set the pitcher on the desk. "Fair enough," he said. "Does that mean you have a plan?"

"I will," Chalis said curtly, and it sounded like an oath.

The company worked through the night readying the facility for attack. Namir toured the processing center, walked among the ranks, offered his strength or advice where he could be useful and stepped back when he was unwanted.

On the lower levels, the engineers scrambled to undo the adjustments they'd made to the magma extractors. Flooding the facility was no longer one of Twilight's short-term objectives, but the molten rock might prove integral to the facility's defense: If the Empire tried to imitate Twilight's previous strategy of sending in burrowing vehicles below the compound, the attackers would find Twilight ready to rechannel the magma flow.

It was the sort of dirty trick that won wars—unpredictable, unfair, and deadly. Namir smiled grimly when Vifra—Twilight's new head of engineering since M2-M5's destruction—described what she had in mind, and he challenged her to take it a step farther. "Were you here for the fighting on Cartao?" he asked.

Vifra flinched and glanced toward her comrades as they dismantled a control terminal. She seemed to be seeking support. "I really
just got here," she said. "I joined six months ago, off Phorsa Gedd."

Namir had probably been there for her recruitment, he realized.
But she was an engineer and so he'd never trained her, never called her
fresh meat. She must have been blasted good to rise so swiftly through
the ranks, even considering the company's rapid attrition. He made a
note to get to know her.

"Doesn't matter," he said. "Keep us alive, and I'll tell you about Cartao after."

When Namir returned to the upper floors, the distant thunder of
Imperial bombs made the facility sound as if it were weathering a
storm. On a lookout post above the main wall, he could see flashes all
about the peak of the mountain, see streaks of light in the sky where
the bombers passed. The Empire wasn't attempting to destroy the
facility—it still wanted to preserve the infrastructure—but it was
doing all it could to contain Twilight Company.

Still, Namir thought, that meant more time to prepare.

The barricade mazes at the facility entrances had been transformed
over the past few hours, reorganized to funnel enemies into kill zones
and allow snipers a line on attackers. The mazes were works of art—
a junkyard of sabotaged loadlifters and spare parts and toppled bever-
age dispensers—but Namir ordered most of the soldiers constructing
them to another task. "If the enemy gets this close," he told one group,
"we're bound to lose anyway. I want squads around the perimeter in
positions they can *hold*. Keep the Empire down the slope, make them
fight for every meter they climb."

That meant, of course, digging trenches and assembling artillery
pieces near the sites of the bombings, hoping dust and night and caution gave enough cover for safety. Namir didn't ask for volunteers or
offer the troops a chance to back out. He saw that they were afraid—
the young and old, veterans and fresh meat. Yet the job had to be
done, and they went without complaint.

He felt a mixture of pride and guilt as he continued his tour. He saw
the soldiers put their losses—the deaths of their colleagues and the

destruction of their vessel—to one side, determined to do their part in an impossible situation. If they survived, there would be trauma and grief. Some of them would break: They'd put themselves in the line of fire, request noncombat duties, or walk away on a mission and never return. Yet he trusted all of them to hold together until the battle was over.

He'd led them to Sullust with a promise to strike against the Empire. He was responsible for their fate. But if they could hold together, he could, too.

A gray dawn arrived, and Namir met briefly with the squad leaders and senior staff, sketching a plan of battle for the coming siege. Hober and Von Geiz had counted the dead and wounded, quantified the company's capabilities as well as they could. It hardly seemed to matter in the face of a planet's worth of attackers, but Namir and Carver and Gadren and Mzun and the others pretended the battle was winnable anyway.

"Should Chalis be present?" Von Geiz asked abruptly. He'd cleaned the blood from his face and wrapped white gauze at an angle over his forehead and left eye. The others looked to Namir, who shook his head.

"If she had a plan ready, she would be here," he said. "Let her work."

He'd seen bitterness and fury in her during their meeting, but not the despair he'd witnessed on Ankhural. He trusted she would do what she could.

He had no choice but to believe she would hold together, too.

Namir slept on the floor of one of the upper-level offices, leaving instructions with Hober to wake him if anything happened. No more than two hours passed before a runner arrived with a tray of food and the news that Chalis wanted to see him.

He ate hastily—pooled in the tray's compartments was some sort of noodle soup apparently scrounged from a worker's locker—and tried to gauge his strength. The rest had boosted his energy levels, and the food would do so as well; but the boost would fade fast, and his legs were still sore and throbbing from marching to and from the *Thunderstrike*. He almost hoped to see combat. At least adrenaline might carry him through the day.

Chalis had rearranged the administration office, moving the couch and boxes to one side and tiling the floor with maps of the mountain and its vicinity. In one of the niches now rested a bronze bust of a stern-looking man. Namir didn't have time to examine it before Chalis picked her way across the floor to his side.

"I want to go to Pinyumb," she said.

Namir frowned, tried to place the name—all Sullustan names sounded the same—and cursed his sluggish mind. Finally he found what he sought. "City at the base of the mountain?" Chalis didn't correct him, so he assumed he'd guessed correctly. "What for?"

"We know there was a resistance on this planet," Chalis said. That was true: The files aboard the *Thunderstrike* had indicated as much, though Alliance High Command didn't know, or didn't care to share, more than the bare bones. "Luko's records show they attacked this facility recently and are active in the city."

"Luko? You on a first-name basis with the ex-administrator here?" Namir asked, glancing toward the box of records again.

Chalis seemed inured to the joke. "I've had time on my hands. We can't maintain a channel to the *Promise* for more than a minute without being jammed, which makes formulating an extraction plan difficult. Not that the *Promise* has room to take us aboard, but we'll need a defense when we manage to get offworld—"

"I get it," Namir said. "What do you think the resistance can do for us?"

"Just about anything would help." Here, she did smile—a bitter, nasty twitch of her lips. "I'm not expecting a starship, but even information would be an asset."

"Fine. Pick a squad, grab any vehicle in the hangar, but be prepared to slip through the perimeter on foot—"

"I'd advise you to come along," Chalis said. "All you can do here is wait, and if we *do* locate anyone you might want a word with our potential reinforcements."

Namir grimaced. He didn't like the thought of leaving. "You might be overestimating the strength of the resistance. If we haven't heard from them by now . . ."

Chalis stepped to the door and looked over her shoulder at Namir. "You can't win this battle," she said. "Our only hope is an exit strategy. Take whatever chance you can get."

It was a blunt argument, but she wasn't wrong.

Together with the three surviving members of Twitch's squad, Namir and Chalis climbed into a boxy Imperial troop transport that hummed softly out of the hangar and toward the facility's main entrance. It was one of a handful of vehicles Twilight had made operational since the *Thunderstrike*'s crash. It nearly ran over Roach as she hurried to wave it down and pulled herself up and through the hatch. "Gadren sent me," she told Namir, squeezing onto the bench beside him.

He frowned. "That leaves Gadren with, what—just Brand?"

Roach shrugged. "Said you needed protection." She wasn't wearing her helmet. Namir noticed a patch of her scalp was bare, as if the hair had been burned or cut away to treat a wound.

"All right," Namir said. Another set of eyes could be useful, and Roach was skinny and quick. Useful on a stealth mission.

She nodded firmly, adjusted her comlink in one ear, and retrieved a second earpiece from her pocket. She inserted it deftly, and a moment later Namir could hear the muffled, tinny sounds of music accompanying the transport's voyage down the mountain.

Toward the base of the mountain, they abandoned the vehicle and changed into ill-fitting civilian clothing—whatever garments the workers at the processing facility had left behind during the evacuation. They stashed their rifles with the troop transport, switching to knives and snub pistols small enough to conceal in boots and under vests. Comlinks were deactivated and stowed in pockets. Any close inspection would give Namir and the others away, but from a distance they might pass as Pinyumb locals.

First, however, they had to *reach* Pinyumb. It was dusk when they began creeping down the slope, half squatting and half crawling as the terrain permitted. The Empire's perimeter was intended to stop infantry units and speeders, not catch lone travelers, but scouting a path was neither swift nor safe. Twice, Namir came within a stone's throw of a stormtrooper patrol and had to wait for the enemy to move on. The rebels scattered and regrouped over and over; apart, they would draw less attention, but they were vulnerable alone.

Roach stayed at Namir's side more often than not. He wondered if Gadren had instructed her to do so or if she'd decided to play bodyguard on her own.

Once they were through the blockade, reaching the city was comparatively easy. Namir saw no civilian vehicles descending into the underground through the transport station, but a steady trickle of Imperial military vehicles and cargo carriers still flowed. In two teams of three, the rebels slipped aboard the carriers and squeezed between supply crates, letting the repulsorcraft carry them onto lifts dropping below the planet's surface. Namir expected the air to grow thinner, to turn unbearably noxious in the bowels of Sullust, but instead it seemed to grow pure—fresher even than the stale air of the *Thunderstrike,* reminding Namir of the dewy atmosphere of Haidoral Prime. He removed his breath mask with cautious excitement.

Then the six travelers emerged furtively from the vehicles onto city streets, and Namir had his first glimpse of Pinyumb.

The city sat within a great obsidian cavern, its roof dimly gleaming with refracted iridescence from tower lights. Its buildings were sleek, tapered and curved instead of rigid, rising along turquoise waterways lined with footpaths and pedestrian bridges. The walkways, in turn, wove among rows of plants that glowed with phosphorescent bulbs and archways carved from the cavern stone. Namir caught himself staring in wonder. He wondered if his companions would scorn his reaction as naïve: the ignorant amazement of a child from a backwater world.

But Roach was grinning, unashamed, as she craned her neck and took in the cavern vista. That comforted Namir, even when Chalis murmured a warning to Roach and the girl's face became stony.

"Why's it quiet?" Twitch asked through her teeth.

Namir swore to himself and broke the city's spell. Twitch was right: There was no traffic in the streets except the receding transports, no civilians using the walkways or the bridges. The buildings were lit, certainly, but no sounds arose from inside. He felt suddenly exposed on the street, as if marked by a sniper.

"The city is in lockdown," Chalis said. "Typical procedure—it probably has been since we landed. Come on."

Chalis led the way into an alley, and they started their journey through Pinyumb—once again in twos and threes, once again sending scouts at every junction. They soon discovered that stormtrooper teams were stationed on every major throughway. Floating, bobbing, cam droids combed the back ways. But the Empire seemed to be patrolling as a show of force, not actively searching, and the squad had no difficulty remaining hidden. Here and there, Namir did spot a civilian— always moving briskly but not running, always with one hand holding up a datapad that doubtless served as authorization for travel.

The squad's destination, Chalis had explained, was an old resistance safe house mentioned in Howl's files. "We won't know if it's still active until we get there," she said, "but it's our best lead."

She navigated into a section of the city that appeared to have been erected in an earlier age. Among the metal structures were buildings made of stone, and the narrow streets were cracked and thick with yellow sulfur. The group descended a stairway into an alley beneath ground level and found a door built into the wall.

"An icehouse," Chalis explained. Twitch began toying with the keypad. "This would've been a wealthy district, once. Primitives stored meat, milk, anything they wanted to keep cool here."

The others looked puzzled, but Namir remembered the icehouses on his homeworld. He wondered if Chalis recalled such things from her childhood. She didn't glance at him once.

Twitch made a triumphant sound. The door swung open and they proceeded inside. The building's single room was devoid of life, furnished as a sparse apartment with a cot and stove and a portable sanitation station. "Someone's been here," Twitch said, scuffing the dust on the floor. Namir agreed with the assessment, though it was hard to guess whether the safe house had last been used hours, days, or weeks before.

A thorough search turned up scraps of food and medical supplies and nothing more until Roach—guided by some instinct Namir couldn't even guess at—fished a datapad from one of the sanitation station's filters. Chalis took possession of the prize, apparently untroubled by the bacterial slime clinging to the screen.

After a few moments of study, she looked pleased. "Someone was here," she echoed, "tracking the coming and going of ships on Sullust. Presumably gathering intelligence for an attack on a spaceport. I can use this."

Namir held out a hand. Chalis passed him the pad and he tried to make sense of it. He skimmed through lists and monthly reports, unsure what he was looking for. He wondered briefly if he was reading the data correctly: Surely there shouldn't have been such a massive difference between departures and arrivals? It seemed like for every hundred ships that reached the planet, a thousand left.

He asked Chalis about the discrepancy. She shrugged and reclaimed the datapad. "Manufacturing," she said. "Sullust isn't Kuat, but it does handle small-scale production of starfighters and assault shuttles. Nothing important."

"Thousands of ships a year is small-scale production?" he asked. His voice was low, but he felt the others glance his way.

Chalis didn't even look up, her eyes on the pad again. She only grunted in acknowledgment, but he could hear the words she'd spoken to him once before:

You still think like a man from Crucival. You don't understand the scale of the enemy.

No one else seemed worried. Even Roach looked more concerned about Namir than any revelation about Sullust. Namir supposed Chalis was right, though the thought bothered him for reasons he couldn't place.

They decided to wait at the safe house for three hours to see if anyone from the Sullustan resistance appeared. After that, they would return to Twilight Company regardless of the outcome. Chalis sent two squad members to scout the Pinyumb spaceport—an underground facility connected to the surface by a kilometers-long shaft—while they waited. "I'd like to know our options," she said.

That left Twitch, Roach, Chalis, and Namir in the cramped hideout. Chalis seemed content to study her datapad or stare at the wall, lost in thought. Roach chattered at Twitch as they guarded the door, describing in intricate detail the items she'd purloined from the workers' lockers at the processing facility and what she imagined those items said about the workers' personalities. Namir relieved Roach after half an hour, partly for something to do and partly out of pity for Twitch.

"When did she get so talkative?" he asked as quietly as he could, turning his snub pistol over in one hand. "She barely said a word in training."

Twitch shrugged. Namir had been expecting derision, but Twitch seemed to take Roach's attitude in stride. "After you left, I guess. She comes to the Clubhouse, lucks out at cards. Awful player. You get used to it."

"Sorry I missed it," Namir murmured, only half joking.

Thoughts of Roach drew his mind back to Haidoral Prime. It had been, what—two months ago? He felt the gap in time vividly. On Haidoral, Howl had still been in charge. On Haidoral, he hadn't met Governor Chalis and she hadn't yet fallen upon the company like a curse. He bitterly remembered the mission to her mansion, the opulence Gadren and Brand and Charmer had bristled at . . .

He stepped away from the door and waved Roach back into place. He spoke Chalis's name, drew her to the far corner of the room where she looked at him questioningly.

"When were you on Sullust before?" he asked.

She cocked her head and let the hand holding her datapad fall to her side. "Why do you ask?"

"The statue," he said. "The piece in that administrator's office. It was yours."

"I visited here, several times, during my apprenticeship under Count Vidian." The words were flat and cold, a recitation of facts. "The bust was a gift to Administrator Luko Oorn, *of* Luko Oorn, in gratitude for his assistance implementing my designs.

"I imagine he saw fit to remove it after my betrayal. I put it back."

Nothing about the explanation seemed less than sensible. Still, Namir felt unsatisfied. The gears of his mind were scraping and grinding, failing to produce the thought he needed. He spoke, knowing it wasn't what he needed to say, knowing he sounded petulant. "What about Mardona Three? Or Nakadia? You visit there before, too?"

"No," Chalis said. "But I helped make them what they are now." She smiled, and it looked like a snarl. "Is this a surprise? That I was involved in building what we're trying to dismantle? It's possible my connections to our targets are what allowed Prelate Verge to predict we'd hit Sullust—and that much is unfortunate—but my intimate knowledge is why Howl wanted me in the first place."

"It's not—" He had to stop himself from arguing. Again, she was right. She was *always* right. Chalis was smarter than him and sculpted conversations like clay. But somewhere in his head, something still bothered him. Whatever it was, it had nothing to do with Prelate Verge.

"How much of this plan," he began, fumbling with each word that emerged, "and I mean all of it, from Ankhural to Kuat—how much of it is about you taking back what you gave the Empire? How much is this all just revenge for you not getting the respect you wanted?"

Chalis drew in a breath that sounded wet and rough. Namir could see the pulse in her neck. He kept talking, unsure he wanted to hear himself, let alone any answer.

"You keep telling me that I don't understand the Empire, that I don't understand the scope we're operating on. So fine, you're right. But is Kuat going to be any different? If we make it that far, if we live through everything and destroy the shipyards, does it even *matter* to the war? Because this is feeling more and more like a suicidal vendetta."

The governor stood before Namir, her expression severe and unchanging, her chest heaving as she seemed to force down a fit of coughing by sheer willpower. "It will matter," she said, "as much as *anything* we could do would matter. As for my *motives,* those are my own and have no bearing on our success or failure." She seemed to flinch, and her voice became smaller as she added, "I would have expected that question from a rebel. From you, I expected more."

Namir had no answer to that. Chalis saved him from trying. Suddenly she sounded confident again, as matter-of-fact as she became when briefing the senior staff or as she'd been during her first meeting with Howl. It was a voice of impersonal charm, and Namir felt strangely hurt that she would use it on him. "Besides," she said, "I already have an idea of how to get us off Sullust intact. I'm not the sort of woman who would martyr herself."

They were interrupted by the buzzing of their comlinks. Namir frowned, retrieved his from a pocket, and reset it in his ear. The others were doing the same.

"Get out," a voice whispered harshly. One of Twitch's scouts. "They're right outside the safe house. Get out now!"

Twitch struck the door controls with a palm and moved outside, followed instantly by Roach. Namir glanced at Chalis and pulled her toward the alley.

Crimson particle bolts struck the top of the alleyway, sending sparks and flecks of stone onto Namir's face. He tried to get a look at the attackers and couldn't. Instead, he saw Twitch and Roach on the stairway at the alley mouth, crouched low and firing potshots with their snub pistols. Twitch was yelling something. All Namir heard was "faster" and some swearing.

He dragged Chalis to the stairs, grabbed Roach's wrist, and put her hand on Chalis's arm. "Head for shelter," he spat. "We follow." Roach turned toward him—*Focus on the fight,* he wanted to say—as if to protest, but he cut her off. "Twitch and I can cover you better."

He assumed as much, anyway. Roach might have become a chatty, reliable part of the team while he wasn't looking, but he was still a better shot than she. She took off with Chalis, and Namir took Roach's place, firing in the direction Twitch had targeted.

"On three?" Namir said.

Twitch nodded, and after another few shots they ran, back the way they'd first come through the city. Across a street and down an alleyway, blaster bolts still streaming toward them. Namir spotted glimpses of white armor when he glanced back but couldn't pinpoint the foe. He fired wildly, one-handed, in the hope of slowing pursuit. He didn't see where Roach or Chalis had gone.

He swung around the wall of a stone building and nearly bowled into Twitch, who had stopped running and was looking toward the safe house. She shoved him aside roughly. "Keep going. Catch up in a bit."

Namir cursed and sputtered. "What are you *thinking*?"

Twitch smiled her nasty little smile—the one Namir had seen on occasion in the Clubhouse before she took a swing at a fellow soldier. "My team," she said. "Still back there."

"Those two are dead," Namir snapped. "You *are* your team."

"Go to hell, Captain," Twitch said, and charged past him back into the fray.

He told himself he couldn't have stopped her. He felt for her. He wanted to chase her—but Roach and Chalis needed him just as much. "Good luck," he muttered, and sprinted away from the stormtroopers.

When he tried to cross the next street, he didn't hear the grenade until his body was in the air, burning and aching in every muscle as if he'd slammed into a steel wall. Then he hit the road and blacked out.

CHAPTER 32

PLANET VIR APHSHIRE
Day Four of Operation Mad Rush
Nineteen Years After the Clone Wars

Private Hazram Namir had been in his bunk disassembling and reassembling a DLT-20A blaster rifle when word about Alderaan came down. It hadn't meant anything to him. Only the fact that Howl had announced it over the *Thunderstrike*'s intercom indicated the planet's destruction was anything out of the ordinary: In the two months since Namir had joined Twilight Company, he'd seen weaponry that could melt gleaming cities into slag, fought beside more species than he could name, heard stories of a Galactic Empire that held millions of stars in its grip. If he'd been told that planets were a common casualty of war, he'd have believed it without a second thought.

In the mess hall that night, however, he'd seen the bitter faces of his comrades and heard their stunned oaths. Whatever had happened, it was something new.

"You said they'd bombed and gassed planets before," he'd asked Gadren. "What's different about this one?"

Gadren had looked at Namir with his alien eyes and said, "This is the difference between the hope of life and absolute death. *Everything* that was Alderaan is now gone."

He hadn't understood entirely, but he grasped enough. He'd seen the Malkhanis and the Creed and others eradicated, purged until only the tattoos of the exiled and the dead remained.

Days later, when word came of the destruction of the Empire's planet-razing battle station, Namir was manning a trench in the honey fields of Vir Aphshire. He heard laughter down the line, someone shouting, "They blew up the damn Death Star!" and the raucous cheers that followed. He hadn't shared in his comrades' terror and astonishment, but he shared in their joy.

He was coming to know the people of Twilight Company. He had no stake in their war, but they deserved a victory.

Vir Aphshire fell to Twilight shortly thereafter. The boost in morale might have played a role, though the Empire's decision to burn the hives and abandon the world entirely probably had more impact. Namir took no special credit, though it was the first campaign in which Twilight permitted him command of a recon group. He'd felt the bounty hunter—Brand—observing him, second-guessing him from the shadows as she'd been doing since Kor-Lahvan. Either she didn't trust him or she'd recommended him for the position and wanted to see the outcome. Maybe both.

Regardless, the battle was won. Namir was alive. The orchards and hives of Vir Aphshire belonged to the Rebel Alliance, whatever that meant.

The evening of Twilight's triumph, Namir was on watch when Sergeant Fektrin returned from scouting the nearest settlement. The creature passed him a report and told him to run it to Captain Evon. "Everyone needs to meet Howl sometime," Fektrin said, shrugging his tendrils.

Namir didn't ask how Fektrin knew he hadn't already met the captain. He felt confident the answer would be unsatisfying.

Namir had seen Howl from afar once or twice, heard his rare declarations over the *Thunderstrike*'s intercom, but all his knowledge of the captain came from the stories of his colleagues. The troops possessed a reverence for their commander, a faith in his decisions unshaken by the actual outcome of battles. Namir had seen such reverence before, more than once. He'd *felt* it before, though he'd been barely more than a child then.

It was strange, to see veterans like Gadren and Norokai acting like newly recruited Malkhani clansmen. They might claim cynicism, yet they still believed in the myth of their commander.

It would have bothered Namir more if Howl's grip on the company had been more demanding. But there were no rallies under his watch, no war cries in his name. He was the cornerstone of Twilight, yet ask the troops why they fought, and none would answer, *For Captain Evon.*

So for two months, Namir had had the luxury of ignoring the captain. That was no longer the case.

At the command tent, Lieutenant Sairgon directed Namir back along the tessellated, papery walkway toward the clay hills of the hive. He found Howl at the outer perimeter of the camp and handed over Fektrin's report, explained that the scouting party had seen neither damage nor fortifications at the civilian settlement. The captain nodded, studying the report briefly before looking back down the path.

"Private Hazram Namir," Howl said, enunciating each word as if savoring it. "Walk with me." He started moving without waiting for acknowledgment, and Namir hurried to keep up. At nearly a head taller than Namir, Howl forced a brisk pace.

"The 'Song of Lojuun,'" the captain said, "has been rattling about my brain for the past thirty-six hours." He tapped his skull to emphasize *brain*. "I can remember less than half the lyrics, and the entire opera is banned by the Empire. I've searched and searched and can't find a single copy."

Namir kept his face forward, his expression flat. "I'm not sure I can help with that," he said. No one had ever suggested the captain might be dangerous—eccentric at worst—but he intended to pick his way carefully through this conversation. In Namir's experience, power made men unpredictable.

Howl gestured sharply, dismissively. "You're helping already— nothing triggers buried memories like clean air and new perspectives. With any luck, I'll be recalling boyhood lunches with my aunts by the time we finish talking." He was grinning, though whether in humor or mere enthusiasm Namir couldn't guess. "I hear good things about you, Private. Sairgon informs me you keep saving the new recruits' lives. And those of some older soldiers, too."

"I've been doing this longer than most of them," Namir said. "Still having trouble judging firing ranges, though; not a lot of artillery on Crucival."

"I'll let you in on a secret: It's a rare individual who can tell at a glance how close to the enemy he can afford to get. You've got the in- stincts. You'll pick up on the facts."

"Yes, sir," Namir said.

The walkway began to squelch underfoot as the landscape turned to yellow-gray clay. Howl looked about thoughtfully, as if assessing the hills for some hidden purpose, and slowed his pace. "We'll be leav- ing the system in a day or two. Given your experience, I'd like to hear your thoughts on what we should do in the meantime."

It was a test, of course. The captain had no interest in the advice of a private two months out of Crucival. Namir saw no profit in games, however, and chose to take Howl at his word. "Threat seems pretty well contained. We could go hunting, but the enemy's on the run. No need to get our people killed backing Imps into a corner.

"I'd say keep it simple. The *Thunderstrike* is short on supplies. So we send a few squads to that settlement, grab all the food and equipment we can get. Don't think we'll see resistance."

Howl began to laugh. Namir wanted to bristle, but the sound was too guileless, too warm to give offense. After a moment, Howl turned to him and grinned brightly. "That," he said, "is exactly the sort of fresh perspective that sparks neurons in a man's brain. I think I just remembered my first schoolyard crush—pretty Twi'lek girl, name of Iania."

"You think I'm too harsh?" Namir asked, voice maintaining its even keel. He'd come to realize that the rebels really were convinced of their own righteousness, their claims to be fighting for *the people of the galaxy*. He hadn't expected their captain to share that particular delusion.

Howl's voice became sober. "I think you misunderstand this war. Treating civilian settlements with respect isn't about mercy versus pragmatism—it's a precondition of victory, no more or less.

"Twilight Company is fighting a battle for the heart of the galaxy." His voice softened to a whisper, as if he were sharing a secret. "For the spirit of every ordinary man and woman and Imperial stormtrooper. Stealing food won't help us win. Killing enemies won't, either. Against might on the scale of the Empire, conventional victory is impossible—when our objectives become purely military, we've already lost the larger fight."

It sounded like the contorted justifications Namir had heard inside the Creed: a philosophy meant to disguise its own hunger for war. Yet looking at Howl, Namir believed the captain was sincere. And somehow, Howl had kept Twilight alive through conflicts that had decimated other rebel companies.

He forced himself to smile. "Of course," he said. "No riling up the locals, then."

Howl clapped him on the shoulder and laughed again. "Good enough for now. You'll figure out the rest in time."

CHAPTER 33

PLANET SULLUST
Day Two of the Siege of Inyusu Tor
Three Years Later

The first sensation that came to Namir was the feeling of cool stone against his cheek. After that came a sudden and intense wave of nausea and the realization that his arms had been yanked behind his back. He tried to lift his head, to fight against the pull, but he wasn't sure he moved at all.

"You sure he's worth taking in?" a voice asked. Low, male, with a static hiss behind it. "He's been under rubble at least an hour. If he dies on the way to holding, it's a waste of everyone's time."

"He's not as hurt as he looks. Stunned, I think." A second voice. This one was a woman's, but the static was worse, garbling the words. She said something more that Namir didn't understand.

He'd been attacked. He remembered the ambush, being separated from Chalis, Roach, and Twitch.

He'd been out for an *hour*?

He groaned and forced his eyes open as he was lifted to his feet. The cavern roof glimmered far above him and white silhouettes gripped his arms, half throwing him into the open bed at the back of a large landspeeder. He tried to sit up and once again failed. He tugged at his wrists and felt a sharp electrical shock. He was bound in stun cuffs.

"This is SP-Four-Seven-Five," the woman's voice said. "We have a rebel prisoner incoming."

The man—a different man, maybe? Namir wasn't sure—cursed softly. "Protocol twenty-four is now official. Soon as we make delivery, it's on to door-to-door searches and roundups. Random arrests, lethal force authorized against any resistance. Let's hope this isn't an uprising."

Rough, gloved hands pulled at Namir's body, set him upright in the speeder bed. The city streets blurred past him and the gentle vibration of the vehicle set his guts on fire. Two white stormtrooper helmets stared at him.

"They didn't even make contact with anyone. Far as we can tell, they were a search party." The woman again, speaking to her partner. "Do we really have to—" The rest of her sentence was too garbled to make out. Namir saw that the lower corner of her helmet had been burned away.

He suspected she could thank Twitch for the damaged vocalizer.

He wondered if Twitch was still alive. And Roach and Chalis . . .

He couldn't help them now.

The woman removed her malfunctioning helmet, revealing a young face etched with hard lines. She gripped Namir beneath his shoulders, hoisted and propped him higher. He could have kicked her if his legs had been cooperative, but what then? He needed to escape, but he also needed a plan.

"Hey!" the stormtrooper said, her voice no longer scrambled. "Rebel! You want to keep the bloodshed down, tell me what you're doing."

Namir shook his head, confused. He started to pull at the cuffs again when instinct kicked in. He flinched reflexively instead of taking the shock.

The woman scowled. "If there's an attack planned," she said, overly emphatic as if trying to demonstrate her tolerance, "you should tell us now. You people signed up to die. The rest of this city didn't. Don't get everyone caught in the crossfire."

"Even if we were planning something," Namir said, his lips stinging with the words—*did I fall on my face?*—"I still wouldn't tell you."

He expected the woman to strike him. She didn't. The speeder abruptly stopped and he slid half a meter forward in the bed as he heard shouting at the front. He tried to make out the details. Something was blocking the road.

Then he heard the sounds of blasterfire and a stormtrooper screaming.

The two troopers near him were looking out to the road now, ignoring Namir. Praying he wouldn't pass out or vomit, he lurched forward, bowling over the still-helmeted trooper with his shoulder while keeping his body low. The woman started to turn to him, but then crimson bolts swept over the speeder bed and Namir was no longer her most urgent problem.

He didn't see whether his captor survived the volley. He swung his legs down to the street, ran in the direction of the blasterfire. He hoped to spot Roach or Twitch, glanced up and saw the shots were coming from the roof of a low building. By the time he made it to the structure's wall, the shooter was already dropping down and gesturing for Namir to follow.

The shooter was a Sullustan: It had a broad, hairless head with mouselike ears, eyes like two globs of black oil, and jowls that gave its face the appearance of a helmet. This was the closest Namir had been to one of the creatures, though he'd seen them among the workers when Twilight had captured the processing facility.

Disappointing or not, it was still a rescue. Namir pursued the creature as it dashed into an alleyway, scooped a duffel bag up from the ground, and began a dizzying series of turns. Hands still cuffed behind his back and his vision swimming, Namir had difficulty keeping up and at last—knowing it might be his death, but unable to control his body—slumped against a wall and began to retch.

The vigor that had come with the need to escape seemed to leave him along with his bile. He was in no shape to fight. He was certainly in no shape to battle his way out of Pinyumb, and after an hour his comrades were either out of the city, safely hidden, or dead. He barely kept himself upright, and was surprised when he felt a soft hand steadying him.

The Sullustan guided him back to a standing position and spoke in a language Namir couldn't understand.

Namir didn't dare shake his head for fear of vertigo. "There were others," he said. "Others who came down here. Are they safe? Do you know where they are?"

The Sullustan replied swiftly and simply, in no more than a few alien words. It couldn't have been anything but a *no,* but the creature watched Namir and seemed to see the incomprehension in his face. Carefully, with an exaggeration that suggested the gesture was unnatural to it, it shrugged its shoulders.

It—*he,* Namir supposed—didn't know anything about the others. Maybe the Sullustan hadn't even known they'd come, had only stumbled across Namir.

Maybe that was a good sign, as these things went.

"Could they be hiding? Maybe made it to another safe house?"

The Sullustan hesitated, as if he wanted to speak and offer some hope or explanation to Namir. Instead he shook his head in that same, exaggerated manner. Then, with one hand, he gestured broadly in the direction of the lifts out of the cavern city. Namir couldn't tell if it was an explanation or an indication of hope.

"I should look for them," Namir said.

The Sullustan took a step back and lowered his head. Refusal.

I could go alone, Namir thought. Hobble his way through a city he didn't know, searching for comrades who weren't likely to be in reach in the first place. And if he found them—if against all odds he didn't collapse on the way or get shot by stormtroopers less merciful than the first squad he'd encountered; if his friends had moved so slowly and hidden so poorly that a concussed and hunted soldier could find them—what *good* could he do? In his condition, he'd be more of a burden than an asset. He'd slow down any attempt at flight, and his brain was too much of a wasteland to let him formulate a plan.

He had no chance at all of making it to Twilight Company.

"Okay," he said. "So where are we going?"

The Sullustan led him away. Namir thought of stopping him, asking the alien to at least remove his cuffs, but the only available tool for the task was the Sullustan's blaster and a shot would be heard from blocks away. So instead they moved together, the Sullustan lending what support he could, through the shadows of towers and among stalagmites at the cavern's edge. During the course of their journey, the towers' lights turned bright, making Pinyumb's evening seem like day. For the sake of the stormtroopers' search, Namir assumed.

Now and then they heard shouts and screams, pleas to Imperial security agents as doors were forced open and citizens marched away. The roundups had begun. The Sullustan hesitated every time, and every time continued on.

They descended a short flight of steps hewn from the cavern rock and through the entrance of an unmarked building. Inside was a cantina, empty of customers and its chairs stacked atop tables, barely lit by a handful of emergency lights. The Sullustan drew Namir into a small kitchen and then down a second flight of stairs concealed behind a cooler.

In the basement of the cantina awaited a terrified crowd. They were mostly humans and Sullustans, crammed so tightly together that many stood instead of sitting. The youngest was a small child, but most were old: withered figures who had learned to face fear with dignity, whose uncertainty showed in their eyes and nowhere else. Namir noticed the uniforms of the processing facility workers on a handful.

When they recognized Namir's companion, the crowd's tension eased only slightly. The Sullustan descended the steps and spoke softly, soothingly, as he reached into his duffel bag and passed out foil-wrapped rations and palm-sized envelopes of medicinal bacta. The old men replied to Namir's companion in his native language, their voices transparently grateful.

When Namir's companion drew a blaster from his bag, however, and held it out in both hands, the crowd seemed to shrink back. He was insisting on something, arguing in the face of terse, bitter replies.

Namir edged around the crowd to the nearest other human, a green-eyed woman with callused hands. "What are they saying?" he asked.

The woman looked at him askance. Maybe she thought Namir should have known the language. Or maybe it was his cuffs. Finally she said, "If the stormtroopers come, carrying weapons will only make things worse."

"They're already going door-to-door," Namir said. "They're rounding up people out there. I'm not sure how much worse it can get."

It wasn't advice. Namir had no stake in these people's choices. Maybe that was why the woman studied him, nodded, pushed forward, and accepted a blaster.

Namir wanted to ask questions about his rescuer and about the city, but his companion drew him back toward the stairs long before the duffel bag was empty. The Sullustan took a moment to shoot through Namir's cuffs before leading the way out of the cantina. The bracelets remained on Namir's wrists but the stun mechanism seemed disabled. Namir's arms and shoulders ached as they walked.

Their second stop of the evening was the dormitory of a housing block, where a similar crowd sheltered. Once again, Namir's rescuer meted out emergency goods that were accepted with a mix of gratitude and reluctance. This time, however, they were interrupted when the door opened to admit another half a dozen civilians: men and women whose faces were swollen with fresh, purple bruises, who limped and sucked breath between their teeth. One man's upper arm was burned through; Namir recognized the effects of a blaster bolt immediately.

"We were in the Swift Market—we ran out of food," one of them said. "When the stormtroopers came, they said we should've been at home . . ."

Namir's rescuer glanced between the wounded and the door, as if torn between the refugees before him and other huddled crowds he'd intended to visit. Then he began searching his bag for bandages, bacta, and salves. He looked to Namir and over to the man with the burnt arm, waiting expectantly.

Namir wasn't a medic, but he knew what needed to be done.

Namir spent the next hour applying bandages and disinfectant to the wounded, smearing bacta over scorched flesh and checking for broken bones. He told each of his patients—even the ones who couldn't speak his language seemed to understand—that his ministrations were a stopgap at best. No one seemed troubled. "You think we have a lot of alternatives?" the man with the burnt arm asked. "You think the Imperial clinic will fix me up?"

"Point taken," Namir said.

After Namir and his companion had tended the worst of the injuries, they moved on to their third stop of the night. In a public bathhouse where wretched and moaning victims lay along the edges of a bright-blue pool, they went to work again. For the first time, Namir felt unwelcome; he listened and wrapped a boy's bleeding leg and heard a voice asking why the *rebels* were allowed to help. The rebels who had caused the Empire to work Sullustans like slaves. The rebels who were responsible for all the pain in Pinyumb.

He kept his eyes on his patient until he heard footsteps approach him from behind. He turned and stood, ready for a fight, and looked into the eyes of a broad-shouldered, leathery-faced man who scowled angrily. "You heard me," the man said. "You shouldn't be here. Not the rebels, not the Cobalt Front, none of it."

"We didn't do this," Namir said.

"You are to blame," the man said.

Namir recognized the man's stance. He looked for it in every recruit who asked to join Twilight, rarely saw it in anyone under forty years of age. The man had the carriage of a trained soldier.

Namir braced himself for a punch that didn't come. The leathery-faced man turned away. Namir wanted to say: *This isn't the Clone Wars. These people are fighting for the likes of you.*

He even believed it, in a way. This wasn't his father's war. It wasn't the war of Crucival. He'd seen dark and terrible things the last time he'd been concussed underground, in a cave watching his friends die. The Empire really *was* a different sort of enemy.

But not so different that he'd changed the way he fought.

He resumed his work, accepting that he was responsible in some way for the wounds he bound—responsible for the plan that had driven the Empire to desperation, reassigning overseers and storm-troopers from the shipyards of Kuat to worlds like Sullust. He felt no guilt, but neither could he deny the accusations of the Sullustans.

Namir and his companion continued their rounds over the course of the night. Whenever they walked the street, they kept to the shadows; they watched the march of stormtroopers and heard distant blaster shots as the Empire's roundups and searches went on. At each site they reached, they saw the number of wounded grow and the desperation of the people increase. They did what they could and moved on.

Namir's fatigue was profound. His nausea and vertigo came and went. At certain moments, he believed he was still rescuing his com-rades from the wreckage of the *Thunderstrike*. At others—in the city, when he sucked in the pure alien air of the cavern and let the gratitude and terror and resentment of the civilians wash over him—older memories flickered to life in his brain. Memories of Crucival and memories of Howl.

He should have been guarding his companion, watching for troops or cam droids. Instead he was merely intent on staying upright. He barely noticed when the Sullustan led him inside a mining hangar built into the cavern wall, or wove between vehicles toward a back office. There, however, he forced himself alert.

He'd been expecting another civilian shelter. Instead, only three people sat in the office—all human, or close enough to pass—each with a blaster in his or her lap. They jumped to their feet as Namir and the Sullustan entered, but the tension swiftly vanished.

"Took you long enough," a brown-haired woman said before embracing the Sullustan and clapping him on the back. "Who's the guest?"

A rapid-fire exchange ensued, half in the Sullustan's language and half in Basic. Namir's companion appeared to be explaining the night's events. The woman finally turned to Namir and asked, "You're with the rebels up the mountain? The ones who took the processing facility?"

"We planned to destroy it and evac," Namir said. "We hit a snag. Who are you?"

"I'm Corjentain. This is Nien Nunb," she said, gesturing toward the Sullustan. "He's in charge of the cell. Until you came along, we were it for the Rebellion here."

Namir looked among the four. They looked weary but unhurt, welcoming but cynical. They were dressed as civilians, yet even their disguises were ragged and dirty. They smelled as if they hadn't washed in days.

"I thought there was a resistance movement," he said.

A young man with skin the color of chalk answered. "The Cobalt Front hasn't ever been much of a resistance," he said. "Their heart's in the right place, but . . ."

"Sit down," Corjentain said. "You look like garbage. We'll swap stories."

So Namir sat, and as he drank a foul greenish liquid the young man assured him would help his head, Corjentain explained the rebel cell's activities with occasional, incomprehensible additions from Nien Nunb. The cell had come to Sullust in the hope of formally allying the Cobalt Front—a workers' association that had become increasingly anti-Imperial—with the Rebel Alliance. Instead, they'd found the most militant members of the Cobalt Front already imprisoned and the remainder reluctant to take up arms.

"I'm *from* Sullust," Corjentain said. "So is Nien. No one likes the Empire here, but you can't force frightened people to revolt. So we figured we'd help Pinyumb how we could—smuggle in supplies the locals can't afford, medicine the Empire won't allow. If that won people over, got them thinking the Rebellion was worth something, great. If not, we were still doing good. The Empire wanted us dead, but we could handle that."

Namir smiled bitterly. "Then the Empire decided to make up for production losses elsewhere. It increased the workload and security on Sullust, and you were in over your heads."

Corjentain didn't seem to register his tone. "The Empire was going to work people to death sooner or later anyway. That wasn't the big problem. Dropping your ship here, though ... that'll have consequences."

"The second we find a way offworld," Namir said, "we'll be out of your way."

Corjentain swore softly and shook her head. "Right. Bit too late. The crackdown's happening, and I'll bet good credits that after they arrest anyone who's ever said an unkind word about the Emperor, they'll implement mass reprisals. Permanent curfews, workers separated from their families ... anything it takes to quell the *possibility* of a future uprising."

It wasn't anything that surprised Namir. He'd heard enough stories at night in the Clubhouse. Imperial crackdowns were why recruits joined Twilight Company.

Instead of offering condolences, he told the rebels Twilight's story. He kept the company's ultimate goal oblique, made no mention of Chalis, but talked about Twilight's campaign along the Rimma hyperlane and its intentions on Sullust. "My squad came down to the city looking for support," he finished. "Doesn't look like you're in any shape to give it."

"Not really," Corjentain agreed. Nien Nunb spoke rapidly, and the two conferred before the woman continued. "We can try to get you back to the facility at daybreak, though. Least we can do."

"I appreciate it," Namir said. He drew in a long breath, tried to focus on his surroundings. Four rebel fighters, a handful of weapons, and whatever was in the vehicle hangar. "What about you? What's the plan here?"

This time, there was no consultation among the rebels; they just looked at one another as if confirming something they'd agreed to long ago.

"We'll rally anyone left from the Cobalt Front," Corjentain said. "Try to fight back one last time, protect Pinyumb from what's coming. Can't let them round up all our friends and neighbors." She smiled a bleak smile. "Shouldn't take too long."

"No," Namir agreed. He drank the astringent mush from the bottom of his cup and stood up, legs aching at the effort. "But if we're stuck until dawn, you may as well show me what you've got. I can look at your plans, give you a fresh perspective. Maybe drag out your war a little longer."

The green sludge, whatever it was, quelled the swimming in Namir's head and warmed his insides. His muscles still ached, but it was more bearable somehow: He was able to *think* as he studied the rebels' maps of the city and debated with Corjentain over where to deploy snipers, listened to the chalk-faced boy's fantasies of breaching the Imperial jail. Namir knew the rebels wouldn't survive, and it was evident they knew as well; still, there was something comforting about their shared choice to pretend otherwise.

Despite Namir's clarity, old memories still leapt to his mind like the random sparking of a wet battery. He thought about all the planets Twilight Company had left behind: Haidoral Prime, Phorsa Gedd, Coyerti, and Vir Aphshire under Howl; Mardona III, Nakadia, Obumubo, and now Sullust under Namir's own leadership. The differences between them seemed stark.

Those memories led him to think about the planets to come. The march to the Core Worlds wasn't over, and Chalis had promised that the campaign would grow more punishing. Namir tried to picture Twilight Company fleeing Sullust; the subsequent battles on Malastare;

living through Malastare and at last reaching the rings of Kuat. There, among the skeletons of Star Destroyers, they would fight day after day, block by block through the orbital city, working to obliterate the ground they stood upon.

Like the Sullustan rebels, Twilight faced an impossible battle, if not a hopeless one. The Kuat shipyards truly might be destroyed. A scattered few squads might remain intact. But Twilight Company, as a unit, would be broken. Namir saw no other possible end anymore.

Maybe he never had. He'd never given much thought to what came after Kuat.

Nien Nunb watched and listened as Namir and the others plotted. Namir wondered if the Sullustan stayed silent for his sake. He suspected not. Maybe Nien had other things on his mind.

More memories sparked. Memories of Howl and of what Namir had been *told* of Howl.

Gadren said the captain believed sacrifice was the strength of Twilight. Brand claimed that Howl had never done anything for a single reason. Howl had been a madman, but he'd understood the needs of his troops better than they did—the moment he'd died, all purpose and hope in the company had gone with him.

Our goal isn't conquest, but alchemy. Where Rebellion comes into contact with Empire, change must occur. The substance of oppression becomes the substance of freedom.

When our objectives become purely military, we've already lost the larger fight.

Namir had emulated the form of Howl's purpose without the substance, the drive to stop the Empire without the foundation that drive was built upon or the methods Howl prized. The company had been fooled; the company was willing to die to reach Kuat.

You don't understand the scale *of the enemy.*

Chalis said the Kuat shipyards were worth it.

All of this danced through his concussed, green-sludge-addled brain in the hours before morning. Corjentain left to make preparations for Namir's return to the processing facility. Namir walked among the great mining vehicles in the hangar—grim-looking blocks of metal affixed with monstrous drills—and gave up on sleeping.

He understood what Howl wanted to achieve with Twilight. He still didn't understand how the captain's calculus had worked—how it had resulted in anything but the company's annihilation.

Then again, he didn't understand how a blaster worked, either. He just knew how to fire one.

When Corjentain returned, Namir called Nien Nunb's tattered rebel cell together and carefully, deliberately extinguished the sparking in his brain until what remained was certainty.

"I have a plan," he said.

Shortly before dawn, the ash angels woke in the upper reaches of Pinyumb's cavern and fluttered through crevices in the rock wall, navigating the labyrinthine path to the surface on talons and wings. Namir crawled behind them on hands and knees with only a night-vision visor to guide the way. "Follow the birds," Corjentain had said. "You've got about an hour before they finish migrating to the surface."

"And if I'm not out by then?" Namir had asked.

"Then you can wait until dusk to find your way back."

Namir had never been claustrophobic, and though the crevices narrowed until rock pressed against both his stomach and his spine, he found the constant scrabbling of the ash angels above and below to be a strange comfort. He was never alone in his journey.

He was surprised how high he'd climbed when he emerged onto the mountainside. The Empire's blockade had crept up the slope since nightfall, but he'd still managed to bypass the perimeter. That only left the half-day-long trek to the peak, avoiding the attention of airspeeders and Imperial scouts while the enemy masses followed him upward. They appeared to be in the final stages of preparation for an all-out assault, methodically bringing the last of their weapons and troops into position. Yet when Namir neared the processing facility, buoyed by his newfound resolve, he felt almost refreshed. He smiled broadly when he recognized the Twilight sniper targeting him fifty meters up the slope.

The sniper met him halfway, her mask in place and her rifle gripped loosely in one hand. "Chalis made it in last night," Brand said. "So did Roach. No word from Twitch and the others. Thought you went down together."

"Missed you, too," Namir said, and clapped the older woman on the shoulder in a half embrace. She neither returned it nor pulled away, and Namir soon released her.

"Not long until the attack starts." Brand turned and began climbing the slope. Namir followed. "Empire's been testing us all day, sending bigger and bigger sorties. Chalis says she's got a way offworld, though. Something about the spaceport."

"Doesn't surprise me," Namir said. "Either part, really. I need a favor from you."

Brand said nothing. Namir wished he could read the woman better. The last time they'd talked had been in the bowels of the facility, above seething magma. That conversation hadn't ended well.

Was she still feeling bitter? Had she ever been bitter, or had he misread her then? *You've always been impossible,* he wanted to say.

"I'm not ready to talk to Chalis," he told her instead. Second-guessing Brand would get him nowhere. "I want the old squad together: you, me, Gadren, Roach." *Pretend we've all forgotten Charmer.* "Can you fetch everyone, find us somewhere private?"

Brand didn't stop walking or turn her head. But she nodded briskly mid-stride and increased her pace.

That would have to be enough.

Gadren sat in the shadows of the small piston control chamber, green and red lights winking on a panel above his head and reflecting off his crest. He'd greeted Namir warmly but briefly, as if reluctant to approve of the gathering without first understanding its purpose. Roach, legs splayed on the floor and back to the wall, watched Namir with confusion. A thin crimson scrape ran over her nose—an almost laughably minor scratch, given what she must have gone through to return to the surface. Brand stood in the corner, a small frown on her face. At least, Namir thought, she wasn't in her mask.

"We don't have a lot of time," Namir said, pacing before the doorway, "and we have a lot to discuss. But first of all—"

He thought of Gadren gently dragging him out of the cantina on Heap Nine. He thought of his last meeting with Brand, just days prior. He thought of how much Roach had changed since his departure for Hoth, and how he'd missed it all.

I'm sorry I disappointed you.

"—I know things have been rough lately. I know I've made mistakes. I wish I could have done better by you. At the very least, I should've given Charmer a better sendoff."

Roach studied the floor between her knees. Brand didn't react. Gadren said, "No one expects a captain to live among his men. We feel your absence, but we know it is required."

Namir smiled bitterly. Gadren was correct, in a way—but the alien was envisioning Twilight Company as it had been, when Howl had surrounded himself with Sairgon and Von Geiz and the others. Namir had removed himself, too, but he'd listened only to Chalis.

"Thank you," he said. "Right now, though, I need your support. I need the company's support. New orders from the top aren't going to cut it today."

Gadren spread two hands, waiting for Namir to continue.

"I don't know if you noticed," Namir said, "but there's a pretty big city not far beneath our feet. The people there are terrified. The resistance is weak. Like it or not, we've made their lives hell and it's about to get worse.

"Now, we can pull up stakes and leave, keep moving forward and try to throw a spanner into the Imperial machine. But even if we do make it to Kuat, if this whole campaign succeeds, we all know it won't win the war. Take away the Empire's Star Destroyers and they've still got more people and weapons and resources than a hundred rebellions.

"So I've been asking myself two questions: What are we doing this for?" He kept his eyes off Brand. It had been her question first. "And what does it take to keep Twilight alive?"

"And what answers have you come to?" Gadren asked. He spoke delicately, deliberately. Howl would have been proud.

"I don't *have* any answers," Namir said. "I'm not sure I'm capable of finding them. Maybe that makes me unfit for command—maybe it means I shouldn't be a part of this rebellion—but we're way beyond that point now. It doesn't matter.

"What does matter . . ." He was fumbling, and he feared he would lose his audience. This was why he'd come to them instead of the company at large: in the hope that they would forgive his awkwardness and understand his intent. "I got us here by finding a goal that seemed worthy of Twilight Company. I think that was my mistake. I should have focused more on finding a way to fight worthy of all of you. If we'd done that, maybe the goal would have appeared without trying. Maybe the answers would seem obvious."

Maybe Howl's invisible calculus would keep us alive. But he couldn't promise that.

"That's all background now. The point is: I think it's time to forget Kuat. I think if we're going to die, we should do it here, helping the people of Sullust, instead of marching to the Core Worlds and spitting in the face of evil. That's the best way to do right by the company and everyone in it."

No one spoke for a while. They might have been waiting to see if Namir was finished. Gadren and Brand watched him. Roach pulled her feet in toward her hips and looked up.

"Howl would've approved," Brand said at last. "I'm in."

Roach smiled limply and shrugged. "This a vote?" she asked.

"I'm not doing this if the company isn't with me," Namir answered. "However it comes out, I'm okay dying. It's the rest of you I'm worried about."

Roach's limp smile became a smirk, as if she was laughing at a private joke. "You're cute when you're awkward," she said. "Sure. I'm in. Bet the rest of the fresh meat will be, too."

Namir wanted to question her, root out the source of her soft-spoken confidence. But she'd given him what he needed, and he wasn't done yet. "Gadren?" he asked.

Gadren folded first one, then another set of arms across his chest. His voice sounded abnormally low, entirely free of his usual joy. "I've thought a great deal about the peoples and species we leave in our wake," he said. "This will come as no surprise to you. My heart aches for the Sullustans, and I nearly wept when I saw the faces of the men and women we forced from this facility.

"And yet I am reluctant to turn away from our path. Not because of the blood we spilled to come here, but because—" As the passion in his voice rose, the alien templed both sets of fingers. When he resumed, he spoke softly again. "If there is any chance of our mission to Kuat succeeding, any hope that it might change the course of this war for the better, surely we owe it to the galaxy to see it through?"

The words struck Namir like a blow, reminded him of his exhaustion. He had expected someone to make that argument—possibly Brand, maybe Roach. But he'd also thought that if anyone would back him, it would be Gadren.

Yet the alien wasn't finished.

"You claim that the ultimate outcome of Kuat's destruction would be insignificant in this battle. If we knew that to be true, I would not hesitate a moment to give you my support. As it stands, it is your word against the word of Governor Chalis."

"Shouldn't be a hard choice," Brand said.

"Has she not sacrificed enough?" Gadren asked. "Proven her dedication to the company?" He shrugged. "Even if not, you must still grant that she is best suited to judge the true harm we do to the Empire.

"I will prepare the others as you recommend. But we will not act unless she gives the order."

"Fair enough," Namir said. "Let's go."

"You're back," Chalis said. "Good. Check the squad assignments and make whatever changes you need to; I want to start in five minutes."

She didn't look up from her desk as she pushed a datapad in Namir's direction. Her voice was more brittle than it had been in weeks, as rough and cracked as it had been on Ankhural.

Roach, Brand, and Gadren had gone to spread word of Namir's plan. Namir and Chalis were alone in the administrative office. "Start what?" he asked.

"Evacuation." Chalis still didn't look at him, studying a screen on her terminal instead. She paused as if trying to decide whether explaining was worth the effort. "A dozen squads will proceed to the city and hijack ships in port. Half will return here to try to retrieve survivors. The others will break for space under cover of the *Apailana's Promise.*

"We'll have a fleet of merchant ships. Not the *Thunderstrike,* but better than dying on a volcano. And it spreads the risk, allows us to suffer a few losses without a catastrophic failure." She tapped a button on her terminal and spoke into her link in a crisper voice: "Groups one and three to positions."

Namir had come with the intent of winning Chalis over, of convincing her of his plan and bartering if he had to. He was willing to maneuver through whatever verbal maze she might construct. Yet Chalis seemed to have no interest in conversing.

And she was giving orders to his people.

"You're taking direct command now?" he asked, fighting to keep the ire from his voice.

She looked up at him then, and he winced. Her eyes were bloodshot and surrounded by dark circles like bruises. Her cheeks were sunken. She looked old but not fragile, as if she'd been whittled down to a knife's edge by the events of the past days.

"You were gone," she said. "I'm glad you're alive. Doubt my motives later."

He winced again. He'd crossed a line with his accusations in the rebel safe house. Whatever bond he'd built with Chalis over the past months was now cracked. "I have another idea," he said. "Some of the troops are behind it, but I need you—"

"There isn't time." She tapped another button. "Chalis to sentry five—where are they?"

A static-riddled voice announced, "Four hundred meters and closing on the peak. Just outside our firing zone."

Chalis looked at Namir expectantly, as if that pronouncement ended any possible lines of discussion.

She was right. There wasn't time.

"We need to give up on the shipyards," he said.

Chalis tapped something into her terminal and rose slowly from her desk.

"It's not your fault," Namir said. "But the plan is killing Twilight, and we both know it won't win us the war." Maybe she'd crafted the campaign to avenge herself on her former colleagues and maybe not. He didn't care anymore. "If we stay here—you saw what the city is like—we can do some good."

Chalis began trembling. Her lips twitched. Namir had never seen her yell, never seen her lose control. Was that what was coming?

"You know better than that," she said, almost too quiet to hear. "Reinforcements will be here in moments; that's the only reason they've held back on an attack."

He tried to speak as she walked around the desk, but her rough, nearly inaudible voice silenced him. "Kuat is still in reach. When we get there, you'll thank me."

In Governor Chalis's hand was a snub pistol aimed at Namir's chest.

He was no longer angry. He should have been, he thought—angry over the way she'd taken control, angry that she would betray him. But he saw nothing of the woman he'd become almost *fond* of in the bitter creature that stood before him. The woman who'd saved Howl's life, who'd advised him over breakfast, who'd seemed to have a genuine, inexplicable passion for art.

"Hard to thank you if I'm dead," he said.

"When I want to murder someone, I don't drag it out," Chalis snapped. "You've seen that." She gestured him toward the doorway. "Third compartment down. You'll leave Sullust when I do."

Namir looked at the blaster, judged his odds of lunging and grabbing it before Chalis could pull the trigger. They weren't in his favor. He turned and walked toward the door, followed by Chalis.

He'd barely stepped outside the office when he saw his salvation. He gestured to one side with his chin, hoped his eyes would convey the rest.

When Chalis crossed the threshold, two impossibly powerful alien arms wrenched her wrist up and to the side. Two more hands closed around her head and waist, immobilizing her. Gadren looked down on the woman from beside the doorframe, his expression mournful.

"I rescind my request," Gadren said. "If I must put my faith in a commander, it will be you."

Clasped in a leathery hand, Chalis gazed at Namir with hate.

Namir made no speech to the company. He had no faith in his own words; Gadren, Roach, and Brand would win over the squads more effectively than he could. His only concession to rhetoric was a brisk outline of his plan to the company's senior staff. Von Geiz seemed almost relieved and only a few voices spoke against him—his opponents included Carver, who declared Namir mad but smiled grimly nonetheless. Hober clasped Namir's hand tightly after the meeting adjourned.

Namir chose not to think about what would become of Chalis. For the moment, she was locked in the third compartment down the hall from the administrative office. In all likelihood, Namir wouldn't have to worry about what to do with her after the battle. Or about anything else.

Less than thirty minutes after his confrontation with the governor, her prediction of an imminent attack was proven correct. Namir had positioned himself atop one of the facility's spires—an access point for piston machinery that Twilight had converted into a sentry post—when a runner arrived from below.

"We just intercepted an Imperial message," the runner said.

"The attack's starting?" Namir asked.

"Yes, sir," the runner said. "But the source of the order—"

Namir looked at him, tried to remember the boy's name and failed. One of Hober's assistants, officially a noncombatant. Probably should've been aboard the *Thunderstrike* instead of in a war zone.

"What was the source?" Namir asked.

"Prelate Verge," the runner said. "The Star Destroyer *Herald* has arrived in the system."

CHAPTER 34

PLANET SULLUST
Day Three of the Siege of Inyusu Tor

The senior squad leaders finished passing on Namir's new plan—the plan he'd hastily composed with the rebel cell the previous night, refined in the back of his brain during the long trek up the mountainside, and finally detailed in his too-short meeting with Twilight's command staff—just as the first wave of the Imperial attack began.

He watched the assault from his position atop the facility spire, macrobinoculars clutched against a rising wind. A few hundred meters below, a ring of Imperial stormtroopers was climbing slowly upward, ranks closing as armored figures scrabbled over obsidian. Imperial airspeeders whipped about the mountaintop in increasingly swift passes, taking quick shots with their blaster cannons at retreating Twilight scouts.

Twilight Company's own forces were divided into three rough lines between the Imperials and the processing facility. The outermost line consisted of little more than a few dozen troops stationed in fire teams behind boulders and in crevices—anywhere the landscape would provide concealment. The outer line couldn't possibly hold for long, but a few bloody ambushes of Imperial forward infantry would make the foe cautious.

The middle line, halfway between the facility and the outer line, was entrenched in a narrow ditch the company had expanded from natural breaks in the stone. The trench would provide cover while—Namir hoped—reducing the effectiveness of the Empire's bombers; it was close enough to the facility that heavy ordnance might damage the structure, something the Imperials still seemed determined to avoid. Almost a third of the company was positioned on the middle line, along with a smattering of portable artillery: swivel-mounted blaster cannons, mortars, and light missile launchers.

The third and innermost line encircled the facility's perimeter. The inner line resembled in both form and function the defense the Empire had erected during Twilight's own invasion; it had worked well then, and it would work well for the Rebellion. Another third of the company occupied positions there, and the remainder of the company's artillery had been placed on the line as well. If the enemy made it past the inner line to the facility entrances, the time for heavy weaponry would be over.

It was a formidable defense, all told, capitalizing on the two advantages Twilight Company possessed. The terrain would give the company higher ground and shelter while slowing the enemy considerably, leaving opposing troops vulnerable to sustained fire. The Empire's continued reluctance to simply obliterate the processing facility was key, as well—if enemy commanders chose to cut their losses and sacrifice the facility to rid Sullust of the rebel presence, the tide of battle would turn in a moment.

Neither advantage changed the fact that Twilight Company was outnumbered ten to one, or that the stormtroopers were better equipped, better trained, and better rested than Twilight had ever been. The horde of white-clad enemy soldiers seemed to cover the dark mountain like snow, separated by wedges of black-clad, lightly armored Imperial fleet troopers. Giant, vaguely insectoid forms hobbled behind the masses, occluded by clouds of yellow dust without the enhancement of Namir's macrobinoculars: two-legged Imperial AT-ST walkers. Namir suspected that only the difficulty of the slope prevented the Empire from deploying the four-legged behemoths it had used on Hoth.

Twilight Company had fewer troops, fewer vehicles, and no air support to speak of. It had nowhere to retreat aside from the facility itself. There was every possibility the engagement would result in a slaughter.

Yet Namir found himself unafraid, even for the soldiers under his command.

There were worse ways to die than fighting to defend one's comrades.

"That Star Destroyer is approaching the planet," Hober said.

Namir had chosen the old quartermaster to act as his aide during the battle, passing along orders and messages via comm. It was rare that Twilight fought as a single unit, rare that it *needed* a strict hierarchy of communication. Howl had preferred to command such battles from the *Thunderstrike,* studying holographic maps of real-time battlefield data and allowing droids to send orders to Lieutenant Sairgon and the squads. But Hober knew Twilight intimately and he had no more pressing duties; Namir was content with the old man and his own eyes.

"How's everyone holding up?" Namir asked.

"For now?" Hober snorted. "They know their jobs. Ask me again after the fight."

Namir grunted and returned to observing the front.

The Empire struck the first hammer blow of the battle. As one, a dozen airspeeders released miniature scatter bombs over Twilight's outer line—explosives small enough not to imperil the facility, powerful enough to tear armor and skin. Namir saw a hundred bright flashes among the rocks, pictured his friends pierced by shards of obsidian or deafened by the blasts. But the squads were sheltered and well hidden;

the damage would be bearable. Two airspeeders plunged down in greasy black trails as Twilight missiles found their targets.

Before the echoes of the bombs had faded, the Imperial infantry charged. It was only the foremost troops who surged upward—a test, Namir supposed, of Twilight's defenses. Red flashes licked the mountainside as the company's middle line fired down at the assailants, doing little harm from such a distance.

The outer line remained dormant until the charging troops were only a stone's throw away. Namir observed through the macrobinoculars, saw white boots seek purchase on black stone and rifles sweep for targets, and gave the order:

"Open fire."

He needn't have said anything. The outer line knew its duty. With the enemy so close, every blaster shot felled an Imperial soldier, sent a body tumbling down the slope. Crossfire tore stormtrooper squads apart, forced fleet troopers to seek shelter among the dead. Yet every blaster shot also gave away a Twilight soldier's hidden position. The mass of the Imperial forces, withheld from the charge, trained assault weapons and sniper rifles and cannons on the newly revealed opponents. Airspeeders swept in, evading Plex-fired missiles as best they could and scarring the mountain with cannon fire.

"Tell the outer line squads to break off as needed," Namir said. "Cede the territory, but do it slowly."

He heard Hober speak into his comlink, observed squads—or surviving pairs, or individuals—peel off one by one and retreat to the middle line trench. He flinched when a Twilight soldier dragging a comrade's body was incinerated in the flash of an airspeeder's blasters. He reminded himself that this wasn't a guerrilla operation but a pitched battle: Casualties would mount swiftly, and the losses so far were within an acceptable range.

The Empire was acting carefully, rationally—neither overplaying its hand nor visibly underestimating its opponent. Predictability and caution were precisely what Namir had hoped for. He could drag out that sort of battle. No use regretting the cost now.

The mass of the Imperial army began to advance. Volleys of particle bolts from Twilight's trench line slowed the attackers, forced them into cover as they crept up the slope meter by meter. They passed over positions abandoned by the outer line and Namir squinted at the sudden blue-white flashes that ensued: the explosions of ion mines left over from the Mardona III mission, recovered from the *Thunderstrike*'s wreckage. Traps wouldn't stop the Empire, but they would slow the enemy forces further.

For long minutes, the battle seemed frozen. The advance proceeded imperceptibly gradually, like the movement of a shadow at dawn; only when Namir forced himself to register the passing of time did he see the incremental changes at play. The Empire was closing in on the trench despite the rain of blaster bolts, and a hundred fallen stormtroopers made no difference when more could follow.

Yet the Empire *did* pause, perhaps fifty meters from the trench line. Namir didn't understand the decision until he saw the lower sections of the army part, making way for a dozen two-legged scout walkers that sprinted up the rocks. Only one was downed by artillery fire before making it to the trench. A second was caught in the blast of an ion mine. The others swiftly wreaked havoc among the troops, and Namir swore to himself as squads pulled into the open, evading the walkers only to be cut down by stormtroopers.

"Tell the inner artillery units to fire. I want the walkers *gone*," he said.

"What about the trench teams?" Hober asked.

"They'll survive," Namir said. "Some of them. Order a withdrawal to the perimeter."

The artillery teams didn't hesitate. Namir was proud of them for that. Cannon fire streamed into the trench, followed by crackling plasma pulses and the trails of mortar rounds. Walkers screamed as metal buckled and cracked, and those that endured fled either down the slope or up toward the facility to their destruction. But the cost was high: Namir swept his macrobinoculars across the rocks and saw whole squads burned and torn on the ground. How many of them had died under Twilight's own firepower instead of the walkers' he didn't dare guess.

He adjusted the settings on the macrobinoculars and studied the Imperial forces. The infantry was moving in to secure the swath of ground leading to the trench, but it wasn't yet making a final push toward the facility. That made sense. Regroup, reassess. So far as their commanders were concerned, time was on their side.

"I'm heading down," Namir said. "From here on in, we may as well watch in person."

The wounded were packed tight in Von Geiz's makeshift field hospital, but they weren't so many that the facility cafeteria couldn't hold them. That didn't surprise Namir. The sort of combat taking place on the mountain didn't leave many wounds: It left people unscathed or it left them dead. He warned Von Geiz that the battle would be coming to the gates soon, and to keep a weapon close at hand. The old medic only nodded and went back to his patients.

Outside, Twilight soldiers were huddled tight around the walls of the processing facility, taking cover behind jagged rocks and split boulders. Red particle blasts—suppressive salvos by Imperial troops— streaked over Namir's head as he walked the line. Often a Twilight soldier would return a quick volley down the mountainside or call in a location to a nearby sniper. Plex-armed anti-air gunners kept a wary eye on the sky, firing at any Imperial airspeeder that dared make a pass. Namir knew the gunners had to be running short on missiles, but there was no point conserving ammunition.

The troops' mood seemed tense but not grim. Carver had somehow acquired an enemy's belt laden with grenades, and he grinned as he passed out bombs like holiday treats. Commander Tohna, lacking a ship to captain, had organized the *Thunderstrike*'s bridge crew into a team of runners carrying supplies to squads in need of water or fresh blaster packs; along with the supplies, he bore boasts and challenges and obscene jibes from team to team, creating ad hoc competitions among the soldiers. Namir hadn't seen Gadren, but word was he'd been singing in the trenches as the bombs fell.

Occasionally Namir stopped to speak with the men and women of the company. Corbo, the fresh meat who'd brought a knife to Chalis's air lock after Haidoral Prime, asked if the company was really fighting for the benefit of the Sullustans.

"The city under the mountain is in lockdown," Namir said. "Every stormtrooper out here is one who's not rounding up the locals."

"Good," Corbo said. "That's what I signed on for."

As one of Vifra's engineers updated Namir about the timetable for the next stage of the defense, Namir spied a figure skulking alone among the ranks, her hands clasping an assault rifle behind her neck. He excused himself and hurried toward her.

"Twitch?"

Twitch pulled the rifle over her head, toyed with it in both hands. "I'm not sorry," she said. "Had to go after my team."

She'd abandoned him in Pinyumb, raced off to save her scouts who'd almost certainly been dead already.

"Forget it," Namir said. "How'd you even get back?"

She shrugged. Her knuckles were scraped and her breath mask was covered in yellow dust, but she looked otherwise healthy. "What's Twilight Company do best?" she asked.

Namir laughed, loud enough to draw glances from the squads nearby. He didn't mind. "Survive," he said. He could have stopped there, but it felt right to finish the sentiment. "Whatever meat grinder we walk into, win or lose. Twilight Company—" *Howl's Twilight Company.* "—always survives."

"Damn right," Twitch muttered, and resumed her aimless march. Yells of approval rose from nearby.

Namir was glad to see Twitch alive. He tried not to wonder about Gadren. Counting the dead could wait.

He continued his rounds, chatting about tactics or long-lost friends or Sullustan weather along the way. He felt at ease; as if he were in the Clubhouse, watching debates and laughter and card games. He hoped the company shared that sense.

Eventually the suppressive salvos increased in speed, but the air-speeders held back. He checked his rifle's power levels and returned to Hober's side, looking up into the dreary gray Sullustan sky.

At the limits of his vision, he made out a wedge-shaped shadow among the clouds, ever-so-slowly increasing in size. "They're coming for us," he said, and smiled grimly. He spoke so only Hober could hear. "Who needs airspeeders when you've got a Star Destroyer?"

Hober nodded slowly. "Do we pull inside?"

"Not yet," Namir said. "I talked to the engineers. Just a little longer, now. But do call our friends upstairs."

The streams of blaster bolts overhead intensified. Namir pulled Hober into a crouch and watched the squads steadily return fire. A calm, unembellished exhilaration began to fill him.

He'd been off the front lines for too long. And live or die, the battle felt right.

CHAPTER 35

PLANET SULLUST
Day Three of the Siege of Inyusu Tor

Images of the firefight still flashed inside Thara Nyende's skull: rebel spies, caught surveilling the Pinyumb spaceport and tracked to their hideout; wild shots in deserted and silent city streets; a prisoner dredged up from rubble in the aftermath.

She remembered the speeder humming beneath her, its gentle vibrations causing her kneecaps to buzz through her armor. Her helmet had been damaged by a stray bolt, causing the vocalizer to cut out. In frustration, she'd taken it off, tried to find out what the rebels were planning. "Don't get everyone caught in the crossfire," she'd said to the prisoner, trying to sound reasonable, trying to appeal to the compassion of a criminal and a killer. "You people signed up to die. The rest of this city didn't."

There were career interrogators at the holding facility, middle-aged men and women with bloodshot eyes and soft-spoken demeanors who never associated with the troopers. There hadn't been time for their methods—not when roundups had already started and shots were being fired. Not when the rebels could move at any time.

"Even if we were planning something," the prisoner had said, twisting his bloody lips in a sneer, "I still wouldn't tell you."

She'd wanted to scream at him, *Everyone who dies tonight dies because of you.* She'd wanted to show him the scar on her forehead, list the stormtroopers who'd been torn apart in the explosion aboard the rebel ship. She'd wanted to blame him for her uncle, still in a holding cell somewhere, probably forgotten in all the chaos.

It wouldn't help. She'd forced herself to stay calm. She'd told herself she would find a way to make things right. That was her duty as a stormtrooper, as SP-475.

Then the sniper had started shooting.

She remembered all this because it was easier than thinking about the pain.

The sniper's blaster bolt had just missed her right lung, fusing plastoid and bodysuit mesh to her skin. A medevac team had retrieved her within minutes and moved her to the garrison's emergency ward. There, she'd spent the early morning twitching anxiously, terrified of death and pain, as droids cut away at the wound and administered bacta and anesthetics. She'd whimpered and begged one of her comrades to stay with her, but no one could be spared from the patrols and arrests and roundups in the city. She'd been left to the machines and her nightmares.

At some point, she'd been placed on a gurney and moved to a civilian clinic. She knew she'd asked why, but she couldn't recall the droids' answer—something about new wounded incoming, about a battle on the mountain. The painkillers were warping her memory. Now she sat on the crinkling sheets of a hard mattress in a room lit by rows of blue-white bulbs. She was shivering, goose bumps sensitizing her bare arms; on her top, she wore only a bandage wrapped around her chest. No one had bothered to remove her armor below the waist.

The clinic was staffed by a skeleton crew of Sullustans and humans. Any droids would have been transferred to the garrison months earlier, and the remaining workers were surely locked in their housing blocks. Still, a young Sullustan checked over Thara's bandage once an hour, and she could hear voices in the corridor.

She'd been listening as much as she could while drifting in and out of lucidity. The voices were the only source she had for news regarding the lockdown, the roundups, and the rebels. They spoke about distant sounds and blaster shots, about emerald fires burning along the riverbank. They seemed to know little more than she did.

"I want to *do* something," a woman's voice said. "Before they come for us."

"There is nothing to do," the young Sullustan replied.

"You're lying," the woman said.

The voices faded away. Thara closed her eyes and tried not to feel the ache of every heartbeat.

When the building shook, she woke up from a dream in which she was lying on the ground repeatedly taking shots from a sniper. She'd felt quakes before, tremors through the caverns, and this one was minor; but she pushed herself upright, caught herself on the edge of the bed, and focused as if it meant the end of civilization.

The medics in the corridor were speaking again.

"You knew Corjentain," said the woman.

"Yes," came the Sullustan's reply.

"We're not doing this anymore," the woman said. "We're not sitting this out. Get a message to her, tell her the clinic is open to anyone who—"

Thara swayed when her boots hit the ground, balanced herself with a light touch to the bed. She forced herself to move into the corridor, one hand unclipping the blaster from her belt and bringing the cool metal in contact with her bare shoulder and chest. No one had taken her weapon away. No one *dared* to take a stormtrooper's weapon away.

The blue-white light on the metal walls made the corridor look like a hologram. The two speakers, the human woman and the Sullustan, stood at the far end. Thara licked her dry lips and hoisted her weapon.

"I don't care what's going on out there," Thara said. The two medics turned, terror plain on their faces.

She tried to sound as authoritative as she could, half naked and drugged and unsure of her own identity.

"So long as this place is under my protection," she said, "it still belongs to the Empire."

CHAPTER 36

PLANET SULLUST
Day Three of the Siege of Inyusu Tor

Brand looked at the magnified face of the Imperial Army captain—young, black-haired, blue-eyed, soft-featured—and pulled the trigger of her sniper rifle. The rifle transmitted its scope data to her mask and, superimposed over the mountain vista, she watched the captain's head burn. By the time anyone returned fire she'd already dropped off her boulder perch and scrambled to a new hiding place.

She imagined a list of the captain's crimes: corruption, spice possession, assault, slave trading. Common among Imperial authorities. Not altogether unlikely.

She missed bounty hunting. But working alone behind enemy lines, eliminating the opposition one by one, was almost as good.

She was sandwiched into a narrow crevice, knees pulled to her chin while she waited for any pursuit to pass her by, when she heard a high-pitched hum beneath the sounds of the wind and distant plasma pulsers. Risking exposure, she lifted herself and scanned her surroundings for the source: a speeder bike flashing down the slope.

She blinked, magnified the vehicle on her mask's display, compensated for its speed, and tried to track it. She recognized the pilot and swore inwardly before opening a comm channel.

"Sergeant," she said. "Need to talk."

She balanced her torso on the edge of the crevice, lodged her boots against the rock, and took aim with her rifle, trying to judge the speeder's heading. It wouldn't be an easy shot. She might still make it.

Namir's voice came through a hiss of static. "We're kind of busy up here," he said. "You having fun?"

"Yes," Brand said. "You're missing Chalis."

"What?"

She aimed down the slope from the speeder bike, steadied her rifle. Particle bolts moved swiftly, but so did speeders. She'd need to lead the target.

"She got out," Brand said. "She's got a full gear pack and a speeder bike. Don't know how she passed the enemy front line."

"You managed it," Namir said. *Fair enough,* Brand thought. "She's probably heading for the city."

She kept her rifle positioned as it was, glanced at the speeder bike again. If she'd aimed correctly, she had four seconds until she needed to fire.

"Dead or alive?" she asked.

Three. Two. She began to pull back the trigger.

Namir said nothing. She liked Namir, but she couldn't wait on him. One.

She finished the pull, felt the rifle surge, saw the muzzle blaze.

Namir swore softly. "Let her go," he said. "You've got other targets, and she doesn't know our plan."

The speeder bike and the particle bolt blurred toward convergence down the mountainside. The rock of the crevice bit into Brand's chest as she stayed propped in place, watching.

The bolt missed. The speeder swerved awkwardly, too late, then regained equilibrium.

"Copy that," Brand said. "Back to hunting."

She turned off the comm, scolded herself for missing. She supposed it was for the best.

Still, she'd never trusted Namir's judgment about the governor. He'd gotten too close, and he'd never really understood the crimes of the Imperial aristocracy.

CHAPTER 37

PLANET SULLUST
Day Three of the Siege of Inyusu Tor

The Empire's infantry and airspeeders kept their distance from the facility as the Star Destroyer descended. The reason why became obvious when the first emerald turbolaser blasts rained from the sky onto the mountainside, cratering the black slope and turning stone into cracked, sizzling glass. The few Twilight Company scouts and snipers who prowled about the peak's upper reaches rapidly withdrew to the innermost perimeter or were disintegrated by the lasers' atomizing spite.

Namir felt a wave of heat billow across his face and tried to shield himself with one arm. Even through his breath mask's filter, the burning air smelled like sulfur and ozone. The emerald rain closed in on the troops, accompanied by the glowing spheres of guided proton bombs encircling the processing facility. How close could the enemy strike without destroying the compound? Namir wondered. How precise were a Star Destroyer's targeting systems?

"They're in position!" Hober yelled into Namir's ear. He could barely hear the quartermaster over laserfire and shattering rock.

Namir saw a squad of soldiers nearby begin to back away from the crest, glancing toward the facility entrance.

"Hold the line!" Namir called.

If he'd judged wrong—if the Star Destroyer's gunners could vaporize the troops without touching the facility—he would die with the rest of Twilight, and the battle would be over in an eyeblink.

But a moment later, the laserfire stopped.

Namir raised his gaze to the gray sky and laughed, the scorched air burning his nostrils.

The dark wedge of the Star Destroyer was beneath the cloud layer now, larger than Sullust's dim and distant sun and close enough to display the lines of its metal underbelly. Red and green lightning flashed around it, but the weapons fire wasn't targeting the ground anymore. Instead, the Star Destroyer was lashing at three new shadows descending through the clouds: one a sliver and two mere specks.

Apailana's Promise and its X-wings had returned.

"How long can they survive like that?" Namir asked Hober.

"Not sure," Hober said. "We've been able to signal back and forth, but we can't maintain a channel. My guess? Not long."

"That's all right," Namir said. "We don't have long down here, either."

It wasn't the sort of thing a commander should say, but Hober laughed bitterly.

The Imperial forces down the slope resumed their advance— alarmed, perhaps, by the company's aerial reinforcements and concerned what other tricks the rebels might have planned. As stormtroopers marched over still-steaming rock, Namir walked the line and called out orders, bringing Twilight's full firepower to bear against the foe. The Empire no longer held any part of its army in reserve, and as soon as troops died others took their place. A constant barrage of particle bolts flashed over Namir; he began to scurry about the Twilight positions on his hands and knees. Imperial mortar shells shrieked, some falling short of their targets and others ripping apart squads of Twilight soldiers. In return, red and orange streams of energy, explosive blasts, pulses of light, sparking missiles all poured down the mountainside from Twilight blasters and artillery.

On Crucival, such weaponry would have conquered the world. Here it wasn't nearly enough.

The first Imperial troops crested the peak. Whatever fortune or skill preserved them through Twilight's gauntlet failed to protect them long—Namir burned one through the chest, his first shot of the battle—but the inner line had begun to crack. Namir glanced toward Hober, who raised five fingers.

Five minutes. They needed to hold out another five minutes.

Namir gestured the squads forward. Soldiers rose above the boulders they'd chosen for shelter or dashed a few meters down the slope. Some were cut down instants later, but the sudden offensive forced the Imperial infantry to halt its advance. Namir found himself shoulder-to-shoulder with Twitch, firing bursts from a rapidly heating rifle at stormtrooper teams suddenly caught in the open.

He risked a glance skyward, saw the continued flicker of laserfire between the Star Destroyer and the *Promise*. "If they survive longer than we do—" he began. He took another shot and felt his rifle pulse.

"Be humiliating. I know," Twitch mumbled. The rest of her comment was lost—Namir only heard the word "navy" and a string of profanity.

The Twilight squads that had moved forward began to lose ground almost immediately. Namir allowed the company to abandon the meter it had seized. Any farther back and the squads would be on the slim shelf between the crest and the facility's walls—at which point retreat to the facility itself would be the only viable option.

A deafening blast thrust Namir forward as a mortar shell exploded behind him. He fell against the stones, felt skin tear as his knees slammed onto the ground and he buried his head and helmet in his arms. He felt fortunate not to have broken his skull; he doubted he could survive another head wound.

Someone pulled him up by the shoulder. He didn't see who, but he saw Hober in his peripheral vision offering a nod. "Do it," Namir said.

He heard yells and cheers and screams and finally a roar of triumph. Dragging himself forward to look down upon the slope, he saw the mountain start to burn.

Namir had sent half a dozen dig teams into the mountain. They used the same vehicles they'd stolen days ago to infiltrate the processing facility, along with a handful they'd located in the facility itself. The engineers had warned him more than once that any tunnels they created would be unstable, prone to collapse if they drilled into the wrong type of rock, let alone if the mountain came under bombardment.

"It'll work," Vifra had promised him before he'd left for Pinyumb. "It's not really that *difficult*. It's what half the tools here are built for."

"You don't want to do it," Namir had said.

Vifra had shrugged. "We built a defense against any Imperial dig team trying to come in like we did: Channel the magma, incinerate the foe. You told us to get ambitious, now we're getting ambitious.

"I can make the mountain spill its guts all over the place. But I don't think half the dig teams will survive. I think you're asking them to die, and they'll die pretty horribly. They'll be buried alive. Or caught in the flow."

"Will they do it?" Namir had asked.

Vifra had nodded. The decision was made.

On the mountain, Namir watched lava seep from the mouths of freshly dug tunnels and trickle into the open. Most of the lava streams emerged below the level of the Imperial army, but that was to be expected. Fire rose where the streams touched scrub grass or corpses. Transport vehicles, stationed behind the bulk of the enemy force, rapidly turned aside. Soldiers higher on the slope shouted panicked warnings, fled the heat into the blazing weapons of Twilight Company.

The lava would encircle the upper reaches of the peak almost entirely. The Imperials would be left with nowhere to fall back to. They would be demoralized, terrified, and they would strike at Twilight Company with renewed fury because of it. It might ultimately prove to be in the Empire's favor.

But trapping the enemy army in with Twilight wasn't the lava's only purpose. Additional streams would spring out closer to the mountain's base, and Twilight Company's dig teams weren't the only dig teams operating.

Nien Nunb's rebel cell hadn't had much in the way of weaponry or manpower. But it had possessed mining vehicles. Submerging half a dozen Imperial guard stations in lava seemed like a fine way to start a revolution.

Namir hoped the rebel cell truly could rally the people of Pinyumb. He wondered if he'd survive to learn whether that part of the plan worked.

Twilight's celebration ended as the Imperials redoubled their attack. Stormtroopers vaulted over rocks at the crest, struck Twilight soldiers with the butts of their rifles before being shot down themselves. The press of bodies became too much for the company; blaster rifles drew too much power, overheated too quickly to stop every enemy who reached the top of the slope. Namir signaled the retreat, and squads abandoned portable artillery and dying comrades to back toward the facility entrances and navigate the company's maze of barricades.

It was as orderly as a swift retreat could be. The squads knew a withdrawal was part of the plan, knew who could afford to leave first and who would stay behind to provide cover. They did their duty as white-armored troops tossed grenades and Imperial flame units sprayed death in an effort to force Twilight to scatter.

Namir separated from Hober somewhere in the retreat, caught his breath behind an overturned loadlifter used to block the cavernous mouth of the facility's eastern entrance. He was toward the back of the maze, and he watched squads filter through and take up stations while others found perches on the rooftop. He was swapping out his rifle's power pack when a mighty hand clasped his shoulder and a voice declared in a deep bellow, "When nature itself turns against our foes, how can we lose?"

He turned to see Gadren standing above him and grinning broadly. Roach stood behind the alien, one shoulder inexplicably covered by a stormtrooper's pauldron. She was shifting her weight rapidly from one leg to the other, her smile far more slight.

"Let's try not to find out, huh?" Namir asked, and gave Gadren's side a solid smack. His eyes, however, were on Roach. Part of him wanted to offer her a chance to run, to hide deep in the facility until the battle was over; but that wasn't what she needed, and he suspected it wasn't what she wanted. "You'll do good, both of you," he said.

"Any word from Pinyumb?" Gadren asked.

"No," Namir said, "but we weren't expecting any. We've given them all the support we can—we've melted their jailers and we've trapped the local army up here. If they can't pull off a rebellion now, they've only got themselves to blame."

Gadren nodded. Roach took one of his arms and tugged gently. "We going?" she asked.

"We'll see you after," Gadren said to Namir. "Stay safe, my friend."

"You, too," Namir said.

Roach led Gadren away into the ranks. Namir watched the two go and worked to steady his suddenly ragged breathing and his trembling hands.

Then, as the pair nearly disappeared from sight, Roach glanced back at him. He made himself smile tightly, offer a nod of encouragement.

She winked back, and Namir began to laugh.

The squads on the facility roof were tasked with occupying the enemy's portable artillery and heavy-weapons teams. So long as those units couldn't engage, the Imperial infantry would be forced to funnel through the mazes, into the facility entrances and Twilight's kill zones. Even the total destruction of the facility was no longer an option—not unless the Empire was prepared to sacrifice its trapped army along with the facility itself.

It was mostly stormtroopers who'd survived the climb up the mountain, and it was stormtroopers who began fighting their way inside. Twilight's makeshift barricades didn't last long against a barrage of blasterfire and grenades, but even rubble slowed the enemy down. As Twilight squads lost their cover, they fell back to the rear and let the next row of teams become the defense's vanguard.

Namir fired into the storm of blaster bolts until his rifle was drained of all power, switched to his sidearm and kept shooting until someone tossed him a battery pack. He was lying on the metal-plated walkway leading to the mouth of the facility; he rose to his knees only as long as it took to sight a foe and pull the trigger.

It was the sort of battle he'd been fighting since he was a child. It felt as natural as breathing.

Although squads withdrew and soldiers fell, although the stormtroopers kept coming, Twilight did not relinquish the entrance. For every company member who died, a dozen Imperials died in turn. Attrition was taking its toll on the once-massive horde that had climbed the mountain. The Twilight squads seemed to instinctively understand their success—shouts of encouragement and triumph rose up as, together, the soldiers realized they might actually win.

As Namir withdrew from the burning wreck of the loadlifter into the facility's main hallway, he cast one last look toward the sky and the distant battle between the Star Destroyer and *Apailana's Promise.*

The ground battle could be won. Namir was proud of that.

The aerial battle could not, and Namir had no cards left to play.

It was conceivable that the rebel cell would take the city's defensive cannons. But even that scenario almost certainly wouldn't occur in time to save Twilight. The residents of Pinyumb had more pressing concerns, and by the time they could turn weapons on the Star Destroyer it would be much too late.

As soon as the *Promise* was destroyed, the Star Destroyer would return its attention to the processing facility. It would see that the Imperial army had failed. It would realize that sparing the facility was no longer possible under any circumstances. Unless a miracle transpired, it would obliterate the entire mountain peak.

Yet Namir had done his best. He'd given the spirit of Twilight Company its due.

He would die with a grin and a battle cry.

CHAPTER 38

PLANET SULLUST
Day Three of the Siege of Inyusu Tor

It had been too long since Captain Tabor Seitaron had last tasted victory.

He'd forgotten the exhilaration of a proper battle: the joy of calling orders and encouragement to a proud and dedicated crew, the tense thrill of suddenly fathoming an opponent's gambit. The arrival of the rebels' gunship had amused him—he'd foreseen it as a possibility, albeit an unlikely one—but the weaponization of Inyusu Tor's lava had come as a genuine surprise. Governor Chalis and her allies were cleverer than he'd expected.

Not that the outcome was in doubt. He watched the gray sky through the viewport of the *Herald*'s bridge, saw X-wings flash by in clouds of sparks and smoke. The Star Destroyer wasn't built for atmospheric maneuvering; but neither were the enemy ships, and they lacked the firepower to be more than an irritant. As soon as the gunship and its starfighters were gone, the *Herald* would deliver a fresh infantry battalion to reinforce the bleeding and battered army trapped on the peak and the forces suffocating brushfire rebellions in Pinyumb. The siege would be broken, the Sullustan governor's precious mineral processing facility would be saved, and Prelate Verge would recover the object of his quest.

Verge himself seemed an admixture of nervous and eager energies. Where Tabor stood at the center of the bridge, Verge paced above the control pits calling commands to the gunners. Tabor did not interfere; the boy's orders were unnecessary but sensible enough, and Tabor had seen worse battlefield commanders.

"Prelate, sir? Captain Seitaron?"

Tabor turned to the communications officer expectantly. *Barcel,* Tabor thought. *Competent lad, overeager but young enough to have an excuse.* Verge cast a backward glance in the man's direction, waved permission to speak.

"There's a shuttle lifting off from one of the transport stations," Barcel said.

"Escaping the lava, I presume," Tabor said. "Is it broadcasting clearance codes?"

"Yes, sir," Barcel said. "The ones you said to watch for."

Tabor chuckled and caught an approving smile from Verge. "Let this be a lesson to all of you," Tabor called. "You may trick a wise man once, a fool twice—but no one falls for the same treachery three times."

Governor Chalis had used her security codes to approach an Imperial transport in the Redhurne system. The rebels had used them again to bypass the blockade of Hoth. For her to try a third time—to flee her own battle in a shuttle—seemed an extraordinary act of hubris.

"Bring the shuttle in with a tractor beam," Verge said, "before it leaves the atmosphere. Keep it intact, please; we'll meet it in the shuttle bay."

Verge was striding toward the turbolift before he had finished the sentence, yet he pivoted when Tabor didn't follow. After a moment, Tabor grimaced and left the viewport for the prelate's side. He kept his voice low as he spoke. "You don't need me for this. One of us should remain here."

He feared he might anger the prelate, but the boy only shook his head and squeezed Tabor's shoulder. "Do you truly think we're needed for this battle? Our real triumph is in the hangar. I want you at my side." It was almost a plea, like a child might make to his father.

Tabor wanted to refuse, to state sternly that so long as men were dying under his watch he could not walk away. Even victory had a price, and though the *Herald* was unassailable, casualties were mounting below. To bear witness was a matter of respect.

Yet he knew Verge well enough to guess what the boy would think of *respecting* one's underlings above all else.

"I have my link," Tabor called to the control pits. "The moment anything changes, inform me immediately."

"The enemy at last," Verge murmured as they boarded the lift. "Do you suppose she knows the end has come? Will she acknowledge that her own disloyalty inevitably led to failure?"

"She's a bottom-feeding rat, Prelate," Tabor said. "I wouldn't expect gravitas from this confrontation."

"Then we will bring meaning to it," Verge said, "in the Emperor's name."

The tractor beam delivered the shuttle to the tertiary hangar bay. Scanners showed only a single life-form aboard; if Chalis was the passenger, as Verge so clearly believed, she'd come alone.

To Verge's amusement, Tabor chose two fleet troopers for security: Zhios and Cantompa, both men whom Tabor had come to appreciate during his time aboard the *Herald*. They'd watched Verge torment their peers, attended Tabor when he'd taken sick from the change in his diet, stood outside the tactical center in their crisp black uniforms and helmets for hours on end. Tabor trusted them—and if there was any honor to be gained in Chalis's final capture, they deserved to share it.

"Do you expect her to storm out, rifle blazing?" Verge asked as Tabor's escort preceded them through the durasteel door into the shuttle bay. At least, Tabor thought, the prelate wasn't openly snickering.

"I expect a bit of caution does no harm," Tabor said.

One of the men called an all-clear, and Verge led Tabor into the hangar—the same one, Tabor recalled, where he had first disembarked aboard the *Herald*. The shuttle inside had already lowered its boarding ramp. The guards had their rifles aimed at the entrance.

With slow, almost ceremonial deliberation, the shuttle's passenger descended. She wore the black uniform of an Imperial Army captain, though her boots were nonstandard. A breath mask hung unused around her neck. Her arms were spread wide, her palms up, in a gesture that might have indicated either surrender or welcome. Her features broadly matched Tabor's memories, but she appeared haggard and thin, exhausted despite the cruel smile that played across her lips.

"Forgive the outfit," Governor Chalis said. "I borrowed it from one of your men to access the shuttle."

She turned her hips slightly, and Tabor saw the fabric was frayed and burned in one spot on her torso. The mark of a blaster bolt. He stiffened and scowled. *To murder a man and then make light of it* . . .

"Not one of *my* men," Verge said. "One of the Emperor's nonetheless. Another treason for your tally."

But Chalis turned to Tabor first, eyes widening in exaggerated surprise. "Captain Seitaron," she said. "You came out of retirement for me. Your mistress must be jealous."

He'd forgotten about her accent—that awful, exaggerated, schoolgirl Coruscanti, as if she might fool anyone into thinking she hadn't been born in the bowels of a colonial backwater. Count Vidian had been a clever man, but Tabor couldn't imagine why he'd gone to such trouble to uplift Chalis.

"I hoped to keep my mind sharp—" he began.

"And you must be the prelate." Chalis cut Tabor off and turned to Verge, looking the stern-faced boy up and down.

—*but you hardly gave me the opportunity*, he'd intended to finish. He bristled at the interruption, forced his irritation down.

"Truly," Chalis continued, "you must be an extraordinary individual. To have been granted a new title by Palpatine himself—not made a moff or minister or vizier with all those duties and responsibilities, but a *prelate*."

Tabor couldn't tell whether Verge understood he was being mocked. The boy eyed Chalis with disdain, looked at her as if her very existence were a personal affront. "So far as you are concerned," Verge said, "I am the agent of our Emperor in this place. You have not done well by our lord and master."

Chalis laughed, a sound that might have been light and joyful if it weren't for a guttural hoarseness behind it. "You're very keen on styling yourself the Emperor's favored servant, aren't you? Is it true that you built a shrine to him on Naboo? That you like to shock yourself late at night to see if you can endure what he endured to earn his scars? Maybe if you wore a mask, he'd treat you more like he does Vader."

Verge took a single step forward, and Tabor saw his body trembling. The thought of what Verge might do to Chalis didn't concern him—was she looking to bait him into giving her a swift death?—but if Verge's anger grew too great, if he lashed out at others . . .

"You needn't listen to this, Prelate," Tabor said. Verge didn't appear to hear him.

"I apologize," Chalis said, and half bowed. "I congratulate you on your defeat of me. I've come to make you an offer."

"An offer?" Verge said. It was nearly a whisper.

"I've learned more than any spy about the inner workings of the Rebel Alliance: its leadership, its plans, its vulnerabilities." Chalis's voice had suddenly lost its playfulness and dropped an octave. "Grant me a pardon for my crimes, and I'll share it all with you."

Verge's trembling increased. His lips half parted as he drew long, hissing breaths. Tabor found that his own jaw was sore and clenched; he glanced to his guards to see if they, too, feared what their prelate might do. Although both aimed their weapons at Chalis, their eyes were on Verge.

All at once, Verge's trembling stilled. His muscles seemed to relax.

Casually, confidently, he stepped up to Chalis and reached out to dig his fingers into her cheek and chin—as if he might tear off her face as he would a mask. Chalis gasped in pain but did not struggle. When Verge wrenched at her, sent her toppling to the floor, she rolled but did not rise again, looking up from a face streaked with shallow cuts.

"The Emperor," Verge said, flicking his hand as if he'd trailed it through mud, "has no need of a woman like you. And in your defeat, I have proven myself worthy of a place alongside Vader."

Chalis looked small and crumpled on the floor. Tabor did not pity her.

"If you say so." Her voice was now rough and cracking. With one hand, she reached into one of the pockets of her pants and withdrew a small, flat device with a single button.

Stop her, Tabor wanted to shout, but it was too late. He saw her thumb flex, heard the tiniest of clicks.

For an instant, nothing happened.

Then the shuttle seemed to come ablaze with a blinding aura of blue-white light. Electrical arcs leapt over its surface and the shuttle bay echoed with the sounds of sparks and current. Popping noises emanated from control panels around the hangar as arcs of lightning touched tractor beam generators and docking clamps. A noxious smell of melted metal and plastoid caused Tabor to gag and shield his nose with his sleeve.

When the light faded, spots of green and red floated across Tabor's eyes and he blinked harshly to clear them. Somehow words came to him as his stunned, aging brain realized what had occurred.

"An ion bomb," he murmured.

The deck shuddered beneath him and the hull of the *Herald* seemed to groan.

"About twenty of them," Chalis said. She was on her hands and knees, slowly climbing to her feet. Her voice was suddenly desiccated. "Everything Twilight had left."

The deck shuddered again. Verge glanced about, legs gently bowed for balance and lips twisted into a sneer. "This is an Imperial Star Destroyer. All vital equipment is shielded. Even twenty bombs will do nothing."

But that wasn't true. Tabor shook his head, trying to organize his thoughts. *Why* wasn't it true? *Think, Tabor.*

"We're in atmosphere," he said, embarrassed at his own urgent tone. "We need full power to stay aloft. Any disruption at all—" Star Destroyers were extraordinary vessels, capable of razing mountains and carrying armies. But their mass was measured in millions upon millions of tonnes, and their energy requirements were vast.

He made an effort to compose himself, to speak in a manner befitting an Imperial captain. "We must withdraw immediately," he said. He tapped his comlink. "Transfer all weapons and auxiliary power— anything we can spare—to the engines. Get us back in orbit."

In return, he heard only Chalis's guttural laughter.

Of course. The *Herald*'s systems were largely shielded, but his comlink had been disabled along with anything in the hangar more complex than a light fixture. He turned to the guards, ordered the message carried to the bridge. They ran together to the hangar door, which did not open.

Tabor spat a curse. The guards set to removing the control panel and searching for the override. Verge stood unmoved, staring at Chalis, as if the ion blast had broken him, too.

Why did you do this? Tabor wanted to shout at Chalis. *What do you gain aside from bloodshed?*

Did she really mean to give her life for the rebel cause?

"Still think you've won the Emperor's favor?" Chalis asked, eyes locked with Verge's.

"You still belong to me," Verge said, though he sounded uncertain.

"And in capturing me you've put one of Sullust's most important assets in the hands of the Rebellion." She shook her head slowly. "Not in a calculated trade, either—but in a bungled act of ego and idiocy."

The deck lurched, sending Tabor hard onto his knees. A sharp pain burst up his legs, and he wondered how much damage he'd done to his bones. He glanced to the guards, who were sprawled on the ground with the door only open a crack; to Chalis, who was kneeling once again.

Only Verge had retained his balance. As klaxons began to sound outside the bay, he lunged forward, grasping Chalis by the chin and striking her across the face. Again, she did not struggle, only turning to ease the pain of the blows as they came in a swift, repeating blur. When Verge—blood speckling his knuckles and his face, his eyes wide as a rabid animal's—paused to catch his breath, the governor laughed again.

"I've seen Vader," she said, a red smile on her lips. "Next to him, you really are pathetic."

Verge froze with one hand curled like a claw above Chalis's eyes.

"We're through!" one of the guards called. The other was attempting to squeeze into the narrow gap they'd created between door and frame.

"Stop," Verge said, his voice almost gentle. "We will not withdraw from the battle."

Tabor was too confused to protest.

Verge kept speaking. "The Emperor will not forgive this failure, nor should he. Have the bridge direct all firepower at the rebel army. Destroy the processing facility if you must. But we will not allow Sullust to fall."

Implications crept over Tabor much too slowly. "Prelate—" he began sharply, scolding. He forced himself to moderate his tone, but he could hear his own strain. "Sullust will not be lost. We can fight the battle another day. To sacrifice our men and the men on the ground . . ."

The *Herald* had a crew of thousands. They had given everything to Verge, but this was too much.

This was madness.

Why did you do this?

"Do not question my orders, Captain," Verge said. His voice remained childishly gentle. "We have *all* failed, and we are *all* responsible. We will fly this vessel into the mountain before we suffer another defeat."

Then Chalis struck Verge while his head was turned and he could argue no more. The two grappled fiercely—the boy in his prime against the governor twice his age. Yet sheer savagery offered her an edge Verge could not easily overcome. Tabor called to the prelate, but his voice was lost in the struggle and the klaxons.

The guards stood where they were, unsure of what to do. But they were good men, dutiful. In a moment, they'd accept their prelate's orders and head for the bridge.

Tabor cursed and drew his sidearm, leveled it at the fighting pair. His pistol was a Merr-Sonn B22, mechanically activated. It might still be capable of firing after the ion blast. If he could end the fight, he might be able to talk sense into the prelate, and the *Herald* might yet escape.

His hands were trembling as he squinted, tried to acquire his target. In the back of his mind, he considered what he could say to sway Verge, what argument he could make to demonstrate that the deaths of so many good men were unnecessary.

He searched his memory, sifted through conversations with the boy over breakfast and while observing interrogations. He tried to fit the pieces of Verge's crazed philosophy together, to find something in his vision of the Empire that Tabor could use.

He imagined the crew of the *Herald* dying for the boy's passion.

He pulled the trigger. The hold-out pistol's muzzle flashed red. The combatants separated, and Verge looked at Tabor with wide, mystified eyes—the look of a hound cruelly struck by its master—before falling to the ground. Flames licked at the hole in his chest.

"Tell the bridge to pull out. All power to the engines," Tabor said. He heard the guards moving, scraping through the crack in the doorway.

They were good men. He could count on them.

Chalis's face was a mask of blood. He aimed the pistol at her breast. She was smiling.

Why did you do this? Out of spite? Out of rebel loyalty?

"Captain Seitaron," she said. "Tabor."

"You are responsible here," Tabor said. "Not the boy, whose madness was given to him, not chosen." Dead, Verge no longer seemed threatening or unpredictable: He was a victim of circumstance, a bril-liant mind and an eager patriot.

Verge had believed he was doing Tabor a kindness, bringing the old captain out of retirement.

Tabor found his vision blurring. He prepared to fire.

"One question first," Chalis said.

"One question only," Tabor snarled.

She shrugged, as if she'd expected that answer.

"Tell me," she said. "If I shot the prelate while you and your guards were trapped outside, how could I then shoot myself in the chest with my own pistol?"

Tabor stared at Chalis as if she'd gone mad.

CHAPTER 39

PLANET SULLUST
Day Three of the Siege of Inyusu Tor

When the Star Destroyer withdrew above the clouds, Twilight Company cheered over the sounds of explosions and blasterfire. Why it happened, no one could guess: The odds that *Apailana's Promise* had defeated the *Herald* seemed nil, and no weapons fire streamed skyward from Pinyumb to suggest Nien Nunb's cell had captured the city defenses. But whatever the reason, it was a welcome gift and seemed to inspire the rebel troops as much as it demoralized the Imperial infantry.

Yet the fighting at the gates of the processing facility dragged on—would have to drag on, Namir knew, until the Imperial Army had been reduced to chaff. He'd lashed the two forces together, bound them in chains of lava, and one would be completely destroyed before the day was over.

Namir fired his rifle until his fingers cramped, until his hips grew sore from crouching. As afternoon approached evening, he fell back with the squads into the facility depths, until the mouth of the entryway was a distant spot of daylight. The metal floor that stretched before the company was littered with debris from broken machines once used as barricades; with the bodies of stormtroopers and Twilight soldiers; with broken guns and discarded power packs and cracked helmets.

And still the foe came. Sometimes by tens and twenties, sometimes in smaller teams augmented by portable cannon fire and repulsor vehicles. Namir saw friends and comrades rent by blaster bolts, immolated by flamers, pierced by shrapnel. A stormtrooper drew a line of blood across his chest with a vibroblade; someone else wrestled the trooper away, gave Namir the chance to bind his shallow wound and return to the fight. He had no idea who'd saved his life.

Occasionally a voice would speak in his ear through his link, reporting on how the fight proceeded at the other facility gates. Namir sent reinforcements where they were needed, called for aid when the fighters at his entrance were hard-pressed. But for the most part, the tactics both sides employed were simple. The time to be clever had ended on the mountainside.

Once, during a lull between attacks, Namir saw a body move beside him and moan. In a haze of exhaustion, he didn't realize the wounded woman was an Imperial until after he had passed her his canteen. She crawled away, only to be shot by a Twilight sniper.

But as evening turned to night, the lulls between attacks became steadily longer. Nearly an hour passed after one furious assault, and Namir and the others glanced uncertainly at one another, unwilling to leave their posts and afraid to break the spell. They no longer heard distant shouts or the rumbling of explosions. The gateway to the mountain was dark. In the silence of the battlefront, the truth eventually became obvious:

Twilight Company had won.

CHAPTER 40

PLANET SULLUST

Two Days After the Siege of Inyusu Tor

Thara Nyende should not have been alive.

Being transferred from the garrison's emergency ward to the civilian clinic for recuperation was the only thing that had saved her. She'd held the medics at gunpoint throughout the day while hunching forward on a chair, allowing them to treat the handful of stormtroopers and civilians who trickled in but ensuring they couldn't join the uprising. Too exhausted and pained to hold back, she'd wept when news arrived that the garrison had been flooded by lava. If she'd had the strength, she might have joined the security forces in the street. As it was, she could only watch from the sidelines and listen to the raucous celebrations that told her Pinyumb had been captured.

Captured by the same people she'd been trying to protect and clothe and feed.

She didn't understand. When the time came, she surrendered to the rebels without a fight.

Now, two days after the fighting had ended, she was officially a prisoner of the Rebel Alliance. Due to the number of captives taken during the uprising—everyone from Imperial administrators to security force members to civilian overseers of Pinyumb's industrial enterprises—she'd been permitted to serve in a limited work-release capacity with the supervision of an authorized volunteer.

Unofficially, she was working at her uncle's cantina.

The cantina itself had become a refuge in the aftermath of the crisis. When Thara's uncle had been released from holding, he'd immediately begun using it as a distribution point for donated supplies; while some of Pinyumb's residents were untouched by the revolution, others had seen their housing blocks burned and their possessions confiscated. They needed help that other residents were glad to give. And as volunteers flocked to the cantina, it also became a place to exchange information about Pinyumb's rebuilding, to organize meetings and discussions on how the city would run without the Empire. It was busy at all hours, and therefore Thara was busy, too. She tracked goods as they came in and out, repaired broken machines, passed along messages. She served drinks.

Her uncle watched her closely, though he tried not to show it. She could have sabotaged his operation, but what was the point?

She felt the eyes of the cantina regulars on her as she carried a tray to a table occupied by mineral processing workers. The facility wouldn't be back online for a week or more, so the old men had time to spare.

"I know who you are," one of the workers said.

She recognized the speaker—a withered Sullustan with drooping ears and jowls. He'd been the first to speak openly against the Emperor in her presence, months earlier. The others had been terrified. She hadn't reported him.

He reached out with a wrinkled hand and gripped her wrist gently. She wanted to slap him away, but she made herself smile. She couldn't afford to make trouble. "I'm not trying to hide it," she said, low and sharp.

The old Sullustan patted her wrist twice and let go. "We all pick sides," he said. "No shame in picking the wrong one."

Thara stared at the Sullustan in surprise. Then she left the tray on the table and walked away.

Not everyone was pleased that Pinyumb had joined the Rebellion. She knew how to interpret disquieted murmurs, weary asides that held a subtext of displeasure. *Instability* was the watchword among Sullustans who feared what the Rebellion might do to their home.

They didn't dare speak their defiance openly. Neither did she. But she wanted to turn back to the old man and ask for all of them: *Who says I picked the wrong side?*

She loved her uncle and she loved Pinyumb, but her colleagues were dead. She wore a bandage over her stomach and couldn't move faster than a hobble anymore. If the Empire came back, she had every intention of rejoining the stormtrooper legions.

And yet . . .

. . . the very thought of taking up a rifle against the people in her cantina made her tremble. Drops of water and tea and ale spilled down the sides of the glasses she carried to and from the bar.

She hoped the peace lasted a little while.

CHAPTER 41

PLANET SULLUST

Three Days After the Siege of Inyusu Tor

Over a third of the company was dead. Another hundred Twilight members, give or take, were hurt badly enough to be off the active duty roster. Namir was certain some would never return to Twilight. Others would retire from combat roles and join the decimated support staff; there had been no noncombatants in the siege, and Twilight Company was now as short on medics and engineers as it was on soldiers. Even the loss of domestic labor droids aboard the *Thunderstrike* left the company wanting chefs and translators and mechanics.

Gadren was among the wounded. He'd lost an arm to a grenade during the final hours of the conflict. "We're built sturdier than humans, with limbs to spare!" he declared more than once in the days after, in the same tone every time—as if it was a mantra instead of a joke. Despite the injury, despite Von Geiz's disapproval, he spent his mornings with the *Thunderstrike*'s salvage crew, searching the wreckage for supplies and equipment and the personal effects of friends.

Roach was among the dead. Gadren had told Namir the story of her heroic final charge. "She dived into the flood of combatants, red hair flying like a banner, silent and determined. A speeder bike laden with explosives raced toward us without a pilot. She vaulted over stormtroopers, stung by bolt after bolt but never hit full force, until she had a clear shot at the speeder. Then everything flashed in fire and she died our savior."

"Is any of that true?" Namir had asked.

"There are no certainties in battle," Gadren had said, his voice low and haunted.

No one else Namir spoke to had seen Roach fall. He let Gadren tell the story the way he wanted. He didn't think Roach would mind.

He did wonder why she'd chosen that name.

He wished he'd known her better.

He said as much to Brand as they picked their way along the upper slope of the mountain. Officially, they were checking for anything dangerous that might impact workers traveling from Pinyumb to the processing facility—unexploded ordnance or dormant mines—though neither was especially suited to the job.

"Not much to do about it now," Brand said. Namir started to snap at her, but she kept talking. "Roach was okay. Didn't need you. You did your part."

Namir nodded and knelt to the rocks, picked up a dagger of slate and tossed it down the slope. "I get that. But the only reason I'm still here—"

I don't want to fight alongside strangers, he thought. What was the point of being worthy of his friends if they all slipped away? But he couldn't bring himself to say it.

Brand didn't seem to hear him anyway. They continued their descent, occasionally passing a mortar-pounded crater or the body of a soldier that had been picked apart by ash angels.

"I miss them, too," Brand said after a while. It sounded like a denunciation, as if she expected better of herself. She stopped walking, and Namir drew close to her side. They stood in silence until Brand spoke again.

"Why do I always survive?"

He studied her, found that her mask was no more revealing than her face. "I don't know. Some of us just do, I guess." It was an unsatisfying answer. All he could do was commiserate. "*I* survive."

"You're still young. Practically Roach's age."

"I've been doing this—"

"—longer than most of us. I know. But it's not the same."

She started to walk again, but her strides were slow and measured.

"I need you, you know," Namir called. "We're still here because of you." Because of things she'd said. He indicated the mountain with a gesture of his chin. His tone was somber. It was a statement, not a question or a plea.

"Not me. Because of Howl," Brand said. Then she turned to him, locked eyes as well as she could with her mask on.

"We did *good*," she said. "I'm not going anywhere."

Pinyumb was free and its Imperial masters had fled, surrendered, or defected. The city's not-insubstantial defenses were under civilian control, guaranteeing at least a brief stay of execution. Pirate broadcasts and intercepted Imperial signals indicated that other insurrections had begun across the planet; those, too, would delay the Empire's inevitable counterattack.

Namir knew all this because Nien Nunb's rebel cell had harangued him into joining daily meetings of the city's interim government. The meetings were torment, full of debate about who was to administer what water treatment system and whether the cavern's artificial night should be shortened during reconstruction. Namir's only role was to speak up when military concerns arose and to occasionally volunteer his troops for menial tasks.

Namir was relieved, at least, that neither he nor the other Twilight soldiers who spent time in Pinyumb were celebrated as heroes—the

Sullustans were too busy and too pragmatic for that, and had suffered enough of their own losses. Yet now and then a Sullustan would approach and murmur quiet thanks, or an old human woman would press a gift of flowers or fruit or etched metal into his hands.

"Sullust will change," Nien Nunb told him at the end of each meeting. Corjentain translated it the first time. The others Namir figured out for himself.

After the meetings, Namir would walk through the streets of Pinyumb—streets that had been empty only a few days before and were now packed with people—and absorb the sights of the weird and wondrous cavern. He strolled along the banks of the turquoise streams and ran his fingers through the yellow dust that coated the rocks. Without his people around, he had no need to feel embarrassed.

Yet there was no escaping his responsibilities. Along with the meetings in Pinyumb, Namir faced the burden of predawn conferences with the remnants of Twilight Company's leadership. "The interim government wants us around for two more weeks, at least," he told them on the fourth day after the siege. "Once they feel secure, we'll get out of the way; ease the threat, make the Empire a little less eager to reduce this area to slag. Not a lot of time, I know, but it should be enough to either get the *Thunderstrike* working or find alternative transport."

"Let's stick with the second option," Vifra muttered. Namir winced. The dig teams' efforts to unleash the mountain's lava had left her with only a handful of engineers.

"What about after?" Carver asked.

"You mean what about Kuat?" Namir replied, as casually as he could.

Carver nodded. Hober averted his eyes. Von Geiz stared intently at Namir. The others watched and waited.

"Not an option anymore," Namir said, "for all the obvious reasons."

"Then what—" Carver began.

Namir interrupted him. "We've got plenty of time. Start thinking. If we're lucky, maybe we'll get new orders. If not, we'll find something that works."

There would be grumbling, among both the senior staff and the rank and file. That didn't concern Namir—there was always grumbling, and he'd done his share when Howl had been in charge. But taking into account everything lost in the prior months, Twilight had become a shadow of its former self. So many dead, so many wounded, so much equipment destroyed and resources expended . . . optimistically, the company was at one-third strength. For the moment, its ambitions needed tempering.

Namir listened to updates on salvage operations, on the recuperation of the wounded, and on the repairs of the *Apailana's Promise*— the gunship had escaped its battle with the *Herald* with its laser batteries drained and its deflectors overheated but its hull, stunningly, intact. As the meeting drew to a close and the attendees filed out of the facility conference room, Namir caught Gadren by the shoulder and drew him aside.

"You going back to the *Thunderstrike*?" Namir asked.

"That was my intent," Gadren said. "It seems where I can be the most use."

He might as well have said *My squad is gone*. Except Brand, but Brand didn't take orders.

"*I've* got another use for you," Namir said. "You're good with civilians. Want to be my liaison to Pinyumb?"

Gadren smiled slowly, sadly, as he looked down on Namir. "That is not necessary," he said.

"It is for my sanity," Namir said. "I'm doing twice the work I was before and I have no one to gripe to. You know this company as well as anyone." All of which was true. His desire to share the burden was genuine; as was his desire to keep Gadren close, for both their sakes.

Gadren closed his eyes and flexed three sets of meaty fingers. A low hum came from his throat, deep enough that Namir seemed to feel it in his bones. "Very well," he said. "For now. But I cannot be your lieutenant, or . . . *her*."

Namir smirked and shook his head. "Fine. But you couldn't do a worse job than she did." He said it because he hoped to win over Gadren and because *she* was an easy target.

It was, however, a lie.

For all Chalis's faults, she had done well by Twilight Company. The mistakes had been Namir's.

Namir had not heard any news of the governor since Brand had reported her flight down the mountain. He suspected she was alive, though it was only a hunch; her body might have been incinerated by the lava or lost to scavenging ash angels. Either way, she was no longer his responsibility. Even Howl, he suspected, would have conceded that point.

For reasons he couldn't explain, however, Namir found himself often looking to the bronze bust in his office, studying the stern face and wondering about the hands that shaped it. He was eyeing the statue five days after the siege when a voice announced through his comm, "Captain? There's a recorded message coming in for you. Source unknown, rebel encryption codes."

Namir frowned. "Specifically for me?"

"Yes, sir. By name."

That seemed unusual for a message from Alliance High Command—had anyone even told the rebel leaders Howl was dead?—but it was a mystery easily solved. "Send it over," Namir said.

The holodisplay on his terminal flickered to life. Azure static coalesced into a once-youthful face invaded by the gentle lines of age. The woman lacked the darkness under her eyes Namir had grown familiar with, though her hair seemed grayer than ever and long, half-healed scratches marked her cheeks and chin.

"Sergeant," the recording of Everi Chalis said. "I hear you won on Sullust, so I'm assuming you're still alive. Congratulations."

Namir realized his shoulders had tensed and forced them to relax. Chalis's voice was rusty, but it wasn't only the usual hoarseness he heard—her accent had changed, and for the third time since they'd met it was neither entirely foreign nor entirely familiar. Namir had come to think of it as her natural inflection, native to whatever world, like Crucival, she'd once come from.

But she spoke with the casual haughtiness that was her manner around men and women she disdained.

"As for me," she said, "I'm very far from Sullust and I won't be returning to Twilight Company or the Rebellion. We never really were a good match, even when our goals looked similar. You made that clear to me in the end.

"I thought I owed it to you to say so in person." Her lips twisted into a wry smile. "Or as close as I can get, under the circumstances. Where I'm going next shouldn't and won't concern you. It's best that our paths don't cross again."

For several seconds, the message continued in silence. Chalis's eyes flickered to one side, then back to the recorder. When she spoke again, her matter-of-fact tone was replaced by something colder.

"Since I left Haidoral Prime to join your company, I've been humbled," she said. "I've been humiliated. It's not the first time, and I accept that as the price of survival.

"But *you*, Hazram Namir? I thought we recognized something in each other. I thought we had a kinship. Instead, you judged me the same way the Empire did: You thought my talent was for making promises instead of keeping them."

She seemed to tremble for a moment. Then she stilled herself and went on.

"I could have won at Kuat," she said. "I could have hurt the Empire. But you didn't trust me."

Then the hologram flashed into nonexistence and Namir was left alone.

CHAPTER 42

NUMESIRA SECTOR
Five Days After the Siege of Inyusu Tor

For the first time in as long as she could remember, Everi Chalis—former governor of Haidoral Prime and emissary to the Imperial Ruling Council—was free to do as she pleased.

The hardest part about escaping Sullust had been swaying Captain Seitaron. The man had been surprisingly slow to permit Everi to take the blame for Prelate Verge's murder; even slower to accept that Everi's disappearance—not her death, which would leave contravening evidence—was the best means to erase all doubt as to her responsibility. Surely no one would be surprised by her traitorous flight from the scene of her ghastly crime.

The old man loathed her. He doubtless still wanted her dead. But his priorities were his crew and his desire to return to the comforts of his Academy; perhaps not in that order. And the more incompetent

Verge appeared, the more attention would be diverted from Seitaron and the *Herald* to Everi herself. She had won the blind eye she needed to seize a fresh shuttle and depart, all using an argument barely plausible enough to pass muster.

Here's to the malleable brains of guilt-ridden old men, she thought, and raised her canteen to the million stars beyond the cockpit of her ship.

She thought of her last drink—her last *real* drink—back in Captain Evon's quarters after the campaign on Mardona III. She thought of the company she'd kept and her mood curdled.

She could have told Namir in her message that she'd saved him and his whole company by forcing the *Herald* out of Sullust's atmosphere. But what difference would it make? Let him think of her as he would. She owed him a farewell and nothing else.

No, she was done with Twilight Company. She was done *thinking* about Twilight Company. She'd invested too much effort and emotion into those people and received only pain in return.

She felt a tingling in her throat, the familiar start of a coughing fit. She made her body rigid, hissed a breath through her teeth, and forced it down.

The rebels were no longer looking over her shoulder, terrified she might betray them. The Empire was no longer sending spies and political officers to keep her prisoner in her own home. Since leaving Sullust, she'd spent the last handful of days ensuring her security and anonymity: trading the *Herald*'s shuttle for a civilian starcutter, draining the offworld financial accounts she'd set up years before . . . doing everything she should have done months earlier on Haidoral Prime before being forced to turn to the Rebellion for aid.

She had neither authority nor wealth, but she was free. She had all the tools she needed to build a new life.

She just needed to decide where to go next.

She had told Namir once that all she really wanted was time to sculpt, reasonable comforts, and a measure of respect. Maybe that was still true. She could find herself a forgotten little world at the edge of known space—something like her own homeworld—where she could afford a patch of land and provincial luxuries. She could pay children with treats to fetch her clay and spend her days relearning her craft. She had been a *good* artist once, before Count Vidian had taken her from the Colonial Academy and redirected her talent for visualization. She could be a good artist again, hidden on a planet beneath anyone's notice while the rest of the galaxy fought and burned and fell into chaos.

What was the name of Namir's homeworld? She could sell a few technological trinkets there and be set for decades.

Crucival.

Everi tapped at the ship's console and began searching the navicomputer for coordinates.

As she did, she sipped her water again, imagined dampening a lump of clay and shaping it beneath her fingers. With enough time, she could fill her own gallery.

A gallery no one would ever bother to come see.

There were many reasons people might seek her out—her schematic of the Empire's logistics, the secrets of Alliance High Command—but a viewing of her artwork was not among them. She smiled bitterly at the irony: She possessed information men would sacrifice armies to obtain, yet she was choosing to retire to a galactic backwater.

There *were* other options open to her. She could find buyers for her secrets despite the risk. She could play all sides in the civil war: not just the Rebel Alliance and the Empire, but the Crymorah, unaligned worlds. She could become a power broker, operating in the shadows but grudgingly respected by those who knew her name.

Respected by the self-declared rulers of the galaxy at last.

It was tempting. Of course it was tempting. It was past time her detractors understood what she was capable of.

She drummed her fingers on the console, drew in a long breath, and winced as the air touched the scars inside her throat.

She had decisions to make. A new life to build.

But there was no rush.

CHAPTER 43

PLANET SULLUST
Five Days After the Siege of Inyusu Tor

Much to his surprise, Namir felt an emptiness after viewing Chalis's final message. It was the same sort of emptiness he had felt years before after learning of his father's death. He was mourning, to be certain, but he wasn't sure *what*, precisely, he mourned.

Chalis had accused him of failing to put his trust in her. There might have been some truth to that—but true or not, the outcome would have been the same. He was responsible now for Twilight Company—not just its people or their goals, but the ideals Howl had set forth. The ideals that meant victory in sacrifice if the fight was worth fighting.

The worthy fight had been on Sullust, not Kuat. Choosing one over the other hadn't been a betrayal of Chalis. If she wouldn't see that, the fault was hers.

Still, there was no one in the company who would understand why he would miss her. He kept the message to himself.

That afternoon, he walked among the wounded in the medbay; among the salvage crews still picking at the wreckage of the *Thunderstrike;* among the mountain patrols lugging Plexes in case an Imperial airspeeder dared to approach. He tried to take in the mood, interpret his soldiers' complex mix of pride and uncertainty and frustration and sorrow. He felt no regret over his most recent choices, and he sensed no anger directed toward him. That was something, at least.

He allowed himself to think about the dead only briefly. He'd asked Hober to prepare a funeral for that night—something using the resources on hand. The Pinyumb interim leadership had offered the assistance of Sullustan crypt masters and formal burial space in the caverns, but Namir had declined the offer; Twilight took care of its own, even after death.

As it turned out, the service took place in Pinyumb anyway, broadcast to the processing facility for those unable to attend. Instead of a vehicle charging station, Hober drained the last sparks of exhausted blaster packs into an array of emergency generators he'd somehow acquired from the Sullustans. "We'll have a new ship sooner or later," he told Namir. "It'll need emergency power, and I'll make damn sure these get used."

The funeral went on almost four hours. Somehow, Hober and Von Geiz had found a speaker for every dead soldier, no matter if all his teammates had fallen. Namir stepped up three times for recruits he'd trained over the years. Gadren delivered four eulogies, including Roach's: "Child of an age of Empire and war. Never broken and fiercer than us all." Even Brand spoke out for an engineer and one of the ensigns from the *Thunderstrike's* bridge crew.

The droids, too, received send-offs, as if they had been as alive as the rest of the company. Namir didn't entirely understand, but it seemed to comfort the others. Even the *Thunderstrike* received a moment of honor as Hober drained one of its laser cannon plasma cells. "Ugly girl and meaner than sin!" Commander Tohna called, and the assembled soldiers cheered.

Afterward, a few dozen attendees filtered into a Pinyumb cantina that had volunteered to host a reception. Gadren, Brand, Twitch, and Tohna quickly located a deck of cards and began a game. Namir sat nearby, observing the hands and calling out corrections over his shoulder as Carver sat at the bar recounting the battle on Phorsa Gedd.

"The cards are lucky tonight!" Tohna declared after a competitive round. "You should join us, Captain."

"I'm busy," Namir said, and jutted a thumb back at Carver. Carver shouted something obscene. "Don't let me slow you down."

"You'll never get him to join," Brand said with a smirk. She'd been drinking just enough to loosen her lips.

Twitch snickered. Tohna looked to Gadren, who shrugged gently. "He thinks we do not know," Gadren said.

"Know what?" Tohna asked.

Gadren glanced sidelong at Namir, who scowled at him. "I have spoken out of turn," Gadren said, placating. "The captain's choices are his own."

Brand jumped in. "No sabacc games where he grew up," she said. "He can't admit he doesn't know how to play."

"I know how to play," Namir snapped.

Twitch burst out laughing. Gadren looked contrite. Brand just leaned back in her chair and played a hand that won her the pot.

It wasn't a bad night.

When most of the others had returned to the processing facility or to lodgings offered by the Sullustans, Namir walked with Gadren through the quiet streets of Pinyumb. "I want to hold an open recruit," Namir said. "Noon tomorrow, if the Pinyumb council approves."

Gadren nodded slowly. "You mean to continue Howl's tradition?" he asked. "You have had concerns in the past."

"Still do," Namir said. "But Howl knew what he was doing. If this is how we fight, then that's how we endure."

He spoke with certainty. He'd already chosen the path; this was only the next step.

The citizens of Pinyumb trickled slowly into the market after the announcement went out. Some only came to question the Twilight recruiters before walking away. Others watched fearfully from a distance. But soon the line grew long, filled with a motley assortment of young and old, pampered and desperate. Namir recognized a few of the locals from his rounds with Nien Nunb on the night before the battle. He saw a withered Sullustan offer his expertise as a mechanic; an eager human youth who'd never fired a blaster volunteer to take up the fight against the Empire.

The open recruit continued into the evening and night. What the coming weeks would bring—for Sullust and for Twilight—remained in doubt, and the end of the war was no longer even the distant dream it had been on Hoth. Yet one thing was absolutely certain:

Twilight Company lived on.

ABOUT THE AUTHOR

Over the last decade, ALEXANDER MARSH FREED has written dozens of short stories, comic books, and videogames (including a lengthy stint at videogame developer BioWare). Born near Philadelphia, Pennsylvania, he endeavors to bring the city's dour charm to his current home of Austin, Texas. *Star Wars Battlefront: Twilight Company* is his first novel.

alexanderfreed.com

@AlexanderMFreed